# Beatrice's Commonsensical Approach

Maureen Mitson feels she is fortunate to have two other novellas published, won creative writing competitions, had a number of short stories selected for radio in Adelaide, Brisbane and Cairns, and poetry selected for popular anthologies and school magazines. This is her third book published by Ginninderra Press and her first full-length historical novel.

I0601940

Also by Maureen Mitson and published by Ginninderra Press

*Paper Chase*

*Jumping the Cracks*

*Take Time…* (Pocket Poets)

*Insulae* (Pocket Places)

Maureen Mitson

# Beatrice's
# Commonsensical Approach

# Acknowledgements

My profound thanks for patiently reading the manuscript and for her informed and valuable guidance on Mary Lee, her life and times, must go to Elizabeth Ho OAM, former Associate Director of the State Library of South Australia, who has commissioned various women's suffrage history projects, and to Elizabeth Mansutti for her reading, editing and wonderful knowledge of Mary Lee.

My thanks also to Frances Bedford MP for her early encouragement and the use of her bookshelf; to Anthony Smith and the management of the Bridgewater Inn; to my publishers Brenda and Stephen Matthews of Ginninderra Press for their unfailing professional guidance; to my friends and colleagues of the Tea Tree Gully Library Writers and North Eastern Writers Inc. for their encouragement; to the Tea Tree Gully Library for its continuing support of local writers; to my family for their tolerance; and, last and certainly not least, to my Phred for his patience and his pride in me.

This is a work of historical fiction based on fact. With the exception of Mrs Mary Lee, her daughter Evelyn Lee, son John Benjamin Lee and certain other political and society personages of the time, some of whom are listed in the bibliography, and events familiar from history that are mentioned in the context of the story, the names, characters and incidents are the work of the author's imagination. Any resemblance therefore to other persons, living or dead, is entirely coincidental.

First published 2015 by
**GINNINDERRA PRESS**
PO Box 3461 Port Adelaide 5015
www.ginninderrapress.com.au

# Contents

For David, of Elsewhere, who believed in me

# 15 December 1879 – Adelaide

## 1

'This wind quite takes my bonnet, Mrs Lee. It is a hot one, is it not?'

Mrs Lee was less concerned about the breezes dislodging her bonnet than maintaining a dignified foothold. Her bonnet was more for convention than style. She mopped the perspiration running down the sides of her face. 'So it is, Mrs Beauchamp. Not like a December back in County Monaghan, I assure you.'

The two women were standing with their boxes on the narrow deck of the SS *Orient* waiting to disembark.

Stifling her impatience and waiting to be called, Mrs Lee stood politely as befitted her dignity, trying to ignore the increasing hustle from behind. She gripped the rail tightly and, lifting her face towards the land, inhaled the pungency of dry eucalypts and tea trees warming in the sun. *Better than the smell of those mangroves over the other side o' this port, they're like dead cabbage leaves...*

As the family immediately ahead of her started a tentative shuffling, Mrs Lee eyed the broad gangplank bridging the narrow strip of water, and assessed its gradient with not a little relief. In her opinion the shorter gangplank would permit a more graceful and economical use of a mature lady's energy. Her skirts were proving enough of a problem to manage. She cast a sideways glance at Beatrice Beauchamp. That young woman was eagerly scanning the crowds on the wharf and busy tucking a wayward curl back under her bonnet.

Mary never ceased to be amazed at how young women could be more interested in their appearance than in their comfort. She was never thus. Thankfully her daughter Evelyn was of a more practical nature than this young flibbertigibbet wife – well, mostly. And Beauchamp – what sort of name was that for a soldier, captain or not? Spelt one way and pronounced another, making fools of folk? Oh dear, she was feeling more irritable with each minute...

She took out her kerchief and wiped her eyes then pulled off her gloves and fanned them around her features, permitting herself a cooling exhalation and a few 'tut tuts'. 'Mrs Beauchamp, there is much of difference awaiting us. Are we prepared for it all, do you think? At least we are not without friends – unlike some of our fellow passengers who know no one here in this Adelaide.'

'Oh, I do agree, Mrs Lee. You have your daughter with you and your son is in this new place, while I have my dear husband meeting me. We can look around, observe and learn while staying in moderate comfort. I admit the prospect is more exciting than fearsome.'

Mrs Lee smiled. 'I do agree. And those distant hills, with that purple haze smudging the green, are really quite attractive.' She tilted her chin towards them almost in defiance, remembering a derisory comment made to her before she sailed. *That Mrs Coghlan called this country the 'back end of nowhere'. One day it'll know itself and be a significant 'somewhere'. We'll show them!*

The shouting increased from the wharf, some crates were dropped and dust flew up and across peppering her face. She flicked one of her widow's ribbons across to shield her eyes. *One of those carriages lining up must be ours. John said he would order one. I should think so – how would I know where Albert Park is from here, and manage this luggage on a horse tram? Can't see him in that crush along there, so why isn't he here to meet us?*

Nor was Evelyn being a help to her mother as a dutiful daughter should. Instead, she had moved to talk with a pair of young officers along the deck. Mary frowned; she was of the opinion that calling them 'young gallants' was a misnomer – some were decidedly less so than others. She looked beyond her daughter. *Ahah, that nice young Lieutenant Symonds is coming this way – doing a patrol, I suppose. He's a nice, well set-up young fellow and not straight out of school either. Evelyn is almost twenty, after all, why not…?*

A bellow from up on the bridge interrupted her thoughts.

'Lieutenant Symonds! Done the telegraph?'

'Yessir! Telegraph officer been aboard, will transmit within the hour, sir – London tomorrow!'

Symonds knew the cap'n was mentally and physically rubbing his hands in anticipation of the owners' gratitude at their speedy transport – only thirty-seven days and twenty-two hours from England! It was almost unbelievable.

He saw the comely Mrs Beauchamp was even now gathering her travel boxes around her feet in preparation for directing their removal across the gangplank and he decided there was nothing to lose by playing the gentleman. 'You are being met by your husband, Mrs Beauchamp?'

She smiled. 'Yes, Lieutenant. My husband and I will be staying with friends in Woodville for Christmas, after which we are to hire a carriage from the wheelwright there to take us to Cock's Creek – some now call it Bridgewater. I collected a letter from the shipping office at the Cape in which he informed me of a property investment he has made.' She couldn't restrain her excitement. 'Oh, Lieutenant, we are to grow orchards! He is to leave the Militia! I so anticipate seeing this place – and simply all that is different.'

Her joy was infectious and he smiled.

'Mrs Beauchamp, I would be pleased to escort you to your meeting with Captain Beauchamp,' he began, only to be interrupted by a raucous yell from among the crowd clustering at the landing end of the gang plank.

'Cooee! You, sir! Please, sir? *Sir!*'

Blast! The lieutenant raised his gloved hand and nodded in acknowledgement to the boy in an apprentice's apron who was doing the yelling. 'Wait there, boy…'

'Sir, yer 'ave a Mrs Bowchomp on board, sir, they say. 'Ope I catched 'er. Er 'usband's been run down. 'E's dead, sir. Will youse let 'er know, sir? *Sir?*'

Even as he realised the import of the message, Lieutenant Symonds turned to the young Mrs Beauchamp. He was just in time to catch and support her head as she sank to the edge of the gangplank, grasping vainly for the rail as she fell.

Mrs Lee bustled over and bent over her friend. 'Oh, Mrs Beauchamp, Beatrice. Oh, my dear girl, I heard! Oh, you sweet lamb.' She turned to the lieutenant, who despite the circumstances seemed quite at ease holding his comely burden. 'It's just the shock, Mr Symonds, and her knees giving way. As they do. Poor young lady.'

Beatrice was already stirring. Her head was still within the safety of the lieutenant's arm. As her eyes opened, it was evident she was not only distressed but confused with embarrassment. Tears started to roll down her cheeks. 'Aunt Wilkes! Oh, please, will you find Mrs Wilkes for me? She is family and my companion…'

Mary Lee stroked her arm. 'She's been met, my dear. I saw her leave… did I not see you both exchanging goodbyes? You'll come with me and Evelyn, my dear girl, till we get you sorted out. We can perhaps find Mrs Wilkes's family for you… Lieutenant, would you be so kind?'

Somewhat reluctantly, he straightened and relinquished his pathetic bundle to the sturdy bosom of Mrs Lee. He signalled to a seaman to come help him steer a passage through the jostling passengers, and they quickly found themselves on the solid stone of the wharf.

Beatrice was moaning and shaking her head as if in denial. 'Oh no, James, my darling James. How? Where? That cannot be true…please… I need to see him…'

During this sad little cameo, the young lad who'd brought the news stood waiting at an arm's length, a paper in his hand, a fearful look on his face.

Symonds snatched the paper from his grip. *As if the usual landfall chaos is not enough. Some of these immigrants are poor specimens but thank the Lord bad fortune like this isn't too frequent.* 'You! You are a careless oaf, lad, know that? An oaf!'

# 2

He scanned the paper. 'Ahah, I know where your husband is, Mrs Beauchamp. Please wait here and I'll find a carriage.'

He turned to the young apprentice again. 'You, lad. Finish moving this lady's belongings, and her friend's, onto firm ground away from the traffic. THEN…then you'll stay here with them until their carrier turns up for them. I will be back later. You don't deserve it but I'll make it worth your while if you guard them properly. If not…!'

Mary Lee now had Beatrice sitting on one of her crates, supported by Evelyn, so he beckoned her over to read to her quietly from the paper in his hand.

'It seems, Mrs Lee, that Captain Beauchamp has indeed received fatal injuries. This was yesterday the fourteenth and the Sabbath but nevertheless he was taken to the casualty hospital by the police barracks. However, his b— Erm, he is now lying in the morgue adjacent, I believe. This certificate of death is authorised by Doctor…oh, not the Dr Duncan I have met before.' *That's a pity; him I knew. A true gentleman.* He nodded to Mary. 'However, Mrs Lee, it is properly authorised. I wonder, if I escort Mrs Beauchamp, could you possibly come with us? That would enable the due proprieties.'

'That I will. I'll speak to Evelyn and she will organise things from this end. Evelyn is a good young woman, though I say so m'self, with an independent head on her shoulders. We have a carriage due to collect us,. Perhaps if I can arrange for Mrs Beauchamp's trunk and bag to come to my son's house? John's been living in South Australia for some years now – Albert Park, which I understand is not far – he was ill y'see, and is convalescing, which is why I'm here in the colony.'

The lieutenant nodded abruptly in thanks and strode off. A carriage was drawing up and he used his rank and authority to commandeer it ahead of a harassed family man. 'We need to go to the morgue.'

'The Dead 'Ouse, sir? I knows it.'

In very little time, Mary Lee had organised her daughter to wait on the wharf to supervise their belongings and the subdued young apprentice, and was helping a blank-faced Beatrice into the carriage, allowing herself the whispered assurance, 'He'll get us sorted, my dear. Fine young man like that, with a good set to his shoulders. Got authority he has, for sure.'

*

They were met at the morgue by Dr Duncan's successor, a younger man with a dark beard. Lieutenant Symonds had met Dr Duncan and dined with him and others at a friend's house only three years earlier and was sad to learn the gentle-natured, white bearded old doctor had died the previous year. Only death had stopped him working! He mused that his gentle demeanour was lacking in the brisk efficiency of the new man. *But then we are in an era of change and a place of change.* Or so he consoled himself.

The lieutenant accompanied Mrs Lee and Beatrice into a small room, where Beatrice broke down at the sight of her husband's misshapen body placed tidily on a barouche. To Mary's relief, most of the damage was hidden by a shroud of sorts. He was quite obviously in a state of undress beneath the covering.

Hesitantly, Beatrice stepped forward and gently turned down the sheet from her husband's face, thwarting the attendant's attempts to prevent her. Only the trembling of her fingers betrayed her composure and she bent down and kissed his forehead. She remained motionless, staring at his face. It was evident that his features had not escaped injury, and the bruising and dried blood was remarkable in its disfigurement, so Mary stepped forward and released the sheet from Beatrice's tightening grip, and carefully re-covered his face.

'That is your James, is it not, dear girl?'

'It is, Mrs Lee, but not as he was once…'

'Let us leave him now, dear, and allow these gentlemen to observe the proprieties.'

Beatrice started to cry, her eyes wildly circling around the room and back to James's body. Sobs broke from her and the tears flowed, she trying to halt them with her gloved hands. Mary put a protective arm round her shoulders to lead her away as the young doctor addressed her.

He was respectful but businesslike. 'Pardon me, madam, but what are the widow's wishes? I am able to organise a burial in the new cemetery at Cheltenham if that would be preferred.'

Beatrice broke into a fresh bout of sobbing so Mary suggested that Captain Beauchamp's friends might be consulted because they could have an opinion. After conferring, it was decided to wait until Beatrice felt able to properly discuss the changed situation.

The young doctor addressed the lieutenant. 'I shall ensure that the captain's personal goods are given the protection of the police station next door – if that is agreeable…'

Mary heard this and, ever the practical one, asked if any money was on the captain's person, as his wife would need to have 'something to fall back on'.

The lieutenant smiled at her in appreciation of her sense. 'A sensible request, Mrs Lee. Because the identity of the deceased has been ascertained and I have been able to verify Mrs Beauchamp as his legal wife, this from my knowledge of the voyage documentation, the doctor will perhaps be kind enough to accompany me to the police station next door? We can then examine the effects and determine the matter.'

Mary sat with Beatrice, who was now crying copiously yet silently into a kerchief. The two men returned to the room in a reasonably short time and the doctor handed Beatrice a pigskin purse. It jingled reassuringly.

'There are some coins, and notes on the Bank of England amounting to one hundred and sixty-three pounds, eighteen shillings and sixpence. I have noted the numbers on this paper, ma'am, £163/18/6, and also, here are some documents pertaining to the captain's regimental service. There are some other papers but nothing such as a bank draft or land title as mentioned by the lieutenant.'

Here the lieutenant interceded and addressed the tearful Beatrice. 'I told the police there might be something concerning a land purchase but there was no such documentation evident on his person, ma'am.'

Mary suggested that such evidence might be with the friends with whom he'd been lodging. This was agreed and so was her suggestion that they take Mrs Beauchamp to Mary's son's lodgings, where Beatrice might be able to collect her wits.

Lieutenant Symonds asserted that he would welcome the short walk back to the wharf along St Vincent Street. 'If Miss Evelyn is still waiting, I will organise her delivery to your son's lodgings, Mrs Lee. By that time you will surely have arrived. I bid you good day.' He gave a quick bow and left, his long legs striding easily along.

# 3

It was not a long walk. Lieutenant Symonds gave a wistful smile as he recalled the turn of events. While on board the *Orient*, he'd thought it deeply unfortunate – for him – that the lady had a husband waiting for her, and a fortunate husband indeed! Beatrice – as he had long thought of her – was deeply loyal. Despite his own best efforts at charming her, hoping at times for an occasional tête-à-tête with which to brighten the voyage – and maybe lead to that closer acquaintance – the lieutenant's best efforts had always been politely resisted.

He recalled lost opportunities and wondered now if there would be hope for him. She was a damned good-looking woman. These were tumultuous times of change, surely an offer of help and support from him would be mere courtesy? Whenever opportunities had presented for a quiet conversation on board ship with 'Madam B', as other officers had named her, he had been treated to various examples of the unassailable qualities of Captain Beauchamp; how initially the captain was transferred from some other regiment to Adelaide because of his stature and reputation as a professional officer. He was apparently posted here as his skills were needed to help discipline the Volunteer Military Forces, also known as the Adelaide Rifles. As Mrs Beauchamp informed him, the colony's government feared an attack from Russia during the recent Russo-Turkish war and a second battalion had been formed.

As he headed back to the wharf side and the *Orient*, the lieutenant remembered bits of their conversations. No denying it, the woman fascinated him. She had so completely and in such an inoffensive way thwarted his obvious attentions while on the voyage. Quite unique, in his experience, yet it indicated her qualities… She was a cut above the women he frequently found available and willing; a challenge and a damned attractive one.

He admired loyalty and she'd been unswervingly proud of the

husband; he was apparently with those amalgamated battalions and with, as she explained, the Duke of Edinburgh's Own. However, she had on occasion mentioned that her husband was to join the re-formed Artillery Company under a Colonel Francis Downes. Hmmph...

Nevertheless, he acknowledged that as a seagoing naval officer he was not conversant with the finer points of military regiments, battalions and the like. Also, a young lady newly married might be excused a confusion of information. He reminded himself that even throughout the voyage, as well as under the present distressing circumstances, her courage and self-possession were decidedly appealing and her personal strength an admirable quality in a wife. *Pity I'm contracted to go on to Melbourne, although...*

There was an overwhelming smell of fish in the air as he approached the *Orient*. The bustle around the disembarkees seemed to have lessened only marginally.

Miss Evelyn waved at him quite girlishly, calling his name. The wary young apprentice was eagle-eyed watching the luggage. He made his way to them. Well, at the least he now knew where Mrs Beauchamp – as was – would be staying for a while, and he had perhaps a couple more days before the ship sailed...

*

As they travelled in the carriage, Beatrice declined to rest her head on Mary's shoulder and sat 'po-faced', to Mary's thinking, against the opposite corner. It was with no small sense of shock that Mary discovered Beatrice had no idea where the Woodville friends lived, nor was she even certain of their family name! What was more, neither did she have any idea of where Mrs Wilkes, that chatty aunt of hers, would be staying, or living. Mary tried to remember what news of Beatrice's family she had managed to elicit from the girl during their occasional evening walks around the deck. At the time, she had thought her to be admirably discreet and, besides, her Aunt Wilkes had usually dominated their conversations. Only now that she needed more than idle chatter did she realise she knew remarkably little of the young woman's circumstances; what was more, she was becoming convinced that Beatrice herself knew little more.

Beatrice slid forward onto Mary as they hit a bump in the road.

'Looks like the road's not made-up here, Mrs Beauchamp. Surely just a patch, as I know from my John that where he lives the streets are quite civilised.'

As Beatrice settled back into her corner, Mary realised the girl's eyes were still quite full of tears. *Not only does she have that awful shock of the news, she had to identify his body and him lying there an' all that...hard even to think of, so it is, them married only so short a while. That cart or whatever it was must've gone over his head, poor soul, the mess it was. Yet she kissed it. That takes nerve, must admit. Well she'd be remembering how he was before, o'course.*

She reached over and patted the younger woman's gloved hand. 'Nearly there, now, my lamb. My John will know what's where and if not, he'll find out.'

She was rewarded for her cryptic assurance by a tentative smile.

Mary looked out over the roadway. There were houses here, all single-storey, some even wattle and daub. Dear God, have they not gone any further here than the poorest bothy? Even as doubts began, she was relieved to pass by a tall sandstone building with arched windows and imposing double wooden doors above a stepped entrance.

'Ah, Mrs Beauchamp, dear, at least the authorities here would appear to have built according to their functions. An' so they should, as the colony's more than sixty years now established. I was beginning to get quite worried. Is there much to see your side of the road?'

Her solemn companion gave a tentative shrug and Mary settled back in her seat, marvelling that a gentlewoman could travel to the other side of the world unaccompanied and so ignorant of what to expect. Nor had she realised, during their shipboard conversation, the extent to which Beatrice had placed her life and trust in the hands of her husband. Yet, though well reared, she understood the young woman to be a farmer's daughter so, however prosperous the family, she was not from the upper echelons of society and therefore removed from everyday realities, as she herself had found so many so-called 'county folk' in England to be. With that background, this one should have a bit of common sense about her – Mary valued 'common sense' – yet, in many little ways, Beatrice seemed uncertain, naïve.

At John Lee's lodging, the ladies gathered their skirts to dismount from the carriage and enter his narrow gate. Mary eagerly scanned the frontage of the house, pleased that it looked respectably appropriate to be the home of her John Benjamin. He was not the most descriptive of correspondents but he had often enough sung the praises of the city of Adelaide despite the protracted illness which, according to his latest letter, was becoming less manageable. She needed to satisfy herself of his recovery.

A young serving lass answered the door and Mary introduced herself and their guest, indicating as she bustled inside that Mr John's sister would be arriving shortly. The young lass informed them that Mr Lee had gone for a short constitutional in the fresh air but had promised to return by four of the clock. Mary's ever-transparent face obviously demonstrated irritation at this, so with a frenzy of bobbings up and down, the lass offered that his walks were on doctor's orders, ma'am, and also a dish of tea if madam required. Madam did, so without delay she quickly showed them to the dining room and pulled out some chairs.

Beatrice sat down, looking blankly around her. The serving lass readied the table for the teacups and Mary ascertained she was called Alice. She said she had been placed with Mr Lee to learn good service habits and be a good girl. The explanation fascinated Mary, who resolved to speak to John to learn more about her.

However, young Alice obviously had her wits because, leaving Mary to pour, she suggested most sensibly, in Mary's opinion, 'After refreshments, ma'am, I can clear out the small box room and make up a chaise longue with blankets for Mrs Beauchamp if she were to stay a while.'

'Good girl for thinkin' of it. Mrs Beauchamp, my dear, you take your tea and – yes – rest on the bed awhile for now. You've had a terrible shock, so you have, but that cup of tea might help a little. I'll wait for John and then Evelyn to return. We can sort things out after.'

Beatrice was led to the bedroom by Alice. Mary took the pot into the kitchen to get it topped up again and had a look around the space. There was a tap over a clean, stone sink, a small bench well scrubbed, and a little table pushed to one side, all under a small window. Taking pride of place was a small enclosed fire, painted green and cream with an oven door next to it and flat round metal lids atop, over a blazing wood fire.

'A curious contraption it is, to be sure, but nice an' neat. Now, Alice, sit here at this table with me an' we'll have a bit craich while the kettle comes to the boil again and I watch it.'

Not afraid of asking, Alice queried 'craich'.

Mary laughed. 'Miss Evelyn tells me here in Australia I must leave my "Irish" behind, and I have to admit in my native county – that's Monaghan – it isn't often heard but the word means to have a chat, a good time. I have Irish friends, from south of the border, and it's too easy to pick up their ways of talking. Now first of all, tell me what is that huge tin contraption outside the window? Does it hold water?'

They shared another pot of tea while Beatrice was left to rest in the bedroom. The lass gave her age as fifteen years old; she had sailed from Plymouth, England, five years earlier on the *City of Adelaide* with some other orphans. She had no knowledge of her parents and Mary was saddened to hear that. Yet the girl was quite self-composed as she told her. Mary was highly impressed, however, that young Alice was quite at home sitting in company. Not for her the timidity that characterised the usual English servant. *This young lass knows her worth to the household. She's not cheeky nor loud, neither. Best wait and ask John Benjamin any more about her background, though. Don't want to hurt her feelings, nice young lass like her…*

'Now, Alice, tell me how you do the laundry here, will you? I do like to know what's what…'

So passed a couple of hours until Evelyn arrived with their trunks, baskets and carpet bags, escorted by and vociferously grateful for the organisation of Lieutenant Symonds. To Evelyn's obvious disappointment, the lieutenant declined refreshment, saying he would return to the ship with the carrier. The vessel was being made ready to continue to Melbourne and the captain was apparently wishing to boast in that colony over there about its quick passage.…

On being told Beatrice was resting, he expressed his regrets but asked that Mrs Beauchamp please be informed that he had looked through the passenger records but regrettably could not ascertain an address for Mrs Wilkes. He did ask that Mrs Beauchamp receive his continuing felicitations.

Almost as he left, and on the dot of four o'clock, John Lee arrived. He was more ruddy of cheek and healthier-looking than his mother had feared, and that delighted her. He was volubly so welcoming to her and his sister that he insisted upon opening a precious Spanish sherry. Arms around each of 'his girls', he led them into a noisy jig around the sitting room floor.

From the relative seclusion of the little bedroom, Beatrice bemoaned their family reunion and reminiscences as typically Irish, noisy and joyful. She was not a little resentful. How could they be so happy when her heart was breaking? So much sadness in so short a time! Unable to prevent the tears, she fell along the bed, stifling her sobs as much as she could in the feather pillow, remembering those last few precious months. 'Oh, Mama! If only you had come with me... Oh, Papa!'

# Earlier in 1879 – England

## 4

Robert Fletcher, Beatrice's father, proclaimed himself a 'prophet of Edwardian freedom'. Certainly he relished the prospect of the old Queen's passing and was quite certain it couldn't be long before her son took over the throne. In his opinion, frequently expressed, Victoria had reigned too long. She'd been queening over them nearly as long as he'd been alive and he was now eight and forty. Rightly or wrongly, whenever he had to sell off some of his stock at a lower price, she was to blame. The Corn Laws and the Irish troubles were both down to her, or so he maintained when arguing with his overseer, Bill Dent.

'What a man has to contend with: a shortage of Irish labourers because they've all tekken ship for the colonies, and his oats and barley down to only thirty shillin's a quarter! Soon be hay-timing an' harvest an' ah can't get labour.'

'Coom on, sir,' argued Dent. 'Our folk were starving when they couldn't buy bread, and t'Irish workers only coom 'ere when they wuz starving. I don't blame 'em for catching t'boats for a better life. I 'ear many a tale of a man being successful over there. If I were a younger man an' me family not around me, I'd join 'em, I would that.'

'Huff and puff,' snorted Fletcher in his local dialect. 'Tha knows when tha's well off. Just get those bags checked and sewn up.'

He strode off to the stables, gaiter leathers creaking, wishing yet again he'd sons of his own. Dear Marjorie had done her best but three lads had died when little – or been lost in the making, as he put it to himself. 'Why's everyone talking about those blasted colonies' was his constant grumble. Especially since he now had a connection there himself – his son-in-law James Beauchamp was on his way there. 'Posted with his regiment', so they called it and he'd even offered him the farm if he'd stay.

'Not for me, Pa-in-law. Don'cha see, the future's over there not here!'

What Beatrice had not overheard of her father's regrets to her husband, she was promptly apprised. Even his opinion of James was passed to her by Father himself, frequently. 'A head full of ideas and little else,' Papa had proclaimed after James first came calling. Papa was always free with his opinions to those close to him.

As the relationship developed, he took consolation from the knowledge that when the young man went to sail to the colony, Beatrice was to wait here at home until he could send for her. Then, her papa had proposed, her mother would sail with her as was proper and his Marjorie would return home at least content she'd seen her daughter settled. The French woman could be their maid for the trip and with luck they'd leave her there. 'Mamzelle' was not one of his favourite people! The plan was intended as a surprise for Beatrice but she had overheard her parents making the plans after James had declared himself. She knew Papa had been reluctant to consent but Mama, dear, dear Mama, considered him a good match.

Their wedding was in the local church on a lovely bright Easter Saturday, 12 April. They went back to the farm until the Tuesday, when they took the coach to Morecambe-le-Sands for a brief honeymoon.

Only a few days after their return, James left for his regiment down south. He managed to pay only one other visit before taking ship for Australia on the twenty-seventh of the month. Then Mama died…

That awful day. Yet it started well enough – blue skies and already summer warm. Papa consented to ride with her over the fells, realising future opportunities would be few.

'Can't keep thee away from t'hosses long, can us, Missy? Tha' mother expects you indoors today, tha' knows. French conversation with that Mamzelle Hoity-Toity-Cost-a-Lot, in't it? Now she's yer "companion" instead.'

Beatrice's smile widened and she gestured widely while mimicking her erstwhile governess. 'Oh, Papa! "Mademoiselle 'av a meegren, Madame"… so Mama sent her to her bed and Maisie took her up some of Mama's potion…est la la! She's all of a dither because she is accompanying me to Australia, Papa.'

Joe had already saddled Gemini for her and knew to 'get t'maister's horse fettled' so in very short time they were headed over the cobbles and out the farm gate.

Papa set Big Red to a canter. 'Let's make for't tarn, lass. I need to check some ewes. Been some late lambing, I'm advised. Bit odd that.'

Beatrice whooped in delight; it was one of her favourite rides, low hills opening to the fells and higher ground. The tarn was set high; it drained from the high tops of the Lakeland mountains. Their Yorkshire Swaledale sheep, sturdy and hardy, were the best animals for such high pastures.

It was a full three hours later when they returned, both exhilarated by the ride and the freshness of the uplands air.

Papa yelled to Dent, 'Best get shepherd up top to keep foxes off t'lambs. Only a couple or so for now, but gradely enough.'

Beatrice felt tired but invigorated; she loved this life and her horses. However, James had promised her a horse over in the colony. South Australia was the name of the part where he was to be stationed, nowhere near that Botany Bay where the convicts went.

She tossed the reins to Joe. 'Give Gemini a good rub, will you please, Joe? She's had to work up those hills today.'

She laughed and shook down her hair as she ran to the house. A good hot bath, then she'd better buckle down to that embroidery to placate her mother. She ran up the front steps to be met by the little housemaid, red-faced, swollen-eyed and sobbing as if her heart was breaking.

'Something up, Maisie?'

The little maid bobbed. 'It's the mistress, Miss Beatrice, she 'ad a turn. Doctor's been sent for…'

Her father heard this as he walked in the door, and still in his boots and gaiters clattered up the staircase to his wife's room.

The housekeeper was standing at the door wringing her hands.

'Mrs Willis, what is it? Now, out of my way!'

Mama was lying on the bed, fully dressed, seemingly inert, but on hearing her husband's voice, signalled weakly with one hand. He ran over and she whispered to him.

'I was stitching, dear, just that new pattern…new tablecloth…then a pain behind my eye then all went black and the pain is agony…!'

Her voice rose a pitch on the last words and he slid an arm under her shoulders and with his other hand stroked her brow, all the while murmuring soothing endearments.

The doctor burst into the room, pushing Beatrice to one side and unbuckling his bag as he approached the bed.

Beatrice shepherded Mrs Willis out of the room with her and closed the door. 'Now do tell me – slowly and clearly, please, Mrs Willis – how long ago did this happen? And how did she manage to get up the stairs…?'

Events had happened quickly after that. It was imprinted on Beatrice's brain as if it had been only the day before. The dreadful funeral, then weeks of preparing to sail without Mama to guide her; the upset and scandal of Mademoiselle running away with Mr Dent's brother when she found she was expecting his baby; her own doubts as to whether it was proper to plan for a trip when she was in mourning. This last was tempered only by Papa's gladness that dear Mama had witnessed her wedding and the admiration of their relatives and friends.

'Even if I have no great opinion of the man, your dear Mama considered him a catch. You belong now by his side. Hurrummph!'

Then dear Mrs Willis promised that she and the Dents would take good care of her papa, which relieved her mind. Papa travelled with her to London and the shipping office to meet his cousin, a respectable widow who was to undertake the duties of chaperone – all this agreed to, to appease dear Papa. Beatrice had once before met the lady, Mrs Aubrelia Edna Wilkes, now a widow, when, to celebrate her coming of age, Mama and Papa had taken her for a week to London to visit its theatres and the rather frightening Tower. Mrs Wilkes had the vapours when asked to ride up the river with them; to her it was a place of 'evil miasma and always being dug up by the lower classes hoping to find treasure'.

However, this Mrs Wilkes was now sailing to live with her daughter's family in the town of Adelaide, named for the old King William's wife. They had arranged to meet on 1 November, thus allowing nearly two whole days and nights to become acquainted before embarking on the *Orient*, which was scheduled to sail on the third. The dowager Mrs Wilkes happily agreed to be her companion and thus Papa was appeased.

# 15 December 1879 – Adelaide

## 5

A timid knock came on the door and Evelyn entered with a glass of water. She put it carefully on the little box table, lightly laid a wet flannel on Beatrice's forehead then, with a sad smile, left the room.

Beatrice sat up, wiped her face again with the refreshing flannel and, realising her whereabouts, tidied her hair and straightened her bodice. *Oh goodness! Here I am worrying about those distant proprieties and forgetting to observe my obligations to this good emigrant family. Dear Mama, help me in this...*

That had to be it; no more mourning her own situation, no more playing the fragile maiden bowed down with shock. Poor James deserved her memories but prompt attention must be paid to her own, current, situation. She had a brain, and fair common sense – as her father had always allowed – so she must set to and find out 'just what is what', as her mother used to say. And just as this family were 'emigrants' so was she. Somehow it didn't sound too friendly, that word. 'Immigrant' sounded better – somehow it had a sense of purpose about it.

First: no more of this wishy washy behaviour. What had happened to James – and her – was an unexpected tragedy. However, she had to look ahead; maybe she could find Aunt Edna Wilkes, not quite an aunt but her only known relative – however distant – in this colony.

Second: she should also admit an emerging truth – although she was shocked to the core at what had happened, she felt able to deal with her own situation more coolly than perhaps others might expect. Naturally, marrying James had been exciting. To marry was expected of her and she had loved him. Yet, though it was generally considered a good match, and he with prospects, she had never been really in love with him in the same intense ways Miss Austen described in her stories. She had thought a lot of this deficiency in her feelings, when travelling on the ship, standing on the deck and watching the water, the waves and the clouds. Nor had she been immune from the attentions, even flirtatiousness, of some of the young officers on board, and more than once she had enjoyed their company walking around the broader rear deck, though careful always to maintain her reputation.

Now here she was, ready to take steps to a room full of new friends and thence to a new life. She exhaled then breathed in again, slowly, then out again. Of course, she had been excited at the prospect of seeing James again, at making a life with him, elsewhere. Now she had to ask if she was deeply in love with him and when learning of his death and seeing him there so wounded, should she not have felt the awful depth of despair as when she lost dear Mama? Of course she cried, but did she cry more for the loss of her plans, their new life, than for James? Sitting now, gazing at the wallpaper, making ready to rejoin her new friends, surely she should be suffering a greater sense of loss? Of course, her James had been lost to her many months ago; was it therefore unnatural that she felt she could cope on her own? Had she perhaps been living only her romantic dreams, believing that, too, was expected of her? *Oh dear, what a confusion. Well, Beatrice Fletcher, decisions are now to be made and you are the only one to make them.*

As she steadied herself she realised she had used her maiden name. *I am outwardly at least, to these people, Beatrice Beauchamp. Oh my goodness. That is a portent in itself.*

She stiffened her shoulders and adjusted her lace. The family was talking in the next room. From Evelyn's delighted squeals responding to a deeper, masculine voice, she assumed that voice to belong to Mary's son, John. Best to wait until their reunion was completed. Mrs Lee always seemed a most intelligent and empathetic woman, she had thought so as they had walked the deck on the journey; perhaps in due course she might be able to advise…

They'd quietened a little, now. To be true, listening to their excited exchange was a welcome distraction from her own thoughts. Tea cups were again clinking on saucers and then it seemed – from more of Evelyn's happy squeals – that her brother had managed to procure for her the employment position she had spoken of while on the *Orient.*

Mentally chastising herself for her lack of the courtesies owing, and after some more minutes waiting for a lull in the others' conversation, Beatrice recovered her composure enough to emerge from her retreat.

Evelyn was nearest to her and reached for her hand. 'Oh, Beatrice! How are you feeling? I am so very, very sorry, my dear.' Then, failing to restrain herself any longer she exclaimed, 'My brother has secured me a position with the Telegraph Department, a marvellous situation and I will be able to contact all the cities and even London!'

Before Beatrice could respond, Mary took the floor.

'Evelyn, my dear! Manners, if you please! Beatrice, my dear, brave girl, Mrs Beauchamp, may I present my son, Evelyn's elder brother, John Benjamin Stedham Lee?'

Beatrice turned to the son and bobbed in response to his courteous greeting.

'My condolences, Mistress Beauchamp. It is most regrettable that you should be greeted by such a situation in a new land. Whatever my family may do to help you adjust to your new circumstances will be our pleasure.'

'Thank you, Mr Lee.' As he kissed her hand in welcome she had no inkling that he considered her a wish-washy type, not at all strong-looking enough to sail back to England on the next available berth. For that was what his mother had already explained would probably happen.

'She's no reserves to fall back on, poor young lady,' she'd hissed at him sotto voce.

John was aware that his mother was herself recently widowed, but bearing up very well, though severely clad in the mourning black. He decided to ask her more of her own feelings when alone with her; now was not the time.

Beatrice accepted a chair and a freshly poured cup of China tea from Mary as Evelyn once more beleaguered her brother with rapid questions about her new situation. John couldn't know his less than favourable first impressions of this very newly widowed younger visitor were reciprocated. Glancing at him sideways, she thought him truly a sickly-looking fellow, with an unhealthy flush of face reducing at times of quiet to a strange pallor. She tried to remember what illness he was prone to, that Mary had described while on the *Orient*. As if on cue, the conversation among the family swung to the ladies' experiences on that rapid steamship voyage.

Later, over a meal, when it was agreed Beatrice would stay the night at least, Beatrice thanked her friends for their caring and support. Evelyn remembered to pass on to her the lieutenant's message about her Aunt

Wilkes. She absorbed this, joined in the conversation but then sat back, obviously in deep thought, allowing the family chatter to surround her.

She was quiet so long, Mary gave her a gentle tap on her knee.

She sat up, smiled then stunned them to silence, announcing, 'Dear people, I have decided to stay in the colony.'

Mary's surprise registered almost comically upon her elastic features, although she managed to restrain from comment as Beatrice outlined her plans.

'Firstly, I must find out the wheelwright's address at Woodville from whom James had purchased the hire of a cart to take us to the property. I will, later, try to contact Aunt Wilkes but she is only remote family to me, she has duties to her own daughter in this colony, and I mean to be independent and self-sufficient. I am sure the wheelwright would know the friends with whom James had arranged for us to stay. Equally, I am confident they would allow me to stay with them until I can learn more of the property James has purchased – or was planning to when he wrote. It is in the place Cock's Creek, or Bridgewater as I believe it is being called. From his letter to me at the Cape, it appears to be not far from settlements and villages occupied by German people who have established good dairy farms which supply milk, butter and cheese. Cock's Creek has a mill I believe for flour-making, a post office and a school. Also orchards. So he wrote in his letter. Then, depending on whether it has a suitable building, I should be able to engage some help and stay in it to become established and manage the orchards.'

Mary was moved to make some remark. 'Well, my dear young lady, you have courage and determination, I'll say that. Permit me to advise you to first find lodgings locally, near to us, at least until my John can perhaps do some investigating for you.'

Quite the gentleman, John agreed to his mother's suggestion. He was surprised that this namby-pamby-looking woman had some strength of will, of purpose. She was perhaps made of sterner stuff than he had supposed, or could it be just a reaction to her bad news? He found himself feeling genuinely sympathetic and hoped this Captain Beauchamp had everything signed sealed and delivered, as was the phrase.

'Mrs Beauchamp, I feel that the "investigating" Mam speaks of should not be delayed – it is very nearly the Christmas closing of some businesses. Also, I am familiar with much of the Woodville area. Mayhap I can find the wheelwright for you and then the friends of your husband. I can leave in the morning. If you allow, I can advise them of the demise of your dear husband. I do wonder if they may be holding documentation of sorts on his behalf or know where such papers pertaining to your property are being held. That way, we may gain some knowledge by nightfall tomorrow of how things stand for you. Meanwhile, please do not hurry to find other lodgings. If you can make yourself comfortable here in my house, with my mother and sister, you would be welcome to stay as long as you would wish, and so have time to organise your thoughts.'

# 16 December 1879

## 6

Next morning, before the ladies of the house were awake, John set off for Commercial Road, where he knew the ostler at the First Commercial Inn. He had considered taking the horse tram through to Albert Park, rather than hiring a mount, but as he was uncertain where he would be directed at the other end, it seemed more common sensible – to use one of his mother's words – to have independent transport. Though still early, the heat of the day was promising to increase markedly and he was glad to be given the choice of two reasonable animals, one a hack with a gentle eye.

'Going far, Mr Lee, sir? This one got plenty staying power but ain't fast, nor by a long chalk.'

'Only over to Woodville, to the wheelwright there, Jonathan. Quite looking forward to a bit of fresh air from a horse's back.'

With a smile and a tip of his cabbage tree brim, he turned the horse's head to leave the yard. *Good fellow, Jonathan, but a terrible tittle-tattler. And there's no need for him to know that poor lady's business.*

Barely an hour later, John was approaching the Halfway House inn. The smell of baking bread assailed his senses. It was irresistible. For him, it was a rare feeling to be hungry and certainly not one to be denied. Lashing his mount to the rail by a well filled trough, he entered to see what they could offer to break his fast. For a shilling he ordered a plate of black pudding, eggs and a trencher-sized piece of new hot bread, all to be washed down with a mug of small beer. The molasses was strong in the beer, and it was a bit cloudy, but still lip-smacking with the hot meal. He also learned quite a bit about the local community and gained the quick route to the wheelwright. Afterwards, clambering back onto the horse, he realised it had been a long time since his stomach had allowed him such enjoyment.

The day was going to be a hot one. He leaned forward and patted the horse's cheeks. Its eyes were almost closed and long lashes curled on to his fingers as it opened them, realising his touch. It was content. Jonathan called it a stayer; he sure knew his horseflesh. John was pleased the horse had drunk well at the trough; even at the thought, he raised his own water bottle and took a swig. Despite the wide brim over his eyes, he had to wrinkle his eyes against the glare.

His stomach began protesting its breakfast and he emitted a chorus of noisy belching. *Okay, horse, prick your ears forward again, a belch is a plain honest compliment to the cook! Christmas is only, what, nine days away and it'll certainly be a hot one. I must remember not to eat too heavily of the rich stuff I know Ma will stir Alice to baking. And to be honest, I shouldn't have had that breakfast back there; too heavy for days like this one. I don't want more ill effects and Ma only just arrived...*

At least, mine host had known of the wheelwright. John followed his directions and reached the yard before the sun had reached midway overhead. He drew his mount to a halt and looked around. The business seemed more smithy at heart, the clang of heavy hammers indicating hot metal. He noticed a couple of carriages that looked ready for hiring over at the opposite end of a big barn from the forge.

'Need a shoe, surr?' From over to his left came the deep-voiced English country twang. A burly fellow, wiping his hands on a cloth came over to stand by John's stationary horse.

John dismounted, holding the horse with the rein. He explained the situation as the smith listened, occasionally nodding.

'Looks like they'll not be needing the carriage then,' he declared matter-of-factly. 'Reckon the friends the cap'n were talking of, yer needs ter see, them'd be the Taylors.' He directed John to their home, went to resume his business then turned back.

'Surr, I'm no old woman tittle-tattlin' but it might be good that you know of a certain fact, surr.' And while John still held his horse's reins the smith told him something of an unsettling circumstance. 'Just be prepared for the Taylors not to be best pleased at the capn's untimely death' – he crossed himself like a good Catholic – 'and they'll be telling you the details of their own disappointment that I'm not at liberty to say, surr.'

Following the smith's directions, John walked the hundred or so yards up a sandy lane, becoming increasingly curious about the whole situation, the stoic horse clip-clopping behind.

A stout man walked down to the lane from beyond a wooden gate. In a superior tone, he addressed his caller. 'Sir, this is a private lane. You are…?'

John gave a quick double bob of the head in acknowledgement of the greeting and introduced himself. He apprised the man of Captain Beauchamp's death, expecting an outpouring of regret if these were truly Beauchamp's friends. To the contrary, the received emotion was anger; it was a totally unexpected tirade at the inconvenience! John was at a loss for words. The rant – it was no less – continued for at least a minute.

Taylor suddenly composed himself and gestured a weak apology. He wiped his sweaty brow with a large spotted kerchief, then turned and, without a word, beckoned John to follow.

Assuming it would be the only way to determine the matter, John vexedly looped the rein over the gatepost and then loped up the path to the shade of the house walls. Some wicker chairs were arranged under a decorative tree and Taylor plonked his body into one, signalling John to follow suit. At his call, a woman came out carrying a tray of homemade lemon cordial.

Mr Taylor practically spat the words: 'Beauchamp's dead, Eleanor. The man's gone. Not only that, so is our money!' He turned to John. 'Where is Beauchamp's wife, sir? And what do you know of the circumstances of her arrival?'

John outlined the events of the previous day up to his arrival at their gate as the Taylors sat, listening intently, without interruption. As John finished, and after sipping his cordial, he broke the silence. 'Mr Taylor, sir, will you not tell me the sequence of events? I need to relay the story to Mrs Beauchamp.'

His own drink despatched, Taylor sat forward. 'We jointly bought this orchard, James and me – up in the hills, more Lenswood than Bridgewater. Don't know why the lady thought it was just James. He, Beauchamp, didn't have the funds for the entire purchase so it was agreed he would pay me half if I paid the full amount in order to secure the property. We drew up a friendly agreement that we took to Beckett's. They're in Rundle Street and they're in land brokerage also. I paid a hundred pounds deposit as surety.' He paused.

'This was back on the sixth. James was to set off for the property early the following day taking with him a draft for £500 – my money, you understand – as required by the vendor's man of business. Yes, yes, strange arrangement perhaps, but the vendor was a European immigrant, not English – he did things differently from us, sir. Still legal, so Beckett assured us. James was military and took with him two pistols. I had no doubts at all the business would be transacted, and that we would then jointly own a very profitable apple orchard, sir!' His voice rose an octave and became louder with each syllable.

Then he quietened as if he realised he needed to compose himself, and resumed. 'He was then to bring back to me the official contract and receipt for the monies so we could return to Beckett's to finalise the deal. His share was half of that amount, sir. As long as his signing occurred before the tenth, our purchase was secure. I have known him for a good few years. We served together, until I retired in the middle of this year. I hadn't heard from James, but I knew he was making plans for housing so assumed that was the reason for the delay. My signature was already on file at Beckett's. Only Beauchamp's was needed to finalise the deal. His wife was to come on the *Orient* – oh yes, of course you know that – so I thought he might make his way here sometime and we would meet the lady. Then, yesterday in the morning, Julius Beckett's man rode up, enquiring about the circumstances of our gentleman's agreement. It transpired Beauchamp had not been to the office at all.'

Taylor leaned forward, eyes glaring, hands knuckled on his knees, then he reached over and smacked John on his leg with emphasis. His face became almost apoplectic in his rage.

John leaned forward. 'Mr Taylor, sir, this heat… Do control yourself…'

'How dare you, sir! A friend, an officer and gentleman of my regiment has cheated on me, and on himself, sir. Yesterday the Beckett's man told me that another purchaser had come forward with the money after the tenth and as the vendor needed to sell and take ship to France – or wherever – the property was no longer available. Beckett's did refund my own deposit but I lost the property, sir! Not only that, sir, my £500 was not placed with the Beckett's office! Beauchamp left here with my money. It is not an insignificant sum, sir!' He exhaled loudly and sat back in his chair.

'You saw him at the Dead House. Was he carrying funds, a bankers' draft mayhap, anything to enable me to recover my investment?'

John knew from his mother that there had been nothing other than some cash on Captain Beauchamp's person, and no land brokerage material or other valid documentation. He said so without detailing the amount of cash.

'Mr Taylor, sir. We had assumed the good captain was staying with you all this while but it seems he has been missing since 6 December. That's all of ten days ago. Do you know where he might have been lodging in the interim?'

Taylor was now calmer and becoming increasingly hangdog of feature.

Mrs Taylor came and sat in the adjacent chair, her calming hand on her husband's forearm. 'Mr Lee, we understood that Captain Beauchamp had only his friends from the regiment and none are still here in this colony, having moved on. I had assumed that he was inspecting the properties in readiness for his wife's arrival. We are entirely at a loss to understand any of this unfortunate happening, sir, and indeed, it is a loss to us.'

John felt the question needed to be asked. 'Mr Taylor, sir. Captain Beauchamp may be interred at Cheltenham. As you are his friends, Mrs Beauchamp wondered if…'

He couldn't finish. Taylor rose and looked as if he would suffer that apoplectic fit.

'Mr Lee, you may pass on to Mrs Beauchamp our sympathies at her loss but I, sir, I, have no compassion for the man.' He stalked off into the house.

Mrs Taylor tentatively signalled John to stay and she followed her husband into the house, reappearing in only a few minutes with a large tapestry fabric bag with a clasp at the top. 'These are the captain's personal effects that he left with us, Mr Lee.'

Her husband walked down the path and stood by his wife as she continued, 'I understand you were unaware of any of these matters and ask only that if you find out where our money has gone you inform Mr Beckett's office, if not ourselves.'

Her husband's only comment was a combination of a humph and a grunt.

John dipped his hat to her then thanked the volatile Mr Taylor for his time. He was quite thankful to remount his sleepy hack and exit that unhappy and angry household.

# 7

John debated turning up the Port Road to journey into the city, to Rundle Street and Mr Beckett's office, but decided against it. Best first to inform Beatrice Beauchamp of the result of his investigations and, not only that, the day was advancing. He considered the late captain's bag of effects rolled before the saddle. They were none too expansive, but the widow deserved to be able to draw from them whatever conclusions she might.

It was also a very hot day and a warm wind was setting up dust. His fob watch – more reliable than looking at the sun on a glary day – indicated ten past three of the clock. So he had missed luncheon and, more to the point, that lemon cordial seemed a long time ago. *My wretched digestion playing games again, I'm not really hungry and if I eat, I'll be sick.* Deciding he needed to drink, he took a last draught from his warm water bottle, then trickled the rest between the horse's ears. It tossed its head and snorted and seemed to pick up its step.

*More than I am able.* 'Let's get you back to Jonathan, old girl. Been a long and tiring day, no? I think my illness is catching up with me. Time to go home in the cool and have a long, cold drink.'

Later, and by the time he had walked the short distance from the carriers, John was quite exhausted. It would soon be evening, and a trifle cooler.

He was pleased to reach his home. The ladies were gathered around a couple of scones and empty teacups when he walked into the house. The tension of the previous evening seemed absent; even Mistress Beatrice seemed more relaxed. She seemed brighter in the face and, not a little to his surprise, greeted him warmly. Evelyn went to find another cup and saucer as his mother ushered her son to a chair.

'Come on, son. If you're feeling all right, let's be hearing the story now.'

'Oh, please, Mrs Lee do let him sit and sip some tea first. He looks so hot and dusty.'

'Tush, my dear girl. We are gone beyond such formality, I feel, though I commend your good manners. Here in our own company, please let us use our Christian names. I will be Mary to you and you will be Beatrice to me, unless you wish otherwise?'

'No, no, Mrs... erm, Mary. I do prefer.'

John was interested to note this exchange. He approved. *So the Mistress Beauchamp has already accepted our more relaxed ways and become Beatrice, casting off that stiff and starchy Englishness.*

He gave Beatrice her husband's carpet bag and she set it on the floor by her feet, looking askance at it. They all sat quietly and listened as he recounted his conversation with the Taylors and, before that, with the wheelwright. Their only movement throughout was Beatrice covering up a quiet gasp with her hand to her mouth as he described the Taylor man's belligerent attitude, even though he modified the man's remarks concerning the captain's funeral arrangement.

When it became clear James's whereabouts between the sixth and yesterday were still a mystery, Mary Lee tut-tutted, though waved him to continue. His other concern, expressed after he drained his cup of tea, whether James could have deposited a bank draft or another financial agreement somewhere else yet to be disclosed, caused his mother and sister to lift their eyebrows in enquiry but Beatrice seemed sunk in her own thoughts.

Then she spoke. 'Are you saying that the money on my husband's body is not mine to spend as I wish, that it belongs in part-payment to these Taylors?'

'No, Beatrice,' responded John, feeling free to call her by her Christian name in this company, 'I believe I have determined those funds can be argued to be yours. Mr Taylor gave the captain a draft drawn on the bank and that is the sum he wishes to regain.' He swallowed his tea. 'I suggest that it is more to your interest, Beatrice, that the land you believed your husband had purchased is no longer yours to pursue. Mr Taylor will pursue the matter of the draft with that firm, Beckett's. It is not up to you, nor me, to take any other initiative.'

Mary intervened. 'Beatrice, dear girl, this changes things. Will you not consider now returning to England, to what is familiar to you? This is a young colony and growing quickly enough but a lady on her own, short of funds, must endure a distinct disadvantage. Also, perhaps you feel that being in full mourning may prevent certain enquiries by you…'

'Dear Mary, believe me, I have thought hard on this matter. If I were to return, I would be an embarrassment to the family I have remaining. I have no funds there. My dowry was paid to James and was to be invested – he said – in this colony. I had only an extra allowance from Papa for the journey. As he also gave money to my companion, Aunt Wilkes, I cannot expect more. I wish to be independent, yet in England I cannot seek employment – it would be considered unseemly. I would return to my father's household and be only a drain on his resources. I have been known as my father's daughter for most of my life, then it was as the wife of a regimental soldier. Am I mistaken to feel that here in the colony I would not be looked down upon for seeking out opportunities for advancement, as a single woman, as a worthy individual?'

She stood and surveyed her new friends. 'I feel I must explore what happened to James between the sixth and the day he…he died, Sunday the fourteenth. It is already the sixteenth and there are working days before the next Sabbath and, tomorrow being Wednesday, I shall make the acquaintance of this man of finance, Mr Beckett, and determine for myself what may have happened that he is – perhaps – not telling Mr and Mrs Taylor. I will also investigate the bag of possessions the Taylors gave to you, John. There may be something helpful in those.'

As Mary moved to speak, Beatrice waved her forefinger gently in a stopping gesture, smiled tentatively and bade them all a gentle goodnight. 'Forgive me but I am weary and have no appetite for supper. Please, all of you, excuse me. I need to think some more and then to sleep.'

# 17 December 1879

## 8

Next morning, after a substantial breakfast insisted upon by Mary, Beatrice set out in the cab John had found and directed to the house. Despite her protesting she must manage things for herself, John accompanied her.

Mary was adamant that his presence would be an advantage. 'Please, my young friend, it is wise to remember we are newcomers to this place. Different in some ways it may be, but in many ways it retains some of the Old Country traditions. I do know that some men of business will not talk to a woman, much as in the Old Country. John has written of this. Is it still so, John?'

He nodded. 'I understand your wish to be independent, Beatrice, but I can perhaps be helpful if questions are asked about the Taylors and, also, I have met them.'

Beatrice agreed to the sense of his suggestion and after a relatively short ride, during which John pointed out various attractions, he paid off the cab at the junction of North Terrace, near to Government House.

Looking to the east along North Terrace, she was impressed by the imposing buildings lining the gracious boulevard but John was eager to make their way to Becketts.

'They've taken over an upstairs office in Rundle Street over Ballantynes and Gerke & Rodeman. Number 40, they are, but are planning some move to more salubrious premises, I believe. There's a lot of buying and selling going on in that part. They are two of the most useful shops in the street for things I like, but first we will see your Mr Beckett.'

They stopped outside Gerke & Rodeman, a double frontage with windows full of utility household articles and barrels on the footpath outside. Beatrice would have liked to study the goods more closely but John was already indicating and opening a narrow doorway with the number 40 painted on it and set between the two shops. He beckoned Beatrice to go first and they climbed a narrow steep stair to an inky-smelling office.

'Not the imposing edifice I imagined, John. I see that monetary, usury, premises are as ready to understate their prosperity here as in London.'

He smiled and nodded. *She'll eventually sound less stuffy; give her a few weeks here – if she does stay...*

A bell rang as they reached the top stair and walked into a large room divided into small screened office spaces. A young male clerk left his desk and came up to John. He in no way acknowledged Beatrice and she bristled at this, particularly when the clerk indicated, 'Madam may wait here on that settle as she pleases while the gentlemen conduct their business.'

John was determined to avoid any protest so, to the clerk's consternation, he quite forcibly steered Beatrice by her elbow towards a larger office with glass windows.

Consternation was evident also on the plump and bewhiskered face of Mr Beckett when John introduced himself with his lady guest, Mrs Captain James Beauchamp.

They were invited to sit, their two chairs opposite Mr Beckett, who relaxed in his own chair, fingers entwined and resting on his substantial stomach; all hidden behind an untidy pile of ledgers and documentation. As they were seated, Beatrice had a spontaneous desire to laugh because the top of his head was the only part of him readily seen above it all! She pretended a sneeze, at which movement he cleared a central passage through which to see and be seen. The only space cleared for any writing that Beatrice would see was a small blotter, itself bordered with pens and inkwells. She maintained her solemn face with difficulty.

'Aah, dear lady, please allow me to express my sympathies. I recognised your dear husband's name of course in the *Register*. Now...'

Beatrice nodded gracefully but John interrupted the flow of sympathy. 'Mrs Beauchamp is anxious to determine her position, as I am sure you understand, sir. As to the business also, please do address your comments freely to her.'

Mr Beckett's eyebrows shot up at the unfamiliar request but his sympathy seemed genuine and, as his later remarks demonstrated, was indeed so. 'Your husband, madam, was to come to me with the documentation and the signed receipt from the vendor by the tenth of the month. This had been agreed as I had another buyer most interested in the property and wishing, because of the season, to make headway with the orchards. They were apples, madam, according to the Taylors. Have you met the Taylors?'

At this point John outlined what he had learned from the Taylors the previous day. Mr Beckett was pleased to explain the entire proceedings and produced documents showing freedom to purchase. All were signed by the vendor and various actuaries per pro with maps in explanation; so many that Beatrice's head was swimming despite the sweet sherry she had been given by Mr Beckett to sip – as a 'restorative' . He asserted there had been no cover-up, nothing untoward in the transaction; simply it was a highly sought-after property unsurprisingly lost to the Beauchamps and the Taylors because of the captain's non-appearance.

Resigned now to the lack of positive outcomes, considering that at least this man of business would be able to advise on proper procedures for a man of the Militia to be buried, Beatrice decided that at least one problem must be resolved. 'I do have another concern, Mr Beckett. I would wish my husband to receive a proper burial, though it would appear none of his friends could be found in the time to attend. I have been advised there is a cemetery at Cheltenham...'

'Dear lady, a man of the Militia has earned a dignified burial and I am sure his regiment would wish to be involved.' He picked up and rang a bell from his desk and a clerk came running. He was given instructions, called another lad who was also directed and who took off, grabbing a coat from a hat stand to run down the stairs.

Mr Beckett stood as if the interview was over, came round the desk and, as John and Beatrice also stood, she a little surprised at the abruptness, he shook hands with John and then gave a little bow to Beatrice.

'I have an appointment elsewhere, sir, madam, but be assured my clerk will make the proper enquiries and we shall send a message to your lodgings tomorrow with suggestions as to what procedures are recommended. Rest assured, dear lady, we are at your service in all things.'

# 9

Back down on the pavement, John braved a smile and whispered, 'Well, he's a bumptious little man but I suspect he knows his business. We shall await his advice tomorrow, Beatrice. Now, if you will excuse me, I wish to make a purchase. Perhaps you would care to accompany me into the store?'

'If you don't mind, John, I'll wait outside to take a look in this store's window. It is interesting to see what one can buy, and where.'

He went into the store beneath Beckett's office, Gerke & Rodeman. Beatrice was more interested in the contents of Ballantyne's window, next door. Above it, on the wall – on a parallel level to Mr Beckett's premises, she supposed – was painted 'Robin & Birks'. Looking up and assessing the space along the width of the two stores, she wondered if Beckett's had not taken over the total area. In the window of Ballantyne & Company was a large display of commodities whose labels were familiar from her market shopping back 'home'. They looked clean and shiny, not dusty, and she wondered if they had just arrived – perhaps even on 'her' ship, the *Orient*.

A ding of the adjacent shop's door bell and John emerged with a small paper-wrapped parcel containing what smelled quite pungently of tobacco. He took his place on the outer edge of the pavement and then moved to take her elbow. She forestalled the familiar gesture by casually placing her hand behind her back as if to adjust the fit of her coat and immediately reproached herself. *I know that really John is merely being courteous and a friend. I am allowing myself to be foolish and overwhelmed with my own thoughts. My imagination is running alarmingly along its own way. I must be less precious in my dealings here with these people. Mama was always so proper in her instructions, she would be unable to accept this casual politeness yet I cannot find it objectionable in these surroundings.*

John was already drawing her attention to another shop of interest across the street and, with no change of inflection or demeanour, was explaining the history of its beginnings. He also indicated the upstairs office adjacent to Beckett's saying that the Birks family had recently opened the department store next to Gerke & Rodemann. 'I think it was about three years ago. Quite a coup for Adelaide and I believe very popular with ladies, as much of its haberdashery comes from Sydney and Melbourne as well as from London on the shipping.'

They continued eastwards along the wide frontage of Charles Birks's store. Quite a showcase range of windows, she thought. Some of the women's styles in the window quite caught her eye and she thought she would look on another day, when she was not so absorbed in her own situation and wondering about her finances. Shopping for anything new really had to wait. At the very least she had no debt to repay, other than to the Lees, though she doubted they would accept any recompense for their generosity. *Just how long will that one hundred and sixty pounds last? Oh my, how much will his interment cost?* Then the thought came into her mind that when her father had paid for her lavish wedding, the cost had been more than what was now her sole wealth! Dear Papa.

She stopped, stood still, and John took her elbow again. 'Beatrice?'

She smiled and shrugged, signalling they should walk on. *He is a good friend but I cannot confide in him yet how I feel when I am not sure myself. Why do I think of my wedding in terms of Papa and Mama more than Jamie. Oh dear…* She sighed and John this time took her arm without resistance.

'Beatrice, you are troubled, I can see. Rest assured we shall help you all we can. I too was a newcomer a few years ago and I remember how lonely, so very alone, I felt in a strange country. What I can do to help you, and my mother and sister, overcome strangeness, I am glad to do.'

'Oh, thank you, John. It is just that Mr Beckett made me realise how final my financial situation will be. Also, there are still questions as to where James went after the sixth and that is worrying. I do thank your dear mother, you and Evelyn for proving the very best of friends. It is just that I must now make some decisions and I am the only one who can make them.'

'Beatrice, may I suggest the most pressing matter is the captain's burial? Let us await Mr Beckett's advice – it is promised for tomorrow morning. He is a man of organisation, well-known and approved in the city.' He paused and looked into her eyes. 'Do allow me to take this opportunity of showing you more of the city. If we walk under the verandas, we will avoid the hot sun and, Beatrice, see this – an enticing little tea room. If I may further suggest, let us take advantage of it and enjoy a cup of tea or chocolate and a scone.'

It did look a pleasant little place, centrally placed along Rundle Street at her estimation; more bakery than tea room perhaps.

James was soon cheerfully explaining to a lady behind the counter how he was walking Beatrice around the city because she was newly arrived in the colony. Beatrice was a little embarrassed at the informality but the lady gave a cheery welcome and introduced herself as Mrs Calder, and in no time they were ushered to a tiny wooden table by the front window and seated either side of it.

'I will gladly offer you a cake, we have a wide selection, and a pot of tea will take no time. Please make yourselves comfortable…' and she bustled off to give a request to a young lass wrapping a large loaf of bread for a woman at the other end of the counter.

Beatrice leaned towards John. 'This is a very busy little bakery, John. I am surprised they don't build a proper tea room here. The atmosphere is delightful – and the smell of the bakery from beyond this room, even more so!'

'The Calders have a big biscuit factory in, I think it is Twin Street, and when the Duke of Edinburgh visited some years back, Calders made a special biscuit they called the Albert – in you-know-whose honour! And I do believe there's talk of a tea room for there.'

She was impressed.

A young lass in a baker's apron brought a small teapot with a little jug of cream and a small dish of lemon slices, put them on their table and disappeared to return shortly with two cups and saucers into which she poured the tea. 'Mrs Calder says you won't 'ave room for the cakes if I leaves the pot.' And off she went again to reappear with two small plates with cake knives and a two-tiered glass cake stand piled with a delicious variety of iced cakes and slices of fruit buns.

They had barely decided whether lemon or milk when she bustled back, with two snowy white starched napkins. 'Mrs Calder says she 'opes you enjoy and will you ding-dong that bell on the counter over there, sir,

45

please, when you wish to go.' She turned back. 'Oh, an' there's no rush, sir and madam. We don' usually 'ave folks sitting down.'

Beatrice laughed delightedly. 'This is simply charming, John.'

She opted for the lemon slices in her tea and was amazed to learn from the young waitress that a lemon tree grew in their backyard.

'And a pomegranate, madam. For the cakes, you see.'

John drank his tea with a drop of milk in it and four sugar lumps. He saw her watching and smiled. 'Keeping me sweet, Beatrice.'

*Oh dear, we are not that close.* 'John, do tell me about your position here and why you came to South Australia.'

He obviously loved his work with the Telegraph Office. From his enthusiastic account, she surmised it was a mix of clerking and geography. He spoke of charting routes and costing transport mileages until she was hard put not to allow her attention to wander. Luckily he realised this.

'Beatrice, I am sorry. I run the risk of boring you and I know you are concerned about your husband's last days and the missing money. Shall we go? We can walk along the rest of Rundle Street and then a short walk along King William Street.'

She smiled and thanked him for his thoughtfulness. He was only being a friend. And it had been a pleasant little halt to their ramblings.

Despite her preoccupation, she could still appreciate the decorated frontages of the variously designed single-storey houses and cottages along their route, even stopping at one to smell a glorious red rose abutting the paling fence, edging onto the footpath.

'Roses in December, John, how exquisite! And those verandas, how wide and long they are, and close to walkers along the pavement...'

'Must be second flowering after pruning. First ones come about October hereabouts. And I doubt the houses will last long along this boulevard – many businesses own the land and when that kind of development happens, then houses must go.'

The thought of houses steered her thoughts to her own homeless situation. 'John, I am sorry if I seem unappreciative of your kind hospitality. It is just that the question of the missing money is both perplexing and vexing. I just know that James went into the hills to look at the property as agreed. The money has to be up those hills somewhere, it has to be!'

On arriving back at John's house, Mary was agog with curiosity and concern so, leaving John to outline their discussion with Beckett to his mother's satisfaction, Beatrice shed her boots and gloves in her little box room.

*Of course, why didn't I think? James's bag from the Taylors! Did I miss something last night, I wonder? I was weary. Perhaps...*

This time she upended it onto the coverlet of her chaise longue. From a pocket in his trews was a paper receipt for 'Meals, Refreshments and two nights' bed 7/8 Dec'.

Excited and still in her stockings, she rushed out to interrupt the Lees' energetic discussion about Becket and the Taylors. 'Look! It's signed by – I cannot read it – but it's from the Bridgewater Inn and James stayed there on the seventh and eighth. He must have been on his way back to Adelaide on the ninth – surely in good time to see Mr Beckett! Dear friends, I must make some preparations to travel to this place. There may be some information to be found there.'

Mary just smiled and returned to the large teapot. *No point my saying she can't do that when I'm always saying there's no such word. Oh, dear God! She is one determined young woman, this one. I didn't think she had it in her. Hope she knows what she's doing'.*

# 19 December 1879

## 10

Beatrice found it strange: only a few days before Christmas and the day boasted bright blue skies and warm sunshine. With John as escort, she was riding up the Hills road heading for Bridgewater and wondering at the sun's warmth on her face. She relished the familiar seat and pace of a horse again. At Mary's suggestion she had spent some of James's hundred and sixty-three pounds only yesterday on more sensible wear for riding; this included a skirt that was cut and sewn up the middle like men's trews – with two legs – quite unlike anything she had seen before, and was called simply 'a hacking skirt'. The lady salesperson, also a dressmaker though Beatrice didn't have time to be fitted and tailored, had received a consignment from Sydney and assured her it was 'quite in keeping, madam, not to ride side saddle when embarking upon a country hack' and had then gone on to speak of women in Sydney riding bicycles in baggy leggings called 'bloomers'. The very thought of her dear mama sanctioning such garments and habits prompted a tender smile from Beatrice even as she registered their comfort on this hack.

During a lull in the wind, she called out to John, 'This is all so good of you, John. I do thank you for all your attention. I am quite overcome by your friendship, and dear Mary and Evelyn's. Even Lieutenant Symonds attended James's committal in the Cheltenham cemetery yesterday afternoon before taking his ship for Melbourne. People are so very kind.'

John smiled and waggled his fingers in acknowledgement. He was still bemused at this young woman's – he had to say it: sensible – response to her unfortunate circumstances. At least Beckett had pulled strings and achieved a prompt burial. He realised, though Beatrice did not, that burials in summertime were usually expedited due to the rapid deterioration of the body. And not a tear had Beatrice shed at that brief service. At least she had been spared any expense; the Militia – as he knew the Adelaide Rifles were more popularly called – had granted her husband a military funeral. To his great surprise, the acting Administrator, Sir William Jervois, had sent a representative to the service, and though his presence necessitated some hasty refreshments and energies from the girl Alice and his mother, Beatrice seemed quite unaware of the honour.

John himself was a little mystified because, to his hazy knowledge, the government had concluded that the threatened invasion – due to the distant Russo-Turkish war – was too unlikely a prospect to justify the maintenance of two battalions. Beatrice's James may have been appointed to boost the company training, but from what John had read of the political harangue between Jervois and Premier Cotton, the expansion of the Rifles – by whatever name – seemed to be a non-event. Mayhap that was the reason Beauchamp had decided to become an orchardist. Yet James's position had been publicly acknowledged by Jervois's presence at the burial and to Beatrice's apparent satisfaction.

And she was herself a puzzle to him. Surely with all the emotion of the last few days Beatrice must have suffered. One would expect some tears, some feminine sensibilities perhaps? But no, she seemed confident and determined on making what she called 'a new life'. John found it strange that mention of her husband was swept aside so thoroughly when it seemed her time in the colony could be measured in hours more than in days. Also, having pondered the matter, he acknowledged he was wary of her; such a resolve – and logic – were attributes quite too 'masculine' for her to appeal to him in a more intimate way.

This trip was part of that resolve. Her husband had stayed at the hotel in Bridgewater for not one but two nights, and less than two weeks ago. He understood she needed to know why and where he might have gone from there, and yet… She was quite unlike most of the young women of his acquaintance. Was it an immigration reaction?

He cast a look at her over his shoulder. Her mount seemed to be coping well with the steep incline. So was she. Jonathan had no side saddle available and John was still a little shocked at her readiness to ride astride. He couldn't know of her riding over the fells at home. He supposed her outfit modest enough; the ankles were covered with what he assumed were leggings worn beneath. Modern women were so unpredictable; even his sister had expressed a wish to buy some long leggings she called bloomers and to buy herself a bicycle – to John they were the subject of music hall mirth and quite regrettable on ladies of taste, and totally inappropriate…

He was still trying to reconcile his earliest impressions of Beatrice with this contrary person who seemed to be set on flouting convention. Could it be an attempt, as a migrant, to cope with strangeness? To prove herself? She had presented earlier as rather pathetic, but now he was quite confused.

Still, no proper saddle or not, the horse seemed well shod and foot-sure, which was an advantage. Beatrice seemed relaxed enough, reins slack, as she was sensibly giving the horse its head. She had assured him she could ride, and so she could. Her expression was one of interest and fascination at the little farms and cottages they passed on their way. As they climbed, she exclaimed at the view, apparently intrigued by the plants and trees by the roadside, in fact taking note of everything around her. John considered that a hopeful sign.

'John, is there not a plan for railways up this road and eventually through to the colony of Victoria? It would seem a godsend to travellers, would it not, as this hilly roadway may be a good surface, but surely it is hard on coaches and carts?'

'Correct on both counts, Beatrice. There is a railway planned and I believe construction has started further down and over the hill. It is my understanding it is planned to be in Aldgate by 1882 or 1883 or so! There is now a huge bridge built over the River Murray and within a few years it is hoped to have a through line to Bordertown – not the best name apparently as the police chief set the town up as a staging post between Melbourne and Adelaide for the mails. He thought it would be called Tolmer, after him. Also, it's about fifteen or so miles to the actual border with Victoria. To tell the truth, I'm a bit vague on the planning but I do know the government has given priority to roadways up to now. This stretch – right through Stirling and Aldgate – has been the official coach road for a number of years now and is, I admit, in need of some maintenance despite the toll house you saw at Glen Osmond. Some years ago the toll house was closed because travellers refused to pay for the dubious privilege of using a road in shocking condition. Talking of which…' He stopped to allow her to draw alongside.

'Maintenance is still not the best. A rail route would be a godsend but the gradient so far has involved much discussion between government and private enterprise as to the need for tunnels and such huge undertakings, if a railway is to be profitable. This road is well used, as you will have noted from the other riders, though some of the traps dare to travel with wheels too fragile. However, that is not our concern.'

Beatrice tried to look as interested as she knew she ought to, but this young man to whom she was genuinely grateful was a little long-winded in his enthusiasm, as Papa would say.

John continued. 'I hope you don't mind, Beatrice, but Mother and I thought you would appreciate the ride, and it allows you to learn something of the countryside even more than the coach might permit. Also, to have our own mounts as we go from Aldgate tomorrow to Bridgewater will surely be an advantage. Are you not enjoying the view?'

'Yes, I am, John. The trees and the grasses even – and those spiky ones – and look at the view behind over to the sea! It is all magnificent.'

'We are approaching Stirling village now, Beatrice. There aren't many homes here yet, but it has been laid out for such. It's mainly market gardens and orchards, as I understand it. Also, that valley, down there,' he gestured with his riding crop, 'is already being called Adelaide's food bowl. I understand a Peter Peckerd, who deals in land brokerage and that sort of thing, has named it Piccadilly Valley. Certainly, the ambience here is suitable for such industries.'

'It's lovely scenery, John but didn't you say Stirling is near to Aldgate, where we stop for the night? I assure you I am quite comfortable, being well used to horseback, but a stop soon would be welcome. Also for this mount, I don't doubt, after all this hill work.'

Beatrice was sure John must be ready to stop. Yes, they had both made use of their water bags, and the hard-boiled eggs Evelyn had packed as refreshments, but apart from a quick stop near that toll gate, it had been non-stop in the saddle. She had noticed he seemed to strike a weary shoulder now and again, and until this last discussion had been quiet for longer periods. She reminded herself that it was John's lack of health that had prompted Mary's own appearance in this country.

An approaching herd of goats broke into her reverie and her horse pricked up its ears. John moved ahead to go single file. He cautioned her that horses and goats didn't like each other, that goat smells spooked the horses at times. She'd never known that but took a firm rein just in case. Surprisingly, the animals were being herded by two young girls, perhaps in their teens and of sturdy build.

*Goodness! As are their clothes. And surely those are wooden pattens on their feet and their skirts don't even cover their ankles – they are quite exposed.*

Each girl goatherd wore a cloth cap with flaps down the back of the neck and carried sticks which they brandished cheerfully in silent greeting. As they passed, they broke into a cheerful singing, unfamiliar to Beatrice.

John turned and smiled. 'They're Germans, or from the settlement anyway. They keep Adelaide in fresh meats and often vegetables and dairy cheeses and, as I understand, until about twenty or so years ago, their women would walk to the Adelaide markets in bare feet! I have been told they would stop just down the hill at Beaumont, down that way,' he flourished his crop in a direction vaguely downhill, 'to wash and cool their feet before reaching the market. Incredible stamina, I feel. After making their sales they then returned home carrying not only such needles and pins and things as they wanted but also – believe this, Beatrice – each carried two bricks for building their new church!'

He called his animal to halt until Beatrice was once more alongside. 'The goats might be the reason they are on the road because, as I understand it, their produce now reaches the market by carriage. There are families of them farming just beyond Bridgewater, near Hahndorf. They are farmers and orchardists and their produce is sought after in the markets. There are other settlements in the north of the colony, up above Williamstown. They are industrious, cheerful people and are free here to practise their own religion, Lutheranism, I understand. And those bricks – well, they built their church in Hahndorf and I think it's been complete ten or fifteen years. Ahah. Here we are approaching the Pump. It is our shelter for the night, Beatrice. It was set up I believe in the mid-forties as a coaching inn used by diggers on their way to look for gold. The owner then put down a water pump so all men and beasts could have a drink. The hotel is actually newer but is still known as the Pump. Quaint, is it not? Let me help you dismount. Ah, here comes an ostler to help, so I will go inside and register for accommodation.'

Beatrice was glad to get down and even more pleased at her choice of the hacking skirt; it provided both modesty and comfort, with its soft lawn leggings that fastened under her foot in the boots. She smiled as she remembered showing them to Mary, who was scandalised by the immodesty, then Evelyn had spoken of the bike-riding bloomers! She and Evelyn had howled in most unladylike laughter as Mary stuttered in protest. Greater humour ensued as both younger women tried to argue with Mary about needing to move with the times!

'Don't say you can't, Mam – you say there's no such word!'

Beatrice was still smiling as she dismounted, even though she couldn't help but wonder if the Hills coach from the city might have been quicker. *My derrière requires hardening up; more horse riding would be a good thing… I've grown soft since leaving home!* However, three shillings for the coach was expensive and monies had to be guarded. Also, the coach did not apparently travel on to Bridgewater but horses could. She resolved to pay the fee for their accommodation and not allow John to do so. It was important to act as independently as she had declared herself to be. Perhaps they could have continued to Bridgewater, as it was so near, but this way they could rest and she could think what might eventuate – about James and his two days of business at the Bridgewater Inn.

# 20 December 1879

## 11

Her room in the Pump hotel had been by no means elaborate, but fresh water was in her toilet jug and the bedding clean and the mattress soft enough.

Beatrice woke the next morning refreshed and eager to get on with the 'investigation'. She met with John Benjamin in the small parlour and they were served a breakfast of bread, cheese and small beer. Beatrice opted for goats' milk to drink instead and found it cool and palatable. They were mounted again, their horses well fed and watered, by nine of the clock. Beatrice had to compromise on the fee as John argued vociferously that his mother would not like the lady to be seen to pay, so although she paid for herself she allowed John to hand the money to the hotelier as a sop to his masculine pride. Four shillings was her charge and she hoped the next place would be less rather than more expensive!

It took less than an hour on the fresh horses to reach Bridgewater. 'Only a small settlement,' Beckett had cautioned, but it seemed a veritable township had sprung up around the inn. Signs indicated a post office and there was evidence of other street traders. Small, but busy.

'We are in good time, Beatrice. It was only a short ride and I wonder if a hack around the little township might be an idea. Finding the management of the inn might be difficult too at this early hour. Also, the air is fresh and I feel it is quite a delightful place. Shady trees, and surely there is a creek that feeds the mill. Shall we explore and then return here for a lunch?'

'Look at those little green parrots, John! Yes, let's.'

They rode down the length of what was seemingly the main street and a small group of men clustered around a cart, doffed their hats and grinned 'Good day.' Further along, a small number of children in pinafores and boots were playing ball in what seemed to be a school yard and under the watchful eye of a matron holding a large brass bell.

'John, this is so like some villages I know at home – in England, that is. It warms my heart to know this…'

His answer was delivered with a slow smile. 'Shall we make the inn now? We need to hope they have vacant rooms and we may be able to determine the circumstances of your husband's stay here.'

He turned his horse round and she followed slowly.

*I am too wrapped up in my own thoughts. I should have realised he might be tired. Mary is concerned for his health, I know.*

They dismounted in the yard of the inn and a bustle of stablemen rushed to attend them. Beatrice had to smile. In England, a lady would not be expected to dismount from astride a horse, she would be side-saddle. Here, these men were unconcerned, thank goodness!

'Oh!'

At the very thought, one who was old enough not to care, simply reached up, took her by the waist and planted her without ceremony feet-first onto the cobbles.

John led the way into a small hallway.

A stout lady in a frilled cap and apron was talking with a group of young men and she bustled over to meet them. 'Yes, sir and madam, what can I do for yers?'

So John explained and made the bookings as Beatrice looked around at the pleasantly oiled timber of the skirtings and the floor and the spotless canopy over a small reception table. Nice and clean, well cared for, then started as John addressed her.

'Beatrice, you must sign the book and then Mrs Woof will escort us to our rooms. But first, Mrs Woof, we are wondering about a past guest of yours – in fact, this lady's husband.'

'When you said your names it rang a bell in me 'ead, it did. Mr Beecham, was it? Yes, 'e was 'ere only a week or so ago. 'Ere, look – it's in the book…'

John couldn't see the name but Beatrice, looking over his shoulder exclaimed, 'Yes! It is spelled B E E C H A M and that's strange… I cannot understand that. James was always careful to spell it B E A U C H A M P. He was proud of his name, his heritage.'

Mrs Woof turned the book. 'No, madam. I remember that was writ by his friend. See under it: George Taylor.'

Startled into momentary silence, John turned to Beatrice, who had no such inhibition.

'What? Mrs Woof, did this Mr Taylor and my husband arrive together seeking accommodation?'

'As I recall, dear lady, they come tergither. From Adelaide the first night, then the next day they was off to Lenswood way – to see a property, I understand. They came back late that Sabbath day – I gave 'em late dinner, I remembers, an' they was making merry so I thought all had gone well. They left tergither early on the Monday. As I understand, they had to see a man of business in the town in a hurry.'

'But…'

John thought other ears might be turning in their direction. 'Come, Beatrice. Let us find our rooms. Perhaps we can have some refreshments,' at which Mrs Woof nodded energetically, 'then perhaps we can discuss matters in more detail.

*

After splashing her face and brushing her hair, Beatrice returned downstairs looking for John, to find him in the small side parlour drinking an ale in the company of the avuncular mine host, who was introduced to her as Mr Anderson.

'Anderson the Younger, ma'am. I succeeded my father in the business. Please both of you be seated and Mrs Woof will bring a dinner.'

Seeing the potency of curiosity and impatience on Beatrice's features, John signalled it was best to leave any discussion until they were alone and eating their meal. At least they were the only ones occupying the small parlour, although there was the noise of busyness in the adjacent dining room.

'John, this is not dinner, but luncheon. I see I have a lot to grow accustomed to…but to the point, that Mr Taylor made no mention to you of him travelling with James, did he? There is a mystery here and when money and land is at the heart of the matter…oh goodness me, I fear it is not a pleasant situation!'

'Beatrice, I understand how you must be feeling but let us enjoy this meal. Sustenance after the morning's efforts are necessary, I feel.'

With a surge of guilt, Beatrice attended to the meal on her plate. It was tasty, but she wasn't very hungry. She reminded herself that John was not a well man. He would need to maintain his constitution.

He finally put down his knife. 'Beatrice, if you will allow me, I shall return to town in the morning – well, to Woodville anyway – and speak to Mr Taylor. From him, I shall hope to gain some answers. I admit to weariness and will rest this afternoon and then perhaps would you care for a short walk before dinner?'

'That is a lovely idea, John, and then in the morning…'

'Allow me, Beatrice.' He held up a cautionary finger. 'Please will you stay here tomorrow in a modicum of comfort as I will make me a quick descent. Then I shall return with what news I determine next day.'

'No, John, I cannot prevail upon you…'

'Please, Beatrice. I have no doubt of your abilities and certainly I know you to be a good horsewoman, but I fear there may some unpleasantness underlying this unexpected verification of Taylor with your husband – hidden from me quite skilfully as it certainly was! You are also new to the colony and I know people who may be able to supply some answers. Trust me, Beatrice, do – as my mother does, and you know her well, do you not?'

Beatrice refrained from further argument by giving a lot of attention to her plate.

'This is certainly a busy little inn, Beatrice, if the noise from that front bar is anything to go by.'

She dabbed her mouth with the kerchief. 'And that music – they seem to have a fortepiano in there, or is the sound coming from that dining room, John? I don't know the melody – well, it's not so much a melody as a singing-along session, I think. A happy sound, though, I do agree.'

'A branch of my family in Belfast – or was it in Newry – is in the music business, with various keyboard instruments including even the majestic organs. I think the one playing in that other room might be more of an everyday instrument but, if it cheers people, why not?'

He raised a finger as she started to comment. 'Please excuse me, Beatrice but perhaps…to business? Tomorrow I hope to determine more information from Mr Taylor and if necessary revisit Mr Beckett. Your husband had no significant funds upon his person, nor any form of receipt or documentation regarding the property. Yet Mrs Woof seems to think the men had been successful in their dealings for the orchard, is that not so? I have a feeling Mr Taylor knew much more than he imparted to me on Tuesday – in fact, I am beginning to be altogether suspicious of that friendship, Beatrice. Striking while the iron is hot is a metaphor for action, my dear friend, and it is called for now, I do believe.'

'Which is why I should come with you and meet this man, John.'

'No, Beatrice. Do permit me. Speed is of the essence – yes, I speak in clichés, I know, a habit I gained from my dear mother, I believe!' He grinned, quite disarming Beatrice of another planned protest.

'If all goes well, I shall even hope to return late tomorrow and brief you on events. But do not be concerned if I do not come until the following day. In a few days, it is Christmas. Places of business will be closed and, if one trail leads to another, I'm sure you would prefer we make every effort to settle this curious matter.'

'I must defer to your greater knowledge of this place and its business practices, John. I must also admit to an increasing sorrow – for my James, for you and your family in being hindered by my affairs, and also for myself. Now while you go for a rest, I might do just the same and then perhaps we can meet later and have that walk before dinner.'

# 21 December 1879

## 12

Next morning as a distant cock crowed, the cry raucous on the still morning air, Beatrice rose from her bed, splashed her face to wakefulness and bustled along to the parlour, where breakfast was to be served.

Mrs Woof was directing a young girl how a place was to be laid correctly at the table. She looked up and bade Beatrice a good morning. 'Mr Lee left very early, Mrs Beauchamp. And settled for two nights' accommodation for you, should he be delayed. And your meals of course. I trust you slept well?' She came over to speak quietly. 'My daughter can help you dress, should you wish. She is quite adept with laces, though perhaps not with stays…'

'Thank you, Mrs Woof, but I have to admit to an increased freedom in my dress here in Adelaide. The young lass in the shop when I bought my hacking skirt gave me very useful advice, particularly in this very hot summer weather.' She leaned towards Mrs Woof. 'I must wear stays but only for whatever more formal occasions may demand – not that I foresee any exclusive invitations! Also, I am in mourning but I only have this grey silk with me to wear, so I hope you will not think me unfeeling.' She gave a tentative comment. 'The lass in the dress shop sold me some stays of a new fashion for me, ones that lace quite loosely for comfort, and also from the front of my bodice. Or so she told me, as it was a very hurried visit to the store and I had no time to try them on.'

Mrs Woof gave a conspiratorial smile. 'Thankfully, the rather stuffy English ettikwetty rules have given way ter common sense here in this climate, Mrs Beauchamp. Mourning is from the heart here, not the dress. Well, in most sensible places, anyway. Now do eat a good breakfast. The eggs are fresh from the German girls only this morning.'

Once again alone in the small parlour, Beatrice was able to tangle with some of her worries about money, her position in whatever society she might find herself, what would follow after John spoke to the Taylors, and not least, what action she must now take to become self supporting. Sighing, she tapped the top of her boiled egg. *First things first, Beatrice.*

*

A few miles down the coach road towards Adelaide, John was already bypassing the small settlement of Crafers. The distant sea was a thin silver line on the horizon and the township seemed nearer than the twenty miles he had calculated. He pulled in to a small cutting as the coach came haring up the hill, too fast for the poor horseflesh and scattering gravel and dust.

He remounted, thinking they could have made better time had they used the coach but... *This Beatrice is a strange woman. So recently bereaved, so suddenly on arriving in a new land, and yet she seems impervious to any emotion. Ma said she was terribly shocked at the first, but by the time I arrived home – well, perhaps because she had rested – she seemed quite in control of herself. Not natural. She's a cool fish, for sure, as Ma would say. Last night at dinner she seemed bursting with questions; was it me worrying about being overheard that put the cap on her expressing any sentiments, I wonder? But at the end when she pleaded an early night, she talked of sorrow, but speaking it ain't experiencing it, dammit! Mebbes it's that stiff upper lip Mother mentioned and the formal way she still talks, like English ways. Ahah, I see the toll gate, soon be there...*

John crossed roads to get to Woodville and decided to water his horse at that wheelwright's place before checking on the Taylors and also cadge a drink for himself.

'Hello, surrrr! Yon horse is not one o' mine again, sir. Don' suppose you here for the Taylors again?'

'What? Oh, hello. Erm, well, yes, actually.'

'They'm gone, surr. Early next mornin' after, 'twas. Hired my trap and driver and bound for the port they were. An' they told the driver they'd already settled up. They 'ad not!'

'The port? Port Adelaide? Come, man, what do you know?'

'You saw them yourself, surr. They were terrible upset. Well, they wus in a shockin' hurry. Said he was to catch the ship to Melbourne. Or Sydney after that. I fergit. See over there? That's their boxes there, an' they ain't going anywhere's till I'm paid! Didn't yer see all their packed boxes at their 'ouse when yer visited?'

'I saw the Taylors, yes, but…ah…we sat outside. Did you know they were to take flight?'

'Not so, surr, but I knew of troubles, yers. I think I told yer, didn't I, not to expect a happy reception, like. The house is cleared out, empty, surr.'

John was nonplussed. He accepted a mug of cool water then walked over to the stack of what were apparently the Taylors' boxes. There was a household of contents here, to be sure. He wheeled his horse, a brief salute to the wheelwright and he set off across the busy roads again. He intended to get to Beckett's. Surely that agent must know of Taylor's business?

# 13

Mr Beckett noted his visitor's warm and dusty state and called for refreshments. John outlined his increasing suspicions and concerns for his mother's female protégée.

Beckett looked horrified. He opened a ledger from the side of his desk, traced an entry with his finger then looked up, his expression concerned. 'It seems it was the seventeenth. The timing seems to be just after – soon after – it was that same morning you and the charming Mrs Beauchamp visited. The note here is not mine…' He tapped a bell standing on his desk and the elderly senior clerk scuttled over.

'Mr Tripp, there is an entry here of Mr Taylor's appearance on the morning of the seventeenth when I was visiting the Calders about their expansion. What was Mr Taylor's purpose?'

'He asked for the release of his funds made earlier, sir, as he wished to make ship for Melbourne and was already late for embarking. I checked the ledger before taking action. Mrs Taylor had substantial funds.'

'Mrs Taylor? The wife? What was the nature of this note – was it the collateral version or cash transaction only? Show me the page recording the transaction, if you please.'

'Here we are, sir. It was late on the Saturday evening, sir, back on the thirteenth of December sir. Mr Taylor and Mr Bowchamps – as he writ his name – came to transact a loan and repayment of same from one to t'other, after deciding not to purchase some property which you had recommended, sir.'

John was beginning to fear that Beckett was another apoplexy waiting to happen, his colour became so high.

'Tripp! Why was I not advised of this when this gentleman and Mrs Beauchamp came to see me – when? On the same morning…the seventeenth. And who is the man sent to the Taylor's on the sixteenth.'

'Well, sir, it all seemed in order, sir, yourself having approved the transaction prior to the sixth of December…and I sent no man to the Taylors, sir.'

By now, John was decidedly confused. 'A loan, sir? Who was the applicant?'

Mr Beckett was scrutinising the notes. 'It appears, sir, that Captain Beauchamp and Mr Taylor did purchase the property in time and also it appears the captain paid his half share in full. It would seem that because the captain was expecting his wife to arrive and was low in cash funds until the transaction was complete, he borrowed from Mr Taylor the £500 share he had put into the property, as he wanted to purchase some household effects towards a comfortable reception for his lady. An agreement was drawn up in which, should anything befall the captain, the property and all its entitlements would revert to the Taylors.'

'That's as may be, Mr Beckett, and what a confusing arrangement we are asked to believe… May one enquire from what source the captain hoped to make good the debt?'

Beckett scoured the inky pages and columns again and Mr Tripp intervened. 'If I may, sir. Captain Bowchamps was expecting his wife to bring with her substantial funds that would suffice to buy the property and other goods and chattels considered necessary for settlement in – where was it now? – Hahndorf.'

Beckett finished his reading. 'This is, I am afraid, Mr Lee, quite legal and above board. With the captain's unfortunate demise, the property and its advantages reverted quite legally to Mr Taylor and his wife. Though, admittedly, it is unusual for monies to be under a lady's name – that's Mrs Taylor – usually the husband controls a family's finances. However, if he was happy with the arrangement, it is not illegal, merely, er, tut tut, er, irregular.' He dismissed Mr Tripp with a wave of his hand. 'It seems, despite the similarity in pronunciation, Mr Tripp in hearing the name Beecham – and look, here it is written as such – in no way connected it with the discussions concerning the name Beauchamp. He pronounces it as Bowchamps, I regret, so brought nothing to my attention. Most confusing. Also, it was most unfortunate, inter alia, that I was absent on other business when these items of business were carried out. Nor did I send a man to the Taylors. That would have to be a concoction of the man's imagination. My sincere apologies, sir. Yet the agreement is certainly legal, if complex. I am pleased to examine it further, sir, if you will allow, to ensure... Do you wish me to write to Mrs Beauchamp explaining the sequence and implications of these events?'

By now hungry, thirsty and completely bemused, John agreed that would be best. He farewelled the regretful actuary and decided to make for the comforts of his own home and the practical common sense of his mother rather than return to Beatrice.

*

Later that evening, Mary brought her teacup over to the table where Evelyn and John were speculating about Evelyn's forthcoming position with the Telegraph Department.

'Listen to me, please, my darlings. We have talked ourselves silly about Beatrice's situation but I am really worried about her. Married woman she may be but worldly wise she is not. I've been thinking – do listen, this is important. Did that Taylor fellow do away with Beatrice's husband, d'you think?'

Her two offspring stared at her.

John spoke first. 'Ma, it did occur but I thought it the product of my tired imagination. Yet I cannot see how, when Taylor was back home on the fourteenth when Beauchamp was killed by the cart...'

'Was it a cart, John? Were there witnesses?'

'The lieutenant from the *Orient* spoke with the peelers down the port, Ma, and there were witness statements. Also the report in the *Register*, according to Beckett, made the verdict conclusive.'

'You said that Mr Taylor fellow said the Beckett's man had come to his house. Beckett knew nothing of it. If so, what did he actually tell Taylor that made him so soon afterwards flee to take ship? And wasn't Taylor curious – to you – about what documentation may still have been on the captain's corpse? He was, wasn't he? It seems a bit suspicious to me, son.'

'Ma, do ease up. Mr Beckett has promised a detailed account of proceedings for tomorrow. We can do no more than await his decisions.'

'That's as may be, John Benjamin Lee, but I'll not quietly stand by and let a nice young woman like Beatrice be diddled at her time of greatest need! For that's how it looks to me...'

# 22 December 1879

## 14

After her breakfast in the inn's parlour, Beatrice sought some paper and ink from Mrs Woof. It was time she set down on paper all her news for her father. She had despatched a letter from the Cape but not since, and so, where to begin? Time flew by as she repeatedly dipped her pen and then, as she wrote of the effects of James's death, she realised she could not express fears too broadly about her situation. *Dear Papa, he cannot receive such a missive of misery! Yes, I must tell him of James, but I must express hope for what I intend...* The thought nurtured the deed and suddenly she felt overwhelmed by unhappiness and misfortune. The tears flowed as she hastily lifted her screed to her father out of their path.

The ever-observant Mrs Woof stepped in, brought over a clean kerchief and a small tot of brandy. In her opinion, this young woman was a good 'un, and to pot with silly class attitudes. She patted Beatrice on her cap, now tilted askew but still pinned on to depict her married status if none other.

'I know you're a lady, Mrs Beauchamp, but women together we know of each other's sensibilities an' if I can help cheer you up, I will. Nor do you fear I blab an' tittle tattle, for I don't, ma'am, nor never will. You sit 'ere long as you want and if you want to eat in your room just tell me an' I'll tell my Lucy to bring it to you.'

Beatrice looked up, eyes still wet, but strangely she felt better, clearer in the head after shedding the tears and indulging in a cry, as she remembered her dear Mrs Willis back home would've said.

'I thank you, Mrs Woof, but I will feel easier when Mr Lee returns with news of my affairs. It is then I think I will be able to finish writing all my news to my father.' She stood and rolled up her missive. 'It is passing the time in waiting that is hard.'

'As to that, Mrs Beauchamp, may I ask if you play the fortepiano at all? We have a machine, or so it is called by me, and was left here by a long-term stayer in payment of his accommodation. Mrs Bones calls it a mix between a harpsichord – I think that's what she said – an' a pianoforte. I call it what the original owner called it.' She grinned. 'Well, among other things, if yer know what I mean. It has been set to rights, I believe. You may have heard it last night? You would be welcome to play should you wish, on your own, as I can direct to the other bar any travellers until this evening…'

'I would like that, Mrs Woof. You are very kind. I am a little rusty, though – the weeks on the *Orient*. However, thank you. Do lead the way.'

Mrs Woof scuttled across the small parlour and into a larger dining area wider and with more tables than where Beatrice and John had sat the previous night. 'There's some sheets of moosic there, Mrs Beauchamp. But I must leave you to find out about it yourself as I know so little and I am to be busy somewhere else now. Anderson calls it a square pianer and it means little to me. I know it has twenty five o' those black keys among the white ones. Mrs Bones from the school comes to play sometimes and makes a happy toon or two.' She scuttled away.

It looked more like a side table than a piano, with a boxy bit at the end, but Beatrice remembered vaguely seeing one somewhere before. She thought of the minister's wife back home – she had a clavichord. Yet this square piano, she noted as she lifted its lid behind the keyboard, had hammers and not strings to be plucked. Hmm. She lifted the lid over the keys and saw that music –'moosic', she smiled – could rest upright. And yes, it did seem to be a five-octave instrument. She lifted the lid of the stool. There were some sheets of music therein; none looked very recent. She decided to play something from memory and, hesitatingly at first, explored the keyboard. *What's that schooldays one… 'Won't you buy my pretty flowers…'*

It was only when young Lucy crept quietly into the dining room that Beatrice realised how time had passed.

'I must get the tables ready for luncheon Mrs Beauchamp, but please don't stop playing, it sounds so pretty as you do it. Mrs Bones plays tunes sometimes the men and their ladies like to sing to, but your music is softer and slower and prettier, like.'

'I assure you, Chopin can be quite sprightly, Lucy! And his music I have found here would seem to differ from what I have at home, as if it was written for this instrument. But yes, I have enjoyed playing. It's been a while.' She turned to watch the lass placing the napkins by the plates. 'Have you ever folded a napkin into a swan? No? Would you like me to show you?"

'Oh yes, please.' Lucy was fascinated and quick to copy; soon snowy-white napkins folded to represent swans nestled on each side plate on the long table.

'Oh, Mrs Beauchamp, that's lovely. Real classy – Mother will be pleased.' She ran gracefully over towards the kitchen.

Beatrice decided to make a tactical withdrawal and made her way in the other direction to her little room. John Lee should be back here before long, as time seemed to have flown.

A clattering in the yard outside drew her to a window. A coach? No, only a chaise – of course. But…but that was Evelyn Lee climbing down! She ran to the reception area and was at the door as Evelyn came in, laden with a huge carpet bag.

'Evelyn! Lovely to see you! But…?'

'Hello, Beatrice. I'm so glad to see you and we really made good time but I had to change my transport… Let me see if I can stay here overnight and then we can talk.' She turned to a rapidly approaching Mrs Woof. 'Is it possible to have a room for one night?'

Beatrice hastened to introduce them as Evelyn continued. 'My regrets, Beatrice, but John could not come…'

Mrs Woof smiled and held up a finger to interrupt. 'Then there is a room, miss: you can have your brother's. Lucy! LUCY! Prepare Mr Lee's room for this lady and also a place at Mrs Beauchamp's table for dinner – er, luncheon.'

Lucy bustled off and the two young women followed. The young kitchen lad puffed and panted behind them bearing, almost dragging, Evelyn's huge carpet bag.

Evelyn barely looked around her room before she undid her bonnet ribbons then opened the bag, fished around and extracted a cream-coloured letter wrap, sealed with wax. This she handed to Beatrice. 'This is what Beckett's office sent round very early today. I understand it may give details about the conversation he had with John yesterday.' Some more delving into her bag. 'This is an epistle from John, probably saying the same thing. However, I'm sure you are eager to read, Beatrice, so if you like to seek the privacy of your own room, I will freshen myself a little, wash off some of the dust – I swear those horses galloped up the hill – and then maybe we can see about luncheon and talk more then.'

Sitting at her own bedside table, Beatrice first unrolled the two pieces of notepaper from John. Quickly despatching his apologies for having to revert to writing it down, she absorbed the essence of his meeting with Beckett, and his knowledge of the Taylors' departure, then his concerns for her and suggestions as to 'moving forward'. *What a ridiculous term. Unless one walks backwards, moving is usually to the front!*

Mr Beckett's documents were obvious copies of a legal agreement between her husband and the Taylors and then between Mrs Taylor – Mrs Taylor? – and her husband for a loan... *A loan? Oh, James. My dear. What...?* Then as she read on, a conclusion not known it would seem by John but later yesterday discovered and authorised by Mr Beckett, there were no monies at all to come to her, none due to her, despite the Taylors' unseemly – or so it seemed – dispersal from this state to another. Beckett had attached a personal note and his rather ornate handwriting was proving difficult enough to translate without absorbing its contents. He wrote that his Mr Tripp had contacted the police station and spoken with the serjeant who remembered her and Lieutenant Symonds identifying the body. *Oh, mercy me, it seems that Captain Beauchamp 'took to the tables' at a local hostelry and played the game through many hours. No! Nonsense! James was no gamer – he once told me of incidents in his army barracks and had told me so many times that gamblers were fools.*

Becket wrote that he was enclosing the witness report prepared by the serjeant from the cart driver's testimony. She read and it seemed one of the miscreants had been tripped up and held by a sturdy passer-by who saw the two men robbing the inert victim lying on the road. *Oh, what a painfully laboured account and my poor James...!*

Beatrice looked up as Evelyn entered. Seeing the unconscious tears streaming down her friend's face, she ran over, stood by her chair and held her friend's heaving shoulders.

Beatrice held up the documents. 'Please read, Evelyn. I cannot...'

'Firstly, this Mr Beckett writes, "...the captain had lost badly. Upon realising he had lost all the money, the loan secured from the Taylors..."'

She stopped and looked at Beatrice, who tearfully signalled her to continue.

'"Fleeing the room, he was set upon by some lower life persons and in speeding on foot, in the dark – it was a close chase – he ran into the cart in question and was trampled by the panicking horse…"'

'Oh no! Oh, dear James…'

Evelyn continued. 'He was then run over by the heavy wheels despite the driver's best efforts. The other gamblers caught up with him lying on the street. The driver was some paces away trying to quieten the horse so they roughly rumbled the body… Erm… He goes on, "The miscreants poached Mr Beauchamp's pockets – this was described by the driver but he was in no way able to prevent them. It seems they emptied his pockets of some money they considered he owed to them." I'm so sorry, Beatrice. All this is a rather terrible story. If there is any consolation at all, you have the answers to your questions and need have no more unpleasant contact with any authority.'

# 15

Beatrice sat silent for a moment or two then looked up at Evelyn. Her eyes were glistening still and red-rimmed. 'Evelyn, I have been so concerned with my own matters I have not asked you why John could not come. Also we should allow you to have a meal after your travel. Let's go into the dining room and then we can talk.'

There was only one other couple having luncheon. The young women each took a seat and agreed their meats with young Lucy.

'John intended coming here today, Beatrice, but awoke quite unwell. Mother says he has a very sensitive digestion. I hope it is nothing more because he told me that in the past months, with only the housemaid to care for him, he's had a number of mild spasms of sickness, as he calls them. Thankfully, now we are here, Mother will organise him some proper treatment, I'm sure. He was most concerned that I bring you this documentation and information about your husband's misfortunes as soon as possible.'

She put her warm hand over Beatrice's cold one. 'Also, my friend, Mother asks that you come back with me and share Christmas with us. John assured me he will be feeling better even as we now speak and I know it will be as a cheerful time as we can make it, considering…'

'Oh, thank you, Evelyn, that sounds most enjoyable but mine is a strange situation. I am in mourning and in desperate financial straits, though I can be honest with you: I am concerned that I must find some means of employment. I'm sure you understand, as you have secured an employment, that I too must look to the future. Unpleasant perhaps, the results of Mr Beckett's diggings, but it means I can draw a line under that page in my life's ledger. I think that is the meaning of that phrase Mr Beckett used – "moving forward". Come,' as Lucy arrived with two steaming plates, 'let us eat and refresh ourselves. You must need it after your horribly busy morning!'

Later that afternoon, as a lovely breeze blew through the shutters bearing the perfume of the sun-warmed lemon gum trees, Evelyn having retired for a nap to her room, Beatrice sat down at the funny little box piano, or square piano as Mrs Woof called it.

What could she play – what would not remind her of Mama, or home. Strange how no singular piece of music could she associate with James, although he had listened to her playing before they married and went away. Did she play for him after their honeymoon? She sat back. Poor James. He had spent time packing and planning for his journey to this place. *Had I played anything more for him before he left? I think not...*

She breathed in and experimented with the keys and the feel of the instrument. She decided to start with the Polonaise – that was the one Mamzelle always pushed for her to practise – but this keyboard was vastly different from her piano. Not only that, the music too – could it have been adapted for this keyboard? Perhaps, if this instrument is old enough... She quite lost herself in thinking of the music and adapting her not very expert knowledge to this strange instrument. She felt a small flush of success when the overall sound proved clear enough.

Then her thoughts wandered to the prospect of Christmas with the Lees. James could not be there but she would not be alone and the Lees understood how she felt, and...well, everything... Her spirits rose, she delved in her memory for something Christmassy and found 'The Holly and the Ivy'. She tried a few notes; it sounded passable, though she needed to change octaves... She became quite lost in concentration when Mrs Woof's voice startled her from behind.

'Do you know the toon 'Silent Night'?

The version she played was quite sprightly and, despite having difficulty finding some notes on the keyboard, she felt flushed with success as she came to a close. To her surprise, Mrs Woof asked, 'No madam, please, can you play it like the Germans sing it?'

'Can you hum it for me please, Mrs Woof? I know it is a German or Austrian melody, but...' She listened and caught the tune. 'Ahah... I know the melody you mean.' She thought for a while, tried a note and then the delicate slow lullaby rhythm of the beautiful song filled the small dining room.

When she finished playing, she was surprised to see Mrs Woof, hands wound in her apron, dabbing her eyes.

'Oh madam, oh Beatrice, that was lovely, really lovely.'

She then scuttled out and Beatrice, a little self-consciously, closed the box lid and made her way out into the garden and the cool breeze. She found a wooden bench and, in a reflective mood and pleasantly at peace with herself despite the bad news of earlier, sat back and watched a pair of small multicoloured birds bobbing up and down on a branch. Like little parrots and how beautiful.

'They call 'em rosellas, Mrs Beauchamp.'

A deep voice broke into her thoughts. It was Mr Anderson. The Younger.

'Forgive me, Mrs Beauchamp, but Mrs Woof has told me of your piano playin'.'

'Oh, Mr Anderson, I am no great pianist but it has been a great pleasure…'

'You play beautifully, I understand, madam. You also gave young Lucy a lesson in table ettyketty this morning, so she tells me. She also tells me something of your situation… Oh please, madam,' as Beatrice stood upright, not knowing whether to feel angry or embarrassed, 'I would very much like to ask a favour of you, madam.'

'Mr Anderson?''

'Would you consider staying on here over the Christmas and Epiphany and New Year to play for my diners?' He hurried to say, 'Not the bar guests,Mrs Beecham, no, no, not at all the place for a lady like you, but in the dining room where the pianner is, some gentle music as they eat and then perhaps some Christmassy songs when it's a good time for such… I would be most honoured, Mrs Beauchamp, if you would agree, and hasten to say you would have your own room and board while you are with us.'

'This is quite unexpected, Mr Anderson. May I think of your offer and speak with you later? But I thank you and… Oh, here is my friend Miss Lee come to seek me out.'

He bowed politely to Evelyn, who bobbed in response, her face alive with curiosity.

She turned to Beatrice as he retreated into the building. 'What offer?'

'It's quite odd, Evelyn, yet not unpleasant.' She outlined Anderson's request.

Evelyn pulled her back down onto the bench and stared at her.

'I have this feeling that everything is moving along so quickly, perhaps too quickly, for me to properly appreciate my good fortune. Yet, playing for strangers, I'm really a little unsure...

'Oh, Beatrice, that'll mean you won't join us for Christmas and I shall regret that. However, I can see it might be a help to you and I am certain that with such a strong sense of purpose as you possess, you will manage beautifully. This playing may lead to other things and relieve you of some of your worries, and I do understand. What is more, it is quite easy for us to meet up with each other – as I have just learned! Perhaps you may be able to visit us after Christmas, even for the New Year – it will be all the eights, 1880!'

'Evelyn, I am so grateful to you and your brother, and to dear Mary of course, for being so helpful, for giving me strength when I felt weak. There is so much that is different here, so much that is the same. I feel that it is all a big contradiction and it has happened so quickly! It is still only about a week ago that we were waiting to disembark off the *Orient*. Do you not yourself have a sense of the unreal? Your dear mother, Evelyn, is a tower of strength. I so envy you having her near. I will certainly visit you all as soon and as often as I can.'

Evelyn gave Beatrice a hug. 'Think it over, my friend, do, and meanwhile, as I am here for the night, let us enjoy our time together. You will wish to empty your dresses from the big bag I brought, and do keep the bag for as long as you need. I shall not be needing it for a while as I have unpacked at John's and shall be working in the city. And you can please let me know if there are others things you need... But let's do the unpacking later. For now, shall we talk and walk? Where does this little wooded pathway lead, for instance! And look at the birds. Oh, my goodness, they are not like our thrushes and blackbirds, are they?' She whispered, conspiratorially, 'Is Mrs Woof true wife to Mr Anderson? Do tell.'

They smiled and, linking arms, set a pace along the path.

# 23 December 1879

## 16

Evelyn made to climb in the chaise; she would pick up the coach at the Pump. 'Dear Beatrice, we will all miss you, and I will more than the others. You know all about my new position from the second of January but I do so hope you may visit for the New Year. It seems from our talk last night you may be occupied. However, if you are free, if there is any chance, please do!' Another hug, and in a cloud of dust from the wheels, she was gone.

Beatrice walked back into the inn to see Mrs Woof approaching.

'Mrs Beauchamp, Mr Anderson has told me of your staying for the pianner. That is so good, believe me. Mrs Bones has arthritis an' says her fingers don't work like she likes. Moosic sounds like it at times, too… An' I understand you like to be kept busy. Erm…I wondered if you were familiar with keeping accounts?'

'Only insofar as I managed the household budgets for my mama, Mrs Woof. Why do you ask?'

And very quickly she found herself in the small parlour working on the daily accounts for the inn. *It seems my employment is to be paid for – by me also! More than playing 'moosic' then! Is it Mary Lee who says there's no such word as can't?*

Later, Mrs Woof explained they needed the guest rooms for the holiday and would she mind changing to a room at the end of the deck. Strange word, sounded shipboard-like, so a question revealed the wide veranda was floored with timbers from some old ship and had become known as the deck. At its furthest extent were the staff quarters.

'It's real comfy, Mrs Beauchamp. My room is next to yours. Nice to be away from the noise, I think. Yes, real private and comfy.'

So it proved. The walls were whitewashed and the windows gaily curtained. Gnat-trap ones, inner ones of muslin, were also there to stretch into place. These allowed breezes to enter but deterred the little evening gnats that could buzz and bite. The bed was narrow and strictly functional, but the sheets spotless and the coverlet brightly quilted in geometric patterns.

The long-suffering kitchen lad dragged along the big carpet bag containing the personal things Evelyn had kindly brought. *Oh, it is good to have them!* Other things such as household items gathered in anticipation of running a home were left behind at John's house in an outside workroom. Evelyn had selected her clothes and undergarments and other small commodities and that was all she needed in the foreseeable future. As she unpacked, she reflected on her earlier English choice of dress fabrics presenting as rather warm in the wearing – at least for the summer weather currently being experienced. She had nothing in black and she should be in full mourning! She had a purple, suitable for half-mourning; that would have to do. Also, she had only the one gingham cool and practical enough to wear in this heat, and it was in pretty pastels..

When planning to live here with James, she had anticipated her lifestyle to some degree echoing that which she enjoyed in England, dressing for calling and for the theatre. She bit her lip, suppressing persistent tears. *Such events are not so likely to come my way now. Nor will I have the funds to spend on gowns. It is consolation I suppose that it is considered quite proper to wear only the one petticoat; goodness in this heat, more would be foolish in the extreme... Oh goodness me, I was such an ingénue. Not ten days in this country yet so much wiser already and feeling so much older. I didn't think of silk not being serviceable; I just didn't understand the heat! Certainly not for whatever work I feel I may be called upon to perform here as I – what was that phrase? – 'go forward'.*

That evening, after dinner, and somewhat embarrassed at the thought of playing for people she didn't know, Beatrice donned her purple silk. It was stylish, well cut and, she thought, would make it apparent she wasn't just one of the hoi polloi. She hated herself for thinking that way and knelt by her bed. 'Dear Lord, I have to be independent. I need to make my way in this country, strange though it may be. Dress is at least relaxed here. They might all know my husband has recently died, but playing the piano is hardly disrespectful to his memory. Independence, or so I feel, is admired here. Dear God, let me not shame my husband or my parents in any way by doing this. You recognise my wish to stay honourable, don't you, and supporting myself? Oh God, oh Mama, oh Papa, oh James...'

Then Lucy knocked on her door and she knew this was her cue.

As she walked in the dining room, she saw that the long table was almost full with as many ladies as gentlemen. They glanced at her curiously but there was no over-long staring as they resumed their talking to each other. Over by the window, some smaller tables had been pushed together to be occupied by a separate group, dressed differently from the other table. They were all in clean but wholesome linen-type shirts and somehow she knew they were the Germans from the settlement up the road. They looked at her more frankly than the other diners and for a moment she felt inclined to turn and run back to her room.

*I can't do this…* She took a deep breath. *Yes I can. I can!*

Lucy's grip tightened on her arm, and she was led over to the piano. Heads turned as she sat down and Lucy bobbed to the crowd before disappearing.

Beatrice smiled and sat down. *This is it then. Chopin's Number 6 – the Polonaise – first, then I'll slow down to a Christmassy number as Mrs Woof requested.*

As she played, she felt the tension drain from her. The room quietened as she changed tempo to the Waltz Number 6 and then conversation renewed but not at all intrusively. Lucy came in and brought her a home-made lemon cordial. It tasted delicious. She sat there indecisive. Most diners had finished eating. Was it time to end the evening? Remembering Mrs Woof's comments, Beatrice slid into the lovely 'Silent Night, Holy Night'.

After she played the introit and moved to the melody, a deep baritone broke into 'Stille Nacht, heilige Nacht'. At the second stanza, other male voices joined in a beautiful harmony. Still playing, she turned to see it was the group of Germans, each one standing. She played a second verse and the male harmony continued. At the end she turned around in her chair and smiled at the group of sturdy men who were now, somewhat self-consciously, resuming their seats. She decided to play a final verse to end and as she broke into the melody proper a single, tentative but glorious soprano rang through the room singing the English words. It was young Lucy! She sang just the one verse in English before fleeing the room to a storm of applause.

Almost at a signal, a scraping of chairs indicted a number were leaving the room. One of the Germans, a tall, blond, stocky man of middle age, turned to Beatrice as she stood by the piano, reached for her hand and kissed it, clicking his heels together in a military fashion. He released her hand and smiled, then followed his friends. Others shuffled out slowly, smiling at her.

Beatrice sat down on the piano seat. She felt emotionally at peace with herself and decided she really must try to encourage Lucy with her music. What a lovely voice. Untrained maybe, but glorious!

Mrs Woof came bustling in. 'Went well, Mrs B. Better than we dared hope, Anderson an' me. Better indeed.' She held out a bundled linen napkin. 'This is for you, my dear. Tips, Anderson calls it, tips. Gratooities. A few shillings there, I'll be bound!'

'Oh, Mrs Woof! I cannot accept this! You have already given me a room, board…!'

'Oh, my dear. This is from the customers, for yer playin'. Usually do this but you're a lot better than the usual hammering on the keys by Mrs Bones, bless 'er. They puts it in the pot set on Anderson's desk. Don't worry, Mrs B, it's quite above board, as they say! Now how about some warm milk, a biscuit or two and then bed, eh?'

Back in her room at the end of the walk from the deck, Beatrice spread the money on the counterpane. Six shillings and sixpence. She sat on the bed next to it and trickled her fingers through the coins. Then suddenly in brighter spirits she sat down to complete her letter to Papa. *No tears on this page or two. It's a strange country and in many ways it has strange customs, but I feel I have regained a measure of dignity.*

It was late when she blew out her candle and sank into sleep.

# Christmas Eve 1879

## 17

Beatrice was lying in bed savouring the early sunlight and the cool breeze wafting through the gnat screen onto her bare limbs. Listening to the pitch and trill of the birdsong coming through her shutters, she wondered if it was a common blackbird, as at home. It certainly didn't sound like the magpies, or a parrot. John Benjamin Lee had talked at length about the native birds as they had climbed that hill on the way here. He was contemptuous of their song but in awe of the splendid colours of their feathers.

She sat up and ran her hands through her hair as she stepped to the window and held wide the curtains and the fly screen – gnat screen, as Mrs Woof called it. She thrilled at the range of greens among the picks of other colours in the shrubbery: yellow-green, glossy green and grey-green of the leaves dappled with the sunlight. There was dew along a veranda rail but no sign of rain, the morning was blooming. Way beyond and through the tree branches, she could peer over the valley to the greenish-lavender colour of the hills beyond. She breathed in the cool air and the perfume of the sun-warmed leaves, sensing the pungency of the lemon gum. This was such a different Christmas Eve to what she had ever known.

*Oops! Here comes a midge or whatever they are called, mozkeeto. Mrs Woof will be closing the gnat screens throughout the rooms – I'd better close mine double quick.*

She swivelled as the smells of cooking meats came to her nostrils. It had to be quite late – to stay in the room could be thought ill-mannered. She twisted her hair up into her morning cap and searched for the piece of flannel by the water jug. There was also some sweet-smelling soap, in a little box, with 'Carnation' written on the lid. The water in the bowl was cool and soft, the soap foamed in a pleasant way as she mopped over her face and shoulders. Before too long she had freshened herself from 'top to toe' as Mama used to urge. *Oh, Mama, if you could see me now, in this strange*

*place where I am finding my way forward – as John Lee directed – and it is not entirely*
*an unhappy experience, Mama!*

Her hair brushed, she slipped into her gingham gown, hoping she might appropriate a clean apron from somewhere to keep the skirts fresh-looking. It certainly felt lightweight and free and easy for walking with only her shift and one petticoat beneath, and in no way immodest. She posed in front of the little looking glass to fix her hair, a second look to check the little widow's cap, and then made her way out onto the deck and towards the enticing smells and the clinking of glass and cutlery.

'Good morning, Miss Beatrice,' carolled Lucy, who was rubbing cutlery to a shine. 'We shall soon be serving breakfast – you in the little parlour please, miss, with my mother.'

Mr Anderson and Mrs Woof looked quite cosy over a plate of mixed cheeses, grapes and a knob of bread.

'Come and join us Mrs B,' invited Mrs Woof, swiping crumbs from her place into a napkin.

*So I'm Miss Beatrice from one and Mrs B from the other. I have some deciding to do... I wonder...* 'Please, if I am to be here for a little while playing the piano, will you two kind persons call me by my name, just Beatrice? I can still be Miss Beatrice to Lucy perhaps or Mrs Beauchamp to any others.'

Smiles all round and Beatrice discovered she had quite an appetite.

Some none too gentle questioning from Mrs W decided Beatrice to reassure them of her background. There had been – so she fancied – some 'certain' looks from a couple of the men on the big table, quite openly suggestive in her book. It bothered her that because she played the piano in the inn, and because it was already known she was a widow – albeit only recently – she might be considered 'available'. If so, the notion had to be scotched straight away. She started to explain something of her feelings as she pulled at the fresh though chunky piece of bread on her side plate but Mrs Woof quickly sensed her concerns.

'My dear girl, Beatrice, do not worry. Anyone of any sense would see you are a young woman of breeding...'

'And any silly business from any man on my premises, you report to me, Beatrice,' pronounced Mr Anderson. 'I'll put paid to it very quick, so I will.' He gave a little cough. 'You might have surmised that Mrs Woof and I are – erm – compatible, Beatrice.'

Beatrice chewed energetically as a spontaneous grin threatened to destroy her earnest expression.

He continued. 'Mr Woof took himself off to the goldfields many years ago and we have good reason to think he is dead, Beatrice. He was a wild character and liked the rum. He useter beat and clobber Mrs Woof terrible, so he did. I knew him and saw what was what. When he took orf, and Mrs Woof was – erm – in the family way, I was setting up here and needed a good housekeeper. I knew her for that and so she came to look after the domestic side of running this place.' He stopped and bit into a chunk of cheese which from then on could be seen churning around his mouth as he continued. 'Beatrice, she is my sister, and Lucy is my niece.'

Beatrice was quite nonplussed. This was a relationship she had not envisaged. She swallowed. 'So this is a family business, Mr Anderson. It looks to be a very successful one. I thank you most sincerely for allowing me to be a part of it.'

The other two seemed to relax, as if they had been worried about how Beatrice might construe their relationship. She concentrated on pouring herself a large cup of tea from the pot and stirring it vigorously.

'I know only that you two generous people have helped me overcome a feeling of despair. Only ten days ago I thought myself a married woman, soon to make a home in these hills with my dear husband. Then I found I had no funds to fall back on. I found good friends and shelter with the Lees – Mary is a wonderfully wise woman – and then circumstances led me here. I feel I am truly blessed. I will play the piano in the dining room and conduct myself always in a way suited to your generosity, my good friends. There are other areas in which I can help and perhaps, until the New Year season is over, I can be of other use to you, helping with the tables, the silver and such…'

'Oh, Beatrice! If you could do that, I would be grateful and so will Lucy. My young lass is ambitious and has asked me if you could stay and give her a few proper lessons on the piano – better than dear old Mrs Bones – and,' here Mrs Woof leaned forward, conspiratorially, 'if you could teach her your ways of talking and ettikwetty things as well, she may one day secure a happy marriage with a decent kind o' man.'

'Oh, Mrs Woof. I haven't allowed myself to consider beyond the near future. I, also, have to find myself a place in this big new world. I had thought to travel wider at some time. May I think of things over this Christmas and New Year period, help with things as you are busy, and then may we speak after the season?'

Mr Anderson's face stretched into his Pickwickian smile as he stood. He eased his waistcoat over his preponderance and gave a hearty burp. Unabashed, he leaned over to Beatrice. 'You will stay 'ere as long as you see fit, m'dear. Mrs Woof likes yer, Lucy likes yer, and I knows a good 'un when I sees one.'

Well satisfied, Mrs Woof leaned back in her chair. 'My own name is Cecilia, Beatrice, but I am called Sissy. If you would like.'

'I will call you Sissy with pleasure, my friend. Now do tell me how I can best help, as I am sure this Christmas Eve that things will become very busy. I can smell the kitchen is well ahead with something that smells like goose?'

'Well, yes. It went in before sunrise, Beatrice, but is for two of the clock this afternoon. We serve Christmas dinner on the Eve and it has become a tradition. It makes for a long day because they sit around and talk until teatime. If you can play for some of that time, it would be champion. You will stop and start as you want o'course, and have drinks an' eat. Some men get the better for drink, too, but Anderson and the outdoor lads stand by ready for rough stuff. We don't have too much. We don't have the Germans of course…'

'Oh? Is there some sort of trouble, Sissy?'

'Bless you, no! They're good lads and lasses – yes, sometimes the lasses come in too and they can drink ale like their men, you'll see. An' they can be loud, oh yes, but always very polite. But this Eve is when they gather together around their own folks an' their church later and sing all their own songs. Sound lovely some of 'em, too. But tomorrer they go all religious all day and that's how they celebrate the Babe's birth. We'll see 'em likely on St Stephen's.'

'Oh yes, Boxing Day, as they've started calling it at home. My papa…' Beatrice faltered, thinking of her father handing out the gifts to the farmhands. *No Mama this year; I hope he'll manage.* 'Sorry, Sissy. Just thinking of my father. Now, you've mentioned today so tell me of your plans for the few days and let's see what I can do.'

'Well, seein' as we're talking, Beatrice – Christmas Day we don't have a Christmas dinner except for residents. Most around here like to spend the day with their own folks, an' that's all right by us. There'll be the bar of course, and Anderson and the men can serve bread and cheese and cold goose to anyone as wants it in there but we'll have our own Christmas. An' come to think of it, Anderson is called just that – Anderson – by everyone, including me. He's never liked nor used his given name so if it sounds a bit, well, formal, it isn't. It's just what he likes.'

Beatrice nodded, understanding.

'Back to Christmas, Beatrice. I like to toddle down the hill to the church – that's at ten o'clock if you want ter come. But it's a quieter day than today. When you've finished today, you'll see what I mean! So today, well, let's see…'

It was a busy couple of hours. The tables had to be dressed, and Lucy had burnished the silver so it shone. The big table had napkins again, white and starched to a crisp.

Lucy held one out to Beatrice. 'I'm not too sure about these, Mrs B, I'd prob'ly crush 'em up. Could you please fancy them up for me, like you know how?'

Laughing, Beatrice showed Lucy how to set the cutlery so that the knife edge faced the plate and that all handle ends were in line with the table edge and each other.

It quite shocked the lass to think that such things mattered. 'Is it really so important to have the choppy edge of the knife facing in, Mrs B? As long as it's there to pick up, that's all right, surely?

'It is Christmas, Lucy. We'll make a show as good as any in the city, eh? And look at these we've just done, how neat they look, and if they're all the same along this long table – just think…'

The two of them were just exulting over the precision of the setting, the polished timbers, the colourful holly and ivy twists around the picture rail when Mrs Woof came in with glasses of cordial.

'Wonder you can't hear the noise from the bar. It's winding up in there and no mistake. Beatrice, do you want to come and share our table now and then mebbes you'll play for the first course o' dinner?'

'Certainly, Sissy. Let's eat and then I must select some music – you can tell me what moods you want… Then I'll make a quick change out of this gingham. Come on, Lucy, let's sample that goose!'

Despite her best intentions, Beatrice found the meaty meal too rich and heavy for the heat of the day and excused herself before the others tackled a spicy pudding. She was pleased to escape to the cooler breezes beyond the deck and the shade of the rustling trees. On the railing, a big black and grey-white magpie was perched. She wondered if he would attack. He cocked his head on one side as she passed but stayed on his perch, unperturbed by her presence as she entered her own room.

The cool water on her dressing table was delightfully refreshing to pat on her face and also to comb through her hair. Her choice of what to wear was a problem. She had a beautiful green silk, the one with the lace décolletage. It was a stylish cut but suitably modest for day wear with the lace. *I think Mama would agree. Mama, how I miss your advice. I wonder how you would consider the relaxed way of things over here? Would you be shocked? I am not in full mourning, though I do wear the cap, Mama. I feel you would want to bring home customs to this place instead of allowing Adelaide to influence you. Certainly at home I would not be playing the piano in public – yet. Am I letting down the standards? I don't feel I am letting myself go but, as to dressing appropriately, I'm sure people here wouldn't mind even if I dressed in my hacking skirt…*

The thought brought a smile and a little shiver of excitement at the promise of a festive atmosphere but quickly dashed as she reminded herself she was actually in mourning. If she couldn't dress that way, she should exhibit some decorum perhaps. How would Mrs Lee feel about all this, she wondered. Evelyn would have told her of the offer from the inn – would she be affronted because she is playing the piano in an inn? *Oh dear, the old rules at Home were so clear cut; here there are so many contradictions…*

# 18

There was a hum of chatter growing and the occasional laugh from the dining room. As she swept gracefully inside in her green satin, the voices quietened and she felt the curious stares like needles down her spine. She quickly assessed the number of diners – a group was at both end of the long table; presumably latecomers were to take the centre places. The little table where the Germans had sat the previous day was made up for six and the chairs were still empty.

As gracefully as she could, she sat on the piano stool and started to play Chopin's Etude in E. She had selected it earlier as a gentle accompaniment to conversation and the guests seemed to agree because the hum of conversation lessened as she played.

Lucy came over and brought a glass of white wine which she laid on the box end. 'It'll stay put, Mrs B. Done it before!'

Beatrice had to smile inwardly at the gesture. Wine at such a time seemed a little daring, but then the diners were indulging. She might be judged unfavourably if she didn't... She paused, took a sip then moved into the Concerto Number 2. One of her favourites; pleasantly trilling and a restful piece, she always thought. The very thought made her wonder if she should at some time break into something more lively. *Not yet: too many were still on the goose and some will still be arriving if the voices through to the entrance hall are an indication.* She decided to leave the instrument for a while and allow the newcomers to settle, so, picking up her wine, exited into the parlour. Mr Anderson was actually asleep in his old chair, leaving the organisation of staff and guests in Mrs Woof's capable hands. He was slouching in such a comical yet comfortable way he looked even more like Mr Pickwick in the papers at home.

Mrs Woof came bustling in, looking harassed. 'Just look at him! Had a few too many ales earlier on with the lads, but then it *is* Christmas, I suppose... I'll Christmas him!'

She bustled out and Beatrice took it as her cue; she left her wine glass to the not-so-watchful eye of the recumbent Anderson and returned to the dining room. Conversation stilled as she entered and then – huge embarrassment – applause greeted her return.

Bravely, she bobbed her head in thanks and resumed her seat at the keys. There was silence. Oh, what to play. Her eyes caught the holly round the walls. She flexed her fingers. *Oh yes, of course – it's Christmas as well as New Year! Just hope I can… Of course I can. There's no such word as can't, is there, Mary Lee?*

She concentrated her memory, hoping she remembered correctly and broke into "The Holly and the Ivy'. Papa always chortled over this one, teasing her mother by claiming it was an ancient pagan song that pre-dated Christianity. Mama used to get so cross! She smiled at the memory and more broadly as her appreciative audience broke into their own version of the words, singing heartily. *Oh, goodness, they're in a singing mood, I cannot stop. What next?* Her papa would inevitably move into his own dubious rendition of 'Here we go a–wassailing' so she effortlessly segued into what had over the years at home become a familiar festive routine. That seemed popular with the singers, and some women were singing now; one had a pleasing contralto but she couldn't identify who.

Mrs Woof brought her another glass of wine but she was too thirsty to up-end the glass because of its probable effects, so whispered for some water instead.

Lucy brought it in and gave her the glass, which she quickly drained with only one hand.

'Uncle Anderson asks if you know "Nos Galan"? Their mother was from Wales there an' my mother says in English it's "Deck the Halls", so you prob'ly do."

Beatrice did, and broke enthusiastically into the lilting song. It had long been a favourite and she almost burst into song herself. Her audience had no such hesitation. By now, most of them were in the mood for jolly music – even those on the late table were clapping their hands to the rhythm. That stopped as drinking resumed and then to her delight someone started singing the chorus – fa la la la la la la – and then a male voice sang, a few stanzas late, 'deck the hall with boughs of holly'. Then came more fa la las and that was a signal for some rowdiness so, as she'd played a number of repeats, Beatrice stood, bobbed and escaped to the parlour and a plate of biscuits and a glass of cool water.

Anderson was well awake now and rapturous in his praise of her playing. 'Give yourself a rest now, lass. It's nigh on six of the clock and some of them look well ensconced. Mebbes just give them a quieter one, to show them it's the end of the dinner! There'll be a few biscuits goin' out and teapots for those as fancy. The noisy ones can move into the bar, but not you with them, lass.'

Beatrice realised those left behind in the dining room might appreciate a change of mood to end the day so she took her place at the piano and, remembering her tattered copy of the *Hymn Book for little Children*, broke into the beautiful old carol 'Once in Royal David's City'. As she played the introduction, Lucy joined her and in her lovely clear, young voice broke into the words, singing two verses. Then the female contralto in the audience sang the last verse in descant. It was a beautiful end to the session. Lucy blushed at the enthusiastic applause, as Beatrice stood, gave a wide curtsey, smiled at the contralto singer and took Lucy's hand and they both left the dining room.

The bar was still noisy enough that they could hear most of the rowdiness in the parlour.

Mrs Woof was alone and ensconced in her chair, a glass of port in her hand, and floppy old slippers on her feet. 'Take a seat, Beatrice. You did us proud today. There's no more meals tonight, only supper for residents – and you're the only one other than us.' She waved her arms around to encase Lucy and the absent Anderson. 'Mr Jack's seeing to pots of tea for those still in the dining room, Anderson's in charge in the bar. We can forget about feeding anybody except ourselves. I have here some lovely cold bread pudding so take a plate and help yourself, both of yer, and Lucy, with that lovely bit of singing, you've earned yourself a small tot of port. That was a lovely finishing off with that old carol, Beatrice. I useter sing that at Sunday school.'

'Did you, Sissy? Was that in England, where…?'

'No, lass. We Andersons are from Melbourne – well, that's where our parents landed from England. I were an Anderson too, o'course. Our da was from Somerset. His family was clockmakers there and he was for a time in Welsh Wales, in Llangollen. Then in Adelaide he met up with Mr Addison, who'd set up the inn and the mill – no, that was a Mr Dunn, I think – but Addison did quite a bit of stuff round 'ere. Not sure how Da came to buy the inn. I think Mr Addison had other prospects somewhere else. Aye, he was a wealthy man, but I'm glad 'e did! Then Anderson told me our dad got the sale because Addison had been a Somerset man as well! But this Anderson were born on the ship coming over but 'e were old enough to take over from our dad. I'm Adelaide-born an' our mother died soon after. Anderson brought me up, really. He was a good brother.'

'Oh, I'm sorry about your mother. She was Welsh?'

'We think so. She spoke some of their language at times. Her family were from the canal boats. A long feeder came from the River Dee through Llangollen and they met there. They had seven living on her boat. I think her parents would've been pleased she met Da. So I suppose she grew up English. Her name was Lucille, anyway – more French than anything else, but people came from all over to work the canals.'

She poured herself another port. 'I called Lucy after her anyway. She's really Lucille Anna Woof. Her father thought it comical her initials made LAW, seeing as he was always breaking it – the law, that is.' She chortled at her own joke. 'Come on then, ladies, both of yers. Bed and peace and quiet. The bar's getting rowdy but Anderson calls "time" when he's ready. Oh yes, Beatrice, you had some tips in the tin. I took out a portion for Lucy and a smaller one each for the yardies – they all worked hard today. I hope you don't mind. But the main tips were for you – they said so as they left. Loved the piano and the singing, that's why I thought Lucy deserved a little reward too – and she did work hard today.' She stood, gave Lucy a hug and led her off towards the rear door to the deck.

Beatrice tentatively opened the door into reception. Not a person evident, though the noise from the adjacent bar was not noticeably lessening! She smiled, found the little napkin bag of coins, and returned through to the deck and her own peaceful room. Lucy was singing quietly in the next room her own rendition of 'David's City'. Beatrice smiled, tipped out the coins on her bedspread. She gasped. 'So much! And some florins too – oh!' She counted and then again. Three pounds and seven shillings. *Oh my. This is unexpected but…being paid for playing…*

Smiling, she started to free her hair from its pins. It wasn't late – darkness had only just overtaken dusk – but sleep was calling. She felt she would sleep well this night, after all.

# Christmas Day 1879

## 19

The birdsong awoke her and she lay there, enjoying the warblings of what she now knew to be a magpie. Her bed was warm and she flicked off the pretty counterpane – or bedspread, as Mrs Woof called it – and allowed the cool breeze filtering through the gnat screen to caress her long legs. The long fine hair on her shins tickled like goosebumps at its touch and, so provoked, her inner senses quickened. A spontaneous laugh at the sudden memory as she remembered her mother's voice, when in that other life so faraway, Mama had tried to prepare her daughter for marriage. *Well, Mama, I am now no longer 'pure'. I was a married woman but only long enough to start to enjoy its comforts and its teasing. I feel I have been a widow almost a year, Mama, not a mere ten days.*

She sat on the edge of the bed. 'Of course! That's why I don't feel so guilty, not being in mourning. It's horribly sad but in reality James was so long ago…' *Oops – keep your thoughts to yourself, Beatrice!*

She stood, straightened her counterpane then sat down upon it, little hand looking-glass in her hand. 'This is Christmas Day. I have been here – in a very different world – for only ten days. Life is moving so fast I'm asking, woman in the mirror, is it guilt I am feeling? It is enough trying to understand how I came to this place, what I am doing here? Now I'm being asked to stay – can I do that without burdening myself with what is "supposed" to be? Was I really only paying scant attention to the responsibilities of marriage? Did I really understand the implications of marrying James, now seemingly ages ago? When I saw him and those horrible wounds on his face, I still don't know who I cried for most, him, or me.'

She lay back on the bed, flicking her fingers on the glass as she thought. *I feel monstrously angry as I think of his gambling. Real enjoyment and experience was denied me thanks to it – or so it appears. And, I fear, a level of shiftiness in his make-up, deceit. Was I so ingenuous I did not recognise it? Papa had reservations, yes.*

*I just know I can not carry out a pretence of feelings I really no longer have. And perhaps I am just a shallow type of person for those contradictions are apparent again! I have woken this morning with a hunger I cannot describe in proper language. It is so physical yet it is overwhelming in its lack of caring for the finer sensibilities... Oh, Mama, did you ever feel this way? I do so need to learn more of what being a woman, a free woman, is about...*

As she began to question the possibility of finding another man and who he might be in this new and very different place, a loud voice echoed through the door. It was Mr Anderson.

'Beatrice, I have been sent to waken you! Sissy and Lucy and I are in the parlour having a Christmas breakfast and they do urge me, with my loud voice, to waken you and say Lucy will bring you fresh water to wake up and then you can join us!'

'Thank you. That is, I will dress quickly.'

Then came a knock, and a call. 'It's me, Mrs B,' and the door opened to admit Lucy and a bowl of warm water and a towel. 'Mother asks that you just don your cap and morning clothes for we are in ours too. There is no one else to spoil our fun!' She giggled. 'Do come, Mrs B. Don't worry about stays and such. We will only be the four of us and it is a very special day!' She was irresistible, a big happy smile bursting with impatience.

Beatrice shoved her hair roughly into a lacy cap, wrapped her robe around her and joined the girl, barefoot on the deck. *Oh, Mama, you would be blushing and calling me wanton!* The magpie was there, head to one side, watching; quiet now. She noticed he seemed to have a twisted claw, poor thing.

In the little parlour, a huge pot of scented tea was surrounded by teacups and a bowl of apricots and roasted almonds.

Mrs Woof was proudly indicating her table. 'Come in, Beatrice. We've hot toast and ginger jam – made with rum, that is – and ginger biscuits and marmalade pastries! It's Christmas Day and Lucy and I will be making a good feast of it as we are going to the ten o'clock carol service where there is no communion, so we needn't starve first, and will you join us then, as now?' Out of breath, she laughed and sat down.

Beatrice felt imbued with friendliness and belonging and sat down as Lucy poured a huge cup of hot tea.

'Later it'll be a hot one – the day, that is – but we don't expect visitors today so we'll eat cool and drink cool I feel. But now, fortify yourself for a visit to the township, Beatrice, where many who don't know you are waiting to meet you!'

'Oh dear. Sissy, I only have the one walking outfit and it is too warm for today. If I am to be scrutinised – oh, a dreadful thought – shall it be enough for me to wear my long navy skirt, with my lace blouse and mother's brooch? It is only morning, after all, not afternoon…'

'Oh, don't fret, Beatrice. That sounds like very suitable. But a good pair of boots if you have them, suitable for walking, perhaps. The road is rough in places. But worry not and first let us enjoy breaking our fast this way! And it is Christmas. Now, Anderson?'

Her brother reached under the floor-length table drape and presented Lucy with a box tied with long green ribbon and with ivy leaves twisted round – it looked quite festive.

'Oh, Uncle – can I open it now?'

He and her mother exchanged conspiratorial smiles and he reached under the table again and pulled out a large flat, paper-wrapped parcel, similarly decorated with green ivy and string, which he presented to Beatrice with a typical Dickensian flourish.

'My dear sister organised this for you and we hope you will accept it with our pleasure at choosing it for you, Beatrice. Nay, lass, no embarrassment, please,' for she had felt her face rapidly warm, 'this is from all of us because you are fitting in so well that only so quickly we feel you are one of us.'

'Thank you. But my embarrassment is… Well, I cannot reciprocate, and you are so kind and generous.'

Mrs Woof leaned over and patted her knee. 'Our pleasure, Beatrice. You have brought us lovely music and some learning of table niceties and this is small recompense.'

Her brother butted in. 'And our takings over Christmas and expectations of early bookings for the New Year from some of those here yesterday are because of your music, my dear. You owe us nothing.'

Her gift was a pair of dress lengths in cotton, one a gingham, the other a delightful picked print of pale green with a seam of cherries and apples she could already envisage as a hem.

'Oh, truly lovely and the fabric, cotton, is so very, very practical. I came so ill advised for the Australian summer. These will make up into – oh, I can already envisage the cutting.'

'Please, Mrs B, can I help you sew? I do like sewing.'

'Beatrice, our friend Mrs Bones – and I hope you'll meet her this morning – she lets us borrow her Singer machine. She bought it from a newcomer who needed the sale. It has a wheel at the side and it makes sewing a seam so neat and it's so quick! Lucy is quite good at the sewing because Mrs Bones showed us both how to use it and, yes, if you can do the cutting, she is certainly a good little operator of that machine. Now I have a present for Anderson and I know he has one for me, so...'

She reached into the large pocket of her wrap and presented a flat paper package to her brother. Simultaneously he gave her a wrapped box, prettily dressed in holly berries and greenery. Much joking about the contents and unwrapping revealed a hand-knitted nightcap for Anderson and a box of scented soap for Sissy.

'Just off the ship, sister dear.'

'Knitted by me in your favourite colours.'

'And now, ladies, if you will permit, I suggest we adjourn to freshen our faces and dress for church. Mrs Bones will start clanging that school hand bell soon and, believe me, we hear it up here too. We have lingered over-long, I fear!' Mrs Woof smiled at Beatrice, 'Particularly when we have a guest who can't wake up in a morning!'

And laughing amongst themselves, they set off over the deck to their rooms, leaving Mr Anderson contemplating the cooling teapot.

*

Beatrice entered the little church nervously, feeling she would be recognised as a stranger in the little community. Yet smiles greeted her as they took their seat on a long bench. It was only a short service, the format unfamiliar to Beatrice, but the Christmas hymns she knew well and she joined in the singing as heartily as anyone.

Afterwards, when they all congregated around a trestle table loaded with teapots and cups and plates, so many of the ladies came up to say 'Welcome.' No introductions were necessary; word had got around.

Mrs Bones, who'd played the little pedal organ for the service, came over and commandeered her in her eagerness to boast of their little church. She explained that the church had been built about twenty years previously by the owner of the mill. And, over the cup of tea served her by another friendly woman, Mrs Bones was happy to tell Beatrice something of its history. 'A Mr Dunn built the big mill twenty year ago, Mrs Bewcham. Then he built our little town round it like a village and called it Bridgewater after the inn, 'acause that was 'ere first. There was a little township here afore, called Cox's Creek but Mr Dunn set up a post office an' this an' that – an' the name Cox's Creek's been forgotten now. Come the Sabbath, there was no place to hold a service, so he allowed a few local people and workers to sit around on flour sacks and a travelling preacher came – he were Methody, I understand. But it wasn't too comfortable, so they citizens built this little church. It ain't fancy, but it's doing a proper job and we got a pedal organ new, just a bit affected by salt water on its trip over 'ere from Scotland. Some Presbytery types didn't want the music, but then we share the church and when they have their service we cover it with that old plush curtain. We who are Church of England share the rector with Aldgate and then he rides somewhere else for an evening service. We likes the music. You would've heard me playing today, Mrs Bewcham, an' I understand you play the pianner lovely. You're playing at the Andersons on that little machine. Do you play the organ as well?'

Beatrice had to tell her she couldn't play the organ and was pleased to see satisfaction on Mrs Bones's face. The dear old soul had been afraid Beatrice might usurp her own standing in the community! Then the older lady was called over by another lady at the teapot but Beatrice managed to ask her about the Singer sewing machine and, to her delight, Mrs Bones was quite willing to loan it to her. However, Beatrice hardly had time to consider a plan before another smiling woman came over to make her acquaintance.

'I am Mrs Rogers, Mrs Beauchamp. I teach at the school some days and my husband is an assistant postmaster here. We loved your Chopin the other night when you played at the inn – and that lovely singing after from the German farmer,' She paused. 'Mrs Beauchamp, would you consider giving some piano lessons to our two daughters? They are twelve and fifteen and have had some lessons in music at school with Mrs Bones. My eldest, Paula, is very keen to improve. Would you, could you, please, give her some lessons? That's if you have any time of course. I wouldn't want to impose.'

'Mrs Rogers, I am finding my days quite busy helping at the inn and Lucy Woof also wants me to teach her. It would mean using their piano.' She smiled. 'May I think it over? Actually, where do your daughters practise now? Do you have an instrument at home?'

'No, but we are allowed to use the one in the school. Mrs Bones would know if you could use that one.'

The idea had appeal for Beatrice. Teaching piano would not only further her independence, but also help her acceptance into this community – and the country!

'Thank you, Mrs Rogers. I have some letters to finish and post so perhaps within a day or two I may see you or Mr Rogers at the post office and we can speak again.'

By this time, it seemed quite a number of the ladies wanted to make her acquaintance and the smiling Mrs Rogers moved away with a little flickering wave.

Beatrice felt that her welcome by the group was the best thing, if a little overwhelming! She looked over the heads to Mrs Woof, who was watching and smiling. Lucy was talking cheerfully to a couple of local lasses almost her own age, one of whom was tapped on the shoulder by Mrs Rogers, apparently ready to leave for home.

Left to herself for a moment, Beatrice surreptitiously scanned – over her teacup – the male contingent of the crowd. Solid, worthy citizens all of them but none looking unattached… She sighed. She felt they all knew of her recent widowhood – they seemed to know everything else about her – yet it all seemed a bit of a paradox. Back in England, at home, and James dead only ten days, it would still be blinds drawn, mirrors beribboned and that all-pervasive solemnity. She would have been expected to withdraw from public life. Yet here, there seemed to be a practical acceptance of her moving amongst them in a normal way.

She went to place her cup on the table, smiling tentatively at people she passed. *Beatrice, none of them were making sheep's eyes at you. Surely that is not what you want? Mama would certainly be shocked! In truth, it's nearly a year since*

*James and I were man and wife and so to me he feels dead from then till now. That body in the Dead House was not the James I knew. The way he lost his life, lost his money, was the way of a stranger to me. Yet, in marriage, he awoke sensations in me I was eager to renew… Do I miss James, or do I… Oh, am I so wicked to feel this way? And I wonder, where is Lieutenant Symonds now… Oh, Beatrice, you are thinking unseemly thoughts and even in a church hall…*

# 20

An uplifted arm waved, its fingers wiggled and Mrs Woof nodded in the direction of the inn. She held Lucy's hand and mother and daughter started homewards.

Beatrice was starting to feel a little overcome by her silent miseries that were in direct contrast to the overwhelming friendship of the community. 'I feel so welcomed, Sissy. One thing, though, I couldn't help notice that most of the men stood back, talking among themselves, and didn't come to greet me. Should I be concerned?'

'Bless you, no! It's just the way of the menfolk. Gather them together with their wives an' unless they're tied to a table an' a plate, they'll congregate down one end of a room as the ladies make for the other. Sometimes, they only seem to come together when it's time to go 'ome! Just the way it is. Isn't that right, Lucy? You'll see when we get home that the bar will have its usual customers. Anderson will be kept busy. We'll have a luncheon when we're ready and he'll join us if he wants to. Unless we have visitors, travellers, wanting a meal, we don't open the dining room, Beatrice. Me and Lucy do what we want to do. Right, Lucy?'

As Lucy nodded, Beatrice smiled widely. 'I can hardly wait to draft out a paper pattern for my dresses from that lovely cotton you gave me. Lucy, do you know how to measure up for pattern making? I've never attempted that.'

Lucy was delighted at the prospect and Sissy said she had made up a few from sketches, they'd manage, so the three chatted cheerfully all the way up the hill. The cheery noise from the bar could be heard as they approached and there were a pair of traps in the yard, and Zed the gardener, who did yard jobs when needed, was in his apron attending to the horses of one team with Jack rubbing down another animal.

'Looks like company,' muttered Sissy, but Zed told her they were a couple of pairs of young bloods out for a drive and a few ales.

'No mention of a meal, missus.'

So it proved, and while the three ladies had a merry session over port wines and cold meat with pickles, the very masculine voices roaring in the bar gave testament to its being the season to be merry!

Lucy and Beatrice cleared the so-called small table in the dining room and spread the green cotton dress length over it and round it and this way and that way as Beatrice decided where the printed cherries would show to the best advantage. She had sketched an outline of a design and with the aid of some old copies of the *Register* the two of them managed to draft a reasonable pattern shape onto the paper.

Beatrice was nervously flourishing Sissy's big scissors, dreading making a faulty first cut, when Sissy emerged from the direction of her room.

She had obviously enjoyed a brief snooze and quickly took control. 'I've made mine an' Lucy's dresses every time, Beatrice. Let's just see… May I?' She moved a couple of the pattern pieces to take best advantage of the weave and immediately plied the scissors. 'Glad you're not doing the bustle, Beatrice. I read in the *Chronicle* they're going out. Not sorry, me. Designs change week by week, I'm thinking. Look at those two orchard women in church this morning, still in crinolines.'

'Mam, the Phillips girls told me their mother likes the crinoline for best in the hot weather 'cos it's coolest to wear. Better than lots of petticoats.'

'I must admit, Sissy, I like the bustle for special occasions, and never did like the crinoline – awkward thing to handle sitting down. Even the bustle gets in the way then, but it does look stately when worn well. However, I've never had a bustle and have taken heart from some Adelaide women I noticed, who still dart up the bodice so it fits snugly. Must admit, though, I do wonder at the practicality of such tight waists and stays in this summer weather. Blouses and skirts are much freer in wearing, don't you think? I have made a few blouses and skirts with help from Mamzelle but my sewing is mainly the embroidery type, as Mamzelle and our sewing woman did the stitching and fitting.'

'Ahah – I thought as much, Beatrice, but it's nought to be ashamed of. Thing is, dressmakers can be found, but this is a country of make do and mend, and if you can't, well life can be hard. Mrs Bones said her lad will bring her Singer up tomorrow so you'll be able to do some sewing. Lucy's good at that, too.'

Later that day, Beatrice broached the topic of piano lessons for the Rogers girls..

'Oh, Beatrice! Does that mean you'll stay on a while – after this week and after New Year, I mean?'

'To be truthful, Sissy, I hadn't thought much beyond then. However, I do have to stand on my own two feet – as my dear friend Mary Lee would say – so if I do, and I am paid for it, I shall expect you to let me pay for my room, or otherwise it'll be a loss for you…'

'I will talk to Anderson, my dear. However, if you will continue to play the little square piano at, say, weekends and special occasions, teach Lucy that and the ettiqwetty stuff, I am sure he would not want to charge you full rate. Let me talk to him, and meanwhile, you just know we like having you here, for as long as you like. Whatever you decide.' With that, she swept out to check on preparations in the kitchen for the morrow.

Beatrice decided, now the main heat of the day was fading, to go for a walk. It had been a day of surprises and new experiences and ideas; her thoughts and feelings were tangled in her brain and she felt a walk with only Mother Nature might clear her head.

She decided to take the route she and Evelyn had started down the other day. The air was mild, the breeze gentle, the deeply blue sky still wide up above, without a cloud. There were at least four full hours of daylight left before the sudden dusk fell with its 'mosquitos' – as she had seen it written in the newspaper; as an import from the Spanish, it said. Today was unlike any other Christmas Day she had ever known, but if this was to be the pattern for many future Christmases, she could not regret it.

The path was quite steep and she enjoyed the feeling of keeping her balance and dodging the sharper pieces of stone underfoot and brushing aside the twigs and branches that swept the hem of her skirt. It was still her only good skirt so she didn't want to stain it with sap. She thought that if she came this way again it might be an idea to wear her hacking skirt. Still, for now…

Some of the shrubs gave off a pungent perfume that was almost medicinal, and not unfamiliar. They also had tiny pink flowers. She picked a branch, thinking to ask Mrs Woof to identify it. As she bent down, a long snake slithered quickly into the undergrowth and she jumped in shock.

She remembered a shipboard conversation when some seasoned traveller had cautioned that when snakes were seen, 'Ignore them and stand still.' Even as she remembered, she was well into her run! She stopped, bent down holding her knees and laughed even as she caught her breath. She could see the bushes opening out to an expanse of flat rocks and heard the whispering of running water. Must be the beck – the creek – at last!

She stopped, startled, spotting a black and white magpie watching her from a shoulder-high branch. Would it attack? It was a big bird, but merely kept its beady eye upon her as she stumbled along the rocky path. Was it the same one that sometimes perched on the rail near her room? Can't see if a claw is twisted… He was in his territory and fearless of no one. Then a mob of little green parrots flew out of a tree, their camouflage so perfect they could almost have been swift-flying leaves. She laughed at her own ridiculousness.

A baby rabbit shot across her path – so small she felt sure it would fit in the palm of her hand. Anderson had moaned about them only last night because some had chewed at the greens in Zed's vegetable patch – and that little garden supplied most of the greens in their meals. Oh, and carrots and those huge balloon-like pumpkin things Zed was so proud of.

Sissy had told her rabbits were not native to the country but had been brought only in recent years by settlers as a means of meat. However, some had escaped and were being found in the Tiers – for so she had discovered the Adelaide Hills were popularly known. *This little one is barely out of its burrow! No doubt it's a ready prey for foxes, though I believe they too are blamed on the British.*

'Oh *no*…!'

A big, jet-black crow with white under its tail, swooped down and with barely a second's stop caught the little rabbit in its talons and headed up again into the high canopy of a nearby local tree. The little rabbit gave a scream of surprise, a shrill eruption of sound that stopped as suddenly as it had started.

*This is nature without the legendary mother!* Surprised, she lost her balance, skidding but still on her feet down a dry patch of gravelly rocks that seemed to be like little boys' marbles, they moved as freely. She managed to grab a bunch of fronds and halted abruptly, the stones rolling onwards ahead of her under the bushes. Nature in the raw had spoiled the moment.

She stood her ground. She hadn't thought to come so far. Nearby and down a few feet ran the little creek. Upwards, somewhere, was the inn. The little creek, grassy-banked and musical over its rocks, had seemed appealing. Now, the safety of her little room was the more so. She turned to mark the way she thought she had approached; no path was discernible; no buildings apparent up above. *Didn't think I came so far, nor did it feel too steep. Did I come by that bush with the little yellow flowers? Surely I would have noticed it... Well, I must have done because just there is that piece of white rock jutting out that I felt through my shoe...*

Encouraged, she bent over to clamber upwards, pulling on the bushes to maintain a foothold at times. Then she passed the pink-flowered bush near where the little rabbit had been. She realised she had dropped the little sprig she had meant to show Mrs Woof. She pulled another and it tore smoothly along the bark of the branch, leaving a strip of white. She rubbed it with her fingers and realised it had the same perfume Sissy used when washing the sheets, or something very similar.

This country, these plants, were strange to Beatrice She pushed her way through the brush and soon saw the wooden decking of the inn high above. The sky had become paler and over in one direction she saw the gibbous moon, pale but evident in the sky. For the first time, she was conscious of having been gone for a period of time but could not in her mind measure just how long. *Goodness, I hope I haven't had anyone worried.*

It seemed not. She reached the decking and walked along to the dining room. Lucy had relaid the small table on which they had cut out her dress, but Lucy could not be seen. There was a chatter of sound from the bar but nothing like the rowdiness of earlier.

Then Mrs Woof breezed into the room. 'There you are, dear. Have a good sleep? Lucy took herself off for one, too. We'll have a light tea soon, more like supper, I think. Are you hungry?' Then she bustled out again.

*I haven't been missed. Oh my! What if that snake had bitten me or that black bird attacked me and not the rabbit? Would they have known? Perhaps I should have told them what I planned...* Smiling at her own silliness, she decided to freshen up a bit, enjoy her tea, maybe play some piano just for herself and then go to bed. A strange Christmas, maybe, and in so many ways, but one she would remember.

# St Stephen's (Boxing) Day 1879

## 21

Beatrice awoke, her legs stiff from their hilly walk the previous day and her head buzzing with her instructions for this day – this very day, whether stiff-legged or not!

She marked points of memory on her fingers, mouthing silently, 'Only a light lunch and perhaps something for passing trade if required, and for those, the small table in the dining room could be readied by Lucy.' Breathe… 'Then at three o'clock, the dining room has to be made ready for the usual evening guests and I've offered to help Lucy. Oh yes, some seats have been booked already, and the Germans have booked the small table. Dinner will be started at six o'clock, the usual time.' Beatrice sat up in bed, still remembering her instructions. 'And what else did Sissy say? Oh yes, "If you could oblige with the pianner again…" Well, of course I will. I'd better have a really good look through that sheet music in the pianner seat!'

After breakfast, Mrs Bones popped in to say she had brought up the Singer machine and that her lad would put it 'where you want it to be'.

All was soon arranged in the parlour and Lucy brought in a tray of tea and ginger biscuits, which gave Beatrice the opportunity to ask the neighbour about the Rogers girls and piano lessons.

'Mrs Bones, can I ask you something?'

The lady merely nodded and smiled over her teacup.

'I have been asked if I would give some young girls – well, the young Rogers ladies to be precise – some piano lessons. I understand they've been brilliantly taught by you and I was…'

'Oh, my dear Mrs Bewcham. If you were worried about my feelings, do not be. My first love is my little organ in the church. I would be so pleased to have you teach the Rogers girls. They need more than I can offer them in the way of teaching, my dear. I will continue with the basic music lessons to all the children in the school, of course, but outside of school hours – well, I think it would be a great advantage for the girls to have you teach them. Look, my dear, why not use the school piano for their lessons? I admit it is a little scratched but it plays well and has been tuned by the man from Adelaide. I have heard your delightful playing on the inn's square piano, and I know from when I've played it you must've changed the music to fit it in that set o' keys. I'm not good enough at adapting – that's it, adapting.'

She smiled in response to Beatrice's nodding. 'Well, the school piano is an upright, possibly forty years old but came over from – I think – Tennessee in the Americas. It has a date 1860 written on its back and I think it was ordered and shipped over by the Mr Dunn who built the mill, he who set up the town and I think he started the school – with the blessing of the church, that is. It's only a bit scratched and it's a lovely piano. It has a full-size keyboard and a lovely tone. I am sure there would be no problem you using it, or even playing it for your own pleasure!'

'That is lovely to know, Mrs Bones. I thought I might have to get in touch with the school authorities…'

'Oh, my dear! The school belongs to the church. Well, really it is our church who started it off in the other vicar's days. So it's a church school – well, really a corporate school. Oh dear, it's all a bit confusing. We take all the children who want to come. It's compulsory now in law from age seven till age thirteen.' She gave a little frown. 'I do believe there is talk of the government taking it over and extending the school next year or the year after. And there's an advanced school for girls now, in the city in Grote Street. It's the first really public one, as I understand, an' girls who are bright, an' if their parents can pay, can study to be teachers! Isn't that wonderful! They will know all the harder sums and arithmetic for children to learn. I think my days will be over by the time a new school starts here, really I do. I don't mind music, but the rest of the lessons… Well, that doesn't matter now.'

She drained her cup and turned to go. 'Oh yes, I wish you happy sewing with the Singer machine. It is a wonderful asset for the straight seam. I will come and listen to you on the piano this evening, too, as I have booked myself and Mr Bones a place here for dinner. Goodbye till then, my dear.'

After seeing Mrs Bones out of the door, Beatrice sat back on a dining chair beset by a mild panic. What was she doing? Why was she doing this, committing herself in this way to this community? Was this the independence she sought or was it that she felt a need to belong? Was she trying too hard?

Lucy put her head round the parlour door. 'Please, Mrs B, should I put the pudding spoon and fork atop the plate and across or down the side in order? Can you show me, please?'

Beatrice nodded, first giving the Singer's glossy black coat a friendly stroke. *Be with you soon, my friend. You have some work to do for me!*

Later, when changed into her favourite silk and sitting on her bed trying to gather an absent courage and *joie de vivre* – still feeling guilty that she was not at least in half-mourning despite logically rationalising the long-time absence of her husband with old tradition – a knock on the door heralded a rather flushed Mrs Woof.

'Oh, my dear, we have a full dining room and your friend from Adelaide has arrived. We have no room. Can you share your room with Evelyn Lee tonight so she can stay? Oh…'

This last exclamation was due to a silken-rustling Beatrice rushing past and through the door, quite forgetting the niceties in her excitement. Evelyn was still dressed in travelling clothes.

'Oh, Evelyn! How lovely to see you! Are you off the coach? I didn't know it ran today… Yes, of course you can share my room if you can stay.'

Evelyn hugged her. 'Oh, Beatrice, I have missed our conversations… May I change then in your room so I can take a seat and dine and listen to your playing later? Then we can share all our news…'

They separated and laughed. Beatrice led her friend to her room as Lucy brought fresh towels and water.

'I am so very pleased to see you, my friend. This is my first visit from anyone and it is so good, so very good, to see you!'

Evelyn was delighted at her friend's enthusiasm. 'My dear girl, it's only a couple of days since… Hey, you have relaxed much of your Englishness, I notice.'

Beatrice looked surprised at the observation. 'How do you mean? Oh, you can explain later. And I do want to hear how is John Benjamin, and dear Mrs Lee?'

'My mother wanted to know if you are well after the Christmas celebrations, not too saddened, because she knows this is the first Christmas after your mother died, and of course all that unhappiness when we arrived at the Port. Mam cares, Beatrice, bless her. So do I, and I am so relieved to see you dressed so becomingly and readying to play for the guests...'

'Evelyn, it is so very good to see you! Oh, I must go, but please freshen yourself then come up to the dining room. I believe Sissy will have a seat for you. I'll join you when I break and then we'll eat together!'

That's how it worked out. A seat was found for Evelyn at the end of the table nearest the piano and as she was drawn into conversation with another lady, Beatrice left her and moved to the piano.

Her music was greeted as enthusiastically as always but this time, between sessions, Beatrice was able to join Evelyn at the table. Without all the seasonal carols this time, she noticed many of the patrons just enjoyed listening; there was certainly plenty of conversation. So after most seemed to be eating their pudding choice, she decided to finish up with the Scherzo No 2 in B Flat Minor – pleasant but not intrusive – and enjoy talking to her friend. As she stood and curtseyed to signal the end of her playing, the applause was as enthusiastic as last time.

Evelyn looked quite delighted. 'Beattie, that is beautiful stuff. You really can play so nicely. Look, can we withdraw – somewhere less busy?'

'It's a lovely evening, Evie. Let's walk a little way over as we did before...'

A gentle tap on Beatrice's arm prompted her to turn to see the German who had spoken to her on Christmas. She smiled, uncertain how to address him.

'Dear ladies, I would escort you outside so you can take the air?'

Somewhat surprised, Beatrice found herself and Evelyn either side of him and heading for the deck outdoors before they could demur.

Mr Anderson appeared as from nowhere and intervened, placing himself between the ladies and the door. 'Pastor Wilhelm, do allow me to introduce you to these two ladies. They are both very good friends of ours.' He proceeded to name them and to each the pastor extended a hearty handshake and a click of the heels.

Anderson then effectively reassured the ladies they were in safe hands.

'My friend the pastor has the community of Hahndorf in his keeping – with others. He and his friends supply us with the eggs, some fruit and vegetables and even the wooden sabots we put over our shoes in the yard.'

He turned to the German. 'Rauf, my friend, these ladies have not seen each other for a while and have much information to exchange with each other. I do hope they will forgive me taking you away but I have been wanting to speak with you. It is a community matter. May I interest you in a good Barossa wine I am trying…'

He steered his tall friend away but not before the German kissed each lady on the hand and gave his little bow.

Evelyn was quite flattered and smiled excitedly at Beatrice as they headed down over the wooden decking. 'He is really lovely, Beattie, that German. He must be a good man if he is pastor. That's the same as our vicar, you know.'

Beatrice smiled, then, mindful of her scrape down the pathway only the day before, suggested they sit on the edge of the deck and watch the moon and enjoy the breeze. 'Evelyn, I admit to ignorance. I thought vicar was just an English title. When I hear your lovely mother talk of Ulster…'

'Ulster? Well, Monaghan is a border county and part of Ulster but we don't often use that term. And my mam is the daughter of a master of the Orange Lodge so that's her religious leaning. Mind you, here she seems inclined to attend the Wesleyan church.' She chuckled. 'Mam has an irrepressible sense of humour, you know, and she can mimic a strong Irish accent if she wishes. She's terrible for mimicking – I think she just absorbs new words because she can. She's full of funny sayings, my mam.'

In unison they carolled, '"There's no such word as can't",' then roared with laughter.

# 22

Lucy brought them out a hot tisane to sip in the breeze as Evelyn began.

'Mother sends her best wishes, Beatrice, as does John. He, poor lamb, has such a weak digestion, he has suffered terribly the last few days. Yesterday he refused the Christmas pudding Mother had brought with her from Monaghan, so we knew he was unwell. Poor fellow.'

Beatrice made a sympathetic moue. 'I do miss your mother's sound advice, Evie. I hope she doesn't lock herself away from new friendships, even though John is ill. She is a strong woman, I know, but even strong women need friends... Talking of which, Evie, have you seen anything of Lieutenant Symonds?'

'Didn't you know? He was contracted to continue with the *Orient* to Sydney – or was it Melbourne? No, dear, we haven't, more's the pity, I say. He will be a wonderful catch, Beatrice, for someone. You know, I wouldn't mind if he were to return to our company... Must admit I liked him and admired his natural authority. Friendly and efficient he was that day. I wish he was around, I really do. Now, do tell me about that lovely German man. Are there any other beaux in the wings up here in the hills?'

Beatrice really had no comment to make about 'that lovely German man' other than to venture her impression he had very workman-like hands, quite calloused. She had noticed that time he picked up hers to bestow that kiss. That news sent Evie into giggles!

It seemed that after no time at all they were both stretched out on Beatrice's little bed, head to toe. Beatrice had enjoyed playing the piano with Evelyn present and between times they'd had time to talk. Sissy had insisted on that. Afterwards, they had chatted about all and sundry for hours, until Beatrice was sure the early sun would shine through the curtains. She stayed as still as she could, not wanting to disturb her friend snoring peacefully at the foot of the bed.

She had to admit she'd wondered whether the lieutenant would call on

Evelyn; yes, he would be a good catch. There seemed to be no one else in Evie's life – if anything, she was more interested in starting work. She had talked enthusiastically about a Charles Todd – an explorer who'd led a team laying the Overland Telegraph Line from Adelaide to Darwin. The man was now involved in the post office and weather maps, according to Evelyn, who'd never met him but seemed infected by her brother's enthusiasm.

Evie had known nothing more of the Taylors' involvement with James. It seemed to Beatrice that was all over and done with now; perhaps it was the cue for her, Beatrice, to get on with whatever this new Bridgewater life was offering. Evelyn was talking energetically and with great enthusiasm of looking forward to taking up her position with the Telegraph Department, though she seemed unsure of her own role there. However, if enthusiasm is the only qualification… Lucky Evie..

The thought came unbidden. *At least Evie will be independent…* And as suddenly she realised that she too was becoming independent. *Yes, I am! With the money from teaching, I should be able to pay for this room here at the inn and be obliged to no one. I can remain respectable and perhaps save money until I know where I need to go, what I can do to build my life. I can, I can…*

Next thing she knew, it was daylight!

Evelyn dropped the soap and clanged the jug. She was washing herself down with the cool flannel. She turned to Beatrice. 'I must make haste, my dear friend, if I am to take the trap to Aldgate to link with the coach. I wish I could stay but tomorrow Mother has some ladies coming for a meeting or something after church and I promised I would be back for that. Then, of course, on Monday I start my new position! But right now, will you be able to come and have a bite of breakfast with me?'

'Goodness me, Evie, I wouldn't do otherwise. I'll do a quick freshen up and get respectable…' Even as she spoke, Beatrice was worming into her gingham.

'Beatrice! Only one petticoat?'

'I do have my shift, Evie! It is Mrs Woof's idea and certainly more sensible for these summers. Who knows the difference? It's not as if we still have to fight the crinoline, is it? And we are here in sunny and hot South Australia. Altogether more sensible.'

They made their way quickly to the little parlour, Evelyn exclaiming,

'Oh, Beattie, you have certainly landed on your feet, my dear. And among friends. I am so pleased and so will Mother be. I hope you will come to…'

They were silenced by the surprising sight of the tall figure of the German pastor rising from his chair at their approach.

'Ladies, please join me to break your fast. Miss Lee, I have my trap at your disposal to take you to Aldgate and I shall then accompany you on the coach – that is, if you will allow me. I have business in the city market.'

Both young women were quite discombobulated but took a seat as bidden. Lucy brought platters of cold meat and cheese and bread with cold goat's milk to drink. She had the audacity to wink at Beatrice, who simply reached for some bread as the German and her friend started speaking as if they were old friends and had not just met!

Beatrice was surprised that her friend made not even a perfunctory protest at the change in her arrangements. *What a spontaneous place for conversation this place is – no hesitation on Evelyn's part or that Mr, what was it, Wilhelm's? A little unexpected, this immediate badinage about bumpy roads and ladies' comfort, but then, this isn't stuffy old Victorian England with its restrictions on this and that…* She hid a smile as she helped herself to a slice of ham, remembering how Evelyn had earlier admired another man's 'air of authority'. *Goodness me, it could even be the start of a friendship for Evelyn…*

All too soon, Evelyn had her bag ready and was helped into the trap. Pastor Wilhelm sprang in next to her and with the briefest wave goodbye, Evie was gripping the side wall as the trap wheeled round and headed for the yard gate, where they hit the lane in a cloud of dust.

Beatrice watched the dust subside, then turned to go back indoors. She felt 'left behind' – alone. Then a tentative tap on her arm made her smile.

'So, Mrs B, are you going to do any cutting out and sewing today, because if you are…'

*Who can be lonely with Lucy around? And here's Sissy…*

'Beatrice, you didn't collect your tips last evening – perhaps with your friend here and all.' She handed Beatrice the linen bag with its friendly jingle. 'We don't have any big event planned today. Trade has been so good over the Christmas and all due to you. We have already been asked to take bookings for New Year's Eve, and I have accepted them, but if you don't wish to play on that occasion, please let me know. Anderson and me, well, we both know you are thinking of perhaps staying longer, but you are not beholden to us, my dear. Rather it's the other way round! So today, lunch and dinner will only be served to passing trade, as on any other day, so please consider your time your own. The piano is of course yours to enjoy as often as you wish. Lucy, you will ensure the tables are prepared after the cutting out, won't you? Other than that, you can help Beatrice as long as she wants you to.'

'Yes, Mam.'

*So that was my Boxing Day, thanks to dear Evie making the ride here. Different from home. I wonder if Papa gave a present yesterday to Mrs Willis, to the Dents, to… Ah well, that is another world and now I'm here. Papa will receive my letter eventually and hopefully answer it with news of…well, of everything.*

# 23

Sunday morning arrived and Mrs Bones sent up to say the morning service at the church was to be 'for the other church' that morning as it was some sort of celebration. Church of England people would have the space for Evensong instead.

The change of plan was welcome to Beatrice, who was eager to replenish her wardrobe with the new dresses – well, one at least! The cutting had progressed well yesterday, and so this morning was the sewing. Lucy certainly could follow a straight seam on Mrs Bones's machine, and she understood its thread winding and other intricacies. She showed Beatrice various quirks of the needle and explained even its mechanism. Beatrice had originally thought it was one with what Singers called a 'treadle' to operate with the feet, such as one her sempstress-cum-dressmaker at home had used. This model sat on any surface and was operated by the winding of a handle. According to Mrs Bones, the treadle was better because then one could have two hands steering the fabric. However, Beatrice thought Lucy was managing quite well and when Beatrice had a trial run on one of the scraps, she found it reasonably easy to manipulate, though Lucy laughed and said she was too slow!

'Modern technicology, Anderson calls it, and says we should keep up to date.'

Beatrice was quite impressed that for so young a girl, Lucy already had many accomplishments. Her mother might persist in her wish for her to learn 'ettyquetty' – and indeed she was quick to remember things – but her sewing was as practised and certainly neater than Beatrice's. But then, as a girl, Beatrice knew she had been ever ready to pass on the seaming and hemming to Mamzelle. In actual fact, the dressmaker in the village had usually completed a project from start to finish. On embroidery and petit point Beatrice had been compelled by Mama to spend at least as much time as she spent riding her horses. Only now, as she debated what stitches she might employ around the bodice of this dress, did she appreciate her mother's insistence. *Dear Mama…*

The hand sewing she could perform while Lucy concentrated on the machining; it allowed her time to think of her own prospects. Was it too precipitate of her to consider Evelyn's possibly finding a partner in the German pastor – or was that too unrealistic a prospect? And what if the Pastor was married? Lucy would know, but best not to encourage Lucy's romantic thoughts.

Nevertheless, it brought home to her, her own situation. Who and what was she, Beatrice Beauchamp, other than an anachronism, totally out of harmony with her true circumstances? Only two weeks in this country, trusted and accepted and even befriended by this community without question, yet burdened with a sense of being an onlooker rather than a participant in this Bridgewater life.

Also weighing her down was her inability to acknowledge simple friendship and willing help; it felt like charity and she the reluctant recipient. Her unwillingness to acknowledge simple kindnesses without an uncomfortable sense of obligation – was it all, can it be, the product of her own privileged upbringing? If so, was that wrong? So what was the right way of…anything?

'Ouch!' She pricked her finger. 'Oh, Lucy, I shall have to bind this or I'll mark the fabric!' She walked off, muttering, 'Botheration! Botheration!'

*Why I am getting into such a tizzy? I am respectable, only one petticoat or not! I am decidedly fortunate in my new friends. Yes, I play the piano, and it is that which I can now do and be paid for it as if a teacher. There is no lack of pride in that! So what, if at home earning money would be seen as lacking respectability, I am not at home now!*

She resumed her chair with a well wrapped finger and rethreaded her needle. She replaced the thimble on another finger and checked her stitching as Lucy left the machine to go and make a pot of tea.

Life must proceed and in time she knew she would more easily accept her situation. Common sense would dictate that, given the busyness of this inn and the company of Sissy and Lucy, and a level of acceptance by the community – and of course the Lees – she would eventually gain that sense of belonging. That's if she allowed herself the opportunity…

So! She had decided. She would stay a few more weeks and why not? Bridgewater was a pleasant place in the heat of the day, more so than the Adelaide Plains. The local community had welcomed her; the Andersons – or Anderson and Woof, brother and sister – were friendly and accommodating; and with the tips from whenever special piano playing was called for in the inn, plus payment for the piano lessons, she would be able to pay for her room and truly be independent. Then in the meanwhile, she could read the newspapers and decide on whether to go elsewhere to chase other opportunities, or stay here. She rethreaded her needle and started to secure the bodice dart as she pondered…

*It is not unappealing to stay here until the anniversary of our wedding is passed; that was Easter Saturday, the twelfth of April. Next year – 1880 – as Mrs Woof has already worked out because she hopes to make bookings, Easter Day will be the twenty-eighth of March. So maybe until at least the end of April I can stay here. After Evensong today I can speak to Mrs Rogers and arrange when to take on her daughters as proper pupils. We can negotiate times and other necessary facts and I will promise to stay till the end of that school term at least. Also, perhaps Mrs Bones would show me the piano in the school house.*

Lucy brought the teapot and the day progressed much as Beatrice expected. The seams and fitting of her first dress were almost complete by lunchtime. After a hasty meal, she helped Lucy with some tables and then they resumed. Sissy had some perfect buttons in a jar so, with luck, by bedtime tonight she might have something new to wear the following day for playing at the evening dinner.

She saw Mrs Bones after Evensong and noted the school piano. It was a well-kept machine, only slightly scratched, but the keys were in good order and the tone quite pleasant. It was agreed she could use it for an hour on Tuesdays and Thursdays after school.

'Mrs Bewcham, could be other mothers might ask for extra lessons. Mebbes, my dear, you should be prepared to negotiate extra hours. If you pay a percentage of each student's fee to the church fund, that would be enough payment for the piano. The church operates the school, you see.'

'Oh, thank you, Mrs Bones. And do call me Mrs Beauchamp. I know the spelling is confusing but…'

'Bless you, my dear. That's what I'm saying: Bewcham.'

She smiled and went on her way as Beatrice bit her tongue. Goodness, Beatrice. How could you be so obtuse? She has a distinctive and not unpleasant accent. It is only the pronunciation, after all.

Mrs Rogers didn't come to Evensong but hopefully they would meet the following day in the village.

After dinner that night – and they had no transient guests so it was a quietly pleasant time to talk and finish the finer sewing of her dress – she negotiated a price for her room with Sissy. She was offered her present one, strictly staff but at least it left the other rooms free for guests, and at a reduced regular rate. Beatrice felt happier at having fees on a firm basis. Her meals were free, in payment for the occasional playing of the piano and for helping Lucy with 'ettyqwetty' matters. The burden of obligation was eased and suddenly that magic word 'independent' seemed written in large letters on her brain and in indelible ink!

In the quiet of her room later, she hung the completed dress on the front of her cupboard. She relished having the pleasant task of training young Lucy – intelligent, pleasant-natured and a young girl with the promise of beauty. Already she demonstrated a clear singing voice and Beatrice would love to train that, but she herself was not expert in voice production. However, as a girl, she had learned enough from her music tutors that might be of advantage. Also, she had to admit she was growing very fond of Lucy and looking upon her more as a sister. As far as etiquette went, she could easily help with tutoring the girl in such frivolous niceties that might enable her to marry well – as seemed to be the limit of Sissy's expectations.

Things had happened so quickly since she arrived in the colony yet, even so, a pattern was emerging in her lifestyle. It was all positive. She hoped that at times she could go to the city and visit the Lees. Mary had a sound common sense and would, Beatrice was sure, be a fount of wisdom if she ran into problems – hopefully nothing resulting from James's activities, the Taylors and any of that nature. And John Lee: she could rest easy on having that good friend, and his mother, to call on whenever problems might occur.

She smiled in the darkness. *Life is worth all the effort!*

# January 1880

## 24

The New Year of 1880 was celebrated and days became weeks. Sooner than she expected, Beatrice began to feel more settled. The casual ways of conversation, lack of protocols in behaviours that she had grown up with – even the habit of some diners using their fork upturned in their right hand as if a spoon to eat – and certainly the easy grace with which people introduced themselves to another without waiting to be introduced, she found relaxing. There was no lack of politeness but it was without the stiff formality she had always thought necessary to demonstrate good breeding.

Mrs Rogers, Clothilde, was proving a considerate friend and she introduced her to Miss Tweedie, a schoolteacher who boarded with a neighbour. Beatrice sensed in Kate Tweedie a kindred spirit and they became good friends from their first meeting. Kate would sometimes come up the hill to the inn and they would sit outside on the deck area savouring the balmy breezes sweeping up through the gully from the creek. Beatrice had learned to call it a creek rather than a beck – which had been the word in Westmorland. Occasionally they walked down to the water to cool their toes in the water. Together they went on what Kate called 'bush walks' and they would stop and sketch any flower, bush or plant – or bird or animal – that stayed still long enough! Kate was a clever watercolourist and some of her bird pictures hung up around her room were quite beautiful. While Kate sketched, Beatrice would make notes and occasionally attempt some sketching herself of grasses and flowers to enclose in later letters to her papa. She had quite converted her friend into using the hacking skirt for such walks and Kate had ordered one – ready-made – from Adelaide. It was quite an innovation and while Sissy was quite pragmatic about it, Clothilde Rogers gave the new way of dressing a few sideways looks!

One Saturday at the end of January, they set off early for a walk to Hahndorf.

Kate was familiar with the way there; she mentioned she walked that way occasionally. 'It's something like four miles, so good to start early if we want to look around. There are some nice shops there, and not only in the Lutheran settlement. Though I do want to buy some bread from the German bakery and, if I see some, pattens to wear on muddy days over my shoes. They are made by the Lutheran village woodworkers.'

Beatrice was curious about them also, thinking of the muddy, wet yard at the inn on occasions. 'Are they worn instead of boots, or over the top of them, Kate?'

'Not certain about over-boots. I like to kick off my boots and just slip into these in my stockings. You can see which you prefer, perhaps. The Germans carve them from wood – I've heard them called clogs – and they really are most effective, Beattie.'

Beatrice was by now quite accustomed to the shortened form of her name – she found that if any name could be shortened to one or maybe two catchy syllables, it was!

'I've often wondered about the tales of those girls walking to the market, Kate. The ones I saw when I rode up with John Benjamin wore pattens then, but he told me about them travelling barefoot. I feel they must have soles of iron. Evelyn writes that she sees the girls from Hahndorf – I think they are mostly from there – in the city market and they wear shoes when selling in the city. Actually, thinking of Evie, she has never mentioned Pastor Wilhelm again.'

She told Kate how the pastor had kindly escorted her friend back to the city after Boxing Day. 'I did wonder if a liaison might come of that…'

Kate hooted with laughter. 'Oh, Beattie! Pastor Wilhelm is married and has a flock of children! Their village has its own school, you know, nearer to where they live, but they come to our school at times for competitions – well, the boys do, anyway – and they are so very well behaved. I imagine he is a strict disciplinarian.' She giggled. 'He is basically terribly proper, you know, and if he knew what you had thought…well, I wouldn't repeat it if I were you! I didn't know you for a romantic, Beattie! The girls you mention – I think those walks stopped some time ago and now they take their vegetables and things in carts…well, mostly. Didn't you say the ones you saw were herding goats? That could be different – general produce stuff, vegetables and things, because they produce too much to carry, requires carts. They are really busy people and they are so clever with handcrafts and…well, they have lots of skills. You know, one of the wood carvers here came to the school to mend one of our desks and… well, he has come a few times and, er…'

She started to blush and Beattie stopped on the path and pointed merrily at her friend.

'You say I am the romantic? Kate, I detect you are more so than I. Do tell, what is his name?'

'Herbert. Herbert Flach Yes, he is attentive to me, Beattie, and so polite and brings me the little carvings – you must have seen them on my shelf?'

'Kate, did I see him mending the brickwork at your lodgings last week? The one to whom you gave the drink of water? But he is Lutheran. Would your marriage, if he asked you, be permitted by his church?'

'Oh, Beattie, his church is very like the Wesleyan. And he has asked me, Beattie. He is building us a home. In the village. When it is finished, we'll marry. For a while I shall continue as teacher until Bridgewater has a replacement. Then I shall teach at the Hahndorf school. I can happily go to his church and he asks only that our children be Lutherans.' The blushes increased. 'Well, I cannot see anything wrong with that.' She stuck out her chin as if in defiance.

'Oh, Kate, nor can I! I think that is wonderful news. Will you ask me to your wedding?'

'Of course I want you there, Beatrice. There is something… Herbert was married before. His wife – and he loved her deeply – was run over by a carriage.'

'Oh, Kate, like my own husband – so was he. Erm…how old is Herbert, Kate? Does he have children?'

'No, dear Beattie. And he is only four years older than I. But it may seem strange, as a widower it is a custom that if he takes a new wife, she will wear black on her wedding day. I confess the thought is not appealing…'

Beatrice lifted herself up to sit atop a low gate. 'Let's sit here a while, Kate. The sun has lost some of its sting but is gloriously warm on my back and that breeze – oh, what perfect weather! Come, explain to me about the dress. This is so fascinating and I am so happy for you. But –

black? And Kate, are your parents in this colony? You haven't mentioned them…'

Kate sat on an upturned barrel with a chain dangling loose. 'This looks like a guard dog's kennel, Beattie. As for my parents, I don't know who they were. You look shocked. Don't be, my friend, for I have never known them so cannot be upset – well, not too much. Herbert also came to this country alone – well, with no parents, though he had an older cousin with him. He did know his family. They were killed in the old country – there was trouble over religion. Pastor Wilhelm has explained something of it to me. Quite a number of the Germans at the settlement fled from their own country, and I do know that Herbert and his cousin had a friend of some authority who helped them flee and gave them money for a ship. I came from a place called Barwell in England but I don't know where it is. I do know there's a river called Tweed near to it because the nuns told me and gave me the name Tweedie – after the river. I was with a group of girls who had no parents and I cannot remember my mother at all. I was in an orphanage then we were all one day given new clothes and a cardboard suitcase and put on a ship at Tilbury near London. We had two old nuns looking after us and they brought us to a home in Adelaide run by Catholics. The nuns left, and me and another girl stayed there and others went to other places and I didn't know where. I sometimes wonder if I will meet them again. The girl I was with, Shelagh was her name, she died of consumption. I only know she had a cough and couldn't breathe and the nuns sent her somewhere to be cured and she never came back. I asked but they wouldn't tell me anything. I cried a lot for her, then gradually became busy again… I wasn't unhappy – not miserable or anything. They taught me with some other children who lived and came from their homes and paid their pennies. I did arithmetic and writing and geography and they taught me some piano – I wasn't very good at that!. Then they brought in another nun who taught me how to teach and I helped her with other little ones. I loved her, I called her Sister Snow, she dressed always in white clothes. That little place closed and other local children went to a Catholic school that opened. I stayed to look after some of the nuns and then a priest asked them to let me teach and I did and then I heard of the post here at Bridgewater… Ooh, this seat is getting hard, Beatrice.'

Beatrice was moved to clamber down and give her friend a big hug. 'I'm so sorry, Kate. So you are a Catholic, yet marrying a Lutheran?'

'I was never confirmed and never attended a communion, Beattie. I think the order I was with were of a different persuasion and I don't understand at all. I asked once and they said they were an Anglican sisterhood. I only know they were kind and gave me a life better than I would have known from earlier. And I believe in a God and think I can believe in Herbert's God – he's the same one really and seems to make everyone at the village happy. What of you?'

'Kate, you know of my papa and mama, my background. I was happy and certainly had many advantages I'm only now beginning to realise. As for religion – well, we belonged to the local Church of England, and I went most Sundays but not all, I'm sorry to say. Looking back, I think I understand how my mama wanted to marry me off to someone of good family, where I would be safe from other distractions – she said that to me once and I think I know what she meant. She approved of James, though Papa did not and told me so a few times. He just wanted to keep Mama happy – and me, bless him. They weren't to know… But then you know all that, what happened as I got here. Now while we are walking, do tell me about your dress. Sorry I distracted you there.'

'Ah well, my dress… I'm not sure how the custom originated. Herbert says something about paying tribute to memory or, as some say, it is an economy measure because the dress can be worn many times. Mrs Rogers has firm views on the matter and told me it is a symbol of subjugation. I laid awake all night when she told me that, and I spoke with Herbert, who said that in marriage, according to his church, he and I are equals – neither husband nor wife is counted less worthy than the other. And I do see the argument of economy. Beattie, you will come? I am hoping you'll be my attendant.'

'Kate, of course I will and I am honoured, but would I have to wear black too?' She pulled a thistle prickle from her stocking above her boot. 'Goodness, look at the length of this prickle! But…your dress, do you see? To me, it seems like a mourning dress and my husband…'

'No, dear friend. You need not wear black. You will wear whatever you feel happy wearing. That economy spirit again – it need not even be new…'

Beatrice stopped and hugged her friend. 'All that matters to me is that you are happy! Just put me right if the customs are different so I may not put a foot wrong.' She pulled away and, holding her friend's arms, giggled. 'Shall we turn around and go home now or do you want to go on?'

Kate just smiled and pointed over the rise in the opposite field.

Beatrice started giggling then laughed outright as Kate stood and walked off at a brisk pace. 'That's why you wanted to walk this way, Kate. I am so gullible! Not only for bread, nor pattens or clogs or whatever else. You wanted to see your Herbert and we are almost arrived at the Hahndorf settlement. You are so, soooo shameless, Katherine Tweedie.' She bent over, laughing so much she hiccupped and had to run to catch up with her friend, who was by now laughing in delighted anticipation.

## 25

As they neared a large gate, a group of children in linen smocks came running over prattling in German.

A boy aged about six or seven greeted them in English. 'Good morning, Miss Tweedie and the other lady. Have you come to see Onkel Herbert?' Their hands were grasped and they were pulled over to the church. 'He is with the pastor fixing the seats, Miss Tweedie.'

Tightly holding Beatrice's skirt – she had chosen to wear her riding skirt as it was so easy for walking – two of the little girls started singing, 'Miss Tweedie, Miss Tweedie,' and a tall figure appeared at the door of the church.

'Oh, it's the pastor!'

'Mrs Beauchamp, this is a welcome surprise.' He turned to look over his shoulder. 'Herbert, you have a visitor,' and a tall young blond man with a smile from ear to ear rushed to the porch.

He stopped, wiping his hands down his canvas trousers. 'Hello, Mrs Beauchamp and hello, my, erm… Hello, Kate.'

Pastor Wilhelm grinned and took Beatrice's hand. 'Come and meet my wife, Mrs Beauchamp. She will make us coffee. We'll let these two talk.' He chatted conspiratorially as they walked – or rather marched, Beatrice thought – across the compound.

'They are a good match for each other, *die junge*. It is good that they blend our peoples, is it not? We will all be South Australians together.'

Beatrice agreed.

He stopped mid-stride and looked at her. 'Do not worry about your friend. Herbert is a good man and will make her happy. You will attend her on her day?'

Beatrice nodded. 'I am delighted to be asked but it seems there are different customs…'

'Ahah. She told you of the black wedding dress and you know it as mourning and have recently lost your husband. Am I right?'

She nodded.

'You are confused and I understand. But if you attend, you can wear what you will, as bright a gown as her happiness will shine. So do not worry. And with her beautiful golden hair, she will look so beautiful in black it will not strike any one present as mournful or sad. It will add to the brightness of Easter time. Worry not, my dear Englander!'

*Goodness, he is so perceptive. No doubt that's why he's the pastor.*

They had reached his home. Beatrice was impressed by its high gabled roof and tall wooden poles supporting wide spans of mud-brick walls and stopped to admire it. This was no hurriedly put together shelter as she had imagined. Along its frontage was a veranda high enough that the tall pastor would never bump his head.

He smiled. 'You wonder at the small pine tied to the ridge, Mrs Beauchamp? It is from the Richtfest. That is when we celebrate the topping of the building house, when it is a house with the tall roof such as this, which the people insisted on building for their pastor. I hope before long most of our families will have such shelters at the head of their *hufen* – I believe your England calls them farmlets. Aha, we are being welcomed…'

With a wider smile, he introduced his wife, who was waiting in the doorway. It was obvious he was very proud of her. Frau Wilhelm was blonde, rosy-faced, tall and enormously pregnant!

'You like the coffee, Mrs Beauchamp? Perhaps? It is come from the Holland ships and in your city market. Rauf cannot work the day without coffee, so he says, but he must sell much produce to cover costs – that is what this wife says!' She laughed infectiously.

'Mrs Wilhelm, do you know I cannot remember when I last had coffee. I shall look forward to it!'

At the first sip it was hot and bitter to her tongue but the aftertaste was, she thought, of hazelnuts.

Frau Wilhelm laughed. 'Add some honey, Mrs Beauchamp – here you are – and stir it in well.'

'This is absolutely delightful – hot and rich. So much better than tea.'

The pastor had left to enter a large pantry – or at least there were shelves of produce on the wall as the door opened. He returned with a basket and gave it to his wife with a nod. She smiled, then moved over to a narrow door. A waft of cool air blew into the room as she descended some steps, her wooden shoes clattering downwards, then stopped. Beatrice cocked her head in curiosity to listen but could only hear bustling noises.

In a few minutes, Frau Wilhelm clattered back upstairs carrying the basket now loaded with potatoes, a pat of butter, a huge slab of cheese and a round loaf of dark bread with a hard crust. 'This you must give to my good friend Missus Sissy, please?'

'Ohoh – she will be overcome. Thank you so very much. And how cool it must be down there.'

'*Im Kellar? Ja*…erm…keeps well the cookings.'

Beatrice took the heavy basket. 'And I did enjoy my coffee! Now I hope my friend has bought her wooden pattens – it looks like rain and I don't really care to get wet, not with this lovely bread here. Goodbye, and I hope we can meet again soon, Frau Wilhelm!'

Too soon they were all farewelled at the gate, Beatrice pretending not to notice the chaste kiss on the cheek from Herbert to Kate – blushes from both of them this time!

So the wedding was to be at Easter. Beatrice felt a huge lump of sad recollection somewhere under her breastbone. She composed herself and remarked on the basket of food from Frau Wilhelm. It was certainly challenged for the volume of its contents by the basket carried by Kate. Under a linen tea cloth, resting on a pile of brightly red and green vegetables, was a monster loaf of wood-oven-baked bread.

'Rye bread, he calls it, Beattie. I don't know it, do you?'

'I do. It is really very tasty. But you will have to eat a chunk for a fortnight – how will you keep such a huge loaf fresh? Perhaps, I know – the one the pastor gave me for Sissy is half that size, would it be better for you to enjoy it and not have it go stale on you? She has the bar people who eat bread with their ale. That monster loaf would soon be eaten at the inn. If you like, we can exchange – or swap, as Sissy would say. The gesture is still genuine, is it not?'

Walking back to Bridgewater, they were both quieter than before. Beatrice suspected Kate was mentally planning her wedding after talking with Herbert. She was consumed by an unsettling mix of feelings. *The wedding is to be at Easter, a coincidence I'm not sure of – not at all. And black is for mourning and I will think of that and of James all the time.*

It seemed soon that they were at the schoolhouse and Beatrice continued, trudging up the hill to the inn. She was actually a bit weary after all that walking. *I think I'll see if I can fill the tin bath in my room and have a lovely long soak from the big kettles. I must have a big, big think.*

Later, while in the bath, she tried to analyse what personal implications there might or not be about attending at an Easter wedding the year after her own. It should be she wearing black, not Kate. Easter would be early this year – she knew that, thanks to Sissy. She mused on her feelings about that until the water ran cold around her. Her own Easter wedding had been on the twelfth of April. *I'm so glad the dates are different. That way it won't feel so…so…personal. I have to let go – but is it too early? It's hardly three months since James died. Yet Kate has had her share of uncertainties in life. I must show a real happiness for her. It is so long since I knew James, in effect. I have to be honest with myself. Kate is my dear friend, and amongst my mixed up feelings is jealousy – Yes! Jealousy! I am jealous of her!*

She soaped her dusty feet almost angrily then reproached herself. Kate had been subjected to some awful sadness, and not to know her family, that was dreadful. This colony had so many people busy making new lives; some had strange beginnings, even unhappy and miserable beginnings. And all immigrants, even herself with her luckier childhood, experienced strangeness, some trepidation on facing so many differences. Kate deserved every good thing that was coming to her.

She dried and combed her hair. Here in South Australia, new residents were selected from decent ordinary people, not convicts. But from whatever background, they would encounter differences in customs, in expectations, and some arrive alone as she did, yet not all could have the good fortune to meet people like the Lees and the Anderson-Woofs. In years to come, the colony would still need to bring new people here, the distances to fill were so great, and so future generations of immigrants might inherit this strangeness until they assimilated. It was unsettling, even though welcomes awaited them – or should… It was an issue that concerned Mary Lee, she knew, from when Mary had been counselling her, strongly advising her to return to England after James died.

As she prepared to join the others for the evening meal, she mused on the issue of immigration and her own situation. And today's walk with Kate had been such a lesson about the people here; so enjoyable and so full of surprises. Seeing the German settlement, its precision, its cleanliness and the politeness of the children, the friendliness of the adults she had passed by, especially the pastor and his wife, had been most pleasant. On remembering Frau Wilhelm, she smiled that she had once imagined an alliance between Rauf Wilhelm and Evelyn. *Why am I always seeking partners for people? Am I jealous of Kate? Is it because I am, deep down, wanting to find a special someone again for myself?*

# 26

Over the next weeks as summer lost its sting, Beatrice's life assumed an easy pattern and, by and large, a satisfying and friendly one. Her music teaching she enjoyed, as the Rogers girls were quite talented and even Lucy seemed eager to improve her playing, though singing was her first love. Lucy was equally interested in learning to speak 'properly', as she put it. All her achievements had but one goal – marriage, to marry well – and that pleased her mother.

'When I am eighteen, Beatrice' – she sometimes now dropped the semi-formality of 'Mrs B' – 'I really hope I'll be allowed to make my curtsey to whoever it is they choose this year. That is Mum's big hope and we both know I have to lose what Mother calls my rough edges. Mrs Rogers says there is to be a Coming Out Ball.'

Beatrice was intrigued by the way many English customs and traditions had been transplanted – and adapted to be more equal – from the ancient shores of the old world to the new. For a girl to 'come out' and 'be presented' at age eighteen here in Australia required no aristocratic family upbringing; it was enough that the girl was clean-living, nicely spoken and respectful; also preferable that the parents could afford some measure of a dowry. All very egalitarian! Though what would Mama have said?

Lucy's 'improvement regime', as Beatrice mentally referred to it, was constant. One day early in March, Beatrice sat with the girl as she wrote an essay in French – not that she felt her own French the best; in days past, her Mamzelle had despaired of her pronunciation. Clothilde Rogers had also hinted at her daughters being included in these lessons but Beatrice had declined and still felt a bit guilty. Clothilde had been quite circumspect, she wasn't a gossiper, but had indicated that her family were of a slightly more professional class than Mr Rogers's, and her own marriage had been a disappointment to her parents. When Beatrice had realised what the girls' mother was trying to impart – that she needed her girls to comply with certain social standards in order to be more readily accepted by their extended family – it had come as something of a shock. There seemed to be so many contradictions in the accepted social mores, she felt that the word 'equality' was as elastic as Mr Hancock's wonderfully inventive rubber bands. Hence the pantomime of the debutante ball which was so desirable for Lucy – and Sissy.

Lucy sighed loudly as she struggled over the essay. Beatrice had suggested the exercise be an account of a wedding like Kate's to Herbert, now only a fortnight away. Might allow her time to think what she would be wearing for the event. As Chief Attendant, the title Herbert apparently bestowed upon the task, she could wear any gown of her choosing and that made her feel better in herself.

Sissy came into the room. 'Mrs Rogers is here, Beatrice. Has come, she says, to thank you for the girls' piano lessons.'

*What? She's done that a few times already.* 'That's not necessary, Sissy, but I'll come and say hello. Lucy, please finish the paragraph, then we'll read it together.'

Lucy pulled a face but bent down and Beatrice followed Sissy into the small parlour.

Mrs Rogers was not alone. A man was with her and he stood politely as Beatrice entered. He was tall, a man of style and dark-haired like Clothilde. A family resemblance? She smiled and bobbed in friendly greeting.

Mrs Rogers smiled widely. 'Beatrice, I have been showing my brother the township and I thought it pleasant to call in on you and Sissy. May I introduce you? May I present my brother, Simon Brinkhurst?'

There was some small chat as she spoke of Beatrice's elegance, her generosity in teaching piano and... Beatrice coughed politely and gave a little bob.

He made a short bow. 'Mrs Beauchamp, I am pleased to make your acquaintance. My nieces are playing and singing so charmingly and I understand it is due to your tuition. I thank you.'

What a growly voice and an Adam's apple bobbing with every syllable.

'Mr Brinkhurst, I am pleased to meet the brother of my good friend Clothilde. Your sister has been of great help to me in helping me feel a part of this pretty township.'

Mrs Rogers prattled on as Beatrice stood politely – her mind racing. *Why this nervousness from her? It's most unlike her normal friendliness... Oh no, penny drops, as Mary Lee would say. I am being introduced for a purpose. He is actually looking me over – that's a Papa phrase. How can Clothilde do this and is Sissy in on the conspiracy? She knows, they all know, it is far too soon and I thought Mrs Rogers, Clothilde, would have realised that. This is too upsetting, too vulgar even...*

She collected her thoughts and put on a tentative smile. 'Mr Brinkhurst, Clothilde, do forgive me. It is an unexpected pleasure but if you will excuse me, I must return to Lucille. Our time is limited today and she must yet complete an essay.' She made a bob and exited as gracefully as she felt capable.

She read Lucy's paragraphs and forced herself to make sensible comments as the girl read it out to her. Nothing had been said about that Simon Brinkhurst's personal situation, yet she felt instinctively he was looking for a wife. Rather, he needed a suitable wife and she had been recommended. And she played the governess to excuse herself. *Oh, Mama!* It seemed she was considered acceptable. She didn't know if she felt disappointed in Clothilde or simply angry at the presumption. She sat back at Lucy's leaving the room. How dare they think to put her on the marriage market? Conventionally it was just too soon and personally, she wanted to make up her own mind. Granted, this Simon was a pleasant-looking man. She seemed to remember one of the Rogers girls saying he was a secretary, a ministerial type. No doubt she would be considered an asset to his arm at career functions!

As she sat quietly, she had to admit it was pleasant to be admired, and it was obvious he liked what he saw. Paradoxically she broke into giggles *What if he knew I shed my petticoats on hot days? Tut tut – not ladylike behaviour!*

With a twitch of her fingers, she dismissed the episode from her mind. With Lucy's essay on the table in front of her, the forthcoming wedding had to be considered. Would she cope with the event – its sentiment and celebration – if it was sufficiently different from English wedding customs? She was still worried at times how she might react, behave, if the event pulled at her heartstrings, to use one of Sissy's phrases. As far as her dress was concerned, she welcomed the more relaxed attitude. Although her own gown didn't have to be new, because 'economy' was considered an admirable virtue, she thought it would be a compliment to her friend to make a new one.

She had chosen the fabric, an unfamiliar weave of a tightly woven cotton from the sale of what seemed to be most of the contents of Ballantyne's in Rundle Street which she remembered as being under Mr Beckett's office. Sissy had seen a notice in the *Register* about their 'clearance sale'. At only fourpence-halfpenny a yard, it had been a wonderful bargain. As Sissy declared, 'Miraculous!'

It had meant a hurried day in the city but she and Lucy had gone up and down in the trap as Zed had some chores and they'd made it home before dark. Her chosen fabric had a sheen, or so it was described to her, not unlike a silk, and yet it was 'breathable' for when the weather was warm again. An attractive shade of lavender, the drapery assistant remarked how the sheen caused glimmers of a deeper colour in the cross-weave. She had some lace and cord fringing too and was impatient to start the cutting. Some lace fringing had been found that was so delicate she was impatient to start making it up.

Lucy was to have a new dress for the occasion too and she was 'over the moon in delights', according to Sissy. Lucy's material was a deeper lavender shade with a delicate fringing more suited to a young girl. 'Yer'll look lovely together,' Sissy had proclaimed delightedly.

It was the first formal occasion Lucy had ever been permitted to attend. The previous afternoon she had been so persistent in asking Beatrice about 'what is and what is not correct', to such a degree that Beatrice snapped at her and then, conscience-stricken, passed off the tantrum with an apologetic 'coming down with a migraine'.

That had been a mistake! Both Lucy and Sissy fussed over her like a pair of mother hens. Sissy was certain she should take a Steedman's Powder but she didn't know the make and declined quite forcibly. She was sent to lie down and rest and the effect of that was to give her time to analyse her own misgivings about her wedding role and whether she would be able to maintain a sensible, happy demeanour. When meandering through her recollections of her 'day' it was Mama and Papa whom she thought of most, not James, and that realisation rendered guilt and self-loathing in equal measure. A migraine was more a possibility after the 'rest' than before!

However, one happy aspect of Kate's wedding was Evelyn's presence as a guest. She had been invited by an excited Kate during one of Evelyn's visits to Bridgewater.

*Evie is – well, Evie, and she has been part of my life in this colony since that first dreadful day. She'll understand how I feel, might feel, if the ceremony upsets me. I certainly do not intend to demonstrate any weaknesses, any feelings other than happy ones for the young couple. I have a responsible part to play as Kate's attendant. Oh, but it is good to know that afterwards Evie and I can talk over all aspects of the day – and a hundred other things as we wish – after we can make a civilised escape. Then we can enjoy the quiet of our own evening back here.*

# Easter 1880

## 27

The wedding day arrived and the sun looked like shining brightly till dusk. The sky was deepening its blueness as Anderson drove his 'three young ladies' to the Lutheran village. There they were greeted by Pastor Wilhelm and escorted to his home, where Frau Wilhelm greeted them with energetic hugs.

'You look so lovely, *mädchen*. It is so exciting, *nein*?'

Beatrice silently wondered if Frau Wilhelm knew she was a widow – but now was certainly not to time to question.

Frau Wilhelm's enthusiasm was infectious and even the newest member of the family was gurgling in anticipation from his little cradle. His mother was tightly laced and proudly bosomed in lilac silk as she served them what the pastor explained was a 'happy cup of something, to smooth your mouths for the singing'.

'Lavender and lilac,' whispered Lucy. 'We are all matching, Beatrice!'

The pastor loved weddings and wore a happy grin non-stop – it quite put his elegant dress into the shade. His trews and waistcoat were dark and spotless, his boots shone with grease and his mark of authority was a starched white necktie of a folded arrangement Beatrice decided had a legal appearance, yet reminded her of the Church of England minister's dress back home – though her memory of that one was that it was often crumpled and a little askew at times, due, as Papa had been wont to report, to the minister's liking for the communion wine leftovers! Beatrice smiled at the memory as Mrs Wilhelm gathered up her son, laid him on the table and wrapped him up to be admired in his beautifully crocheted shawl.

'It is two young people making life together… Fraulein Kate is at my Rauf's sister's house. We will church first and her come after, *nein*? First, you will have a schnapps?'

Tiny glasses of what looked as innocent and as clear as water were presented to them and Frau Wilhelm smiled at Lucy.

'Take, young Fräulein. Here we make many schnapps but this one is from apples. It is but a sip, as you would call it so, and will help your mouth with singing.'

'You mean my throat, Mrs Wilhelm! But I like it…'

She spluttered as she spoke and they were still laughing as they set off across the compound.

It was dusty underfoot and the girls had to gather their skirts again, to avoid marking the hems, although Beatrice comforted herself that it was so dry, it would be easy to brush off afterwards. Her light slippers were more her worry.

She noticed the efficiency with which the day was to be conducted; everyone had a place in it and a task that befitted them. Two young men in knee breeches and long woollen socks were at the door to escort them to their places. Beatrice noticed the Rogers family on a chair near the back and, thankfully, it didn't seem as if Clothilde's brother was with her.

With plainly whitewashed walls and a row of clear windows along each, the space was flooded with sunlight. The windowpanes were lifted to allow the breeze and large bunches of what Beatrice thought looked like magnolia blossoms interspersed with shiny green and pointy red leaves were displayed in two massive earthenware pots just forward of the two front rows. The total effect was cool, bright and welcoming.

Evelyn and Lucy were given aisle seats opposite each other on the two second rows, Beatrice the second place along the front bench in front of Evelyn, from where, the young usher whispered, she could stand up to greet Kate as she came to the Lord's table.

Herbert came and was shown to a seat on the bench opposite, with his other carpenter friend on his other side. Both were smartly dressed in knee breeches of shiny leather, long woollen socks and brown boots shining with grease. They had white linen shirts with embroidered fronts, long sleeves buttoned at the wrist and open collars. Herbert seemed a little nervous as he muttered to his friend.

Beatrice was wondering if there would be music as she couldn't see any means of playing it, although four men stood beyond the table in a group, with scrolls in their hands. Must be a choir.

At the very thought, one tapped a small rod onto the back of a pew and they synchronised the note. Even as the sound registered, a scuttle at the door signalled an arrival and they broke into a beautiful bass melody, sung in German.

Down the aisle walked Pastor Wilhelm followed by a solemn, black clad Kate. Behind her, the double doors thudded shut.

Herbert and his attendant stood and turned to watch the pastor. So did Beatrice.

*She looks so happy beneath that veil. What I can see of her face. At least it's white. I know why she wears a black frock but it doesn't seem right. I know she's never been intimate with a man, she asked me a lot of questions so I know she is still a maiden. It seems cruel to put her in a dreary black when colours, or even a virginal white, would better reflect the light-heartedness of the occasion.*

They assembled into order at the table as the choir ended on a long note, the pastor welcomed everyone and, with words all too easily familiar to Beatrice, exhorted the couple to stay one with another, to love each other through bad times and good, all at some length, eventually proclaiming Kate and Herbert to be man and wife. That was the signal for some more singing. The congregation knew the music and the words and sang heartily.

Caught up in the spirit of everything, Evelyn and Lucy were singing the melody in loud la-la-las. Kate could hear Lucy's lovely piping voice above all others. It didn't matter she couldn't sing the words!

# 28

Suddenly, seeing Kate's face shining with laughter and happy tears, Beatrice felt tears rolling down her own cheeks. *Oh God, if you are here, help me to be strong but it is less than a year since I stood there, in front of the vicar, making the same promises. And we had no length of time together... Oh no! How embarrassing! Nor can I escape. Everyone will see.*

She wiped her face with the back of her glove. *Be sensible, Beatrice. They'll just think they're tears of happiness for the bride. Everyone cries at weddings, don't they? Well, I am crying for myself, for mine, the one that didn't last and the man I thought I knew who turned out to be dishonest and a gambler. As for myself, I thought I knew him and I didn't, and I want to believe he loved me and only gambled so that we could have a good start and that he wasn't thinking I would have money to pay for it all and yet that's what he did think and I was just a means to an end so he could leave the military and live the life of a wealthy farmer...and all that...and...and...*

'Beattie – Beattie, dear, are you all right?' Evelyn was patting her shoulder.

Beatrice sniffed and whispered back, 'I will be. Just the emotion...'

Then the Wilhelm baby's muttering became a loud persistent howl and the intensity of laughter from the guests – as a crying baby was taken as a happy omen – enabled her to cover up her embarrassment. Any who might have noticed would think them tears from laughing. She had a sideways look from Evie but hearty laughter, congratulations were predominant in the bustle and progress down towards the big doors and the hall where the wedding breakfast waited. She bent down to make sounds at the baby, hiding her face until the tears cleared.

Emotional but blessedly brief speeches started the proceedings and were followed by a riotously energetic event. The tables were heavy with cold meats, cheeses, breads and wine. Determined to drive away her own despondency and radiate happiness for her friend, Beatrice drank a little too freely of the rosy wine so, recognising her over-indulgence and knowing she was no longer as steady on her feet as dancing would demand, headed for the piano stool. The piano was old and only partly renovated, but playable. She flexed her fingers and, yes, it played.

Later on, when trying to remember, she could not mentally replay whatever music sprang from her fingers but she did know the energetic dancers worked into groups and she played folk and country until even Herbert came up to her suggesting she have a break. Some of the dancers were flopping on chairs and the younger ones squatting on the floor, chatting and resting, energies spent! She had thumped that old piano, persuading it and herself to remember old dancing tunes, for two whole hours! Her hair had come undone, her dress was wet in the bodice, but as she joined Evie and Lucy at the table, wondering when dear old Anderson to turn up with the trap as he'd promised, she recognised that she had achieved a personal catharsis by her energetic and at times almost frenzied playing.

As her friends laughed and chatted, the sticky honey bread and coffee Frau Wilhelm pressed upon her freed her from joining in the conversation. She was tired but felt relaxed, more than she had for months. She felt that she was accepted for who she was, at the very least someone who could play music for them, but it was acceptance. She was starting to let herself feel that she belonged. Among this company, there was no need for the stuffy social niceties of the past; no need to act a role. She was Beatrice Mary Elizabeth Beauchamp...No! She was Beauchamp no longer. She had been a Fletcher. She felt more like a Fletcher, though it had to be admitted, as a woman alone, a married name gave protection. However, and important, she was herself, neither daughter nor wife and not a hapless immigrant either! There was life to look forward to. She was twenty-three years old, a mature woman of some sensibility and talent – she would make her life here, from now on. She even smiled tentatively as she bit the last of her bread. *Goodness me – what is in this honey? They say honey is a healer...*

Then Herbert and Kate came over to say goodbye; they were travelling up to Tanunda in the Barossa Valley where Herbert had cousins. Herbert wanted to check out cooperage techniques to see if such business was yet operating in that region. Here it was all imported barrels for the wine and he considered importing them a waste of skills. Kate would be resuming her teaching when they came home. She would live in the Lutheran village but, as Beatrice consoled herself, they weren't going to be miles and miles apart!

As guests left, there were more hugs and goodbyes and invitations to revisit. Evelyn had struck up a conversation with a man who looked to be in his thirties, not one of the German community who she recognised, though, and Lucy was over at another table with a young German kissing her hand in farewell! Ahah!

Beatrice received many compliments for her playing as she tried to remember the musical pieces she had thumped out on the piano. It had certainly been a release from her own emotions, playing out a significant measure of her own grief, anger and frustration as she persuaded the old piano to release its chords and octaves. Yes, catharsis; and the playing had enabled her to hide her own feelings and cushion her hurt.

*

Anderson had been welcomed at the party earlier than Beatrice realised and was well in his cups as they started off in the carriage – but jovial with it.

'Who was that young fellow paying court to you, young Lucille?"

'Uncle Anderson, that was another Rauf. He is studying to be a lawyer and lives in Adelaide behind the office where he does some clerking when he's not in the university."

Beatrice was curious. 'Where is the university?'

'On North Terrace,' responded Evie. 'Quite new, I think, or so John Benjamin told me. Only five years or so since it was built, isn't that right, Lucy?'

'I don't know really, Miss Evelyn, but Rauf is studying for a Bachelor of Arts. The law is somewhere in those studies with philos…philosophy and logic.' She grinned. 'Not sure what they are but he says they teach him to think. Rauf works at the clerking so he can pay his way and he learns a lot of the law stuff from what his office does, too.'

'Hmm,' came from Anderson, who winked at Beatrice.

They were both wondering what Sissy would have to say about this new friendship. She would be pressing them for all the news and gossip when they arrived back at the inn. How much, Beatrice winked at Evie, would Lucy impart!

# 12 April 1880

## 29

To Beatrice's relief, the twelfth of April, the anniversary of her own wedding, came and went without too much heartstring-twanging (a Sissy phrase) on her part.

It was a Monday and a relatively quiet day in the inn. After helping Sissy with some ordering and stocktaking, she decided to go for an afternoon walk down to the creek, just to sit and think. Thinking time had become hard to find with Lucy's 'ettiquetty' and French conversation – and her promised help around the inn. She'd set up a new ledger for Sissy to follow for the accounts which was easier for her to follow and had demonstrated it to Lucy too. She really had been busy! The girls' piano lessons in the school were growing in popularity, too, and she was being questioned about extra lessons for others. She wasn't sure whether or not to commit to those; earlier in the year, she had given herself until after Easter to decide whether or not to stay in this friendly place or try to move on to something, somewhere else. Now Easter was past.

She walked down the steps onto the little sandy gravel track. *There's a nip in the air. Sissy says it's autumn and not to be out after dark unless I have a cape. Hmm – more like an English spring.*

'Hello, Mr Magpie! I've brought you some bits of old cheese rind, gone a bit mouldy. So because I'm now a friend after all this time, you won't swoop on me, is that right?'

The big black and white bird approached, walking over with his lopsided gait, toes turned in (as Mama would have said) coming up almost to her own, his black glinty eye on her with every step. She stood still, hand outstretched; an unexpected movement and he would be off. In recent weeks they had met often just by the wooden steps. Sometimes he would be perching on the little fence top that bordered the wooden veranda floor that Anderson called the deck. Like her, he seemed a lone thing; no mate was ever apparent.

*Oh dear, there's a bit of grey fur stuck to his beak – he's been rabbiting.* His intelligence fascinated her, but she didn't like the fact he caught little rabbits like those big crow-like birds. Young rabbits were so tiny, so playful and such attractive little animals and at times, as long as she sat still, they just frolicked around, nibbling at bushes and throwing themselves onto each other in mock fights. Anderson kept threatening to take some dogs to find the burrows; she hoped not but had to acknowledge they were a menace in the garden.

She grinned remembering Sissy's outrage yesterday at going to pick lettuces and finding them with the hearts quite eaten away.

'Anderson! I want you out there with your shotgun!'

*They're good folk these Anderson-Woofs and really, really good friends. Also I have Evie – and Kate – when she comes back. Yet I feel so lonely at times.*

Down by the creek near the rocks, she stooped to pick up a handful of pebbles. One by one she plopped them into the rushing water. A kookaburra flapped out from one of the low-swinging branches of a willow and winged past her ear a little too close for comfort. She wasn't sure who was the more startled. She found her favourite large flat rock by the creek, pulled off her dancing pumps – s*illy things to wear for a walk, Beatrice* – rolled up her skirt to the knee and dangled her bare feet in the cool water. The fast-flowing waters gushed and frothed around any obstacle and the feel of the froth and the chill of the water bouncing higher up her leg was quite stimulating. Mama would have tut-tutted at such unladylike behaviour. She smiled sadly at the thought. The sun shafted through the tree branches onto the water, penetrating the surface and highlighting the blended earth colours of the pebbles and stones below. So clear, so fresh, so good! So simply, naturally clean and fresh and *good!* She couldn't resist it – slipped down the surface of the rock on her derriere, until she was standing on the smooth round pebbles of the creek bed. With her skirts hitched up even to her knees, she curled her toes among the finer grit underneath and lifted her face to the sun.

'Oh! This is a delicious feeling! James, oh James, would I be doing this now if you and I had set up home together? I don't think so. Just a year ago today we had returned to a special dinner at my home, the Fletcher farm. Had you met me off the ship, would we perhaps have been holding a dinner at our Adelaide home today to celebrate our anniversary? Who would our friends be? Perhaps I might even be newly enceinte. Who can tell what might have been?'

The little parrots were listening to her, heads cocked. *They are a pair, I am but one. I am an anachronism; I've good friends, respect and a measure of financial independence, yet I feel I am the odd one out, the one looking in on the others. Be sensible, Beatrice. You are new here, an immigrant. Yes, much is different but you are coping with it all… I must make myself realise that this is just the start of a new life, a new beginning.*

She sighed and paddled her feet up and down, looking down at the rounded smoothness of the pebbles. The water was fast-moving, explaining the rounded knobbly feel of the pebbles.. She looked up at the sky, gripping her skirts in a bunch in front of her. *Here I am paddling in a creek; if James and I had set up house, would I be hitching up my skirts, barefoot? No – he would have been astounded by such loose behaviour. Though I doubt I would have even considered it – things happened and I am different…*

The little green parrots bobbed at one another, twittering and rubbing beaks, quite unperturbed by her presence.

'That's one of those tea tree bushes you are on, is it not? Oh, little birds, you are lovely. I'll stand still and not frighten you. Keep up that chatter-chattering to each other. No doubt you're saying, "Who is that silly human with nothing better to do with her time?"'

Smiling, she stepped backwards out of the water and back onto her rock. Warmth from the sun-baked granite curled upwards, tickling the soles of her chilled feet and prompting goosebumps under the fine hairs on her shins. It felt delicious. The little parrots sat on the sprig, heads cocked as if ready to listen.

'You are my audience, little birds. Do you know it's twelve months since I married and almost four months since James died? Not long really and yet in some ways it seems much longer since my wedding. I was Mistress Beauchamp, really, for only a couple of weeks or so, no more. Just long enough, little birds, for me to understand Miss Austen's heroines and how their innermost feelings became physical and delightful. I was only just learning but he left me to take ship.'

The two little green parrots were stilled by the sound of her voice and watched her with great interest and no show of fear.

'What then do you think, little birds? Am I supposed to visit the Rogerses and better my acquaintance with her brother? He is being groomed as a parliamentary minister according to Anderson, who likes him well enough as a person. I have seen him with the Rogerses at the post office once or twice but I feel there is something lacking in me because I cannot say that he stirs my feelings in any way. Yet I know very well I am capable of feelings to some degree. Therefore, little parrots, I conclude he is no partner for me. Is it surprising that now, here by this lovely stream, or creek as they call it, as I cogitate and reflect on my life, on who and what I am, I should conclude that I am no longer bound by any convention? By anyone? James came over here and ended up gambling our money – well, money that he didn't have, that he had expected I would repay. Come now, little green parrots, you be judge and jury. Am I the wronged party here in this story? Or am I lacking in humanity and other senses?'

They didn't want to reply; as if at a signal, they winged upwards from their perch.

She gazed at the changing sky. The beautiful sunsets constantly amazed her. They were becoming familiar; she was not a stranger to them, no different from any other person on this huge orb called Earth. She stood, feet apart on the warm rock, stretching her arms out wide. She extended her face heavenwards and exhaled, long and easily, bringing her arms together again as if to embrace the peace, the quiet and the calm. She closed her eyes and breathed in deeply, each breath saturating her body with a newly recognised contentment. She opened her eyes and focused on the lovely evening sky. Oranges and crimsons were strengthening and over to the west, out of her vision from this low point of the land, the sun would be sinking.

She felt suffused by a quiet happiness and knew, though the right words were hard to find, she had reached a special place in her heart and mind…*a place I can live with myself. How can I phrase it…a sort of stepping stone onto – what are the words – tranquillity, serenity. Well, acceptance at the very least! This is the new me. I am finding myself again. I have reached a new stage in my life. What was that funny phrase of John Benjamin's – 'go forward'. Maybe that's what was meant by it.*

She leapt off the granite, pulled on her pumps – her feet dried by the warm rock – and laughed out loud as the two little birds took wing rapidly. The little bushes up the track were starting to cast shadows.

'Old Sol, Mr Australian Sun, is doing his usual trick, plunging below the horizon over there to the west behind the hill. He may be out of my sight but his shadows are casting longer and deeper. It's time I headed homewards.' *Homewards? It feels like home but it is not. I still have that decision to make, but I have found me again, that is a very good beginning to a proper decision. First things first.*

She clambered up the twisty little track, picking a large flowering bunch of the tea tree bush for Sissy on her way. Sissy called it her laundry bush because she liked to simmer a tisane from the twigs, leaves and all to add to the rinsing water in the laundry. Sometimes she used lavender for the staff beds, but said tea tree oils were good to fight ticks and fleas and were good for guests' bedding because she didn't know where some guests had come from!

Humming to herself, Beatrice reached the deck and her little room, pulling herself up by the veranda rail. Magpie was elsewhere but she left her bunch of greenery on the boards till later. *Better freshen up first then see if any guests had turned up requiring attention. Not that Lucy isn't capable but I'd like to have a look through that new music Evie brought for me last time – still haven't tried any of it.* Her smile widened. *If it is a quiet evening, it'll be an ideal time for a private practice session on the old piano, just for me and the new music.*

She washed her face and gave her long brunette hair a brushing to free it from the few leaves and twigs it had gathered on her walk. *Better pin it tidily, I suppose. Can I hear voices round the corner from the bar? Might be a piano evening after all, not just for me but for the guests. Well, f I must, I'll change into a better gown later.* She picked up the tea tree sprigs and was just leaving to seek out Sissy when that lady bustled along towards her.

'Oh, Beatrice! Did you have a lovely walk? You'll never guess, what a lovely surprise and with a message from your friend Evelyn… He's come as he says on the off-chance an' I asked him to wait and when I said you'd be back soon he asked for a room an' said he'd stay an' he's been in the front bar talking to Anderson an' now they're having tea in the parlour, an' this is the message from Evelyn.'

Beatrice chuckled. 'Oh, Sissy, draw a breath, do! It must be John Benjamin. How lovely.'

'Nay lass, it's another I don't know but well set-up he is, an' you'd mebbes better read your friend's note first.'

*Another? Can't be Clothilde's brother with a note…* Beatrice had already handed over the tea tree foliage and broken the seal to read but cast a quizzical glance at her friend's fussy attitude before doing so. She read the opening lines as she walked along and her surprise was still evident as she walked in the parlour to see her surprise guest, rising from his chair. .

'Lieutenant Symonds!'

'Mrs Beauchamp. You look so well…'

# 30

That same day in John Benjamin's house, Mary Lee watched Alice clear up the dinner dishes. It hadn't been a bad dinner, although it was what her old Irish housekeeper had called 'scrag end o' lamb'. Rolled up, with that parsley and stuff from out John Benjamin's garden, it was tasty enough. And young Alice could turn her hand to a good gravy, must be said.

'Tell me, Evelyn, have you heard from little Mrs Beauchamp lately? Lovely girl that, and I do wonder how she's settling down, what she's doing. That Mr Symonds seemed interested in her too, did he not? You know, I did wonder if he was interested in you. I thought he might be calling on you.'

'Mam, dear, I couldn't help but notice how eager he was for news of her. Yes, I am a little disappointed but… Mam, he looks upon me as her friend and that's all. He's a lovely man and I would wish – but there you are… And I would prefer a city man, if one at all. But back to your question. I told him Beatrice seems happy in Bridgewater, that she seems to have found a place there. He was eager to find out all he could about her, I have to say. In fact, Mam, he was really keen and he'll be riding up to see her sometime soon. I gave him a note to take to her. Not that I think he was looking for an excuse…'

'Oh, my dear Evelyn, why are you so certain he wouldn't admire you? You are a handsome young woman, educated, industrious, and caring…'

'Mam, do listen. He was very clearly asking me about Beatrice because she is the woman of interest, not me. And though he is a lovely figure of a man, I'm not so sure I'd want someone who works on river paddle boats and travels all over the country. Like I said, I'm more suited to a city fellow, or bloke, as they say here. Do leave it, Mam. You're always on about women being independent and yet you want me married off! If the lieutenant goes up into the hills to see her, let him work it out for himself and, more importantly, Beatrice is my friend and I would like her to have the chance of happiness again, after James and all that mess. She feels very let down by him, as you know, and he showed his true colours at the end. She has much to work out of her system, Mam. She's finding things very different here, even more than me, I think, though we got here at the same time. Her background was different from ours, no denying. Time will tell.'

'I only want you to have a companion, Evelyn. I'm older than you. I have had a life, children and stepchildren and loved them all and been loved in return. Is it wrong to want something like that for you, m'dear girl? And Beatrice Beauchamp had a different background from us, I'll grant you, but we were never in penury, my family, nor were you deprived of anything. We travelled here on the *Orient* second class with many comforts, not steerage, my goodness, no. That we have to practise economies now is because I certainly do not wish to ask for money from the family in Ireland, m' dear.'

'Oh, sorry, Mam. It's just that you do go on so and I see you worrying. I'll find someone when I'm ready and when I meet him. I can look around you know, and I do. There's no such word as can't – isn't that right, Mam?'

She grinned at her mother, who jokingly pretended a slap to her face. 'I'll always look after you, Mam, as long as I am able. You know that, don't you. Now, change of subject. What's this new committee you want to get onto, or better still what's this plan you have for Alice? She told me something about going to school. If so, where and how, Mam? School costs money we don't have…'

'Alice? Bless the girl. It's not really a school. I know she can read, sort of, and write, but she's keen to learn about housekeeping and money, adding money and accounting as such, and I think she deserves a chance to develop her talent. She's a bright girl, Evie. So…you know that Mrs Horace down the road? '

'The housekeeper for the university man?'

'Mr Hartley, yes. But he's not in a university. I don't think so. I believe he is called the Inspector-General of Schools. He was before that the headmaster of that college – Prince Alfred's – and he came to South Australia to take up that position. How is that! Apparently he's made some enemies because of his new ideas – so Alice says…'

'Alice? Mam, do stop prevaricating. How does all this affect Alice?'

'Alice helps out Mrs Horace – does her shopping sometimes when she does ours. She told Mrs Horace about wanting to learn arithmetic and Mrs Horace told her mistress. Turns out that lady spoke to her husband and he asked Alice to invite me to see him last Monday. I did, an' it turns out he knows of my family, taught for a while back home at the Methodist college an' he knows of John Benjamin. I was well struck with his sincerity, Evie. He's a great believer in – now, how'd he put it? – "wide-based elementary education". He writes his own study books, plans to publish them one day not only in arithmetic but others as well. Alice doesn't know his position but I'm sure I can find out. But listen, Evie: turns out also he's spoken to Alice an' says if she will help Mrs Horace with shopping an' such regularly, he'll let her sit in on Thursday lessons with Mrs Horace's grandson – lessons about money, keeping books, and whatever's useful, so in time she'll be able to take a post as a qualified housekeeper in a good house. Alice says he's got a new way to learn to read, using sounds not names of letters. Makes big words much easier to spell out she says. I'm interested in that… Seems a good chance for the girl, Evie. We can spare her the time and, what's more, she'll get her dinner there on that day an' Mrs Horace is a good cook. Every little helps, Evelyn!'

'Mam, that is excellent. I am so pleased for her. Alice is a good lass, for sure. Now, what of you…?'

Alice knocked on the door gently and came in to clear the cloth. She smiled to Evelyn in appreciation. 'Don't you fret about your Ma, Miss Evelyn. She's got herself organised as well, so she has. An' what she's doin' for me, I'm ever so grateful. I'll not let her down.'

'I know you won't, Alice, and I think it's an excellent way of building your future, as my mother says. Now, as you go back into the kitchen can I ask you to take this napkin as well – I spilled gravy on it, I'm sorry. Now…Mam?'

'That's another thing, Evie. Mrs Hartley told me of a friend of hers, a Mrs Colton – she's a Wesleyan too and she's on the board of the children's hospital. I'm to go for tea, with Mrs Hartley, to the Coltons' tomorrow. Big house, I believe. Mr Colton was the premier until a couple of years ago, so I must wear my best feathers, hmm? House is in Hackney. Not so far to go.'

143

'Right, Mam, but what do you plan to get involved with? You aren't one to sit around, as I well know, but with John not so good…'

'Truth is, I don't know, exactly, but Mrs Hartley told me how Mrs Colton is very keen on helping women and girls. You know my feelings on that topic. She was apparently on the servants' home committee. Not sure if that's still going but they helped single girl immigrants find honourable work – and Rabbi Boas knows of her – and also the female refuge and she helps her husband with ideas for the Social Purity Society – you know that group she took me to where they want to add a ladies division…'

'Mam! All right, I get the picture. Changing the subject, how's John going with his treatment from that new doctor?'

'I don't know, Evie. He's fed up with me askin', I think. Keeping up with work, though, so's reasonable, I suppose. He doesn't eat much, though, to be sure.'

'He introduced me to one of their surveyors, Mam. He's one of a team working on the telegraph to Perth that finished a couple of years ago. He's now well past his apprenticeship and branching out. And he's good fun, Mam, wants to take me to the music hall tomorrow night. See? I can meet people…!'

''Course you can. No such word as can't. Hope for you yet, my girl!'

'Mam, I'm in no hurry to marry for the sake of marrying. I'm not twenty-one yet, as you well know! This is a modern place, modern thinking. Now, would you like a sherry as you read your book by the fire?'

# 31

In the Bridgewater Inn, Beatrice could only repeat, 'Lieutenant Symonds! Goodness me!'

He moved towards her and she – with automatic formality despite her surprise – held out her hand in greeting. He kissed it then led her to a chair next to his own. She smiled and withdrew her hand as if needing to smooth her skirts. Actually, she preferred to be on his level.

'Lieutenant, this is a pleasant surprise. You are looking well.' *Oops, he'll think that a bit fast of me. Was he always as tall and well set-up, as Sissy claims?*

Sissy scuttled out. 'I'll send some more tea in with Lucy, Beattie.'

Beatrice tried to marshal her thoughts. She sat down on the edge of the chair.

The ex-lieutenant spoke first – his smile carrying through on his voice. 'So it's Beattie now? They seem good people, Mrs Beauchamp. I assume Miss Evelyn described my return to the fold.'

She nodded. 'Only now, Lieutenant. In this note. And you are not in uniform…'

'No. I am no longer in that role, ma'am. I achieved a discharge from the line and have bidden the oceans goodbye, unless I am later persuaded otherwise.'

'Goodness, that must be a change for you. Please do tell.' *Heavens, I sound like Jane Austen!*

So, as Lucy brought in the tray, her face also alight with curiosity, he did. It seemed he had returned to Port Adelaide on the *Orient*, after visiting Melbourne and Sydney. Those two cities were busy, bustling places and it was only when arriving at Port Adelaide this time that he realised he preferred Adelaide.

'Geographically it seems poised more centrally between east and west and of course the telegraph line – and I heard all about that from John Benjamin – allows communication from Port Augusta to Albany in the west and Port Augusta is near to Adelaide and Albany almost next door to Perth. Adelaide seems to be the hub of it all. These are such exciting times, my friend.'

'So, Lieutenant…'

'No, I am no longer lieutenant, now I have relinquished my commission. May I re-introduce myself?' He stood and gave a little bow. 'I am plain Mister Arthur Francis Symonds and I prefer Arthur, if I might be so bold as to ask that you call me by that name.' He smiled. 'Like you, I think, though proprieties are still maintained, certain familiarities are welcomed – not only allowed – and I do like to invite the use of my name. I wouldn't in England of course but…' His smile widened. 'Though I know some retain a military title to carry weight in business, I prefer to cut my ties completely. I have no relatives left behind in England and I was never easy on my sea legs, strange as it may seem. This is such an exciting country in which to live, I want to stay here. There are opportunities for advancement and so many professions and prospects.' He sipped his tea. 'I took the opportunity of looking up Mrs Lee and her family. I admit I thought you had probably returned home to England after your loss.'

She nodded and looked thoughtful. 'Like you, I assessed my situation. It seemed to me that here I could achieve more as an independent person than back home in England. There I would have to conform to what now seem unnecessary social behaviours and traditions. Mr Symonds, I look about me and see opportunity and, for the moment at least I have – as dear Mary told me, landed on my feet.' She smiled at him. 'Mary would have really enjoyed seeing you again, I am certain of that. She is a wonderful person. In fact, I know that Evelyn was pleased to see you also.' She waggled Evie's brief note in acknowledgement.

He nodded. 'You are correct in that her mother is a remarkable woman, and very welcoming. Mary – she asked me to call her that – is already much involved in good causes, as I understand. She entertained me to tea and was most open with her stories and admiration of you. I was invited to stay while the son and daughter came home from their employment and we enjoyed a convivial evening. Miss Evelyn told me all about your living here and, indeed, most interesting remarks about a wedding in the community and other events that indicated you to be well settled. And I had expected to see you still in mourning! Miss Evelyn is also making headway in this new land, in her new employment. She was quite happy to write to you. I do hope you will not consider my unexpected arrival somewhat precipitate?'

*Precipitate? Strange expression in the circumstances. He still speaks so formally.*

'Please, Beatrice – if I may call you friend, will you allow me, as you allow other friends, to call you by name?' He smiled most engagingly.

She merely inclined her head in acknowledgement as he resumed his story. Anderson's interest was wholly engaged.

Beatrice was feeling overwhelmed. This most handsome man, well spoken – and she well remembered his lovely deep voice – was reminding her in a most factual manner of her less than pleasant arrival in this country. He prompted her remembering with an unwelcome clarity those long days of doubt and uncertainty on the voyage with only dear Mary and Evelyn to talk to in a sensible way. Aunt Wilkes's prattle constantly fuelled her own sense of inadequacy; an inadequacy that flared anew when she discovered James was no longer alive to support her in this new place. Yet James had turned his coat – gambling!

She gave a nod as if listening while the lieutenant – Arthur – spoke about his voyage to Melbourne and back. Anderson asked a few questions and they engaged in a discussion about some parliamentarian who'd been in the news apparently, thus allowing her to busy herself with her cup of tea. Then as Symonds warmed to the subject of opportunities, she allowed a furrow of concentration on her brow; in truth, her mind was racing. As he further outlined his own hopes and prospects, only half of which she heard; he indicated that this was a country open to a man's ideas and initiative. Anderson was giving a few grunts in agreement with him as the notion occurred to her – as prompted by that word, 'precipitate' – that he might be putting himself forward as the ideal replacement for her husband! Just as quickly, she dismissed the idea as preposterous. *For heaven's sake, I know from the tone of Evie's note that she really admires him.*

As he and Anderson argued a minor point on provisions for girls and women – Anderson considering the future need of employing more help in the inn – Beatrice accepted that as a friend Symonds could be solicitous of her welfare but how dare he assume she needed manly support to make good in this country! She had rallied her thoughts, thanks to the Lees' friendship initially – yes, they were good friends – and found a new determination and confidence that prompted her to stay, to prove herself capable. She knew she was accepted in Bridgewater's little township. She also knew she had earned a measure of respect in the community by working for her living and without losing any so-called social standing. She knew that opportunities awaited her elsewhere if she decided to look for them. She was capable!

*I'm being discussed and this is becoming too personal. Am I to be allowed to speak for myself? He sounds as if he has rehearsed this speech word for word on his ride up here! Wants to justify his calling on us unexpectedly. Look at Sissy's face. She has now joined this happy little soireé and, oh my goodness, I know what will be going on in her mind. Now he's answering a question from Anderson.*

Was it really only an hour or so ago, down by the creek, on her special stone, that she had reconciled herself to living here, being recognised for her own nature, abilities – and 'initiatives' –and to stay among this lovely mixed community as a respected member of it, while deciding if and where else to go, later?

*And he, pleasant company he may be, handsome and 'well set-up' though he may be, is reminding me of all the stuffy conventions that I – only this afternoon – decided to rebut. And hardly addressing me at all!*

Beatrice stood and replaced her cup and saucer on the tray with not a little emphasis. 'Lieutenant… erm… Mr Symonds, it is delightful to once again renew our acquaintance. You mention you expected to see me still in mourning. You may not realise, although mourning and grief is held no less in respect here than in the Old Country, it requires no despondency in dress. Grief and related emotions are recognised as no less genuine when held within oneself without an untoward, outward show, I assure you. I have learnt much since coming here. There is a relaxing of many old customs and a welcome given to anyone willing to adapt and become independent. Or so I have found.'

'Oh, Beatrice, do allow me to call you by your name. You mistake me, I assure you. I would not cause you annoyance because I have nothing but admiration for you. Mrs Woof and Mr Anderson have enlightened me of your many qualities including your music and I would not impinge on our new-found friendship by wishing any changes to your arrangements here.'

He stood up to speak face to face. 'Beatrice, your strength of purpose on being faced with such unhappiness on arrival in the colony invokes only that admiration of which I speak. Your friends the Lees also speak most highly of your acuity and determination when confronted with your husband's…erhem…business dealings.'

*This was too much! That her good friends had seen fit to apprise this, this sailor, of her personal affairs was too much, too much!*

Sissy saw her annoyance, muttered about being needed in the kitchen and bustled out.

'Mister Symonds. The Lees are my good friends and I am grateful to them, and shall be ever so, in more ways than you can perceive. So too are these my special friends here at the inn. I am also learning to my cost perhaps that the more relaxed attitudes here can extend also to discussion of certain personal matters. I deplore that familiarity when my personal affairs are discussed out of the acceptable circles. I choose to whom I speak of my situation and I am disappointed that you seem to know more of it than I might choose to tell you.' She stopped and took a deep breath.

He had taken a step back, looking surprised, maybe a little shocked, at the outburst, but with an irritating semi-amused tilt to one eyebrow.

Anderson stood, looking a little embarrassed. His discomfiture angered her even more.

'Mister Symonds, at the most I thank you for whatever level of concern you initially expressed to…to winkle information from my good friends. To you, I assert that whatever you may have heard or chosen to interpret, I found for myself this way of life, this way of facilitating my independence. I also feel that I am accepted as one of this community and…and…I prefer to choose my own friends, sir!' She exhaled and bowed her head. 'You will excuse me. I must now seek out my friend Mrs Woof and ascertain the programme for this evening, which I was about to do when your arrival interrupted me!' She swept from the room, leaving Arthur standing by her chair.

Anderson decided it was time he investigated the noises in the bar, though his man was there in control.

Had Beatrice stayed to measure their visitor's reaction, she would no doubt have been angered further. Arthur, the erstwhile lieutenant, was not in any way upset by her outburst. He merely nodded to himself as if confirming that his estimation of her character was absolutely as he had expected. He resumed his chair and poured himself another cup of the best china tea. This young woman he had admired from afar while on the *Orient* had reacted much as he had expected, showing evidence of considerable initiative. As a married woman of good breeding, she had always commanded a certain standard of polite detachment, and he'd learned she was no prey for his reputed charms. But she was now no longer married. Not only that, but she had developed in only a few months an admirable strength of character. She was also best-looking, which in no way detracted from her appeal. He looked forward to the rest of the evening.

# 32

Beatrice fled to the main dining room, where Lucy was readying the tables. She smiled at Beatrice's approach. 'Did you have a nice walk, Beatrice? You have met Miss Evelyn's friend, I believe. Isn't he handsome? A bit old, but still good'looking... My mother said there are dinner guests, three of them – brothers, I believe. They're the ones noisy in the bar right now. But they don't have a room. Your friend, the one Miss Evelyn sent, has booked a room and I think he's going on somewhere tomorrow. The three dinner guests have to leave quickly, they say, after dinner, so I don't know if you want to play music tonight.'

She looked at Beatrice, who had picked up a bundle of napkins and was folding them with no small degree of irritation.

Lucy, misreading the reason, said, 'Mother says you needn't if you don't want to.'

'Lucy, the gentleman is a guest of the inn. Mr Symonds once helped me and he is also known to Miss Evelyn. You are right to think he is her friend too. Yes, of course I will play the piano tonight during the meal if your mother would like. Sometimes it calms the noisy ones down a bit, doesn't it? The other gentleman may even wish to retire to his room after dinner and then, perhaps, I may be able to practise some of the music Miss Evie left me last visit.'

Sissy bustled in. 'That's a surprise visitor, your Mr Symonds, Beattie. What a lovely-spoken gentleman, too. And intelligent, says Anderson – more so than them three in the bar with him now. Would you believe they been to a funeral today? Not so respectful, is it?'

Beatrice's eyebrows shot up behind Sissy's back. Here she had been telling Arthur Symonds about relaxed social attitudes and now Sissy was going on about the respect owed to a funeral – she was so ingenuous at times.

Sissy placed some water jugs on the one table and tossed her head towards the parlour. 'If you don' want to play piano the night because o' your visitor, Beattie, we understand.'

Beatrice glared at Sissy. 'Of course I'll play, Sissy. Sometimes it keeps the level of loud noise down. And Mr Symonds is a guest and the reputation of the inn must be maintained.'

'About him, Beattie – your time's your own after dinner, you know that, don't you? You choose. I would understand if you want to talk with him.' She suddenly registered Beatrice's expression. 'Or something.' She moved some chairs around a table. 'He was telling Anderson about a friend he has in Creswick near Balaarat...'

'Mam, Anderson told me it's Ballarat, no big "aaa" sound in the middle any more...'

'All right, Miss Clever Clogs, you finish what you're doin'. Beattie, some gold mines are still yielding there. Mr Symonds quite got Anderson interested. Must say I was glad to have the other gentlemen come in to book for dinner and distract Anderson.' She came close to murmur in Beatrice's ear. 'Anderson went off once gold digging. Years ago now. Came back with enough for a ring but the woman, who lived in Adelaide, had found someone else. Sad that. I never knew her and he used the gold, putting it towards buying this place, as I understand it. I don't want him getting ideas again.'

'Sissy, maybe Mr Symonds is intending to go off that way again to make his fortune. I don't know of his plans, I assure you. I have never thought of the goldfields as appealing. To be honest, I read that most were all more or less spent now, I mean used up. I will go and freshen up and, yes, I'll play for the dinner tonight.'

Sissy was quite openly curious, and Lucy was standing and listening quite keenly to what seemed an interesting conversation.

Beatrice felt she should state the true state of affairs. 'Sissy, dear Sissy, Mr Symonds was known to Evelyn, her mother and me when on the *Orient*. He was an officer then. He has become a friend of the Lee family, especially of Evelyn. It is pleasant to see him again, Sissy, but that is all, I assure you. Now I'll go for a drink, then I'll freshen up. See you at dinner.'

As Beatrice left the room, Sissy noted Lucy's face alive with curiosity and she frowned. 'Lucy, that young lady doesn't know when a wonderful opportunity hits her in the face. She's nearer twenty-five than twenty –

she should think on that! And he's heading for thirty, time for any man to be settled with a wife and family or risk being called a rake. Ah well, there's no accounting for tastes. As for you, I need help in the kitchen with some scones, please, young lady. And you've some time yet before you start looking for a man, Miss Lucille! You can think on that!'

*

Beatrice had a short meal then played the piano while the guests ate – including Arthur Symonds who sat alone at a table. She decided not to make a fuss about his presence, but to treat him as politely as she treated all the guests. She expected him to leave as soon as he'd eaten, but he was still sitting when the other diners left. They hadn't paid much attention to her playing anyway, had laughed loudly, and their going was a relief. She took out a sheet Evie had left, it stated 'allegretto'. *Hmm, is that the same as allegro or does it mean increase speed gradually. I should really know.* Becoming interested, she started to pick out some notes.

Anderson came into the dining room, Lucy brought him a plate and he joined Symonds at his table. Lucy brought a drink for Beatrice and after a sip, she noted the two men were deep into a shared conversation so she resumed playing. The melody was unknown to her and she couldn't gauge the tempo to her satisfaction. *I should wait until I have a quiet afternoon for this one, it's intriguing; maybe…* She stopped to pencil in a change to cater for the square piano's fewer keys.

'Lost your touch, Beatrice?' came Symond's question.

She turned, and Anderson, noting her expression, intervened. 'This is new music brought up by Miss Lee and I know Beatrice has been eager to give it a try. I also know that our square pianny ain't the same as a usual machine, so she's adjusting. That right, Beatrice? Lucy told me all about it.'

'Thank you, Anderson. I shall enjoy trying them out on the school piano too, after I teach the girls in the morning. But they are pretty melodies.'

'So you do teaching as well, Beatrice? You have surely become quite an asset to this community.'

'I hope so, Mr Symonds. It's good to know I have useful skills I can

153

impart to others younger than I. It is very satisfying.' *Goodness, do I have to sound as stuffy as he does? It's his influence. The sooner he leaves here, the better.*

Sissy came into the room with her favourite teapot on a tray. 'Do come and join us, Beatrice. Mr Symonds has kindly asked us to share his table. I have the best China for you but if you want a wine, dear, Anderson will get you one.'

*Oh no! She's actually giving me a sly wink! No, no, no – no matchmaking here, if you please.*

Mister Symonds was discussing Adelaide – its opportunities, its populations and various needy groups described by Mrs Lee. As Beatrice listened, it became plain to her that he genuinely admired Mrs Lee and what he termed her 'good works'.

'She is an eminently capable woman. Although only here these few months, she has become caught up with the injustice meted out to some Jewish immigrants to the colony – settling them into decent places to live and stay. Miss Evelyn spoke to me of her involvement already with the ladies' committee of the female refuge and that's for young girls – saving their souls is the catch cry, I believe. Some church ministers – I think of a few different churches – have realised the unpleasant fate of young girls, some who actually come here unaccompanied, hopeful of employment in service, because that also gains them a bed and meals, but find the only employment is prostitution.'

Sissy was horrified. 'Oh, how terrible indeed! Er…Lucy, do go and get on with the pastries, please.'

Lucy was obviously reluctant to leave such an interesting discussion but her mother's frowns expected compliance – or else…

Symonds continued as if there was no interruption. 'Yes, it is, and I believe Mary Lee has volunteered her help to find work for the girls and provide accommodation in the refuge.'

Noting Lucy's reluctant exit, he remarked on a recent case of a young Irish girl made pregnant at only twelve years of age. 'The Catholic nuns have also opened a new safe haven of sorts in Norwood where the young girls can give birth in safe conditions. Mary also told me that a Reverend Kirby set up a Society for Social Purity like one in England but as yet has no ladies' committee… Yes, she has made a niche for herself, has Mrs Lee.'

Beatrice knew something of Mary's activities. 'I do so admire Mary. I believe she wants to help another woman set up a women's committee of that society. The present committee want to raise the age of consent – it is only twelve at the moment and, goodness me, that is far too young and yet she writes of younger girls in the city areas, on their own with no families, being so misused and abused Evie has told me of Mary's wish to become more involved, that she is seeking support from other women, those well positioned with a measure of influence. However, her time is becoming limited, apparently, as John Benjamin seems to need his mother and sister more and more to ensure he eats correctly. He has some kind of digestive or abdominal sickness and increasingly is in pain and not going to work. Evie says that when he has these attacks his mother fusses over him like a mother hen. I asked her if she was not being too critical but she admitted she is also concerned that he ignores the best advice. Last time she came here – it was for Kate's wedding – she said he had found a good doctor, newly arrived from America of all places, who has some fresh ideas he wants to try.'

Symonds nodded. 'Yes, and I think it was a contact of his who told Mrs Lee of a house for rent in North Adelaide. Did you know she'd been looking for one? As I understand it, John Benjamin's lease is running out soon. I believe it's to be Barnard Street – I think that's right. It is much nearer for Mary's involvement with the charities but, as I understand it, quite a walk to Miss Evelyn's place of work.'

An involuntary yawn escaped from Beatrice. 'I apologise. It has been a long day and a busy one. If you will all excuse me, I will bid you goodnight and retire to my room.'

Symonds stood politely, encouraging Anderson to lumber upwards and bend over in a clumsy bow. Beatrice tilted her head gracefully and withdrew.

*Oh, my goodness. I started the day getting all my thoughts in order and finished the day with them all in a tangle. What an anniversary to have one's head singing with thoughts not of one's dear departed, but of the lieutenant – who is no longer such – and who seems to be attracted to dear Evie. As for his being 'precipitate', I'm sure I read too much into it. Well, he speaks enough about her. And that raises the question, I wonder if she knows of it?*

As she energetically brushed her hair, relishing the feel of its lush weight on her shoulders, she admitted to a thrill at seeing Symonds again and recognising a measure of interest from him... *I had quite forgotten how good-looking he is, and none the less for being without his uniform. He is remarkably egotistic too. Still, if his thoughts are on Evie and hers on him, I must be circumspect. As Papa would say, 'Wait and see how the land lies, Beatrice.'*

She climbed under her sheet and pulled up the quilt against the cool air coming through the gnat netting. She could still hear voices from the small dining room. *Certainly Sissy seems to be enjoying being heard. I do hope she too is being circumspect and not letting her enthusiasms run away with her! And it is rather pleasant, despite the man's arrogance, to think I may see him in the morning...*

Another long yawn and she fell asleep.

# 13 April 1880

## 33

Next morning, Beatrice woke to the magpie calling her from the fence post. No shafts of sun were coming through the little east window; this indicated a grey sky and a dull day. She remembered on her walk yesterday wondering whether rain would come. Well, now it seemed to be spotting on the roof above, but not too heavily.

Then she remembered the lieutenant, who was no longer such! She made a hurried but thorough dress and bound her hair in the new attractive way – into a loose knot at the nape of her neck, only a small cap of lace atop, and pinched her cheeks to bring up the colour. *Cannot deny he is an attractive man and interesting – if irritating with it!*

Lucy was at work in the small dining room; she smiled a good morning. 'Mother and Anderson are in the parlour as there are only two – would you like to join them and I'll bring in a plate?'

Beatrice had already made her way. *Only two?*

Sissy was pouring the tea. 'Just in time, Beattie. You slept well, m'dear.' She sat down heavily and cut a slice of bread from a loaf. 'Your Mr Symonds has gone already, even without breaking his fast. He said he had to get the coach – though which, I'm not certain. He said he was leaving from Murray Bridge on a boat because he needs to be in Echuca by Thursday.'

Beatrice accepted a cup and sat down abruptly, her spoon slipping off the saucer. 'Oh, sorry, Sissy. Thanks, Lucy, and where may I ask is Echuca? Is that in the gold fields?'

Anderson eased his bulk on the chair. 'He was talking of it last night, Beatrice. It's a pity you did not stay. It sounds an interesting prospect…'

'That's right, Beattie, an' for a man of the sea like he is, seems natural to take this chance.'

'Man of the sea in the gold fields? I don't understand, you two. What is he planning to do at this place Echuca?'

'It's where the boat is based…'

'Boat? So he's gone back to sea then, has he? So much for all his talk of giving it up.'

Anderson shook his head. 'No, lass – Beatrice, I mean. Echuca's a port on the river, the Murray, and it's away over the border in Victoria. Funnily, the boat he's to learn the ropes on – as he put it, funny thing that – is called the PS *Adelaide*. Built about fifteen years ago an' wooden-hulled he said, an' it's a paddle boat.

'What, one of those like in the Americas with big wheels either side, like a mill wheel?'

'Yeah. Well, not as big, no. The boat's used for collecting the wool from stations lining the river and then taking it back to port for carrying bales o' wool there for off-loading. As Symonds put it, Echuca is a trading hub – like on a cartwheel, I picture it – and boats from there travel the Murray and the Darling, and the Murrumbidgee, to collect their loads like wool and wheat and take to Echuca, where it gets the train to the port of Melbourne. Echuca seems set to be a busy place for him, Beatrice. From what he says, he has some sort of managing job, organising loading and how much to take where and what pays the best price. Then he'll get onshore with the firm – they're called Grassey & Partners, or something like that – who he'll be working for. I've heard of a big hotel there that's a bit wild, but the town's a bit wild too, as I understand. River folk can get a bit over much in their cups, I'm thinking.'

Sissy thought to put things straight. 'He's a big strong fella, though, your Mr Symonds, Beattie. He'll give as good as he gets. An' he's got brains and speaks well and, as Anderson said, as long as he keeps his head straight and doesn't take too much of the local brews. An' he shows no signs of being too much of a drinker, that one… You'll have no need to worry.'

'Sissy, do stop! He's not *my* Mr Symonds. I wish him well. I do wish I had stayed and at least wished him a safe trip, however.'

'Oh, as to that, I nearly forgot.' Sissy dug into her apron pocket. 'He left you a note. Now can I suggest you eat up that toast and bacon Lucy brought you or it'll be cold an' wasted.'

Beatrice was soon left alone. She finished up her breakfast as bidden before opening the seal on her note. It seemed Arthur Symonds had secured a position for three months on trial and then, if he and his employers suited, he would settle in Echuca. As his work involved frequent travels on the river and Murray Bridge was on the riverboat routes, he hoped to take the coach from that town to see them in Bridgewater again about the end of June. He continued, 'If you are still in Bridgewater then, Beatrice, I would welcome the chance of meeting with you again so we can perhaps share news of our various enterprises. I remain, your humble servant, Arthur Francis Symonds.'

Beatrice didn't know how she felt. Surprised, yes, but because of what he had written? Or that he had written at all? Or – and this was more the case – that he had gone so abruptly so she couldn't say goodbye properly?

She leaned her elbows on the table, knuckles kneading her face. There was no denying he was an interesting man but last night she was persuaded to remain circumspect because he might be interested in Evelyn. Y*et this note is to me and he wants, or hopes that he and I can meet when he next comes this way – about the end of June, he says.*

She felt a thrill at the prospect and suddenly blushed like a schoolgirl. *Why pretend to myself? It feels good to know I am attractive to a man like him. I'm like Lucy lusting after Rauf…*

A spontaneous laugh at the thought of dear sweet Lucy knowing the meaning even of the word escaped her just as Lucy came in to clear her plate. She was surprised and pleased when Beatrice jumped up from her chair and gave her a big hug.

'Lucy, my dear, stay as sweet as you are!' And Beatrice skipped over towards the door and back to her room as Lucy ran back to the kitchen.

'Mother, your Beattie just gave me such a squeeze and she's laughing fit to burst!'

Sissy stopped rolling the pastry. 'Oh, is she now? Not weeping and wailing like her love 'as been thwarted, then? There's hope for her yet, Lucy.'

'Mother, if that were Rauf, I'd be crying, so I would. Gone away for so long…'

'Lucille! You are seventeen never mind eighteen and when you are that age and make your debut then we'll think about young men! For now, he can visit you when their pastor comes to see Anderson but we'll leave it at that. Rauf *is* a working man, and learning to be a lawyer. He's not earning enough to have a wife hanging on his arm. He is only paying for his room, board and books. He might be a catch later on but you have to learn, my girl, that good things come to them who wait. Now, to these pies.'

Lucy sighed. At least her mother was allowing her and Rauf to meet on occasion, but never to be alone with him. Funny thing, Rauf respected her mother's wishes in that way but it meant they could never sneak a moment together without either Mother or Anderson around and oh, Lucy did want to feel a 'proper' kiss! She applied herself energetically to frilling the pie crusts with the back of a spoon. *And my birthday wasn't long ago and I won't be eighteen till next March. Even then I have to wait at least another year before Rauf can graduate and be a proper lawyer. But Anderson says I should just look at other lads, too – there are two or three in the town who talk to us at church, but I knew them at school! Edward's nearly served his apprenticeship in the carpentry and I know he likes me. And there's Peter, he has prospects in the bakery but somehow Rauf treats me really nice. I suppose there is plenty of time, but…*

She sighed, causing her mother to smile. She was recognising her daughter's mood swings from adolescent to young woman – Lucy was growing up!

# May 1880

## 34

The cooler days and continuing dry weather as they came into May was a joy to Beatrice as Kate returned and they resumed their walks on most Saturdays.

Anderson was grumbling incessantly about the lack of good, long rains and the forecast shortage of water. He was getting on Sissy's nerves, as she often proclaimed, and Beatrice was glad to accept extra music tutoring away from the inn. She also helped Anderson with the inn's accounts more frequently as he applied himself to planting his garden and watching for rabbits. Paying guest numbers were down, and it was apparently expected at this time of the year – for some reason yet unknown to Beatrice. With Lucy's French language lessons and her own playing, whether for guests or not, her own time was busy enough, yet there was still too much time to think...

And think about Arthur Symonds she did. Evie made no mention of him in her letters, which arrived less frequently, but she knew Evie, too, was busy. Beatrice had been delighted – well, quite overcome – to receive a long-awaited reply from her father.

Then shock, horror! Papa wrote of actually considering taking another wife – a Mrs Gilbert he'd met at a church soireé. Oh, Papa! He asked if Beatrice had ever known her, as she spoke often of Mama and their shared interest in fund raising for the boys' home. Beatrice hadn't known her, nor remembered much of her mother's involvement in such a charity, but had to reflect how she had rarely expressed an interest in Mama's activities; her own main interests had been with the horses.

Papa wrote of the Gilbert woman's qualities at length, saying she could never take the place of her dear mama but it was now over a year since Mama died and the proprieties had been observed. He felt the running of the house required a woman whose 'heart was in it'.

She sat for some time considering her responses. He might even have married already; the letter was already weeks old. How to respond? She picked up her pen…

'Dearest Papa, you surely have as much right to home comforts as any other person. I know all about loneliness.' *I'm learning also about frustration at the lack of the special intimacies of marriage.* 'You are certainly still of an age to enjoy the advantage of companionship and a well organised household. I doubt I will ever come back to direct your household so please put away any hesitation on my part – there is none. I wish you every happiness, dear Papa…'

She sat, thinking what next to write. *I do not have the right to deny my poor papa any such consolations. It doesn't help to know Kate can sleep in Herbert's arms each night and even tries to tell me about her joys and then stops when I wish she would and then I wish she wouldn't! To be held, touched and loved again would make life worth living again. Wait, Beatrice Fletcher-Beauchamp. Do you really want to deny your father such expressions of caring, just because you don't have any one to share them with? This will not, cannot be written!*

Over the space of a few evenings she continued her father's epistle – it needed to be long and detailed enough to satisfy his curiosity. He did ask… So to play safe, she could speak of factual things such as her life as it was now becoming. She mentioned John Benjamin's illness and also wrote of the lieutenant's return to their lives, albeit fleetingly. Apart from her bodily frustrations – and she blushed even at the thought – she had become so settled, complacent even, that it was due time for her to make some efforts for change herself.

She folded up the paper and sat up, splashing her face with cool water. Of course! She would go to Adelaide and take her letter to the General Post Office herself and mayhap stay with Mary and Evelyn in the new house in North Adelaide for a short while. Evie had expressed an invitation because it was a roomy house. Also, Mary might advise her; she was wise in the ways of things and might be able to ease her mind about Papa's apparent hurry to seek another wife, replacing Mama.

She paused at the thought: what did she know of Mary's own marriage? She did know from Evelyn that Mary had to practise stringent economies. Yet surely John Benjamin had allowed some money for his mother's welfare. Yet she had spoken of musical instruments being the wider family's source of income and interest, that at least one relative played a large church organ. Perhaps it might be wise to be more circumspect in conversation about finances and family situations, particularly as her knowledge was all speculative…

However, it would be good to see John Benjamin again – he had been so helpful in those early, frantic days in the colony. Yes, that is what she would do! The inn was in a quiet time; for a few days they could catch up on the accounts and the other business themselves – yes, she could arrange things to go away.

\*

The Barnard Street house in North Adelaide was charming. Set well back from the street, it was of the ochre sandstone brick with the white quoins so characteristic of Adelaide houses and a lush vine covered the fence between it and its neighbour. After negotiating the gravel path, Beatrice climbed the three steps up to the front porch but she had no need to pull the bell because Mary had rushed to the door.

'I saw you from the window, my dear girl! Oh, Beatrice, it is just so very good to see you again, and you looking so well, and I do believe you have put on a little plumpness. They must be feeding you well at that inn!'

She led the way down a long hallway – bemoaning its length the while, 'Though it's good to let the breezes down in summer, so it is.' She signalled Beatrice to leave her bag in the hall. 'First we must have a pot of tea after all your travel! Sit you down.' She poured two substantial cups of strong brown tea. 'Evelyn will be home later straight after work and John's gone off for his walk. Poor lamb, so he is. You will be surprised when you see him and it's not for the better. This doctor – another new one, as John Benjamin has faith in the newest methods, unlike me who likes the tried and true, but there…'

She brought her hand up to her forehead, obviously upset, and Beatrice jumped up to give the plump little figure a hug. Mary was so distressed she even allowed it.

'Beatrice, this new doctor has told John Benjamin that what he has could be a form of a malaria, but I fail to see how. He does have terrible fevers some nights but they don't hang around. Malaria, or so I am told, is infectious and neither Evelyn nor myself are so affected so I feel the doctor is wrong. I do believe John Benjamin tells me tales, tells me what he thinks I like to hear to stop me worrying – but I worry all the more! You know that tuberculosis was in the papers the other day? Now that *is* a worry! When I read it, I even made a full pot of best China tea and drank the lot, worrying about all the worst possible things. I am just a silly old woman and, like Evie says, I am allowing my imagination to take hold, instead of my common sense. Of course, to be sensible again, the doctor has assured me I have no risk of infection. If it was tuberculosis, he wouldn't say that, would he? and with tuberculosis… Oh, my dear, too dreadful to contemplate!'

She lifted her head and smiled. 'Come, I'm neglecting my manners. I didn't offer you a cooling wash and refreshment. Allow me to show you your room. Rooms we do have aplenty in this house!' And even while still talking, she made her made back down the hall.

'This is Evelyn's room but there are two beds and Evelyn said you two like to share your talk after retiring and why not? So yours is the bed by the window, this is your washstand, and here is a cupboard for your clothes should you wish. Please come along to the living room when you wish.' She turned. 'We do not stand on ceremony here, dear girl, as finances do not allow, but I have the time to do our cooking and baking when Alice is at school. I do enjoy it. John has organised a cleaning lady and she also does the laundry once a week and that is a great help. Come when you are ready.'

'Alice, Mary? At school? Is that the same young girl who helped in the other house?'

'Yes, and of course this is so much bigger than John Benjamin's little lodging in Albert Park and more to keep clean, but she manages, does Alice. She's a clever young girl and, though we call it school, it isn't really. The lessons are at Mr Hartley's house. Alice wants the arithmetic and that is the strength of this Mr Hartley. As I was telling Evie a while back, he's the Inspector General of Schools and would you believe he taught in Belfast! Now he's a member of the Legislature – no, that's not it – the Legislative Council. All so very respectable. His wife has become a friend of mine too. Alice is a bright girl, an' with book keeping, an' she can read an' write well enough she should one day be an asset to any house. After her beginnings, she deserves it, so she does.'

Then John came home. Beatrice greeted him enthusiastically but pulled back when he surprised her with a quick hug, and she felt his shoulder bones through his jacket. Her own arms – albeit tentative – encircled his ribs with ease. He had lost a great deal of weight, his face was gaunt. He had grown chin whiskers too, stylishly clipped, but they were grey. The change in his appearance was dramatic; Beatrice could understand why Mary was so concerned. He made a few pleasantries then excused himself and went off into his room. Nevertheless, when Evie arrived home shortly after, there was laughter and chatter and the noise level increased to such a level he came back to join them, laughing and saying he would not accept missing any detail.

And it was a happy evening. Evelyn was enthusiastic in describing her work at the Telegraph Department. She didn't mention any suitors, although it seemed she was one of a crowd of young women who kept each other company for the theatre and the music hall and occasionally grouped together in each other's houses to play and sing the more popular songs. This talk of singing set the plan for the evening. Evelyn took the piano seat as she knew the songs, John joined in and then Beatrice as she learned the words. Mary quite soon begged to be excused from the 'ribaldry', as she phrased it, took up the teacups and left them to their 'naughty devices', which they much enjoyed!

Much later, they collapsed into the cushions and John poured them a small Madeira.

Evelyn wiped her forehead on her kerchief. 'On Saturday, Beatrice, you and I are off to the city. I want to show you some of the new shopping. There are some wonderful stores in the city now and I do so want to look around one with you. Whatever you wish to buy, I am sure you can buy it in Charles Birks department store. It is in Rundle Street – you may have seen it before but not ventured inside, remembering the speed with which you disappeared to Bridgewater!'

'Business first, pleasure later, my friend. I must send Papa's letter from the post office. But maybe I can do that tomorrow while you are working and then have a look around locally. But your mama has asked if I want to go with her in the afternoon. And I do have a list of things for the shops. And I know you are connected to the post office, so that's another reason for going there first. At least I'll see the outside of it. Then on Saturday you can show me around. That will be a handsome thing to do and I'm so looking forward to it.'

Evie laughed. 'Right. Well, wear some good walking boots, Beatrice – we have some distance and hard city pavements to walk on. There is a tram for part of the way but the walk is pleasant and I know you enjoy a walk. And it's typical weather for late May, I am assured. Like the English, unpredictable! Now, let's hear all your news of that wonderful inn you have adopted!'

# 35

Next morning, donning her sensible boots, Beatrice set off to post her letter. Mary said it was quite acceptable to walk unescorted providing she kept to the busy streets. She was amazed at how busy the streets were, how many couples were out walking, not only serving girls doing the shopping as would have been the way at home. There were two young women riding bicycles together and with a small wheel at the front! Surely they must be imported? John had spoken of a George Burston who had ridden to Adelaide from Melbourne earlier that year on a bike with the big front wheel – euphemistically called a 'penny farthing'. *Goodness me. Hardly dignified. Actually quite comical. They are a laughing stock...* Nevertheless, she was interested to note they were wearing those bloomer leggings that her hacking skirt dress shop assistant had described. *So fashions have reached here from Sydney. I can see the advantage of the skirt but no, no, no, I'm not ever riding one of those machines!*

She walked down Barnard Street then turned right and walked the hill down to King William Street. It wasn't far, but Evie had been right, it was hard on the feet.

She quickened her pace as she went down quite a steep hill past the rear of the new children's hospital and finally made her way over North Terrace, recognising the entrance to Rundle Street from her walk with John Benjamin – seemingly now so long ago. The Town Hall was on her left and the post office entrances to her right a little further on. She entered, noted where to pay and post Papa's letter but as soon as that was done, having seen the clock at past eleven, she wasted no time in retracing her footsteps.

'Evie will show me around tomorrow, won't she, little street sparrow?'

It cocked its head to her voice.

'You look the same as sparrows at home, and you scavenge in just the same way along the pavement!'

She walked back down the wide King William Street as the clocks chimed the quarter. *Have I been that long?*

She increased her pace until she reached the hill by the new children's hospital grounds and regained Barnard Street.

Mrs Lee greeted her return. 'Beatrice, you should not have hurried! It is too warm and we will not be late, m'dear.'

By the time they were enjoying a bread and butter sandwich with a cup of Mary's strong tea, Beatrice had regained her breath and was ready to ask about the female refuge committee.

'Oh, it's such good work they've been doing, Beatrice. The women now want to share the membership and form a viable subcommittee, and that's what we're working towards, like in the *Social Purity Committee*. It's startin' to be more of a women's world, thank goodness. I thought you would like to come and listen today – we have some of the women coming to talk of their experiences. I just thought as you were here you might like to see something of what goes on. And to hear how some of these women, once so desolate, forgotten and tempted to do wrong, have turned their lives around – makes it all worthwhile.'

The hall was a small one and lined with a collection of chairs, stools and benches. Beatrice sat with Mary on the front row, four other ladies sat along a bench table at the front, facing the rows of chairs. Beatrice thought the arrangement somewhat confronting, almost like a court of judgement. These young women were victims, not perpetrators but... Those in the audience were invited by one of the four at the front to put up their hands if they wished to share their stories. Some did and were invited to stay behind later to discuss their problems more personally.

Stories of beatings and bullyings seemed the order of the day and Beatrice thought some of the tales alarming. She asked Mary what the later discussions would achieve.

Mary told her how she was hoping to set out some plans for training. 'These young women have no skills and need to learn. Many cannot even read, Beatrice. One wonders how such pathetic creatures could slip through the net. And most come from London – London, the centre of the advanced world!'

She quite obviously retreated into her own thoughts as they walked, none too quickly, homewards. Then, as if coming to a conclusion, she smiled. 'The lucky ones will get a place, Beatrice – depends, it does, on whether they learn before they go off to a post. Yes, training is what's needed.'

Beatrice realised how deeply Mary felt for some of the young women's misfortunes and decided to leave her to her contemplations. Mary being Mary, she was no doubt already formulating a plan or mentally drafting a letter to the newspaper.

*

'On Saturdays the streets are busy, Beatrice, are they not? How do you find them comparing to yesterday?'

'I don't know, Evie. People were no doubt in their offices yesterday when I was down this street but I do remember noticing plenty of carriages turning up Rundle Street back there…'

They were already well on their way up King William Street to the imposing building on the corner of Victoria Square where Beatrice had posted her letter the day before.

'Our General Post Office and my place of work. I do want to show you. I specially love the clock. It has a lovely chime.'

Beatrice laughed. 'I heard it yesterday, Evie, and I do agree.'

'Actually, it's quite new – 1875, John Benjamin told me. He's one for remembering dates. The tower was earlier of course. John said 1867 – and I do know the stone was laid by Prince Alfred, the Duke of Edinburgh. Our royalty – and appropriately so because I think our clock is as grand as Big Ben in London. Well, it was made there anyway, by a firm in Whitechurch which isn't far from where we lodged at one time. The bells were cast by a John Taylor of Lough Keough. Mam thought that was in Ireland. Listen, there goes the half hour! There are five bells so four can chime and one is specially to chime the hour. People say they were tuned to sound like the bells of Great St Mary's in Cambridge and the Houses of Parliament in Westminster.'

'Goodness, Evie – you are positively beaming with pride, as if it is your own!'

'I feel somewhat that way, Beattie. This wonderful building accommodates both the post office and a telegraph station. So, yes, I think it a magnificent building, I really do. Isn't the wonderful half-domed roof not splendid? Your letter could still be waiting here, but not for long – it'll be franked and placed for despatch onto the first available vessel at the Port. We don't need to go up onto the gallery around this hall, which is a relief. It tends to be a busy place and isn't really open to the public.'

Beatrice was enjoying a lazy meander around the spacious hall, remarking the fashions displayed by the ladies. The crinoline was thankfully rare, but petticoats were still obviously plentiful and skirts lavishly decorated. Most feminine footwear was the boot, and having experienced, yet again, the hardness of the pavements, Beatrice was not surprised. Hats and par-bonnets had replaced bonnets in popularity, she noticed. She ventured to Evelyn that was no doubt more practical now but, for the excessive heat of summer, surely bonnets would give more shade to the complexion.

'Let us walk to find this marvellous shop of yours, Evie. And I really could do with a new pair of boots.'

They set off down towards Rundle Street.

'You know, Evie, here in the city I am conscious of my ignorance in fashions. In the Hills township there is a more relaxed air about – well, everything. Do you feel – well, as I do – a little unsettled? So much has happened to me since we came to this place and in my experience, short though it may be, so many changes have occurred, so many differences I have learnt to accept, yet so much I seem to have forgotten. I am full of confusion and contradictions, Evie.' She stopped, caught Evie's arm to halt her friend.

Evie's eyebrows were raised in enquiry as Beatrice continued.

'You mentioned my comfortable dressing – do I, am I, seeming uncouth to you? I would hope not…'

'Oh, Beattie, not at all. Yes, Mother has said you are perhaps more countrified. That is the most she has said and it is not a criticism. I would take it as a compliment. Are we not all of us new arrivals, learning to make way in a new land? You I envy, truly. You have learned to be different yet fit in! Me – where style is noticed among the imposing buildings and monoliths of power – I have a place to keep, to be one of them, and I have to conform. The cut of my skirt is noticed, the colour of my boots, the flattening of my kerchief.'

They walked on.

'You know, Beattie Beauchamp, I do envy you, in truth I do. You are true to yourself and that is an admirable quality. And you are able to enact it, demonstrate it, more than I dare. You are not much older than me. Is it that you are more mature in your thinking perhaps? I do, really, envy you in many ways. Adaptable, that's what you are. Now we are back near Rundle Street, let us cross to the corner. That's it. Take care. The traffic builds up on Saturdays. You came here with John in those early days, I think? And said how yesterday all the carriages were filling up the street? Look, before we go, let's stop here because it's one of my favourite places and I do want to show you. It's called Beehive Corner. There is a lovely drapery lady here and her shop is called the Beehive because she has a lovely gilded beehive decoration on its door. But she has sumptuous fabrics. You may see some you like – or not! Then afterwards we'll walk up Rundle Street and we will become girls again, you and I, seeing what is pleasant to see and maybe buy.'

Indeed, there were some lovely fabrics and trims in the Beehive shop and Beatrice had quite a talk with the young woman behind the counter, learning that she too had been in the country only a short while. She came from Carlisle, north of where Beatrice had lived, but the next county only. Each enjoyed the feeling of familiarity when they spoke of familiar country and knew the names of the mountain peaks and lakes.

'Do come again, miss. It's been lovely sharing those names and places…'

Beatrice was pondering on that 'small world' theory of Mary Lee's – that everyone in Adelaide meets someone else from their own home town, eventually – while Evie pulled her on the way up Rundle Street, talking non-stop.

'I need some stockings, Beattie, and you'll love this shop, Charles Birks. My mother knows of Mrs Charles Birks from Mrs Mary Colton. Mrs Birks is called Rosetta but prefers Rose, Mam says. The Birks have only been married about a year and, of all things, she is stepmother to his six children and,' she paused for effect, 'she was already their aunt, as he was married first to her sister. Mam said they're due back from England soon. But just look at the space here for displays of those fabrics, and the jewellery. And that necklace!'

Laughing together, the two women spent an enjoyable hour or so imagining luxurious and indulgent purchases; their only actual acquisitions pairs of stockings and some ribbon.

'You wanted boots, Beatrice. There is a lovely shoe shop in the Central Market. It's a bit of a walk up past the post office and Town Hall again but do let's find a tea house, have a lovely cup of tea, sit a while in the sun in the parklands or something and watch the world go by. Then we'll be ready to walk to the market. He'll have boots for you, I promise. Then after, perhaps we can walk home if it stays a nice evening. Or would you like to take the tram home?'

# 16 June 1880

## 36

The sixteenth of June and her birthday. Beatrice opened her eyes, felt the cold wind whizzing through her open window and buried under the cover again. *Today I am twenty-four years old. Too young to be a widow, too old to find a husband. So they say.*

She sat up and ran her fingers through her long unplaited hair. *If I am vain at all, it is my hair that pleases me most.* She reached over for her hand looking-glass. *Hmm, my nose could be straighter, my eyes larger. They are learning to wrinkle too, thanks to this Australian sun. Mama used to say my eyes were hazel and matched my hair. Hazel nuts? Dear Mama. If she were here it would be a special dinner being planned for tonight and maybe a gift on the breakfast table with Papa and Mama sitting and smiling as if they were keeping a secret.*

She swung her legs out of the covers. *Well, hello to this world! I haven't told anyone here it's my birthday, so it'll be a normal Wednesday. I can't yet expect any more letters from Papa, and now he is remarried – though he has yet to tell me – I dare say his time will be again in demand. I do hope he is contented. I know that is all Mama would want. And as for today – I don't have any music lessons at the school today so that leaves some spare time. Which is good. I can finish off the embroidery on my new dress. Oh, perhaps cut out that skirt – the jacaranda-coloured twill. Well, that's what Lucy called the colour – like the African tree down by the schoolhouse with lovely heavy blooms that fill the tree around Christmas time; I think I saw it when John Benjamin and I rode around that first day. That seems so long ago now…*

'We hope you have a very happy birthday, Beattie.' So came the chorus from Anderson, Sissy and Lucy – sitting at the small parlour table looking expectant.

'However did you know? I haven't mentioned…'

Anderson swallowed his mouth of hot chocolate. 'Miss Evelyn told Sissy in a note that came yesterday – with a package we had to give you today.'

'And there's one from me, from us, too, Beatrice. Please open it up. Well, maybe Miss Evie's first.'

'You are to be congratulated on your manners, Lucy. Do come and help me undo this knot.'

'Oh, look, it's all embroidery threads, Beatrice. What lovely colours. Oh, how nice, and you wanting to finish those peonies on your dress! How lovely.'

'And now, Beattie, our one?' So spoke Sissy, needing to get on with her day. 'We do hope it was the right choice.'

'Notepaper! Oh, how opportune. You dear people. It's so hard to find nice paper for my letters and this is lovely quality, and envelopes too with the flap for the glue-wax. Bless you all, this is really, really a surprise. But...how? If you didn't know till yesterday...'

'Well, actually Miss Evelyn mentioned your birthday when she was here for the wedding – an' you were then writing to your father and it gave me the idea, so she sent this up some weeks ago, an' I kept it ready.'

'Oh, you are so good to me, you three wonderful people! Let me give you a hug.'

Sissy and Anderson, all smiles, went off then to their chores. Lucy cleared the plates while Beatrice contemplated the toast and honey. She was in the midst of wondering how to approach her embroidery and which silks to use when Lucy ran in.

'Beatrice! A packet for you from the carrier!'

'Goodness me, who else knows today is my birthday?' She split the seal and opened up two large pieces of a rather coarse paper. 'Well, well, well... It's from the lieutenant, as was – Mr Symonds.'

She sat down to read and Lucy, not daring to look too curious, ran off back to the kitchen. *At least, Mother will be pleased to know he's written to Beattie.*

Friday June 11th 1880

My dear friend Beatrice,

I will be leaving here tomorrow and hope to make the stop near the new Murray Bridge by Wednesday 16th June. I will have a load to clear first, after which another can take over my duties for the next stage, so I was hoping I may be able to stop over in Bridgewater for maybe two days if there is a room available. Might I ask you to arrange with Mrs Woof for me to stay from Thursday night the 17th? I will be starting my trip soon, making my way down the river as you read this, though I believe this epistle will have to go first to Adelaide and then sent up to you from there.

As you know, I have been working in Echuca. I don't have an official title but I organise freights of wool and logs – collecting one from the farmers at various ports, and logs from the mills. They can both be hazardous loads – tho' spontaneous combustion is not the problem other than with the hay bales and other feeds; my concern is equal weighting – but I can talk of that later!

You may not know but Echuca is really a centre for a number of smaller towns hereabouts – have you heard of Swan Hill? Of Yarrawonga? Echuca was first settled by a Hopwood who operated a punt across the river at this point about 30 years ago and it was then known as 'Hopwood's Ferry' – you can gather from that what his industry was! It stands on the junction of two rivers, the Murray and the Campaspe – hence its new name, Echuca, which means 'the meeting of the waters'. It's now quite a town. We have a newspaper and some fine big hotels – where I have been living until I knew if I would be staying here or not. The original ferry ran from what is now a magnificent river-trading wharf built only about 15 years ago – a splendid construction. There seem to be boats constantly tied up alongside – my company has its moorings and our boats are kept busy with trade the length of the river system.

Oh, Beatrice, I would really like to show it all to you one day. Perhaps we may discuss your future plans when we meet? I do so admire you, Beatrice, in making of yourself the self-sufficient woman I saw when I visited, and fashioning her from the timid lost soul who arrived here in December last! Do please arrange some accommodation for me. I look forward to talking with Mr Anderson again. I didn't realise he knew so much of the river systems.

Your friend – in good faith, Arthur Symonds

Beatrice laid back in her chair. *Well, he doesn't mention my birthday. So this is just coincidental? And he seems to have retained his position. But what's all this 'your friend – in good faith'? And why should he feel he can discuss my future plans – my plans – when we meet? At least he seems eager to discuss the river with Anderson, that is good. Yes, I'll see Sissy about a room for him. She'll be in seventh heaven to see him again, he who is 'well set-up' and all! There'll be time enough to talk about whatever I want when he arrives – and not only what he wants.*

# 37

Sissy was definitely pleased to know she would be seeing 'that nice Mr Symonds' again. 'Sure, there's a room. Not a busy time, this…'

'Sissy, he does seem to take a lot upon himself – as regards me, that is: infers I have become a stronger person than I was when I arrived! He does have a nerve.'

'In what? Oh – infers. I see what you mean. Well, have to say, he's right, my dear. You were determined enough but a bit wishy-washy compared to what you are now. Look what you are – piano player, music teacher; ettyquetty instructor to Lucille and her friends – even getting them to talk nice! You do the accounts and help me and Anderson in many ways with running this place. You have lots of friends and oh, Beattie, I nearly forgot! Your friend Kate and her Herbert are coming here tonight for dinner, 'cos it's your birthday but it's a surprise so you don't know and, what's more, my Lucy is going to play the piano for you!'

She paused for breath. 'If you like this Arthur Symonds when he comes again and he likes you, my girl, you can put all what you've learnt to good use with a man like that!' She turned back to her egg-beating. 'You talk to your friend Kate tonight about this bloke. She didn't meet 'im but she knows you. I'll get Anderson to talk to him about politics or sump'n an' you an' her can have a woman talk. All right? An' if Mr Symonds don't come tonight, Anderson'll talk to Kate's Herbert giving you an' Kate a chance to talk woman-talk.'

'Sissy, you are incorrigible!'

'No more of them in-whatsit words, if you please, Miss High an' Mighty,' but she laughed as she finished beating the life out of the eggs.

It was so good to see Kate and have the chance for a good friendly talk. Dinner was delightful and Lucy played some of the Chopin quite smoothly, with only a few minor errors. She was so proud of her effort – and why not? Sissy looked almost swollen with pride as she and Anderson actually sat and dined with the guests. There was another couple from the village who were obviously celebrating something quite privately so they were left to their own devices; Sissy served their meals to allow Lucy to play.

Afterwards, Anderson drew Herbert away to talk about cross-cut saws, of all strange things, so Beatrice and Kate were able to enjoy their own company over a glass of port. Lucy had found some other diversion, so she didn't try to join in – an act curious in itself to Beatrice, as Lucy was usually intensely curious about 'adult' conversations.

Kate was similarly curious, in fact uncommonly questioning, about the ex-lieutenant. Beatrice was becoming irritated by her persistent assumption that he was coming back to the inn to see her, that he'd fallen for her and her lovely piano playing!

'Kate, do be serious. I talked to the man on board the *Orient* and he was always so proper. He came here to the inn only to satisfy himself that I hadn't been cheated out of anything – you remember I told you how he helped me after James was killed? He's just a good person, a friend. Goodness gracious, I've only known him six months! I know nothing of him or his family. To tell the truth, I did wonder at one stage if he and Evelyn would make a match. In fact, I thought so then.'

'Beattie, you have been here on land for six months and a day, if I remember what you told me. You spoke with him on the vessel for more than a month before that, did you not? I have known Herbert for not much longer than that. As for James, how long did you say you knew him before you married? Didn't your mother know his family – and him as part of it – for years and years? Did coming from an approved family make him the better man? Look how after he died you found out he gambled, and let you down.'

'No! Don't speak ill of the dead, Kate. I admit to being disappointed in the way things turned out but…look, there's no comparison! This ex-Lieutenant Symonds has never been tested. I simply do not know him well enough for any other opinion. Please, Kate, if my disappointment about James did one thing, it was to make me very, very careful indeed about any relationship with another man!'

Kate held up her hands. 'Whoa! Beattie, I am your friend, we are all your friends here. I haven't met this man but Anderson and Sissy think he's worth another look… So does Evelyn Lee – and her mother had hopes for her and him, so eligible he is…'

'What! You've all been talking of me again? Am I seriously to think you are all trying to marry me off?' Beatrice stood up and stalked over to the door, then as rapidly cooled down, smiled to her friend as if in apology, and sat down again. 'This port is too heavy for clear thinking. We should abstain.'

'No, wait here, Beattie. It is your birthday! Herbert has brought round some of our wine, made in the village. It is a very pleasant, light and happy one, I think.' She left the room in a swirl of skirts to find the wine.

She returned followed by Sissy, who was all smiles.

'Here's some fresh glasses and some pickles and cheeses for you. I'll come and join you later if I may, when I've finished what I'm doing. Seems the men are now busy talking about barrels. Of all things, I mean…!'

She turned to Kate. 'You didn't say that young Rauf was coming with you, Kate. Now Lucy's hanging around the men and it's quite – what's that word of yours, Beattie – disconcerting? I must go and give her something to occupy her mind. He's a nice young man, but that's it, they're both too young… I'll come back shortly.'

Kate grinned towards Beattie. 'Oops-a-daisy! He offered to come to drive the cart back if Herbert had too many ales or wines. I didn't think about Lucy. Oh dear. But she's growing up. What is she now, seventeen? Almost eighteen? Hardly too young! Hmm. Well, it's not our problem. Mine is to find out more about this ex-lieutenant who's coming to call on you. No, don't look all annoyed at me, Beattie. Nobody's trying to marry you off, as you say, but the truth is, to have a good man by your side is a blessing in this raw country. And you admit to his being a help after James's death, and John Lee was very helpful with that Mr Beckett or whatever he was called. It is perhaps unfortunate that Mr Lee has doubtful health or… Look, in matters of money, Beattie, many firms, companies, refuse to talk to a woman unless she has a man as guarantor.'

She topped up their glasses and held out a plate of cheeses. 'Come, try the pickles with the cheese and sip this wine. Know that I am your friend.' She took a sip then leaned forward. 'Now, Mrs Beauchamp or Miss Fletcher, as you will, tell me something, all you know about this Arthur Symonds. First – how much taller than you is he? What colour is his hair?'

Beatrice knew Kate was her friend, and those questions she could answer. By the time she'd finished describing the ex-lieutenant, she almost felt proud, a pride in him as a friend, as if he was her possession. She felt a shock at the realisation.

Kate laughed and leaned forward conspiratorially. 'Be honest with me, Beattie. A man like that? Don't you think he could make you feel special? You are a woman – don't you miss that touch, that special tease of a man attracted to you? You were wed, a wife. Beattie, you told me things. Have you forgotten what it's like? That special feeling with a special man? When he…' She sat upright. 'Ahaa! You are going pink, my Beatrice, going pink!'

Beatrice rolled her cold glass around her cheek. 'Kate, my dear friend, that is nonsense! It's the wine, I have had more than usual. Yes, it is just your "happy" wine. It really is delicious!' Then she giggled.

Kate burst into laughter. 'I think the wine is rather stronger than we are used to drinking but, Beattie, dear Beattie, I am now determined to meet this paragon. For so he seems to be. We will come to dinner on Saturday as paying guests and you can introduce me as you wish. But now, my dear friend, I have some special news. I want you to be the first to know. I am expecting!'

Beattie laughed in delight and clapped her hands. 'Oh, that is such good news!' She cast a wicked sideways look at her friend. 'You didn't waste any time, did you?'

But Sissy interrupted their banter by bustling in looking a little harassed. 'Would you believe that boy Rauf is helping Lucy in the kitchen to polish the silver platters?' She looked defensive. 'Well, I had to give her something to do and you could knock me down with a feather when Rauf offered to help! He's putting some energy into it, I'll give him that, but I said they must leave the door open.'

She walked over to Kate and gave her a little kiss on her cheek. 'I heard the last bit an' I'm so delighted for you, Kate, for you and Herbert. And the good pastor, Anderson's special friend? I know he will be delighted it will be another little one for his church! And today it's my good friend Beatrice's birthday. So pour me a wine, do. Let's try those pickles and we'll celebrate! But you, young-lady-having-a-baby, drink more water than wine, I suggest!'

She winked, and laughing together, they clinked their glasses in a happy salute.

# 17 June 1880

## 38

Next morning as her friendly magpie carolled her awake, Beatrice felt most unready to leave her bed. Why did she imbibe too freely last evening! 'Ooooh!' she moaned as she eased up against the pillows. Cautiously, she stepped over to the washstand. The water was quite chilly and she took the piece of flannel to soak and rub her face until her eyes felt a little less reluctant to face the light.

Last evening had been quite an experience. She could not remember another occasion when she had spoken so frankly with another woman about – well, innermost feelings and sensations. She brushed her hair. Her mama would be appalled, as she considered such female conversation the province only of mothers and daughters – certainly never friends! Oh dear – *in vino veritas*. As she pinned her hair sedately up top, she realised it had in many ways been an unburdening. Airing one's negative thoughts and fears could lessen them and clear the way for new and different insights. And Kate had entrusted her with her news, too; it was a shared trust and a friendly feeling.

She plonked down on her bed. The other week by the creek, in the peace of that place, she had examined her innermost thoughts and reached a sort of catharsis. Last evening, by sharing such thinking with a trusted friend, she had achieved a similarly pleasant freedom of inhibition and anticipation. Anticipation? Yes. Oh dear…

She moved to pin on her lace cap atop her chignon, stopped and flung it onto her bed. Maybe last night's wine had loosened her tongue – and Kate's – but sharing their thoughts and exchanging opinions and reaching whatever conclusions they had reached – well, they were her conclusions and not dictated by anyone else, certainly not a mama nor even a dead husband.

She slipped her feet into her indoor slippers. *No widow's cap, no inhibitions about social correctness are going to burden my thinking any longer. Mayhap it has been only six months but they have been eventful ones, oh yes!*

A last look into the glass. 'You are Beatrice, you are an independent woman and you can exercise your own mind and make your own decisions.' She walked out onto the deck and looked the curious magpie in the eye. 'You are meeting the real me today, bird, and now let's see what is for breakfast!'

Sissy cast a curious look at her as she walked into the parlour but said only, 'Good morning, Beattie.'

Anderson nodded as his mouth was full of breakfast and Lucy gave a cheeky grin as she buttered a piece of bread.

'Good morning, everyone. I had a lovely birthday yesterday, thank you all.'

'Yep, I noticed that you and Kate – that is, Mrs Flach – had a good talk. Nice to see, Beattie. Mind you, if she's expecting, she should not have drunk the wine, I'm thinking.'

Anderson chimed in. 'Oh, come on, Sis! Herbert is delighted, looking forward to being a father, hopes for a son of course. But as for drinking wine, well, you were in your cups once or twice when you were married to that other fellow, Sissy, but Lucy is a darlin' – that right, my pet? – nothing wrong with her!'

Lucy smiled. 'Don't know why it is men always want sons when it's the daughters who seem to work hardest…' She flashed a bread-fuelled grin at her mother.

'Today is the day Mr Symonds is supposed to arrive. Any news at all from the early carrier, Anderson?'

'No, Beatrice. No messages but I don't know how he's planning to get from Mobilong…'

'From where? I thought it was from Murray Bridge. Is that nearby?'

'Same place, Beattie. The bridge over the river there was only finished – was it last year, Sissy?' She nodded as he continued. 'I've always called the town Mobilong – well, it was called that once, still is by most around 'ere. Now it's bigger and lots of the steam paddle boats call there, they call it after its bridge. Or so I've noticed.' He looked up at the ceiling as if for inspiration. 'I still call it Edwards Crossing at times – and that's going back a bit – but I think the Bridge name will stick. And Beatrice, I don't think there's rail from here to there as yet, so I don't know how he'll come over the land. Maybe from Mannum would be quicker – there's tracks through… No, I couldn't say to be sure. If he has a horse, could be done, but to tell the truth, I'm none too sure about that cross-country way at all. We take roads for Adelaide and then from there, whenever we want to go somewhere else. Don't try to cut corners.'

Sissy started to clear the table. 'Well, we'll mebbes see later today – at some time – when he gets here. Come on, Lucy, we've things to do. His room for a start so it'll be ready for whenever he does arrive.'

It was a typical Thursday, with a typically organised pace, for which Beatrice was extremely thankful. Her head cleared as the morning wore on. The men in the bar from midday dinner time onwards were a bit noisy, though, and kept Anderson busy. Lucy and her mother put some pies in the oven, and Beatrice went down to the school after three o'clock to teach piano until five.

It was well after five when she arrived back at the inn. Apparently there was still no ex-Lieutenant Symonds. Lucy had readied the dining room for whoever might need meals – apparently, four guests were expected – and had done an interesting variant on the napkin folding. She smiled in pleasure at Beatrice's congratulations.

After a cup of tea, Beatrice replaced the music sheets she'd used with her pupils and idly picked up some new sheets that Evelyn – dear Evie – had sent up for her to try. Two of the new melodies were fascinating and the scores challenging at first glance. Apparently two were early Brahms Hungarian Dances. Definitely music to be well practised when alone! *I don't know if Evie plays this kind of music. Her tastes are more music hall.* She smiled at the memory of her last visit to Barnard Street.

There was one folded sheet, Brahms's lovely Cradle Song. She scrutinised the bars, slowly, one-handedly tapping out the melody and remembering her Mama playing it at home on the farm. She felt guilty and regretted not sharing in the playing with Mama more often. Piano practice had been a chore in those days; she was more interested in her horse and the farm. *Papa indulged me, lacking sons as he did. Poor Papa! But if it wasn't for Mama's insisting I practise, I wouldn't have found myself this happy independence, here on the other side of the world. Dear Mama.*

She placed the Cradle Song ready to hand. Wiegenlied: Guten Abend, gute Nacht was the title in its original German. She wasn't sure how to pronounce it; Mama had called it Brahms's Lullaby – yet another title! She busied herself spreading a range of music on the stand in readiness for the evening. The Brahms was glorious – but not lively enough for early diners, so she reluctantly decided it would have to be played at the end of dinner, if at all.

All was ready now, so she went off to wash and change and decide what to wear. It was going to be a chilly night if the wind as she walked home from the school had been any indication. The evenings were closing in earlier too, so she hoped the ex-lieutenant would *not* try to ride an unfamiliar horse, on unfamiliar tracks, in the dark. *You silly woman, what does it matter to you? He is a sensible fellow and can make his own decisions, as you now know you can too!*

The magpie was perched on the rail outside her room. It took some broken biscuit from her open palm and she rubbed his grey beak with her finger. 'You are supposed to be a wise bird. Do you think I am acting like a foolish schoolgirl? Like Lucy does around Rauf? Hmm? I haven't decided if I even like the fellow, have I? Well, I shall act like an adult and if Mr Symonds turns up, that will be good. If he does not, well, that is his decision. Me – I must get myself ready for the evening's playing. See you in the morning, Magpie.'

The evening went well. The four guests were apparently Pastor Wilhelm, his wife and two friends newly arrived from Klemzig. Beatrice was introduced to the newcomers and, recent arrival to new arrivals, they exchanged some pleasantries before she started to play.

At some point Sissy bustled in and signalled it could be an early finish as the pastor rarely stayed till late, and did Beatrice want her meal afterwards? She agreed. The small group had applauded the familiar Chopin so when she noticed they were on a coffee, Beatrice decided to play the Brahms for them, and to close the evening.

She was delighted to hear a tentative tenor voice singing the words – the German words. She turned to see, still fingering the melody. It was the young immigrant from the pastor's table. He was standing by his wife's chair, smiling down at her and holding her hand. Sensing an appreciative – if small – audience, his voice strengthened and the lovely German melody rang round the room:

*Guten Abend, guten Nacht,*

*mit Rosen bedacht,*
*mit Näglein besteckt,*
*Schlupf unter die Deck!*
*Morgen früh, wenn Gott will,*
*wirst du weider geweckt.*

He halted, cleared his throat, growing rather pink in the face, and waved his hand in apology. '*Meine Mutter hat mir dieses Lied gesungen* – erm…erm, my mother sang that song to me, is meaning. I am sorry, Miss Fletcher, I remember only those words, that verse.'

'That was really lovely, I thank you,' and Beatrice ended the phrase and walked over to shake his hand.

He smiled and nodded, the pastor gave his usual friendly grin, the ladies gathered their skirts and wraps, and they left the room with Anderson escorting them to the waiting trap.

Beatrice smiled as she reclaimed her piano and tidied up her music. She read the Cradle Song's words, given in German and English on the sheet, thinking of that young German's mother and her mama, both sharing a love of the same melody though so many miles and different cultures apart.

# 39

She didn't see him arrive nor did she hear him but she sensed his presence. She turned from the piano. Ex-lieutenant Symonds was leaning on the door jamb, ankles crossed, a battered straw hat in his hand and a grubby cape skewed around his shoulders. Sissy was hovering behind him smiling stupidly – no doubt applauding herself thinking he was Beatrice's own ex-lieutenant, a lost love, so to speak.

Beatrice opened her mouth to speak but couldn't choose the words. She was wordless.

He was not. 'Hello, Beatrice. I do apologise for being so late. Mrs Woof tells me you haven't eaten either, so may we dine together shortly? I must first freshen myself up enough to be welcome at a lady's table, must I not?'

Assuming her agreement – she was still tongue-tied – he walked over, kissed her hand, gave a small bow and headed for the guest accommodation. She closed her open mouth with a snap.

Sissy followed with a tray. 'Do take your chair, Beattie. Makes it easier for me. And – oh, my dear – if I may presume, do let him have his say. He has come a long way.' She placed the tray on the end of the table. 'And it has been a couple of busy days for me, too. I'm tired to my bootstraps. Here, a glass of that nice Hahndorf wine for you – it was left from last night. So…'

'Sissy! Do I have a choice in the matter? All right, just for you I'll hold my tongue but…he's even left the smell of horse lather behind him!'

She had sipped nearly all her wine and was crumbling a bread roll when he walked in. At least he had changed to a clean shirt. His face shone with washing and his hair was wet, though neatly brushed back from his brow. He indicated the chair opposite her, his brows raised in query. She wiggled her fingers in assent and he sat just as Lucy came in with two steaming plates of stew, her smile from ear to ear.

*Oh, for goodness sake…*

'Beatrice, it is good to see you again. You received my note, I hope?'

She nodded and, remembering Sissy's plea to be pleasant, smiled weakly though with an imperious tilt of her head. 'Yes, I had your note. It is good to meet again. You wrote of your work. It seems very different from deep-sea sailing. I look forward to hearing more. However, may we first dedicate ourselves to this excellent stew before us? I am hungry and I am sure you must be.'

He frowned but took the hint. The two of them ate silently, Beatrice trying to determine a strategy for pleasant conversation. *This is really becoming just too much! I am annoyed – no, I am furious! The way he assumes I will follow his lead in everything. And he's eating as if he is starving – well, at least he can use cutlery and I've seen many who can't. Beatrice, does that really matter at this moment? I want to find out his every fault but why am I so nervous about him? And why do I feel so – what? – inadequate, because he is sitting opposite, lifting his gaze frequently to look at me from under those eyebrows?*

He didn't speak a word, merely gave Lucy a brief smile as she placed pudding on the table. Beatrice couldn't stomach hers, though he applied himself and his appetite to his own plate with relish as she finished her wine. He drank only water.

*I had forgotten the direct gaze of his grey eyes and they are such a warm grey, I must admit. And that lively hair – did it always have that wave across the front, falling over his brow, necessitating that constant sweeping of it back? And he has such long fingers…* She imagined the feel of his hair running through her fingers if she swept it back from his brow…and felt herself pinking up at the thought. One of her father's axioms came paradoxically to mind: 'The best form of defence is attack…'

He had noticed her staring at him. He dabbed his mouth with his napkin, replaced it on his lap then asked, 'Beatrice, have I changed so much that I warrant such an inspection? Or is it that smell of horse lather I heard you mention?

She gave a little cough. 'Erm…Mister Symonds, Arthur, I was merely admiring your hair. Its thickness, its colour and that delightful curl around the ears – they are no doubt the envy of many a female. And though you have been living in that climate by the river, interstate, it has not diminished you, or so it would seem.' *Ahah, got you back! Thanks, Papa!*

He sat upright, sat back, eyes wide, then gave a delighted laugh. 'Oh, Beatrice, I always knew you were no mollycoddled Miss Namby-Pamby. No, I am in no way diminished as a man, I am no milksop. I admit, I have met enough females who wish my attentions, who hang on my every word as they would hang onto my arm. But I like to think of any future partner for me as an equal in all things and as individual as she wishes to be.'

'Oh, stop there, do! If you recognise independence, you will know I am not hurrying to be anyone's future partner. Do not lightly use that term in relation to me. Friend – good friend – yes. We have spoken of such things before and you have learned much of my life here. You must know I enjoy it. And yes, I have spoken of looking for some other employment, of industry, to satisfy myself. I am also aware – have been made so, repeatedly – of the advantages in having a male partner, whether in marriage or business, in order to seek any necessary finance. *This by my friends…!*'

This last comment was intended for Sissy's listening ears just through the semi-open door. The sound of her skirt rustling away was immensely satisfying to Beatrice.

Symonds sat quite still, gazing steadily at Beatrice. He picked his napkin off his lap, folded it neatly, placed it by his now empty glass, exhaled and slapped his thighs.

*Quite a piece of theatre. Now what will he have to say?*

Very little. He stood and replaced his chair. 'Please excuse me. It has been a long day. I mean to retire. Perhaps we may meet afresh in the morning?' He gave a little bow and before Beatrice could compose her thoughts to respond, exited the room.

# 19 June 1880

## 40

Beatrice was not sleeping well. Thoughts of Arthur's thick, bouncing hair and imagined scenarios of how it would feel to her fingers were intruding with a disturbing regularity through the dark hours. She was annoyed – it was ridiculous, it was not possible, or so she kept telling herself – that the ex-lieutenant could make her feel like this. And what was 'this' anyway? Attraction? That was possible: physical attraction. As she had confessed to Kate, she did miss the intimacy of her marriage, newly learned and brief sensations though they had been.

She could hear one of the the local possum family scratching on the roof above. She tried to focus on it so she could sleep. In her half-awake state, she dreamed of Arthur's long fingers, brushing delicately along the side of her bare neck, beneath her pillow-tangled hair; she was swaying on her feet with a shudder and a thrill shaking her to her bones and she couldn't speak and he murmured against her ear, 'You are enchanting. Do you know what you have done to me? I can think of nothing else. Oh, dear God, Beattie, admit it: you are a woman! You need me, want me, as I want you, don't you!'

'Oh yes! Oh no! Go away…'

She sat up in her bed, and put her hands to cover her face. Oh, my God. That dream was so vivid. She was disorientated, where…? Ahah, the possum's scrambling around again, so she was in her bedroom. Every nerve in her body was tingling with that special kind of exquisite pain which had no name because it was not mentioned in polite society. It was still dark; she had a long drink of water and eventually fell into another fitful sleep, waking only when the knock on her door announced Lucy's morning call.

She woke languorously, still savouring the dreamtime sensation of long sensitive fingers caressing her breast…then up under her chin… delighting her, teasing her awake. She sat up and swung her legs over the side of the bed. Oh, why is it morning already?

Lucy poured the fresh water into her wash bowl, casting a questioning look at Beatrice before closing the door behind her. The waiting magpie carolled loudly for its usual breadcrumbs as she left.

Beatrice decided she would be pleasant to Arthur at breakfast. His departure last evening had been abrupt and had unnerved her. *She brushed her hair vigorously, then paused. I was a bit abrupt, I suppose. Abrasive? What's the word? Whatever did I say? Was I as inconsiderate as I seem to remember, so rude?* She prided herself on being even-tempered.

Whatever Arthur was hoping for, it was flattering that he had travelled some distance, in no comfortable fashion, to see her. Sissy was correct: she should have listened to him, as a basic courtesy if for no other reason.

*Ah well. Too late now. I am no easy woman to be taken for granted. I'll be friendly when we meet; at the least, polite. Thankfully it's Friday and there are no school piano lessons. I'll wear the green poplin with the strawberries. Evelyn said it has a softening effect on me. Hmm, now I'm wondering what she meant by that, but I'll need a shawl – it looks quite wintry through the window..*

Sissy was just finishing her breakfast, Anderson was not in evidence, Lucy was singing in the kitchen and of the ex-lieutenant there was no sign. Beatrice sat down and poured a cup of tea from the big pot.

Sissy swallowed the last of her toast. 'Mr Symonds was up early. He's had breakfast and he's in the sheds out the front helping Anderson. They're talking ball bearings or something that's gone wrong in the big carriage wheel…'

'What would a seaman like Arthur know of wagon wheels!'

Sissy looked at her scornfully. She was obviously not in the most friendly of moods. 'You really don't know the man, or you don't listen to him, my Beattie. He's an engineer. That's what he did on the ship, your friend Evelyn told me. But then, those days your thoughts were full of James, weren't they? You mebbes wouldn't have been interested and that's quite right too. But he's more than a mere journeyman, your Mr Symonds.'

'He's not my… Oh, all right, Sissy. I'm sorry. It's just that he seems to think I'm a silly, clinging female, hanging on his attentions and I am not, N O T – not! After breakfast, I'll seek to speak to him and make friends, or whatever you want. Then you might stop calling him *my* Mr Symonds!' She started to energetically scrape butter on a cold piece of toast.

Sissy beat a retreat.

Beatrice had swapped her cup of cold tea for a hot coffee by the time Anderson and Symonds walked into the small parlour.

'Goo'day, Beattie!'

'Good morning, Beatrice. How are you today?'

Sissy brought in hot coffees for the men and one for herself.

Anderson was taking his coffee and wrapping his hands around it. 'Chilly out there this morning. This kind fellow knows about ball bearings, hubs, traction – not bad at all, Sissy!'

'My pleasure, Anderson. I had to know a bit about mechanics and engines because my father had an engineering firm. Father had designed a successful pump engine but did not pursue its manufacture because he was something of an inventor and went from one idea to another. He saw me through school and then I was supposed to take on the firm but he dropped dead of an apoplexy. My sisters' husbands were not in the company.'

Beatrice allowed some interest. With her head cocked to one side, she had to ask, 'So with that background, Arthur, how did you end up a seaman?'

He turned to look at her. 'Fate took a hand. The company contracted to manufacture the pumps claimed they were owed money – despite being able to sell their products and in fact having many orders. They claimed the money we owed was their only means of assuring supplies to fill the orders.'

He waved his hand in a gesture of dismissal. 'We were declared bankrupt and I was homeless. Well, I was staying with one of my sisters. I was fifteen. I couldn't buy my apprenticeship but I had completed school, so I sought other employment. By my sixteenth birthday, I was deckhand on a herring ship for one season…'

'Arthur, sorry for interrupting but if you could not buy an apprenticeship as an engineer, how did you finance a commission in the navy? '

'I didn't – that is the short answer. The brother-in-law I had been living with knew of a new firm in Glasgow branching into marine engineering. I had some practice in pumps and things like that, so they agreed to take me on. By then I was nearly sixteen and quite grown, and my build stood me in good stead. Then the founder, John Elder, died and his wife ran the company…'

'Really? A woman at the helm?'

'A good choice of metaphor, Beatrice! But she eventually transferred control to a new company, Fairfield Shipbuilding. I really enjoyed the work there, developing steam engines – well, to put it simply, ones that reduced the consumption of coal, caused fewer problems due to friction and in general gave more power, more speed. Their marine engines were in demand and when I was offered a chance to join the Orient Steam Navigation Company – in a lowly capacity, I should say – and there was quite a bit of collaboration between companies. I did so, and learned more about the engines and pumps and…well, I really felt that I made up for my lack of learning earlier. The company developed and built ships there, in Glasgow, and also down in Liverpool.'

He paused. 'Please, Mrs Woof, may I have another coffee. I agree with Anderson – it was cold out there.'

'Oh I'm sorry, Mr Symonds, but you have had such an interesting life…' and off she bustled to call to Lucy.

Symonds smiled after her. 'Yes, I have been fortunate. My work with the newer engines is how I became an engineer on the *Orient*, and before that on a couple of others. As you know, this last voyage was the *Orient*'s first, its maiden. It did carry an auxiliary sailing rig, but we really wanted to give the steam a good trial – and we did. A remarkable vessel, that one. I'd visited Adelaide before but the last time we came by the Suez Canal – Egypt is a fantastic place.' He drained his second coffee and smiled at a fascinated Lucy.

Beatrice suppressed a smirk. Now there's someone who *is* hanging on his every word. 'Oh, that's how you knew your way around Port Adelaide so well…'

'Not really, Beatrice. This place has grown and developed in an astonishing fashion since that first visit. So has Melbourne. It was while I was there I realised I wanted to stay in this country but the line insisted I travel back from Melbourne while they organised a relief. They picked up another engineer here and I spent some time showing him the ropes.'

'So you are an engineer…!'

'Yes, Beatrice. That was my function on the *Orient*. Nor am I an eager seaman. I prefer terra firma to heaving oceans.' He grinned at her and she had to laugh.

'So your work in Echuca is as an engineer?'

'Yes and no, really. I applied saying I had engineering experience on seagoing vessels; not so much the operation of them but more their design and recommendations. Seemed they were pleased to have my knowledge. I was asked to advise on a small paddle boat – not so much a passenger vessel as one which tows a barge and is used for freight – and freight of all goods up and down the river is, or was, a massive industry. Coincidentally, that first little vessel was the PS *Adelaide*.' He grinned. 'Seems I passed the test and they asked me to stay and work from their offices in the town as a consultant, though I have to be prepared to get my hands dirty now and again.'

# 41

Arthur leaned back in his chair. 'Echuca is a very busy port and a pleasant town. There is a massive wharf made of river red gum and in a year, so I am told, up to two hundred and fifty boats of all sizes tie up there for trade. Wool and logs mainly are freighted between farms to port and thence to the Melbourne train in many cases. It is a very busy – and somewhat noisy – place and residents boast it never closes!'

His audience was rapt.

Lucy sat, eyes shining as she listened. 'I heard it mentioned once and thought it was a gold town where people made fortunes.'

'Oh, there is gold, Lucy, travelling from the gold field for assay – that's having it valued – and then transported usually onto the train for the city. It used to catch the coaches but of course, as you know, there were too many hold-ups with those – what's the term, Anderson?'

'Bushrangers, like…'

'That's right. We all know of those, don't we?'

Beatrice jumped in at this point. 'I know there are problems with highwaymen and that here they are called bushrangers, but aren't the worst of them now in custody? You are meaning the Kelly gang – everyone seems terrified of them. And I read of a Captain Moonlite hanged in Sydney not long after I came to Bridgewater. A romantic *nom de guerre* perhaps but…

Symonds frowned. 'Thankfully we haven't seen them close to Echuca, though being on a transport route of course we heard a lot of detail from people coming through from Melbourne and other directions where the Kelly gang proliferated. Some could even speak of dealings with and against them and they have many supporters. Their cause is something of a vexed question, as much of their hatred stems from when the British landowners were instrumental in causing the famine in Ireland…'

'Oh yes! I remember, I know all that. Papa had some Irish men coming to the farm looking for work. They stayed a while and our overseer, Mr Dent, found some of them work round about, also. Papa spoke out against Queen Victoria at every opportunity and though he saw a farmer's side of the question, the landowners – they who sought only profit and status – thought he should appreciate their point of view. Papa took the view that no man who never tills the land should seek to exploit others in order to make a profit. There was much of that. The absentee landlords gained an unpleasant reputation amongst many working farmers – landowners also, but only of the properties they worked! Mama was made quite uncomfortable in public by some women who took another point of view. Many of those women were merely parroting their husband's pompous assertions. They probably had few opinions of their own.'

No one spoke and Anderson was looking at her through narrowed eyes.

She continued. 'I've probably shocked you, Anderson. But many English people protested when the famine became widely known. Papa and some other farmers up our way sent wagon loads of flour and potatoes, and oh, lots of useful things, over to the worst affected areas; they were helped and encouraged by the various churches. Papa used to say it was too little too late and I feel that too, but it was a certain class of person guilty, not the normal English people. You know, I remember debating this with Mrs Lee and Evelyn one evening. They hold firm views on that situation. We had some vigorous discussion, believe me! May I say that although I sympathised, and protested along with my father, I do feel it is wrong that such a hatred has persisted and been brought across the oceans to this new country. And I'm sure that robbing and shooting innocent men and women, particularly those who try to uphold the law, is no way of securing any kind of justice.'

No one responded.

She continued, 'I myself have learned how relaxed Australian attitudes are in comparison to my experiences back home – well, in my growing up days. Here I can speak more freely, do work without it being considered unsuitable for one of my class – oh, and in many other ways! For instance, if I dislike some objectionable tall poppy, I can speak against him – or her – and am free to do so.'

Anderson leaned forward. 'In Wales there is a rumbling dislike of

English law dating from even further back in history. I'm glad your father thought like that about the Irish famine, and I have to agree with you about this country but what's this tall poppy talk? News to me!'

Symonds gave a short laugh. 'Beatrice is well read! It is a metaphor for celebrated people, notables. Some attribute the phrase to that worthy ancient Greek, Aristotle. I heard it in Melbourne in relation to a court case and I believe it was used about fifteen years ago here in Australia – there was some controversy over an award…' He paused, looked thoughtful then resumed. 'If I am right – and I am recalling a newspaper report, you understand – it is believed to relate to men whose social position is sufficient to make them formidable, in conflict with the minister of the day. This in the context of being a sort of public proclamation that the recipient is a tall poppy and though, in these days, their head cannot be struck off as I believe was the way in the time of the Greek philosophers. For some, it is worthwhile bestowing the honour to buy loyalty. I would say, with such friends, who needs enemies?'

Beatrice smiled. 'I read it in Livy's *Histories of Rome* – I think that's the title. He writes of the tyrannical Roman king, Tarquin the Proud, who received a messenger from his son Sextus Tarquinius asking for advice as to what to do with some wealthy opposition in the area of Gabii. According to Livy, Tarquin didn't answer but went into his garden, took a stick and symbolically swept it across the plants, cutting off the heads of the tallest poppies that were growing there. The messenger, tired of waiting for an answer, returned to Gabii and told Sextus what he had seen. Sextus considered that his father wished him to put to death all of the most eminent people of Gabii, which he then did.'

A loud clapping of hands came from Lucy. 'Oh, it is no wonder I can learn so much from you, Beatrice. You are so clever. We read some of the ancient philosophers – or rather, Miss Ball read tales out to class to improve us, she said – but they were usually more about battles and between Saxons and Gauls and things to keep the lads in the class happy.'

Everyone laughed at Lucy's enthusiastic appreciation, though Beatrice felt her cheeks pink up a little when Arthur actually gave her a slow wink!

# 42

Sissy suddenly sat up and bustled from the room. 'Oh, my goodness, the potatoes will be burnt and you'll be chopping my head off! Lucy, get up girl and fix the tables!'

Everyone laughed.

Anderson said he'd better check on the stable lad and the wheel and declined Symond's offer of help. 'Nay, Arthur, you've been a great help already. Stay with Beatrice. We'll meet over dinner.'

Symonds looked over at Beatrice. 'Would this be a tactical withdrawal on their part? Must admit, I am pleased for an opportunity to speak with you. There is a lot on my mind, Beatrice, you see, and most of it concerns you.'

She looked at him as if to speak but he put his finger to his lips. 'Please, Beatrice, let me speak first. You see, I know you think me too forward, perhaps unbecomingly so. Am I right? That upsets me, I have to say, but I cannot indulge in pretty phrases – innuendo. I speak plainly. Some have criticised me for being…brusque? But I do want you to like me, Beatrice. To trust me and eventually think of me with more than simple liking. Beatrice, how best to say it? I am paying suit to you.'

She brought her hands to her mouth and stared at him. He didn't flinch, nor pause.

'Beatrice, I have thought of you almost every day – no, almost every minute of most days, to be quite honest! I am soon to be thirty years old. I feel ready to have a dear partner and in due course a family. You are the woman of my thoughts and dreams, Beatrice. Yes, I say dreams, and I cannot believe I am confessing to dreams, yet I do not aspire to fantasy often. In fact, I doubt I have ever done so before.' He leaned forward in his seat. 'I am a decent person, honest, I believe, and well enough set-up financially to be considered a reasonable prospect. Can you not consider me a possible suitor – or is that just too rapid a development for you?'

She sat, her body immobile, her mind racing. 'Arthur, forgive me. Yes, this is too much too soon for me to absorb – I think that is the word I'm looking for. I don't know that I could be the partner you want. You see – well, little more than a year ago, I was ready to marry and become a dutiful wife, following my husband wherever he was made to go. Fate then stepped in, dealt me a few blows and, in recovering from them, I made promises to myself. I didn't know much of anything, so I realised. I felt quite lost… In fact, here at Bridgewater with the wonderful support of these local people, I believe I have found myself.'

Symonds sat, elbows on his knees, chin on his knuckled hands, listening intently. Beatrice was not to know he was as fascinated by her flexible features, as intrigued by the expressions fleeting across her face, by her determination to express her opinions, as whatever opinions she mouthed. But opinions she had – and he made up his mind to listen.

'Arthur, I learned quickly what I can do with my own abilities, talents. I had to. It came as a surprise – and here I am being very honest with you – that with those intrinsic attributes, I have learned to bring to the fore other skills that I think were suppressed by the dictates of my lifestyle, my place in society and by my choice of husband, God rest him. I believe deeply that true partnerships in marriage are more than show pony wedding days and festivities. Marriage requires dedication, loyalty and many other values I hold dear. My husband let me down – he gambled away what he had and expected my dowry to finance our beginnings in this new country, confident that my imagined wealth would be his, as is stated in the Act. To be frank, I have wondered since if it was the expectations of my dowry to cushion a new life in Australia that prompted his proposal in the first place!'

Arthur sat back. 'Beatrice, take a breath, do! Tell me. Are you saying you would not feel it your duty to contribute to a marriage?'

'No, I am not saying that! I would, in all ways, play my part. Yet I had no part to play in James's expectations of my supposed dowry, his apparent intention to finance his gambling – his status. Nor, ironically, did I have the dowry he thought I had! He had no idea, nor did he care how I would feel. That is apparent and it upset and angered me to the point I question the very concept of sharing in a marriage, as described by law. But I would work with and for any man I could respect, would like and, yes, maybe even love. However, this idyllic state would need to be reciprocal. I have learned that loyalty needs to be returned. I would expect no less from a partner than I am prepared to give. I have learned to doubt my own instincts in judging people, Arthur. How can I be sure to choose the right person? I am maybe too much at fault in that only lately have I realised my abilities and learned to value my independence of thought and action. Is it too much for me to expect a partner, and I am meaning husband in this context, to encourage me and support me in pursuing my own interests as I want to do?'

'Whoa, Beatrice! That is quite a speech and you sound like one of those women seeking enfranchisement! No, do not frown at me, Beatrice, please. Your friend Mrs Lee and I have had quite some discussions on the topic and I do agree with the aims of the suffragists – but not with the aggression, the militancy of some. I consider that type self-defeating in that they further animosity to their cause. Yet listening to you, I must ask you – are you seeking a Magna Carta prior to any contract?'

She broke into laughter. 'What kingly aspirations, Arthur. But in a way, yes, I am, I think. As I said, marriage is all about compromise. If I agree to a partnership, I can promise I will not do all the taking, I will also do as much giving as I am given. And more as needed.'

As if on cue, in came Lucy to warn them midday dinner would be served soon. 'But not in here please, sir and miss – the small dining room, if you please.'

Beatrice raised her eyebrows at the formality. 'Thank you, Lucy. I will go and wash my hands. I dare say Mr Symonds will too.'

Despite its prelude, it was a pleasant repast. Sissy left Lucy in charge and joined them, Anderson poured the Hahndorf wine from a stone jar. That led to discussing the township and then the recent wedding.

'It was nearly three months ago, Sissy!' laughed Beatrice. She turned to Symonds. 'You will meet my friend Kate and Herbert tomorrow night – they are coming for dinner.'

'Yes,' giggled Sissy. 'Kate wants to meet you, Arthur, erm…Mr Symonds.'

'Does she now? Well, I hope I'm up to scratch, Mrs Woof! Nice to know you were talking about me, hmm? I'll look forward to talking with Kate, I think…'

Anderson reached over and took Sissy's glass. 'I'll finish that for you, Cecily Woof, or we'll none of us get a meal tonight!' He turned to Beatrice. 'We have no bookings for a meal tonight, Beatrice, so please don't feel you need play the piano. Why not show Mr Symonds something of our little town. It's a fine day, if a bit windy – good for a walk.'

Beatrice had no time to demur, as Symonds nodded his agreement.

'I'll be in on that, Anderson. Thank you. Come, Beatrice, do, and show me something of this pretty town. There is a post office, I believe? I need to send a letter.'

*

Beatrice was a little unsure of walking into the town alongside Arthur. People were always too ready to interpret a situation according to their own wishes and were too ready to do so, in her estimation. She tried to avoid walking too closely together but he took her arm when the road surface roughened, and tucked it into his. Despite her hesitation, she had to admit they fitted well together.

He looked keenly around him and was obviously quite impressed. 'It is a pleasant little town, Beatrice – plenty of trees for shade. It's a busy one too.'

The school yard was emptying and students of all ages were pouring onto the street.

'Don't they stay in school until later? Three o'clock is surely too soon?'

'It's always earlier on Fridays. I don't give music lessons on Fridays either. There is a very good reason – many chores related to the family farms and orchards are planned for the weekend when the children are available. They work hard then – and in summer, depending on their crops and harvest, many of the students, even the youngest ones, are out in the fields before they reach school in the morning!'

'What fruits grow so prolifically that such labour is necessary?'

'Oh, it's not always picking fruit. See that field? It's a poor soil on that hill and they'll be picking up stones – they seem to be doing that endlessly. Other farms have cleared trees and youngsters have to clear the areas of stumps – depending on the trees, of course. I have often thought there isn't much time for play but they are all happy youngsters and everyone seems to be friendly with everyone else. I like the town, I like the people. I really do. What's more, they accept me as belonging to their community. It is a feeling that is becoming very important to me.'

They ambled along, side by side, passing through a rowdy, dusty cluster of boys leaving the schoolyard.

Beatrice smiled. 'Boys cannot talk. Have you noticed, Arthur? Boys shout!'

He laughed. Then became solemn-faced. 'Beatrice, I must tell you, I have to return to Echuca next week. Perhaps leaving here on Sunday. I don't know when I can come next, but I shall make it as soon as I can. Will you be pleased to see me, Beatrice?'

They'd reached the bench under the tree opposite the post office and she gathered her long skirt around her and sat down. She patted the space next to her and he sat.

'Arthur, I was listening, you know. I understand. I do feel you deserve to know…'

His face dropped. 'Oh, I see…'

'No, no, I don't think you do. Arthur, I have given as much thought to your comments as I've been able in the last couple of hours. Please know that I do like you, very much. It's just that – well, I have always believed in honesty and I prefer the direct approach. As you do. It prevents misinterpretation so please, please, let me speak. I have no other gentleman friend I can say is close, Arthur. I know and have learned of myself – we have spoken of all that – I do want a partner I can trust, as well as all the other values, and then eventually have children, being one of a family again. I know I would be a good wife and mother, eventually. I feel it in myself. Now, is that person you, Mr Arthur Symonds, engineer? Would you be the partner I seek?' She turned to look into his face. 'I like you. Very much actually.'

She looked down; his hand was resting on his knee and she picked it up, closed her two hands over it and looked into his eyes again. 'I think I could return your feelings, Arthur. But so much has happened to me, so many changes have come into my life in such a short time – relatively speaking – that, well, I need more time to be certain.'

He lifted his hands and held her face in them, looking intently into her eyes. 'If there were not these noisy school ragamuffins still within hearing and seeing distance, Beatrice, I would kiss you here and now. It might help you decide about me. Do you think so?'

'Hush, Arthur, please. I am trying to be frank with you. I have not been kissed for a long time and I cannot say I would not enjoy the experience, but with Mr Rogers coming out from the post office and you shortly to go in there and post your letter, it may be sensible to be discreet.'

He sat back and smiled. 'Damn, Beatrice. I will catch you later, be forewarned!'

# 43

Beatrice was careful to keep the rest of their walk in full view of any passing people and open window curtains and doors. But Arthur needed to post his letter and Mrs Bones waved from the schoolyard, where she was sweeping up some litter scattered by the students, 'Halloo-oo, Beatrice!' so she walked over on her own to greet her musical co-conspirator.

Within a few moments and his business concluded in the post office, Arthur joined her at the school wall. Beatrice introduced Arthur as Mr Symonds 'from the inn' and pretended not to notice Mrs Bones's questioning look to her, as the latter bobbed in greeting. They exchanged some chat, Arthur stoically agreeing that fourteen-year-old boys could be 'a handful' for a woman teacher.

Other townsfolk familiar to Beatrice suddenly appeared on the road as from nowhere and Beatrice thought if Mrs Bones bobbed her head any more it would drop off! When Mrs Rogers appeared outside the post office, Beatrice only waved in return and quickened her step.

Arthur laughed. 'I met Mr Rogers indoors but I think they will know me by now!'

As they strode up the hill back to the inn, making a fine speed, Beatrice caught a stone in her shoe. He took her elbow as she removed the shoe, which he took and, having shaken the offending grit free of it, gently replaced on her foot. He took her hand, reached for the other hand and, bending, touched her brow gently with his lips.

Beatrice caught her breath. She looked back at his solemn expression while, slowly, her caution dissolved. Her brain registered the exquisiteness of that feeling; her body, deep inside, was more effectively stirred than in any hurried passion. The touch from his lips was being indelibly marked by the breeze upon her face. Her breath seemed to be locked in, somewhere beneath her heart – that same place that had been so chilled when her mother died. And even when James…

He stood back, watching the emotions fly across her face. His hand was warm on hers, holding and waiting, as she tried to draw in air.

'Arthur…'

'We discuss over-much, Beatrice. Did you know that, according to one of the grooms in the yard here – he told me when we were fixing the wheel – that I speak stuffier, that was his word, than even you when you first arrived! Anderson joined in, said that you wouldn't say a word if a sentence would do! I think we need to learn straight talking, Beatrice. My old father used to tell me to call a spade a spade and not a shovel. So, Beatrice Beauchamp – or Fletcher, as you now prefer – I love you. I want you as a man wants a woman, and you are the woman I want to marry.'

'Arthur! Marriage? I'm not ready to marry anyone. I've made one mistake and, oh, please understand! I cannot bear to repeat it!'

His eyes narrowed. 'Beatrice, do not, *not*, compare me with him.' His gentle holding on her hand became a determined grip. He led her at a faster pace the short way up to the inn and behind the walled garden. None too gently he pushed her against its stones; their warmth from the afternoon sun reached through her back bodice.

Time seemed to stand still. The magpie flew near and perched atop the wall, watching curiously. The familiar scents and sounds of the trees and shrubs around her were suddenly amplified, each competing to overwhelm her with its richness. Her legs were weak and she was glad of the wall's support behind them. She didn't flinch at the rough stone against her back; she could feel only the long length of him as he pressed against her.

Finally, she spluttered, 'I wasn't comparing you – marrying him was my mistake and mine only.'

He braced himself against her, his hands on the wall either side of her head. 'Beatrice, I am not James. Just ask yourself – did he make you feel like this?' He crushed his mouth to hers in a hot angry kiss.

She arched against him but couldn't know if it was in protest or pleasure. The kiss went on… Sensations hurtled through her mind and body; it was all heat and light and a hot, hot anger. Yet even though her anger fuelled her, her body betrayed her and she responded – soft moans escaping her as she railed against all the logic, all the sensible, balanced discussion of the past two days.

He released his hold, then came nearer and nibbled her lip, softly, gently. She felt burnt, consumed. This was a new experience. James had never… Her defences deserted her. A storm of frantic emotion swept through her bringing perspiration to her brow and goosebumps to her arms. She quivered almost violently and he released her, his eyes glinting with what she read as success, angrily, exultantly.

He placed his hands on her shoulders, almost apologetically. Almost. 'I love you, Beatrice. I will be your husband and I will make you love me.'

An angry voice bellowed from behind the mulberry tree. 'Sissy! Bring my gun will you! Those dratted rabbits are in the beans!'

*Anderson! He must not see us together!*

Beatrice fought to catch her breath as she turned in panic and ran back round to the front yard of the inn. She was shaking, though whether or not with anger she couldn't think. She could hear Anderson now calling out to Arthur. She lost her shoe again, picked it up and hopped around to the front gates before putting it on. She stood, breathing deeply and straightening her skirts. Some decorum was required. Anderson had seen Arthur and was swearing about rabbits…it carried over the walls. She must go in…

Lucy met her in the reception area of the inn. 'Beatrice, I've put fresh water in a bath for you in your room. I thought you might like it after your walk and I can see now you look a little hot – and windblown.'

*Walk? Ah, yes, that was before…* Windblown? 'Thank you, Lucy.'

\*

As she lowered herself into her bath, she felt as if steam would arise from her skin. He had set her on fire – the presumption of the man! However, the bath was blissful, the water warm, and the perfumed soap worked up a comforting lather as she laid back on the metal. Her lips felt bruised and her bottom lip stung a little but didn't bleed, nor did it stop her musing. *I've never been kissed like that before. Am I so angry because I liked it? Even on our honeymoon James's kisses didn't stir me like that, I didn't feel them, that tingling, down there, not in the very depths of me, as Arthur's kisses did. Oh, Mama, remember when we were reading* Wuthering Heights? *Mamzelle could not understand it and you and I laughed at her? But Emily Bronte wrote of the human soul, did she not?*

204

'Oh, where's the soap…'

*I remember a passage – was it Catherine? 'I have dreamt in my life, dreams that have stayed with me ever after, and changed my ideas; they have gone through and through me, like wine through water, and altered the colour of my mind.' And Arthur Symonds, engineer, once lieutenant, am I to change my ideas? You are going away again soon and want an answer before… I want to say yes. I want to, to promise to wait for you… Oh a serious question he set upon me, a serious answer he deserves. Those kisses reminded me in a way I think no one else can, that I am a woman. I still have a woman's urgings, I have not forgotten. Yes, I could marry him because like he says he is a decent man… What was it Emily Bronte wrote? Erm… 'Whatever our souls are made of, his and mine are the same.'*

A knock came on her door. 'It's me, Lucy. Beatrice, are you all right in there?

*Goodness me!* 'I lost the soap, that's all, Lucy! I'll be out soon. I have latched the door.'

She lay back again. So there was no piano tonight unless she wanted to. Hopefully some time therefore to chat, and conversation with Anderson and Sissy present should preclude any intentions Arthur had of grabbing her in an embrace. The very thought caused her to blush and her fingertips and toes to tingle. She felt her skin grow warm despite the cooling water and slipped further down in the hope her skin would cool also. *Oh, my goodness, my body betrays my mind.*

Typically on cue, Lucy knocked on the door again. Please can I come and take the bathwater, Beatrice? I don't want to be late to dinner either. I might play and sing, says Mother.'

'Just getting out, Lucy. I'll call you soon…' *It's not only Lucy who'll be late. Beattie, 'tis you! I think you should organise your thoughts and actions, define a strategy.*

# 44

Beatrice had so often been in the habit of slipping onto the piano seat and teasing the short keyboard into her popular adaptations, it was strange sitting at evening dinner with the others. At first it was only her and Symonds at table, as Sissy bustled in to explain Anderson was caught up in the bar with some local residents – they wanted only bar food and were making quite a lot of cheerful noise arguing about which team won in a local football match.

'I'll join you when I've sorted the dessert. Mrs Jack's giving me a hand.'

Anderson brought in a stone jar of the Hahndorf vintage for Arthur and Beatrice to enjoy until the food arrived. 'I'll join you as soon as that bar lot clear off! But I've asked Lucy to play and sing for us tonight, so you take it easy, Beatrice. Good practice for Lucy, her mother says. The help's in the kitchen so Lucy can get off and make herself pretty.'

Arthur smiled absent-mindedly in acknowledgement, seeming – to Beatrice's mind – almost subdued. 'Another tactical withdrawal, do you think?' He smiled without waiting for her comment, just continued with polite conversation about the closing in of the seasons, the strange fat sheep a local farmer had brought over from New South Wales to improve his stock, and the busyness of the local post office.

Such a mix of topics! Was he avoiding too personal a conversation? Not that Beatrice wanted anything more personal at the moment, but it occurred to her he might be cast down about her comments earlier; if so, she hoped he wouldn't talk too much about their afternoon walk. She was most relieved when he joked that Anderson needed to buy a more reputable fowling piece to use in his battle against crows and rabbits. She started to relax a little. Not only did the tone of his conversation lighten, he made a mischievous remark, to her mind, about the sturdiness of the stone boundary wall, the one he'd pushed her onto earlier.

She maintained a studiously blank expression. *Papa always said attack to defend, yes, but don't be too ready to rise to the bait...* Despite her inner tension, she was determined to keep up with the more cheerful tone of his conversation and rallied when he asked about the fruit, the apple and cherry orchards in the area and how long they'd been established; she knew something of this. He asked if she knew which property James and the Taylors had wanted and if it was near. She didn't; hadn't enquired further after discovering James's treachery.

He then surprised her by speaking of a proposition put to him in Echuca by an orchardist. 'He was on one of the boats heading downriver and wanting to look at some land near a Lake Bonney.'

She shook her head. 'Bonney is a strange name. Must have been called that by one of the explorers we hear about. Bonny means beautiful, to me anyway.' She considered for a moment. 'Anderson's a store of information – he might know. But why?'

'There's even a vineyard growing up that way, at Napper's Ridge, I believe, and irrigation is well advanced there.'

'Goodness me! James was changing *his* career to be an orchardist. Not you too, Arthur?'

He looked at her quizzically. 'It's all about irrigation for me, Beatrice, and the means of it. Around that Lake Bonney, people are talking of the possibility of the whole area being a rich orchard for food supplies – to help the colony in general. Or both colonies, I suppose, Victoria as well, as it is near to the border. I do feel, you see, that the trade down the river, on the boats and barges, is waning somewhat. The trains to Melbourne are being used more often – by the wool growers, certainly. They use the barges to collect their wool but it's quicker and cheaper for them now to send it from Echuca on the train to Melbourne, not downstream to Adelaide. Not only that, the river levels fluctuate and this drought is likely to continue over the next year – so I've been warned. Irrigators might be in greater demand than river boats. John Lee was talking to me about the geography of the area and water allocations and such, as they affect men laying or planning telegraph cables. Also, I had a man on one of the barges telling me of his uncle, who had a hotel about twenty or thirty years ago at a place called Overland Corner. Doesn't that name ring sweetly in your ears? I asked John about it and he's actually been there. Imagine the geography of the place – named for the drovers who brought their stock through from New South Wales to South Australia – quite poetic.'

He sipped his wine. 'His hotel was the Lake Bonney and he made a good living with the drovers. That name really appeals to me.'

'It's always the hotels, the inns that found country towns here, or so it seems to me.'

He smiled and shrugged but continued. 'That's as may be, Beatrice, but you see, if that area develops, engineers with the special knowledge I have could be in demand. I've heard the present owner, a William Napper, has established vineyards and fruit orchards and intends expanding his irrigation and – this is good news – using steam engine pumps! My very profession, Beatrice, and that is where my interest truly lies. My first career was in pumps and I love the way they can command the river's flow to man's profit and betterment.'

He refilled his glass and topped up hers – she had only sipped her drink, finding herself more interested this time in his future planning.

'You see, Beatrice. I'm more a land animal than I thought. Sea legs I've had, river legs too. I love the power of water, the beauty of it and the way in which we can engineer it to our better good. Don't need to be on it all the time.'

He could see he'd aroused her interest; he leaned over the table and wrapped his hand around hers. 'To work with water from a land base; helping it enrich the soil and then establish a foothold on it for me – and my family – that is what I would really like to do. I think there is a future here for people like me – like us, Beatrice – with specialist knowledge, the energy and the goodwill.'

She smiled but eased her hand away from his and held up a cautionary finger. 'Arthur, I must admit, I am impressed. You have an ability to look ahead that I envy. There is a new word, "trends" – like solving future directions. You seem able to define those trends. It is an admirable skill. As for me… In the last few months I have been concentrating on building up my interests and involvement in what is around me and working out how to fit into this community. I realise I have to move on, but…' She smiled. 'John Benjamin told me to go forward and I have tried to understand the meaning of that. I had tentatively thought of governessing, or even becoming a typewriter or telephonist/telegrapher to obtain a position such as Evelyn enjoys.'

He made no response.

She took another sip. 'I like what you are planning, Arthur. Please do write to me with your plans, your achievements, after you leave here. Do let us be in regular communication.'

He sat back in his chair, obviously shocked by her suggestion. 'Oh, Beatrice. What does a man have to do? Writing, you say? That smacks of distance between us and a long separation.' He slapped his hand on the table in frustration. 'Look, I know I cannot promise when I'll be back but... Aah, here's Lucy... Do, please, let us speak tomorrow.'

# 45

His frown disappeared as he spoke to Lucy. 'You look very lovely, Lucy. Some man will be very lucky to win you one day. Do come and join us.'

Beatrice welcomed the diversion. 'Lucy, that new dress looks lovely on you. You are so clever with embroidery. And you've fixed a semi-bustle. That really makes you look so elegant. Do twirl... Oh yes, that is lovely. Now, come and sit down.' She patted the chair next to her.

Lucy blushed in pleasure at the compliment. 'Mam – erm – Mother says I may have a small sherry and then, if you don't mind, I would like to play. Anderson has been showing me some of his Welsh songs and I have copied the music – I think – so I can sing them to him. And some others he's always whistling, so I've tried to remember them...' She whispered to Beatrice. 'You heard me practising, didn't you, but you didn't know it's his birthday. I thought it'd be a nice surprise!' Lucy rustled off to the piano.

Sissy came in, behind a trolley burdened with plates and roast chicken and vegetables. 'Here's dinner, my dears, and Anderson's on his way now. He's closed the door and Jack can watch the yard. Zed's out there with 'im. Anderson doesn't want a fuss, but it's his birthday today – he's turning fifty and five! Time is catching up on us all – hahha hee.' She giggled. 'Hard to think of my brother as getting old – and me catching up too fast.'

Anderson came in and Lucy broke into a lilting, happy tune, one even Beatrice didn't recognise, to salute his entrance! He grinned and gave a portly bow and that set the tone for the evening. Arthur stood up and shook his hand in congratulations and Beatrice, to her own surprise, found herself kissing Anderson's whiskery cheek.

Sissy beamed and beckoned Lucy to the table. Conversation somehow swung from cabbage tree hats to bushrangers. There had been notices in the newspapers that the Kellys were on the warpath again but where they were heading was only speculation. Lucy looked worried but Anderson said all the talk was of somewhere in Victoria, not around there. Symonds paid attention as this followed on a few rumours he'd heard in Echuca before leaving. Anderson expanded on the evils of Captain Moonlite, who'd been hanged in Sydney back in January. He was delighted that back in April, the Victorian government had withdrawn its offer of a reward for the Kelly gang's capture, as he put it. Lucy looked worried and asked if that would only mean they would be free to do as they liked.

Arthur wanted to reassure her. 'Worry not, Lucy. Ned Kelly and his fellow malcontents seem to have disappeared. I heard that two of his sisters tried to buy passages for some of the men and their families to California, some months ago, I believe.'

Anderson was quite wound up. 'No, Arthur, lad. They don't disappear, not that lot. Jack tells me he heard from that carrier bloke that Ned Kelly's after an informer called Sherritt. Been telling the police about the gang, apparently. Seems he wanted Ned's sister but she wouldn't oblige, so he sought revenge on the Kellys. That's what it's all about. Nasty piece o' work, they feel.'

'Huh. That's pot callin' the kettle black that is,' muttered Sissy, draining the gravy onto their plates. 'So let's enjoy our meal without any of that nasty stuff, if you please!'

Arthur raised his eyebrows at Lucy and gave her a wink. 'A very good idea, Mrs Woof, and I'm looking forward to hearing Lucy on the piano. I'm thinking you may have some special music in mind, Lucy. Is that not right!'

Lucy just smiled shyly at Arthur and tackled her meat with increased energy. Beatrice smiled inwardly. *Dear sweet Lucy. She's fallen for Arthur's charms and has already confided that he's her favourite gentleman, a genuine compliment. Loves his eyes. Hmm. Rauf the younger had best look to his laurels!*

Sissy rose from the table. 'Pudding tonight is Anderson's favourite in honour of his birthday – rice custard and strawberry jam.'

At her speech, in rushed Mrs Jack to clear the table and, under cover of the activity, Beatrice and Arthur exchanged looks clearly stating a lack of enthusiasm for rice pudding. Lucy broke into laughter and Sissy turned, realising the joke.

She grinned at them. 'It's all right for those who don't like it. I have pears and apples to choose from with a piece of goat cheese, an' some of today's bread.'

That was more to Arthur's taste, though Beatrice decided she'd eaten her fill. Truth to tell, she was in a bit of a tizz-wazz, as Mamzelle would have said. These references to the Lees, too… Had he spoken to Mary and John about her? She hoped not but decided not to make a fool of herself by asking. So Arthur wants to talk tomorrow? Hmm. She knew what he wanted, so that meant planning and rehearsing what to say. Also, she was to play over dinner tomorrow night. She would need to decide on the music, concentrate on playing and introduce him to Kate and Herbert. The atmosphere needed to be amicable, at the very least. Oh dear!

Lucy excused herself and moved over to the piano. 'Dear Uncle Anderson. I have been practising some tunes for you with Beatrice helping me adopt – no, adapt – them. You know this first one because I've heard you whistling it and it needed no adapting 'cos it were…was… written for the clavichord and by that big, wicked Welsh King Henry that beheaded his wives.' She broke into 'Greensleeves'.

Anderson was touched and mopped his eyes with his big fat finger, then standing up, called out, 'Again, Lucy, love, please,' and he started to whistle a beautifully clear counterpoint, a descant.

When he sat down, they all clapped, including Lucy.

Anderson swigged a drink then sat, hands waving in rhythm as Lucy started off with 'Lavender Blue, Dilly Dilly…' At the second verse, he broke into the words in a decent baritone that quite surprised Beatrice. And so the scene was set for the next hour. Lucy would play another folksy piece and Anderson would break into song.

Sissy was beaming from ear to ear. 'Aye, he knows most of 'em, 'e does.'

Then Anderson sat down, drained his glass and looked as if he'd be falling asleep, so the ever-alert Sissy pulled his sleeve and signalled it was time for him to get to bed.

'Come help me, Lucille. Between us, an' Jack an' Zed, we'll get cleaned and locked up.'

Beatrice gave Lucy a hug, Arthur stood, bowed and kissed her hand. She blushed in innocent charm, stammered 'Goodnight' and moved to help steer a happy but tired Anderson through the door..

Arthur stayed on his feet. 'If you will excuse me, Beatrice, I will retire too. I have a letter I must write before sleep. We shall meet in the morning as we break our fast, I assume.'

And with that, she too received a kiss on her hand, then he left the room.

Beatrice looked at the vein on the back of her hand; it was a gesture so unexpected. But what exactly had she expected? Discussion? Argument? Whatever she had fretted about, it had not happened. The evening had been most enjoyable, time spent with friends, good friends, and one who wanted to be more than a friend...

The room, so busy until a few minutes ago, seemed unnaturally silent. Beatrice checked through some of the piano music, closed the keyboard lid, and with another sigh walked along the deck to her own room. She smiled widely as she walked by Anderson's; his loud snores were already resounding in the night-time silence.

# 20 June 1880

## 46

Beatrice woke to the warmth of a shaft of sunlight light shining across her bedspread and touching her cheek. The magpie was warbling beyond her door, a sure sign other people were up and about. She stretched, tensing her muscles from neck to toes. Realisation dawned in concert with the day. This was Arthur's last day, or so he'd said, and he wanted to 'talk'.

He'd made his intentions known to her and he was wanting answers. Would it be too hard to promise to wait for him, to be hand-fasted here, to marry at some future date? Even as she asked herself the question, her body answered. She closed her eyes, savouring a thrill of anticipation starting in the core of her body and extending upwards, slowly, leisurely, until she caught her breath. Yes, she was a woman and she wanted a man, an honourable man, one sincere in his affections and, naturally enough, one who could support a wife, a home and, yes, eventually a family. Was that man Arthur Francis Symonds, ex-lieutenant of the *Orient* and a steam pump engineer?

She stood to wash and dress her hair. Those qualities she had thought to find in James. Since James's death she had wondered whether or not such practicalities were enough for a marriage. She doubted she had ever loved him, as love was felt by Elizabeth Bennett for Mr Darcy in Miss Austen's story. And exactly what was meant by the phrase 'in love'? The story was make-believe but other than reading of it and testing her own emotions, how else was a young lady of fine breeding allowed to learn of love? In her own situation, had she been inhibited by her mother's pride and her father's prejudice? Surely Arthur's kiss, the way it made her feel, was significant?

She brushed her hair vigorously. *I admire his hair; I wonder how it would feel to pass my fingers through it… Does he notice mine?* She remonstrated with her feelings of doubt. 'And I contradict them with my wish to impress, and why? Come, Beatrice, do dress, do! The green gingham this morning and a loose bun at the neck, a ringlet each side in front of the ears. You are prevaricating…'

Maybe it was time to try the new style, with a fringe across the forehead? And no ringlets? She surveyed her face in the looking glass, wondering whether the new hairstyle would suit her face. Lucy had obtained a Sydney newspaper, left behind by one of the visitors, in which there was an illustration of it, with the hair cut across in a line above the eyebrows – and no parting. Beatrice liked to keep abreast of new ideas and new styles but this fringe was severe in its presentation. *It seems harsh, gives too much emphasis to the nose and detracts from the eyes and my eyes are my better feature. Also, the new style would need regular clipping and cutting to keep its form. I doubt if I would be bothered…*

Lucy's knock echoed on the door. 'Breakfast's ready, Beatrice!'

Time to go.

Anderson was sitting in the small parlour with Arthur, who was sounding forth about some government policy or other. Sissy could be heard in the kitchen apparently arguing about eggs. Beatrice managed a smile: situation normal. She moved to the table.

Arthur turned, stood and pulled out her chair. He smiled. 'Good morning, Beatrice.'

Anderson just wiggled his fingers and pointed to his mouth full of toast.

Beatrice spooned a small portion of porridge into a bowl and added some honey. Arthur and Anderson were devoting themselves to their own breakfast, and silence reigned until Sissy bustled in with a plate of coddled eggs and fresh toast.

'Take as you wish onto your own plates, if you please. I am guiding Mrs Jack in the art of ginger beer making and cannot leave her longer, so excuse…'

Anderson beamed. 'I deal in ales of many kinds and qualities but there's little to equal my sister's ginger beer!' He picked up a last piece of toast and, with a loud, unapologetic burp, exited the room to watch the process.

Arthur lifted coddled eggs on to his plate. 'Beatrice, the letter I needed to write last night…it was to Mr Napper. I think I mentioned him.'

Beatrice took some eggs and waited for him to comment further. This planning was so practical – so commonsensical, as dear Mary would say, which was good, but Beatrice wanted a cue to introduce some more personal feelings into the discussion. She started to speak but he resumed his plate, completing his repast in short order. She recovered and endeavoured to empty her plate too. He continued with his planning…

'I need, Beatrice, to complete my contract with Echuca first – that is in November. I cannot leave them earlier without penalty and certainly cannot afford to lose money that way. I am hoping this Mr Napper will allow me to join him as late as January. I understand that is when the grapes will be fleshing out and irrigation is perhaps more important earlier in their season. However, we will see… Beatrice, dear girl, have you given any thought to our discussion yesterday? Would you be willing to come with me to the river lands? Will you be with me, both of us expanding our interests? I'm sure I can build a career on my steam pump knowledge and we can also acquire land, a property.'

Aha – this was her cue. She put down her fork and swallowed. 'Arthur, I have thought much on what you said. You now think you will be away until about November and then come and stay until after Christmas before going to your new position? Hmm… I see… You say would I come with you. That has a hypothetical ring to it… Forgive me, but I need security. Are you asking me to marry you?'

'Oh, Beatrice!' Arthur slid from his chair onto one knee, looking up at her serious expression. 'Dear ex-Mrs Beauchamp, ex-Miss Fletcher, my Beatrice, will you do me the honour of becoming my wife? Perhaps on my return we may marry here amongst your friends? Then spend the Christmas season here before taking the boat from the Murray Bridge, one that will be there in early January to take us – me and you – to develop more irrigated acres for an employer and for ourselves?'

Beatrice, laughed, head back, and a fleeting shadow passed over his face as he feared caprice. No, her laugh was as hearty as spontaneous.

'Oh, Arthur, that is certainly a long and non-hypothetical proposal!' She stood, straightened her expression and looked steadily into his eyes. She reached for both his hands with both of hers. 'Yes, Arthur Francis Symonds, I will take your hands in marriage as I do give you my own…'

He had no time to respond – there was a gasp and a thud behind. They turned in unison to see Sissy bending to pick up a set of tablecloths.

'Oh me, oh my! I'm sorry, Beattie, Mr Symonds. Oh, I didn't mean to disturb...but oh! No, I'm not sorry! This is wonderful news!' She turned tail and ran through to the reception.

Beatrice and Arthur were both on their feet, arms around each other and shaking with silent laughter.

Head back, and still smiling, he looked earnestly into her eyes. 'Beatrice, there can be no secret now, my love. How long before all of the town knows of our match? How long before Sissy runs down the main street, skirts flying?'

'Arthur, do hush! Sissy is no garrulous chatterbox, she's a good friend, Until we give her permission, I wager her comments will go no further than her daughter and brother.'

'I'll take your word on it, my love. Quick, let us go out the back way, where you go walking, down to the creek, where we can be alone! And not overheard!'

# 47

The magpie flew off the fence and up into a nearby eucalypt, head cocked, watching the friendly woman trip down the path through his territory. She had no titbits for him. Nor was she alone. He watched as a baby rabbit squealed out from under the man's feet and disappeared into a tangled mass of wild correa, a perfect carpet hideaway for little animals. The magpie knew from past experience not to bother chasing rabbits in that tangle of weeds.

The pair ran down over the gravel and stones, dodging the rocks, then through the wild grasses still wet from the rain; she first and showing the way, holding the hand of the man behind, who was trying to find his feet – or keep them steady. He was on unfamiliar ground. She was laughing and he was urging her to slow down, slow down! The black and white bird continued to watch from his high viewpoint and waited until they stopped their noisy laughing and squealing until, in the way of humans, they stopped in their tracks at the side of the water and held each other close. Sensing that breadcrumbs and shredded bacon bits would not be on his menu this day, the magpie flew off in another direction..

Beatrice and Arthur had come to a stop on her favourite sitting space, the flat rock by the creek. It was wet, as were their shoes from the grasses, so each needed to curl their toes and keep their balance.

Being winter and after a rare good rain, the creek was running freely, stirring up the mud to hide the pebbles and lapping high enough up the rocks to spatter their boots. There was no sitting down this day! An energetic breeze was whirling around their legs and flicking around Beattie's hemline, lifting her skirts against her efforts to retain her modesty. She gave up, uncaring. There was only one other person here with her. He wouldn't care and she wouldn't mind.

She threw her arms high around Arthur's neck and he bent his head to kiss her, while lifting her off her feet. She thrilled at his kiss, at his strength and at the way in which they fitted together. He too registered her ready response yet sensed she was still holding something back; he recognised in her an inner core of strength and energy, qualities quite unforeseen while on the *Orient*. Of course, she had then been playing the role of respectable lady wife to an absent husband. But now…

He lifted her arms from around his neck and, laughing heartily, held her at arm's length. 'You'll know me as husband, my love. You'll recognise in me your match as I know you for mine.'

She threw back her head, her lilting tones reflecting her gaiety and echoing his own happiness. 'Oh, Arthur, how could I have doubted you, doubted myself and my own feelings? You make me feel strong and yet – as if in contradiction – my knees are weak and now I need to sit, wet rock or no.'

She took a skip to the higher, dry end of the rock, tugging him along with her; still hand-fast, he slipped to a seating position, pulling her down with him. They settled down on this part of the sun-warm rock, arms around each other's waist and their backs against one of the stubby little tea tree shrubs that Beatrice had once called Sissy's laundry bushes. The weight of their bodies crushed the tiny pink flowers, releasing the delicate perfume, as they watched the shifting clouds mask the hilly horizon and listened to the rushing of the water and the susurration of the low-growth shrubbery.

Beatrice was the first to break their silence. 'I don't know when I realised I needed you, Arthur. A part of me tells me I should still be in half-mourning. Were I at home, I might have graduated to purple or grey after six months – that is now – but that all seems so false and I cannot feel guilty. I mourn for James, yes, but more for the manner of his going than for the man I try to remember. Is that so unfeeling of me? I have been beset with such doubts, most of them not about how I feel about you but about how I should be feeling, behaving. Do you understand? I conclude it has been my English upbringing and my mother's insistence on being correct. Yet here, after only six months, I feel so ready to shed all those inhibitions, to feel free of them. I realise they are so artificial in my new chosen life. Was I really so shallow before? If I had truly loved the man, would I not still be in mourning, old customs or not? Yet it is over a year since I saw him last and I wonder now, and after…well, after it happened and how, I wonder if I ever did know the man? Did I really love him or was I so eager to please Mama and caught up in the idea of a beautiful gown, the wedding and such frivolities? At the morgue that dreadful day, I felt pity but, do you know, I worried more how I could tell my father and how I could fare out here on my own. I was embroiled with my own selfish miseries. Even since then, I have been fraught with private fears that I might be thought a loose woman for not caring. Do you think ill of me for that?'

'Hush, Beatrice. Do not distress yourself over what might not and might be appropriate. All I want from you is your love for me – that it is the kind that endures. For I am not perfect. I love my work and may in the future need to be away, leaving you at home, wherever our home may be. But I promise I will never give you cause to doubt my love and respect for you. James was…well, he was understandably almost a stranger to you by then. Why should you not have been caught up in the romanticism of a glorious wedding? You were together so short a while and then… All your Bridgewater friends here, and also Evelyn and Mrs Lee who knew you well in those early days, would not expect you to enact the pantomime of formal mourning. I certainly do not. Rest easy, my love. You will always have their respect, and mine.'

He freed his arm and stood upright, then bent over to take both her hands to pull her to her feet. He put his hands to her face and looked deep into her eyes. 'I love you, Beatrice, deeply and honourably. But we must be practical. I suggest as the day is developing, and you have a dinner concert to prepare for, we should tidy the twigs and blossoms off our persons, and walk back up to the inn. Lunch will have long passed but I suspect there will be Mrs Woof's glasses of celebration port to withstand upon our arrival! First, let me kiss you again – out of prying eyes…'

Back on his perch, always hopeful for a dainty morsel of stale bread, or bacon, the magpie watched the humans struggle to walk arm in arm up the narrow little track, laughing and talking together. A kookaburra dived towards the creek and in the mysterious ways of birds, the magpie knew it could mean a possible meal challenge. He swooped off and over the walkers' heads on the way.

'Oops!' Arthur swiped the air in panic as the wingspan brushed his ear and Beatrice laughed at his discomfiture.

# 48

The port glasses were waiting. Anderson and Sissy were standing ready, beaming from ear to ear.

Lucy looked a little overwhelmed. 'Oh, Beatrice, I am so happy for you. And for you, Mr Symonds. I understand why you love Beatrice. We all love her too!'

Anderson was shaking hands vigorously with Arthur. Sissy wiped her hands on her apron and enveloped Beatrice in a pastry-smelling hug so energetic Beatrice nearly lost her balance! However, Anderson was there to catch her and take his turn. Sissy looked a little uncertain at Arthur, who kissed her gently on each cheek then did the same to Lucy causing her to blush furiously.

Anderson raised his glass. '*Llongyfarchiadau* to you both. That means hearty congratulations in Welsh, my boyo. *Llongyfarchiadau!*'

Beatrice was almost moved to tears. 'Oh, that's lovely, Anderson,. Thank you. What a lovely word. Hhkl-ongy…. You must write it down for me!'

Anderson laughed. 'Tonight's dinner is going to be very special, Beatrice and Arthur, very special indeed. You know, when she heard the news before, our dear Sissy and Mrs Jack prepared a goose and Lucy has been beating eggs for those mer-ing-you things for a pudding – sorry, dessert, she says it is! So sip up, dear friends, and do no more than ready yourselves for this evening. Beatrice, we have people coming to listen to you who know your music – will you still play, perhaps a little, for them? Yet you must enjoy the evening yourself. An' we'll see that you do, so we will!' And he left the room.

Sissy smiled and whispered to Beatrice. 'He means meringues, Beattie, little crispy sugar puffs. Lucy calls 'em little wedding dresses an' she does 'em a treat. C'mon, Lucy, we'll let Beattie have some time to herself'

'Here, Arthur, have a lovely apple to bite into, as I will. What with

221

all the excitement, I really do not want anything more to eat, and by the sound of things, we had best retain our appetites for this evening. Oh yes, and you'll meet my dear Kate and her Herbert too.'

Biting into a large green apple, he led her out onto the deck. From apparently nowhere, the magpie swooped to the fence and clung there, head cocked.

Arthur bent towards her, whispering, 'Show me your room, please, Beatrice. While I am away, I can then imagine where you lie down at night, sit and read and write, and it will feel that you are closer.'

She opened the door to her little room. With his height, he dominated the available space.

He looked slowly around, absorbing, memorising. 'Yes, I can feel you in here, smell your perfume, your soap. Oh, Beatrice, seeing and remembering this place, and you in it, will help me over the months we will be apart.' He held her close. 'I will be at Echuca for almost another five months. The time seems long but I shall attempt to organise a freight or a ferry load downriver this way to visit – maybe on the *Avoca* again…'

'Again?'

'Yes, it is the *Avoca* waiting for me tomorrow night at Mannum – that is not too far from here. She was built on the Lakes – you know, the big lake, the one called Alexandrina after the Queen? Built there at Milang, only a few years ago. She is so young and frisky!' He laughed. 'Well, frisky may not be the word perhaps as she is a big one, a cargo tow steamer. She's sound and steady and the owners want her to leave the Murray and and I'll leave her at Mildura to head for Echuca. It's not a quick trip, but I have the task of maintaining and assessing her steam processes en route. I'm not certain which one I'll pick up from then on but there'll be one waiting at Mildura, with no doubt a minor problem I will be asked to rectify. Such is the nature of my work.'

He held her tight against him. 'It can be a good life for a woman on board and, oh, I am greatly tempted to take you with me. But no, we are not yet man and wife and I will not sully your reputation, my love. However, do let us make the most of this brief time together. Come and sit beside me on your bed…'

'Arthur!'

He smiled, and started to fidget in his pockets. 'You mistake my meaning, my love. Beatrice, it is the custom to give you a ring for your finger. I am not well versed in such pretty manners, my love, that I feel confident…erm, I do have a ring which was given to me in part payment of a debt and I hoped… But you may not like it or it may not fit. It is a gem believed lucky by the ancient Romans – an opal. This one is called a precious opal.'

He fossicked in a little pocket on the other side of his waistcoat. 'I doubt you may like it, not because of its value, though it is substantial – oh, danged thing, where is it? – but because of its multicolours, and it flashes its brightness in different hues depending on the light. Aaah, here it is.'

He unbuttoned a little tapestry fabric pouch and extracted a yellow gold ring with a stone of a rainbow hue, shaped in a perfect oval. 'This stone was found at Rocky Bridge Creek in New South Wales, or so I was told, Beatrice, and – here I must be honest – I thought of you and had the ring affixed and measured it by my own little finger in the recommended way and with every wish and hope – so I do hope it fits. Please hold out your left hand, my dear girl.'

Beatrice's hand was shaking but, very seriously, he took her hand in his and slipped the ring over her fourth finger and along over the knuckle.

'Oh, Arthur! It is beautiful, simply glorious! I will wear it with pride and love. Oh, my dear man.'

He stood and brought her to her feet and they kissed, he tenderly at first then becoming more demanding..

Beatrice broke away breathing heavily. 'My every instinct is for us to…to be together, closely together, in every way. And here and now… Well, that would be a mistake. I must dress, make myself ready for the evening as must you. Oh, Arthur…'

His smile widened to a lascivious grin. 'A mistake I'd love to make, my Beatrice, but you cannot attend tonight's dinner looking as dishevelled as I would make you. However…' He bent, his grin replaced by a gentle kiss to the ring on her finger. While holding her gaze, he opened the door. 'I will see you in the dining room and will save your place next to mine for dinner.' Then he was gone.

Beatrice stood, her heart fluttering, and twirling the beautiful opal around her finger.

# 49

Beatrice dressed in the lavender gown she'd made for Kate and Herbert's wedding. Her hair was arranged by Lucy into a flattering coif. Beatrice returned the favour, combing Lucy's into a loose roll swept back over the ears – suitable for a younger woman. Lucy had also chosen to wear lavender.

As Beatrice entered the dining room, she noticed Mr and Mrs Rogers already sitting at the long table. She waved her fingers to them, then sought Anderson. He was in the small parlour, with Sissy straightening his neckerchief.

They looked up and she smiled. 'You both look very dashing. Does this mean you are coming in to dinner, Sissy?'

'Certainly does, Beattie! Mrs Jack's ruling the kitchen for me this evening and…oh, Beattie! You have a most beautiful ring there. Not even waiting for wedding band… Is that….'

'Dear Sissy. As you say, it's done and dusted!' She held out her hand for her friend's admiration. 'Yes. To be proper, Sissy, Arthur and I are now forsworn and I am so very happy. Anderson, I was wondering, has the party arrived from the German village yet? I'm wondering about Kate…'

He smiled. 'I think they've arrived and I'll be off out to welcome Pastor Wilhelm. I think that's his voice I can hear.' Lucy was already there welcoming young Rauf, he noticed. *Ah well, young lass carries herself well and he's an up-an'-coming young feller. Let Nature take its course, I say.*

Kate and Herbert entered the dining room as Arthur came in through the opposite door. Beatrice felt a lump rise in her throat as she looked at him. He was so handsome! She breathed steadily as she watched him move across the floor. He was wearing a worsted cut-away jacket with buttons up to the shaped lapels. His necktie was in a blue chequered pattern and his shirt collar a creamy colour. His trouser material matched the jacket and the flared cut of their hems fell smoothly onto the instep of shining leather shoes. He had an air of authority about him that could easily command her love and, she sensed, the tenderness to win and hold it.

She realised she was staring and blushed as he bent over, smiling, to kiss her hand and whisper, 'Do I pass muster, Beatrice?

She sought a response, but a squeal of delight interrupted from behind.

'Beattie, you look lovely tonight. And it is so good to see you again!' It was Kate, leading a slightly abashed Herbert. 'Beattie, please do introduce me – us!'

This was quickly done and Arthur lightly kissed Kate's hand and shook Herbert's. Kate steered them to one of the corner tables overlooking the deck and by the time they were all sitting down – Beatrice in the outer chair easily accessed – the two men were discussing steam pumps and irrigation!

Kate smiled in apology. 'Apparently there is a coopering position near a mill in the Barossa and all Herbert seems to talk of is water flow and the speed with which it can be harnessed for grinding purposes. I am so weary of the subject and so delighted to be able to talk with you, my friend!' She leaned her head to Beatrice. 'Come, tell me the story: when did he give you that ring? It is beautiful!' She leaned over to whisper, 'How difficult was it in the end to make up your mind and accept him? I want to hear all about it.' She twirled her own wedding band on her finger. 'I've never regretted saying yes to Herbert- I am so happy, Beattie!' She leaned even closer. 'I have even stopped being sick whenever I move from our bed, and that *is* so much better!'

The dining room chairs were filling fast. Mrs Jack and one of the Rogers girls came in with carafes of cold water and a list of wines to choose from. It seemed no time at all to Beatrice before big tureens of vegetables from the garden were placed on the tables with jugs of hot gravy, then individual serves of goose or beef on hot dinner plates. The diners exclaimed in pleasure at the succulent slices of meat. Anderson gave a nod for Mr Jack, resplendent in a starched white jacket over his moleskins, to start pouring drinks.

Sissy and Anderson were sitting with Pastor and Frau Wilhelm and Sissy flushed in pleasure at the acclamation after the plates were dispensed. As the noise level dropped, Lucy walked into the room and up to the piano. She looked proud and almost regal in her bearing but the old Lucy was very much there to make a blush as she passed Rauf's table. He bestowed on her a rapturous smile. As she sat down, she was joined by the other Rogers girl, who was to turn the pages.

Beatrice knew Lucy had been practising often lately and that she had been with the Rogers girls down at the school piano quite often, with Mrs Bones's goodwill. What she didn't know was which music had been practised but now rippling from the keys of the square piano was… Gilbert and Sullivan! From the operetta *HMS Pinafore*. Then Lucy broke into the song 'Little Buttercup', with Isabelle Rogers cheekily miming an absurdly coy female, that brought the diners to laughs – whether chewing food or not!

Beatrice cast a look at Arthur, who was smiling, and she felt herself inclined to burst into giggles. Dear little Lucy didn't know that Little Buttercup was actually the character Poll Pineapple, a rather blowsy older woman who sold tobacco and delights to sailors when in port – hardly the sweet little girl being enacted by Isabelle! She chuckled into her glass remembering the actress in the part when Papa and Mama had taken her to London and the theatre on Mama's birthday. Mama had pretended to be shocked at some of the songs but Papa had roared with laughter!

She slipped another look at Arthur and he leaned over to whisper, 'Do you know the story, Beatrice?' And when she nodded, biting her lip to suppress her laughter – as no way could she laugh and embarrass the two girls – he gave her a slow wink.

Lucy sang her final line, then played the final chords, stood and curtseyed to the delighted audience. She regained her seat, trilled a few bars and then – surprise, surprise, what now – signalled to Mr Jack. He pulled off his apron with a flourish and moved towards the piano at Lucy's cue. After clearing his throat a couple of times, he began singing, in a rich bass tone, not the supposed hilarity of the 'Captain of the Queen's Navee' with all the 'Capn's sisters cousins and aunts', but the tale of the British Tar.

The lyric was obviously chosen to target Arthur. It had been well rehearsed. *But when could they do all this? I must have been down the street or somewhere…*

'A British tar is a soaring soul as free as a mountain bird,
his energetic fist should be ready to resist a dictatorial word...'

*Oh, goodness, hope he's not implying Arthur's a bare-knuckle man.* However, as she flashed another look at Arthur, he was smiling quite widely and tapping his fingers on the table to the beat. When it came to the line, 'He never should bow down to a domineering frown or the tang of a tyrant tongue,' he actually burst into a laugh. This pleased Mr Jack, who postured towards him, wagging his finger and enjoying his chosen role.

It was bright and cheeky and quite set the happy scene – and a few diners to clapping the beat. One or two even took the hint it was playing to 'the chap who's marrying Beatrice' and broke into a humming despite their plates not yet being cleared. And Beatrice herself felt that the so-called tyrant tongue was inferred to be hers – as a nagging wife – and smiled, inwardly!

It came to an end. Mr Jack gave a flourishing bow and with a happy grin donned his apron once more. Lucy had a short break for a drink. She came over to Arthur and Beatrice, anxious that they had liked the surprise.

Beatrice wasn't going to spoil Lucy and Isabelle's impression of Little Buttercup. 'Beautiful, Lucy. And very funny!'

Arthur was still grinning and stood to kiss Lucy's hand in a very grown-up way. *She's positively simpering!* Lucy then returned to the piano – some Chopin again as the pudding was served and bowls of apples and slabs of cheese carried to the tables. Beatrice didn't know *Pinafore* was so popular, or had even thought of a London show being re-enacted in the Adelaide hills! *There's a new one,* Pirates of Penzance. *I wonder when it'll come to Australia, or even if it will? Buying the music is one thing, but the show itself – well...*

Beatrice walked over to the piano with a glass of water for Lucy. '*Quelle surprise!* Lucille, where did you buy the music?'

Lucy smiled. 'Miss Evelyn, Beatrice. She sent it up to me and we practised so you would have a surprise tonight. She knew I would be playing.'

'Lovely! And you played it so well on the little square piano! Now, that did surprise me, as I suppose you had to adapt the music.'

'No, Beatrice. I have two sheets and one was prepared for a clavichord, so…'

'Oh, delightful! And clever Evie for thinking of it. I must have a try myself later.'

# 50

As people started nibbling the fruit, Beatrice wondered what other surprises were to come. Curious, she let the others talk among themselves as she watched Lucy playing. Occasionally Isabelle leaned over to Lucy and the two girls shared a comment. *What assurance she has now and she's certainly a very graceful young woman.* Then Isabelle took over the keyboard and played the intro to 'Greensleeves'. That was obviously the signal for Lucy: in her beautiful voice, she sang the words of that loveliest of melodies, words of love that King Henry VIII was supposed to have written and sung for Anne Boleyn. She repeated the chorus and then curtseyed as the last bars were played by Isabelle, at which cue Anderson stood by his chair and tapped on his glass with a spoon.

'Ladies and gentlemen, Pastor and all our friends, I want to share with you all some lovely news. It is this: our beautiful Beatrice is now hand-fast to Mr Symonds and they will marry – I hope, here in Bridgewater – later this year. Mr Symonds, as you know, was an officer on their ship and that's where they met. Beatrice has become one of our happy family now for well more than half a year. She teaches piano in the village among other clever help she provides to us here at the inn, and I know you would all want to wish them well.'

A rumbling and scraping of chairs heralded a fury – or so it seemed to Beatrice – of people rushing to shake Arthur's hand and kiss hers, and some women even gave her kisses on the cheek! An initial astonishment and then the realisation that although such friendly informality would never have happened at home, this was South Australia where so much was different yet, in other ways, the same! *This bustling about and hugging – well, it all feels so right, so happy.*

Arthur stood, his arm now around Beatrice's shoulders, and spoke briefly of his thanks on behalf of himself and Beatrice for everyone's good wishes, and for welcoming him as a suitable suitor for such a beautiful, worthy lady as Beatrice, after which Beatrice stopped listening she felt so embarrassed! Kate gave her a big friendly squeeze and Herbert said, 'Don't forget you are to be godmother!'

Lucy then signalled to Anderson, sat again at the piano and started to play the opening bars of Brahms's Lullaby and, as if that also had been arranged, Herbert moved over to the little piano with Rauf, both breaking into the German words of the beautiful melody. They received tumultuous applause – a perfect ending to a perfect evening.

Not long afterwards, the diners started moving out, Anderson and Sissy farewelling their customers. Isabelle exited the room and Lucy followed Rauf into the reception area. It seemed no time before the newly hand-fasted couple were alone in the dining room among the clutter of dirty plates, cutlery and empty glasses.

Arthur took hold of her hand and pulled her over to the door to the stairs. 'Let's go to my room, stand on the balcony to farewell the gathering and look at the stars, my love.' He brooked no refusal – even as he uttered the last word, they were on the stairwell, he pulling her along.

On the landing above, he opened the door to his room and pulled her over to the balcony glass door and flung it wide. 'The winter moon, my Beatrice. How beautiful how pale and how clear!'

Side by side, they leaned over the railing overlooking the front yard, waving to the walkers, the horses and the Germans in the Hahndorf carriages. Goodbyes were called, and from under the balcony someone whistled a *Pinafore* song, but finally all the boots, pattens, wheels and hooves had clomped over the cobbles so that Mr Jack could close the heavy wooden gates. The scent of the eucalypts was strong in the night air.

'Oh, Arthur! Can you smell the trees? It's the recent rain. So clean and clear…'

Arthur pulled Beatrice into the bedroom and closed the glass. 'I leave early tomorrow, my love, and I wish I could do more but for now, some last kisses, kisses to remember?' He pulled her to him and made good his promise. But as she began to melt in his grasp he stiffened upright, pushing her tenderly away from him. 'Oh, Beatrice, my dear girl, nothing more now, much as I would wish.' He smiled down at her anxious face, took it in his hands and kissed her forehead. 'I cannot love you as I want to, not now, and leave not knowing if – well, whether you may be compromised.'

'Oh, Arthur! I...'

'Shush, dearest. I promise you that I will remain true to you as I know you will be to me, and the months, the weeks, will quickly go. I shall be able to come again, I think, around the end of August or beginning of September and more able to determine when we can move to a suitably settled township. Meanwhile, oh, Beatrice, do write to me. Perhaps you may be able to read about Overland Corner. Also, Kate's Herbert has learned much of the area and you may be able to speak with him. Then you will know as much about the general area where we hope to live as I. You can tell me when you write!' He laughed and caressed her cheek. 'Come back down these stairs with me. I will see you down to your room and we shall say goodnight. Then I shall bid goodbye to our good friends of the inn and retire to pack my belongings.'

'I will come with you and help you pack.'

'No, Beatrice. That would challenge this gentleman's restraint too far!' He laughed at her disappointed expression. 'You know I am right, my love! One last kiss to sustain me?'

Willingly, she obliged, and again...

# 21 June 1880

## 51

Beatrice awoke at the magpie's warbling and hastily donned her robe. As she peeked around the deck, Lucy came out of the room next door that she shared with Sissy.

'Good morning, Beatrice. Your fee-ahn-say left before the dawn had properly broken. Mr Jack told me in the kitchen. He had been asked last night to make his horse ready. He said – Mr Jack, that is – that Arthur did not want to prolong his goodbye, but he will be back as soon as he is able.'

Although Beatrice knew her now committed fiancé would be off at first light, she had hoped to catch him before he left. Despite her pang of disappointment, she had to smile at Lucy's polished though painful pronunciation of the French word.

'Lucy, your playing and singing was beautiful to hear. And,' she teased, 'Rauf looked quite smitten also!'

'He is really nice, Beattie.' She blushed and lowered her voice, leading Beatrice to think her mother must still be in her room and within earshot. 'We had time to talk last night. Beatrice, he likes me and…and at the end of the year he will be taking his final exam and then starting full-time clerking. I didn't know what it is but it's a sort of as law apprentice. It's supposed to help him decide what kind of law he will work with – there are so many different kinds! And then, well… I'd better get back to the kitchen, I think, and get started like Mam told me to!' She ran off, mentally hugging her romantic dreams to herself.

*Bless her cotton socks, as dear old Mrs Willis used to say. Now, Beatrice, today is not a busy day but you promised a letter to Evie and to Papa. Why not use the time and give them all your news. First, dress, then investigate the company at breakfast, then to the escritoire and your letter writing.*

When Sissy emerged for breakfast, her eyes were puffy as though with crying. Responding to Beatrice's questioning expression, she admitted, 'Not used ter all this drinking, Beattie, and that's the truth of it!'

She sat down and Anderson poured her a cup of hot strong tea, added milk and spooned three sugars into it, winking slowly to Beatrice as he did so.

'Come on, Sis, cheer up. It were a lovely occasion yesterday and young Lucille shone nearly as bright as our Beattie here! Bit of a sore head is a small price to pay.'

Beatrice also had to admit that the strong and very hot tea straight from the pot was a great restorative. She also spooned coddled eggs onto her plate with relish. 'Young Lucy cooked these too, I suspect. She has many talents and will make an admirable wife one day.'

'Hrrmph' came from Lucy's mother as she spooned eggs on her own plate. 'That young miss needs to get into my good books and you two can stop chortling. She wants that young Rauf, she's going to need to practise being as ladylike as you are, Beattie. He's going places, so Pastor Wilhelm told me last night.'

'Cecilia Woof! Still your tongue, sister! She's my niece and she's a little beauty. Playing and singing like that fits into any of your society lady's salons. I'm proud as Mr Punch of her, so I am. She's of age to marry now if she wishes, with your signing the papers till she's twenty-one. All right, I know, Sissy, he's still to get experience, but just give them another year to get to know each other and think of plans and all that, and I know I'll try and convince you that young Rauf and her are a good fit – like a shoe with the right shoe horn!'

With that comical analogy prompting Beatrice to choke on her tea, he picked up his toast and exited the room.

She reached over and took Sissy's hand. 'They are good together, Sissy, and if they still feel that way this time next year, surely you'll be pleased for them?'

Sissy sniffed. 'That's the problem, Beattie. She'll not be able to help me here. She'll be setting up a fancy house in Adelaide somewhere.' She sat up straight, poured another cup of tea from a waning pot and gave a tentative smile. 'I was proud of my girl last night, Beattie, no denying. And it's just my sore head talking. I'll be thinking right soon. I'd better go now and inspect the kitchen.'

Beatrice sat alone, looking around the room, at the fire glowing warm and, through the open door at a corner of the little square piano, a pile of music sheets on its end. *This place, this room and that piano – with these lovely people – have given me a home, some independence and a feeling of belonging. Even when I am with Arthur in the river lands, I will always think of here as my second home.*

She gathered her plates together and decided that her first letter to write would be to Evelyn and Mary and John. *They surely deserve to know about all that has happened, about me and Arthur, and I must ask how John Benjamin is improving. Goodness me, my life is going to be a busy one, that much I do know!*

# 21 August 1880

## 52

Mary Lee sat in her living room in her favourite chair, the window open to a lovely cool evening breeze. She was comfortably dressed in a loosely draped house gown – one of John's indulgences to his mam – and had decided to wait up and find out what the young ones thought of the Town Hall concert. A bang at the front door announced their arrival and she heard Alice urging them to 'Ssshhh!'

'Come on in, you noisy children,' she called. 'Tell me all about it!'

John Benjamin came in first, pulling off his scarf as he did so.

*Goodness, his neck is as thin as a stick – oh, my boy…* 'Come on in and tell me all about it then. Did the organ feature at this concert, or was it only orchestra?'

'Orchestra, Mam, but John went to sleep halfway through. He even dropped his head onto his coat so he did.'

Beatrice chuckled. 'Hey, you two, let this country woman give an opinion. It was wonderful piano playing, Mary. The pianist was part of the orchestra, from Sydney. I play Chopin at the inn. I really thought my playing was reasonable but this pianist's fingers just flew along the keys! It was like poetry. Now…who's brought the programme? I can't remember his name…'

'Sorry, Beattie, I had it but I left it on my seat. He was Sydney somebody, or was that the name of the orchestra?'

'Oh, well, it was beautifully relaxing, Mary,; just right for listening at the end of a hard day. And I'm the one who hasn't laboured all day to be too tired to give an opinion. And truth to tell, Evie, your day was catching up with you also! I noticed when we started after the intermission your eye lids were drooping!'

They all laughed.

With excellent timing as usual, Alice brought in a laden tray and put it on the table and began pouring tea. 'Now this is the best China leaf, and I've even brought in one of Mrs Bell's lemons, thinly sliced. But I cut my finger, Miss Evelyn, so please will you pour? An', Mrs Beatrice. If it's not work, what do yer call riding that bumpy cart down to the market from up in the tiers? An' at an earlier hour than even I would have been awake today! Then walkin' over here to spend the day goin' out with Mrs Mary an' walkin' all round the hospital before you could have your bread an' butter? That's work, that is. Isn't that so, Mrs Mary?'

'Indeed it is, Alice. It's that country air keeps Beatrice so fit!' She held out her hand for a friendly squeeze with Beattie. 'Mrs Colton's on the board of the children's hospital, an' she has plans how I can help out if I want…'

'Oh, Mother! That Mrs Colton will create work for you now her husband has been re-elected to the House of Assembly. He may be a good man, but Mam, please don't go signing yourself up for things that'll have you out day after day for hour after hour. You need free time to do what you want to do, Mam, not what others want all the time. We've only been here a few months. Find your feet first, do. If you want us to make a new life here, you've plenty of time to decide.'

'I haven't said yes, Evie, but Mrs Colton said she'd like it if I was more involved with the female refuge committee and then we women can have enough of us to push for a ladies committee of the Social Purity Society.'

Beatrice thought to interrupt the persistent debate between mother and daughter. They all worried about each other in this family! She sensed that Mary needed goals that captured her imagination, her principles – not only to help others but to prove her worth in this new land. Mary was a woman with the highest ideals, not only for others but most of all for herself. She would not easily be thwarted, it was not her character. Beatrice also knew that Evelyn was constantly on about her mother over-taxing herself in caring and worrying for John. Unfortunately, his decline in health was all too apparent.

She decided on a slight diversion in topic and sat up on the edge of her chair, attracting their attention. 'Dear Alice, do rest assured my early start was most enjoyable, not least the conversation opportunities. Mrs Kate Flach travelled on the cart too. She's brought some of her patchwork she's hoping will sell so she will be helping in the market today. It was so pleasant to chat – that's her Herbert's word for it when women share gossip!'

'Beatrice, dear girl. That Mrs Flach, your friend Kate, is she not enceinte?'

'Yes, Mary. The baby is due to arrive in December, I believe.'

John placed his cup and saucer on the tray. 'Well, Beatrice, I'm so glad to see you and to know you have found your companion. I must say I liked Symonds well enough when we met before he went up to Bridgewater. Even so, our acquaintanceship was fleeting. Are you certain of him, my dear?'

Stupidly, she felt herself pinking up. 'Yes, I am, John...'

'I ask you only because I recall only too well your unhappiness and uncertainty at the turn of events that greeted your arrival from the ship. I also recall your determination and resolve and recognised in you a certain strength that, I confess, quite startled me. My dear mother calls it common sense, and you have that quality, dear Beatrice. However, common sense can sometimes mask a calculated defence.'

'Oh!'

He held up a finger and gave a wry smile. 'Is not December when you plan to marry, Beatrice? You know, whatever happens in this life, if he is the man for you, my dear, marry him with all my blessings. If I have gone away, I will be there, in thought if not deed. '

'Oh, my son, don't talk that way...'

'Dear John, you are the best man friend any woman could wish for... It's just that...'

He stood by his chair smiling at the faces around him. 'As long as I know, and I think I can recognise it already, you have a deep feeling for this man, one that will grow to make him the luckiest man in the colony, I shall relax, my dear. I admit I am envious and, had things been different for me, I would be fighting him every step of the way.'

Mary had heard enough. She pulled herself to her feet. 'You, my son, will get better, I know it. A mother's instinct never fails. However, I do suggest we all call it a night now and get ourselves the sleep we deserve. We no longer say rhymes about going upstairs to say our prayers, but I'll be saying mine and I know they'll be answered. And,' she wagged her fingers in mock reproach, 'tomorrow is another day! G'night, my dears.' She gave her son, now on his feet, a kiss on the cheek then saluted the two young women in the same way before exiting the room.

Beatrice noted Mary's eyes were starting to brim with tears, but she said nothing, other than, 'Goodnight and God bless.'

John followed her out of the door, leaving the two young women looking at each other in consternation. They heard John and Mary speaking in the corridor. Mary was distressed and they knew they must all face an unpleasant truth sooner rather than later. But Mary would worry, no matter what platitudes were offered to her. Evelyn moved closer to the door, listening.

Mary was telling John she had questioned his latest doctor but had been rebuffed. 'He told me it would infringe your privacy, my son! Does not a mother's concern count at all? Is it this tuberculosis as the new doctor calls it? In the newspaper it talks of more than four hundred cases so far this year. Am I not to be afraid, son?'

The voices died away and Evie and Beatrice waited a decent moment before they, too, made for their beds.

# 3 November 1880

## 53

The blinds were drawn and only faint noises came from an occasional carriage outside on Barnard Street. Yesterday, Tuesday, dear John Benjamin had died – in his own bed with his mother, sister and Beatrice attending him. Evelyn was even now in his room, directing the undertakers, Mr Downs and his family, in their business. Beatrice was comforting Alice in the kitchen.

The two of them, Mary knew, would be cooking up some things to offer any visitors who might come back after the funeral. *Bless 'em both. They're good girls. Bless all of 'em.*

John Benjamin was to leave the next day for the cemetery. Evelyn had directed Mary to rest quietly and made her a pot of tea, and Alice was incessantly fussing around her to the extent she felt she was expected to weep and wail and tear her clothes. In truth, she felt drained now of all emotion.

Dear John Benjamin, as she would always think of him, had suffered this debilitating illness, this terrible unnamed disease, for at least two years now. It was the reason she and Evelyn moved to Adelaide last year, after all. He had tried so many doctors, received differing diagnoses and treatments, none of which expedited a recovery. His weakness and acceptance of his fate over the last few weeks had been excruciating for Mary to witness; she could cry no more. The doctor said it was a pneumonia that finally took him; he was too weak to fight it. It was a relief that he was now free of pain and at rest. Dear boy. He was the reason she and Evelyn had come to this country and now, of her seven children, only Evelyn was sharing her life here on this faraway side of the world.

John Benjamin's funeral notice was in the paper today and tomorrow he would be interred in the Wesleyan Cemetery. He was known as Ben to many of his work colleagues and some would be coming to his funeral – that's why there was all that fuss in the kitchen.

Beatrice had been with them since Monday afternoon and had spent time in John's room, holding his hand and mopping his brow. He lost strength but Mary noticed he could still smile and he was happy for Beatrice to be with him, with his mam and his sister, in those last hours.

*Dear God, if things had been different, what might have happened? He would have tried to win Beatrice, that I know. Now I am so glad she is here also to sustain Evelyn. The good Lord knows my girl has been a tower of strength these last weeks; she needs a friend with her. I'm no good; I feel torn to pieces.*

Beatrice knocked on the door and sat on the pouffe by Mary's chair. It was apparent she had been crying.

'Dear Mary, I really do not know what to say. John has been a rock for me – I knew he would always help me sort out my troubles if any resulted from James's money misadventures, that gambling. He liked the Anderson-Woofs and his confidence in them communicated itself to me in those early unsettled days. He persuaded me I was capable of independence when I had doubts. I shall always owe him so much… Oh, Mary…'

'Shush, my dear girl. I know John cared for you and wanted only your happiness. He will be a fly on the wall at your wedding. He told me you took him to see the little church with that funny little pedal organ and he just hoped he could see you married there.'

'Dear John. And Mary, it is so close to his passing…'

Mary knew strong words were called for. 'Beatrice Beauchamp, let us have no crisis of conscience about your marrying when you are… I have no qualms about the juxtaposition of the dates. Nor did John.'

'But the conventions, Mary. When I first went to Bridgewater I used to worry about what I was supposed to be doing, as opposed to what seemed more sensible for whatever circumstances presented. But in the hills, new ways are more readily accepted. You are subject to the old ways here in the city, conventions nurtured by the Establishment, and I could not bear the thought of criticisms weighing down on you from your new acquaintances in the church…and around Mrs Colton…and the others with whom you have established a relationship.'

'Sshush, Beatrice. These last days before John faded from life, he and I were able to speak.' She gave a sniff and dabbed her nose with her kerchief. 'I know how he so enjoyed visiting you that last time at

Bridgewater, when he chartered the coach to come up there. "Hang the expense," he said to me. Yes, he saw the church, and you walked around the township, helping him up the hills – he said the roadways were all up and down in Bridgewater – and you played that little square piano for him. He told me of it all… Music is very strong in our family back home. He was never very interested in playing but one of his cousins even plays the large pipe organ, and very well indeed. John was happy to know of your happiness, Beatrice, and he would not want you to delay your wedding one minute! And he so enjoyed that last visit you made to us here. What was it, only three weeks ago, when you, he and Evie went to that new music hall? You said it would brighten him up a bit. It did. I remember you laughing as you came home that evening. He hadn't the energy to laugh any more, he said – fact was, he just couldn't – but he was so happy. Oh, I hear Evie farewelling that Mr Downs. Come on, girl, wipe those eyes. She'll be in here with the details in a minute. She sees tears an' it'll set her off again.'

# 4 November 1880

## 54

John Benjamin had been laid to rest, Alice and her friend Mrs Horace had done a sterling job with scones and cups of tea, and Evelyn and Beatrice were sitting in the living room recounting their impressions of the occasion. Beatrice had met Evelyn's co-worker and friend for the first time.

'He has a nice, kind face, Evelyn. Oh, I know you're just good friends, but he has, no denying. Does he have aspirations…you know, want you and him to be together?'

'I don't think so, Beattie. We really are just friends. He's not the marrying kind. He's one of nine sons and daughters and has mentioned more than once how they are all so different, they just don't act like a family unit and he wouldn't want to have a cohort of ankle-snappers like his elder brothers have. They all go in for huge families.'

'Yes, I know what you mean. That's the hard part, isn't it, defeating Nature and not conceiving? Only way is not to conjoin…'

'Conjoin? Beattie, you are so strange at times and so old-fashioned.'

'Oh, I'm aware of urges, Evie, believe me. Arthur and I have talked of such things! He's now going to start with this Mr Napper and I am quite looking forward to our setting up home together,' she smiled, 'and…well, you know!'

Evelyn smiled and said she knew of Renmark, that the name came up regularly in telegraph notices. 'When you are living around there, you will let me know when I can come and stay, won't you? And now they've caught that awful Kelly gang, or most of them are dead and gone anyway and he is in Melbourne gaol, I feel easier about travelling in the country areas.'

'Evie, my dear friend, I must mention: you were coming to my wedding to be my chief bridesmaid. However, with John being ill and now laid to rest, I would not be surprised if you had decided not to. I would not hold you to account if so. You've had a terrible loss and…'

'I hope you are joking with me, Beattie. Mam says you feel bad about planning a wedding so soon after John's death. Don't feel that way, my friend! What's more, Mam will be coming up with me. She has an open mind on some of the stuffier mourning customs and knows that John would like her to be with you too. I know you told Mrs Woof no elaborate wedding breakfast and only me and Lucy as your attendants. That is enough deprivation on a wedding day, and John would want you to have a wonderful, wonderful day.'

Beatrice smiled fondly at her friend. 'You are the very best of friends, Evie. And if Mary feels she can attend, she will be so very welcome. I'll ask Sissy to organise a room for her – well, at least a decent bed! But cutting costs would be a bonus all round and if there is a bonus in trimming the celebrations, that is it. Arthur and I are faced with unknown expenses settling in the river lands. The little church in Bridgewater is being decorated for the occasion – I have no say in that and it will look lovely, I'm sure – and I took John to see it, did I tell you? I have decided not to have a new dress to marry in – my lavender will do. Ssshh, Evie, no protest! I will give it fresh ivory-coloured trims and I will carry a mixed flower bouquet. Lucy will wear the lavender she wore at Kate's wedding too and the two of us will freshen our dresses so they will be charming. Do remember I have been a traditional bride once before. Mam ensured I had a lovely wedding but that is behind me now. So, my friend, you will be my helpmeet at my wedding and so please do wear one of your favourite dresses and don't go to any untoward expense. I know you will look lovely because you always do. Mrs Rogers is decorating the church and I think Arthur plans to buy all our flowers from her cousin, who grows flowers for sale in a corner of her farm, so you and Lucy will have the same arrangements as I, well one similar. We shall all link in.'

'Kate will be there, I'm sure, but she must be very huge with those babies she is carrying, Beattie. How does she feel – two for the price of one?'

Beatrice grinned. 'She moans a bit about feeling enormously bulky and cannot bend but she and Herbert are thrilled and eager to see whether boys or girls or one of each! You know, she is a little bit concerned that their due date and our wedding might coincide! I have tried to reassure her on that point but...'

'Well, I suppose it is possible that the babies might arrive but Saturday the fourth of December is your date, is it not, and that's a calendar month away. Plenty of time for twin babies to arrive before your big day, Beatrice! Now, you are staying here this evening and then going back to Bridgewater tomorrow, is that right? On the coach, after…afterwards?' Evie paused. 'I'll just make a fresh pot of tea but have you heard, there should be a train service through to Bridgewater in a couple of years?'

'Yes, and Arthur and I will take a train from Adelaide to Morgan after the wedding – not the next day, though – and there take a paddle steamer. We'll have quite a bit of luggage, you see. He has stuff to pick up in Adelaide first so we may have a couple of days here.' She paused. 'I'm quite ridiculously excited at the prospect of travelling there, of making a new home with Arthur and not least of actually travelling on one of his riverboats!'

Mrs Lee listened to their friendly chatter. She was in the next room, John's room, and she was sitting in his saggy old favourite chair. It rocked back and forth and he had sat down in it quite often in his last few weeks after giving up his work. She looked around. His things were all around her – all his maps of the strange 'outback', as he called it, where telegraph engineers went and he monitored their reports. A pot of that sharp-smelling pomade he would comb through his hair was on the side table. She inhaled its perfume deeply, and the essence of her son's very presence. Tears sprang again to her eyes.

She knew people were speculating about what she would do now John had died. She had been surprised that some expected her to return to Northern Ireland. She had no plans for such a move: Evelyn was happy here and she, Mary, knew there was much to be done in this new colony for girls and young women, and could be done more easily than in England or Ireland where old ideas – and males – reigned supreme, in her opinion. Besides which, even if they had wanted to go, she and Evelyn simply could not afford the return fare.

She rocked back and forth, sipping her cocoa. Yes, there was much that could be achieved here, and John Benjamin liked living in Adelaide and had planned to stay. So would she.

# 4 December 1880

## 55

Saturday the fourth of December 1880 dawned crisp and full of the magpie chortling from outside of her window. The glass was open, only the gnat screen clipped to keep out the flies and the freshness of the breeze cooled Beatrice's bare feet and legs. *It must have been warm last night – I kicked off the covers…*

'Oh, it's our wedding day!'

'Huh? Oh, Beatrice, you gave me a shock!' came Evelyn's muffled voice from the foot end of the bed. 'Do you know you kicked my ear in the night?' Then she pulled herself to a sitting position and gave a huge yawn.

Beatrice broke into laughter. 'Evie, your face is a picture and the rags are all dropping out of your hair!'

'And you never got yours in at all by the looks!'

The two girls chuckled and then Evelyn grinned.

'Well, you got here, Beatrice, you actually got here.'

'You didn't think I'd back out, did you? Evie!'

'Not seriously, but it did cross my mind when you were talking about not knowing anyone in the river lands that you might be having second thoughts. It's not easy, as I know, being a migrant – all right, I know I had my mother with me and my brother here but there is still so much unknown and it's so easy to make a mistake because of… Oh, I don't know what I'm trying to say!'

'Evelyn Lee, you sound a terrible doubting Thomas. Is this how you feel and is this why you steer away from a relationship?'

Evelyn crossed from the washing bowl. 'I do like this lovely soap, Beatrice. I do have a very good friend. He's a very well set-up man and popular with everyone. Mam likes him enormously. But – big but – he really doesn't want to marry. He doesn't like children. And we do have a good time together, he and I, but he does have some firm ideas I don't agree with – as in government. He doesn't like Billy Morgan…'

'Who?'

'Sir William of such name. He's the premier – for now.'

'Evie, do help me with my laces. The premier minister – Morgan – isn't he the one who pushed for the telephones to be operating here? Surely, John was in favour of that! Oh, that's tight enough!'

There was a resounding knock on the door. 'Misses! Both of you! The flowers are ready and so is breakfast. Will you gown up, please – just to be respectable, says my mother.'

'Coming, Lucy. Let's go, Evie. Just put your wrap on or Sissy'll be getting all irate.'

Anderson was there, resplendent in new white breeches, bright red braces and fat woollen socks and already tucking into porridge. 'Don't worry, Beatrice. I'll be all togged up and do you proud. I'm very honoured to be your sponsor, so I am.' He yelled out, 'Sissy! Come on, let's have it!'

In walked Lucy and Sissy, each in morning robes, carrying plates of coddled eggs, rashers aplenty of bacon and a stack of toast.

'Come on, Lucy, serve it up and, young ladies, we'll all of us have us a good breakfast. Lunch, as you call it, will be a hit an' miss affair, I'm thinkin'! Flowers are lovely, Beattie – came up from the old Mrs Rogers about an hour ago. She musta bin up at first light to put 'em in their special bunches!'

Lucy laughed. 'Bouquets or posies, Mama, not bunches…'

'My mother…?' queried Evelyn.

'Bless you, dear, Lucy took her some porridge and honey and stewed apple into her bedroom an' she'll help her dress shortly unless…'

'No need, Mrs Woof. I'll eat my eggs then I'll go and see to Mam. Lucy has promised to tidy up my hair later, after Beatrice. Erm…no Arthur?'

Beatrice was concerned. He'll need…'

Anderson ladled coddled eggs onto a plate. 'He's being seen to, Beattie. Mine host at the Pump is seeing to Mr Symonds this mornin' an' he'll be having the best, I promise. He'll be at the little church come noon with Herbert helpin' him get ready.'

They all relaxed and tucked in and then just as Lucy was suggesting she help Beatrice dress later, there was an almighty knocking on the door and the ostler, Jack, burst in.

'Mr Herbert's 'ad ter go back to the Lutheran village, Anderson. Says 'is babies are comin'.' Pastor Wilhelm said as 'e was comin' anyways, 'e's taken the trap to the Pump an' he'll do the job with Mr Arthur and bring 'im back spick an' span, so not to worry.'

'Oh, dear...' mumbled Sissy.

'Oh, how exciting!' That was the shriek almost in unison from the three girls.

'That is absolutely delightful! To happen on my wedding day. I am so very happy for them. This is lovely news, Sissy. We'll all be organised and maybe by the breakfast afterwards – there'll be two more residents in the village! Come on, Lucy, we'll start the hair... See you in a little while, Evie. Do wish your mother a good morning for me!'

Anderson sat up. 'Babies on a wedding day. Good luck if ever there was. Eh, Sis?'

*

Mrs Bones was resplendent in a long emerald green gown with matching plumes in her hair. She sat regally on the stool by the pedal organ playing a tune Arthur didn't recognise, but it was magisterial, even pompous, no doubt selected for its dignity. A dignity belied, he smiled to himself, by her great aplomb and enthusiasm as she beat out the rhythm on the pedals; their clunk-click detracting in no way from her rippling the bass chords on the keys. *Wonder if Beatrice chose this? I'll have to ask her its name. Bit portentous for my taste but...*

Arthur was pleased to see that Mary Lee was seated one row back from the table with Mrs Woof. They both rated highly in his opinion because he recognised, even if Beattie hadn't voiced it yet, what very good friends they were to Beatrice, particularly over the last few months of great change for her.

*And Mrs Lee has so recently lost her only son – well, only one here in this country as far as I know – yet she's here to support Beatrice in her marriage to me. And she's wearing something very 'Mary', as Beatrice said earlier but it's a blue – not too dark, just subdued, but blue – and I would have sworn she would be in black. Aah, black ribbons trailing down from that top knot thing on her head. Better than a black veil; this is not the occasion... God bless the woman – and I don't say that very often!*

Pastor Wilhelm's wife arrived with a pew full of children. She smiled at the anxious-looking groom as he scanned the congregation but her children retained their solemn behave-or-else expressions.

Arthur didn't know many of the guests and feared the uninvited ones would take up all the available places. Many, he realised, were friendly onlookers from the village. *Seat for Anderson by Sissy, though; and young Rauf from the village – he'll be waiting for Lucille. Good man. This minister came up from Adelaide, knows Mrs Bones, knows Beatrice, but I can't even remember his name. His church is Presbyterian, though, called Chalmers Free Church, or was that earlier? Bit confusing, the organ and all… Anderson did tell me. Minister's a friend of Mrs Mary Lee, I believe. Well she's a good one, respect her choice.*

'All right, Arthur?'

'Thanks, Rauf. Little bit nervous, I think, but that's all. Got the ring. Er, you all fine with this other minister here? I've had a good talk with him – well, he buttonholed me earlier, would you believe. Seems a genuine fellow.'

'Oh yes, he's a regular here because they rotate between Church of England and Presbyterian services in this little building. We all serve the same God, you know.'

The music volume increased, the congregation quietened and Arthur turned round to see the church packed to the rafters, and there, coming in the doorway, the bridal procession. *She's leading Anderson, who's quite majestic in top coat and knee breeches and grinning like the Cheshire cat in Dodson's tales. Quite a corporation on the man – a good man. He's trying to keep pace with Mrs Bones's pedals! Oops. Left right left, not left left oops, Anderson. Not a military man. Oh, Beatrice, you look lovely. That gown, a pale sort of purple, with Evelyn Lee following and she's wearing something that blends in and then behind her, young Lucy in another shade of pale purple. God, they're beautiful, all of 'em. And she's my very own Beatrice… Who'd have thought?*

He held out his hand to her. 'Beatrice, I love you so much.'

She clasped his hand in hers, giving him a smile of such incredible sweetness that Sissy gasped and started to cry. *Well, I allus do at weddings an' look at my little Lucy. She's all growed up – and look at that Rauf boy noticin'…*

The minister waited until the bride gave her lovely bouquet of mixed wild flowers to her chief attendant then, when the two stood before him, he launched into his well-rehearsed script… 'Dearly beloved, we are gathered…' He read to Arthur the prescribed vow and asked him if he would take Beatrice to be his lawful wedded wife.

Arthur nodded, then remembered to speak aloud.

The minister read to Beatrice the sacred words and though she baulked a little at the vow to 'obey', she nodded, then smiled and answered clearly, 'I do.'

They kissed and a loud clapping came from some in the congregation. This startled the minister until he persuaded himself this was the country, after all, not the city! The formal part of the service over, the bride and groom walked slowly, hand in hand, into the tiny vestry to sign the paper work. Anderson and Evelyn, as witnesses, followed. Beatrice had to think as she took the pen in her hand – Fletcher? Beauchamp? Or Symonds?

It seemed to Beatrice that all of the village and most of the Lutheran village had come to the service. She buttonholed young Rauf and asked if there had been any word about Kate and Herbert's babies.

'Not yet. I'll let you know the minute I hear and I'll keep an eye on the pastor because they'll contact him first.'

Beatrice later, at the breakfast, had her own question of Pastor Wilhelm. 'Why the phrase "man and wife"? Is it the same in your church, pastor?'

He looked astonished at the question, peered at her from under his eyebrows and asked, 'Did you not promise to obey, Mrs Symonds?'

'Yes, but why not role and role, husband and wife? That would represent a truly equal partnership.'

'Dear Beatrice, you are his wife!'

Beatrice stored that one away. Today was not the day but she would question the form of service more closely – later would do.

# 56

They walked back up the hill to the inn, all together in a happy crowd, bride and groom, attendants, the minister, and all the congregation coming to the refreshments at the inn – the breakfast, as Sissy referred to it.

Sissy didn't even bother to run; she knew things would be under control. She and Mrs Lee were companions on the hike up the hill and enjoying the chance to talk. Mary was really impressed with how Beatrice had adjusted to all the changes in her life – she bore little resemblance to the timid and tearful new immigrant of nearly a year ago – and seeing her in the surroundings that had helped her was so comforting. She was obviously well thought of. Sissy was quite happy to speak of her admiration for her.

Sissy envied Mrs Lee her stout leather boots; she found it hard work in her new slippers walking up the gravelly road. She looked down at them, getting a bit dusty. They had been an indulgence from Mr Birks's store but she was coming to realise they were not intended for outdoor walking. *They looks nice on me feet, though. Long time since I had some pretties…*

Children were laughing and jostling and Beatrice looked up at Arthur, loving his happiness and admiring him in his wedding suit of fashionable cream-coloured flared trews and a matching jacket, all in moleskin. He caught her gaze and to everyone's rowdy enjoyment, gave her a smacking big kiss, then and there in the street.

Habits die hard and, momentarily embarrassed, Beatrice started to blush, prompting more friendly laughter from those immediately around her. They were almost at the inn when a cry went up, '…on a horse!'

It was Herbert Flach – standing in the stirrups, his face flushed, dusty and streaked with tear stains as he sought to catch up with them.

'Oh no,' muttered Beatrice. *Don't say things went wrong… He looks so unhappy…*

Then Herbert's voice rang loud and clear. 'Miss Beatrice! Everyone! Rejoice! I am blessed! I have the two luffly babies, one girl an' one boy, born together an' the girl came first. Miss Beatrice, you be godmother to Eloise Katherine? Mr Symonds, you godfather to Francis Herbert, yes?'

'Oh, Herbert, lovely news. How is Kate?'

'Herbert, man, I am delighted and honoured – and I'm called Francis too!'

'Kate is really happy an' well an' I will now go back to her but my wishes to you both for your weddings from me an' her both.'

And before anyone could blink an eye, his horse was wheeled round and he was galloping off, lederhosen rump standing well above the saddle; cheers and well wishes from the crowd following his dash back towards the road.

Sissy was crimson with excitement and expended energy. 'That is such good news on a wedding day, Beattie. You are blessed! Oh, and Arthur too, of course!

'What wonderful news, Mrs Lee. Kate is such a good friend of Beattie's…and new babies, one of each, a pigeon pair, isn't that what they say? Right, let's hope Jack's got your drinks all ready and Mrs Jack the plates… Come on, Lucille!'

Lucy went straight to the piano as guests found seats. Some men went out onto the back deck to smoke their pipes. The food was to be served in the new buffet style, where guests helped themselves when they wanted it.

Anderson had arranged times and schedules with his helpers so it wasn't long before he tapped a gavel on the top table and called guests to order.

Beatrice rather cruelly was reminded of Mr Pickwick as Anderson, jacket off, flexed his thumbs behind his braces and launched into a portentous speech about all her talents, intelligence, cleverness in teaching Lucy and readiness to turn to at any time and help Mrs Woof with the guests. He even mentioned how her time in the colony had taught her not to speak in that stuffy, 'PROPAH' English way and recounted a couple of incidents she thought long forgotten when her lack of country ways had given him and Sissy 'a giggle or two'. Beatrice heard Evelyn chortling at a couple of his comments and determined to ask her just what secrets she had let out…

As for Arthur, he was praised as a man of honour, a self-made man of merit who knew how to call a spade a spade and would, Anderson knew well, look after 'our dear Beattie' and make her a wealthy woman who could come back and visit as many times as she wanted!

Arthur then stood in front of the gathering and spoke briefly of his welcome in Bridgewater, his love for Beatrice 'since I first set eyes on her' on the *Orient* but she was someone else's wife and 'a pillar of rectitude'.

Beatrice smiled as she heard Sissy mutter, 'Pillar of what?'

Then Anderson shook Arthur's hand, asked Lucille to 'tinkle the keys' and invited guests to mingle and mix and leave – when they wanted, 'But not too soon 'cause I can allus broach another barrel! An now we'll have some dancing, the new Mr and Mrs Symonds first, then I intend to monopolise my dear sister's dancing steps – seeing as she's got cheeky young slippers on her pins…'

The delicate starting phrase of Chopin's Waltz No. 2 in A Flat echoed round the room and Beatrice was so surprised that Lucy was playing such a complicated piece. Arthur stepped up to her and bowed, extending his arm and drew her to him. Not a word from him but she was very conscious of his nearness and his warm breath on her ear.

Then she noticed – she had not before – that the old school piano had been brought up to the inn for the occasion. *Clever Lucy – she knows the limitations of the 'little square pianny'. How did she arrange that?*

Then all thought left her. Arthur's arm was around her; she felt its warmth through the fabric of her gown, causing a path of heat down to her waist – and below…

He was whispering in her ear, 'I love you, Beatrice, and now you are mine. I mean that, my love, but you will always be yourself as well, so stop giving me that squinty-eyed look!'

She smiled and her feet seemed to follow his effortlessly. Lucy's playing, which she noted out of habit, was smooth and faultless. Beatrice thought she would always remember the rhythm, the melody, the warmth of his grasp, of his hand, at this moment…

The music stopped and some of the crowd clapped at Lucy's playing. She rose and gave a little curtsey then Sissy ran in with a plate and guided her daughter to a table.

Arthur gazed at his new wife. 'Do you want to, need to, eat, my love? Or…'

She laughed. The spell was broken. 'We must eat and we will mingle but not too late. We will go up to your balcony room after six o'clock. That is when it will be ready for us! Oh, Arthur, I love you so, late though I am in knowing it. We can wait to be alone, we have all our lives…'

Reluctantly, he responded to a tap on his shoulder from Anderson. Beatrice scanned the room for Evelyn, thinking she might be with her mother. No, Mary Lee was now involved in a conversation with Mrs Bones. *What other tittle tattle is Mrs Bones passing on, I wonder?*

Beattie noticed Evelyn nibbling from a plate of cheeses and talking with… *Who is that fellow? Ah, think he's a friend of Kate's. Her relieving teacher? I can't remember his name but he's not from our village. Teaches grammar and French language I think that's what I heard from Mrs Bones. Suppose I'd better talk to some of these others.*

'Mrs Rogers, thank you for coming today, and Mr Rogers – why, it is good to see you when you are not behind a counter stamping the post! You know, I took a letter down to the GPO in Adelaide recently and I believe it sat in its box after I left it for nearly a week before getting a ship. Seeing you in the township, stamping and franking so quickly, I simply had not thought about the necessary wait for a ship going in the right direction.'

'Ahah, Mrs Beauchamp – sorry, Mrs *Symonds* – I send to the GPO three times a week so that when a ship is in, my service is as quick as theirs. Sometimes, ships going to Melbourne or Sydney take the post through to those cities to catch ship. We may not be quick, ma'am, but we do get the mail through – and there is always the Cobb and Co., particularly now the Kelly gang has lost its leaders.'

'I know he wasn't a very pleasant person but I was unhappy that such a young man, only twenty-five years old, should have to forfeit his life in such a way. To be hanged – when was it, three weeks ago? – is a bad way to end a life.'

'It was the eleventh of November, ma'am. Yet you must remember he was not at all penitent – and a callous brute to many poor unfortunates and quite ready to end the lives of others. Particularly the police, whose job is hard enough without miscreants like the Kellys…'

'Shush, man!' Mrs Rogers turned to Beatrice. 'Like many public officials, Mrs Symonds, Mr Rogers dreaded the news about the travels of the bushrangers. Too many uncertainties, indeed, when one is responsible for the mail.'

'Oh, I do agree. Now please do help yourself to finger foods, as my friend Evelyn uses the term. It seems that this way of serving a buffet is becoming very popular in the city and… Aah, Mr Jack, could you please replenish Mrs Rogers's cordial?'

# 57

Beatrice wiggled her fingers and then went over to Mary Lee. 'How lovely of you to come today, Mary – in the circumstances. Without you and Evie and John Benjamin, I don't know where I would be today. I doubt I would be here and so happy as I am.' She leaned down to kiss her dear old friend's plump cheek. 'And I do so like that dress. It has the new buttoning down the bodice. Do I detect Evelyn's hand in this choice?'

Mary smiled. 'Indeed you do. And I bought it ready-made from Charles Birks's store! That surprised me to my boot straps, Beattie, that dresses in my size that fit so well are hanging in a shop waiting to try. They're all of a sameness on the rack but if I like it, I don't mind. Rose, Mrs Charles Birks, told me and Mrs Colton they plan to bring lots of new selling ways – they call them marketing techniques, would you believe – over from Sydney that copy London! I wasn't sure about the colour, but Evie said John had wanted me to get one for the wedding and would help pay for it as long as it wasn't black or the darkest blue. I was in a bit of a fix, thinking, but Mrs Colton thought I chose well. And Alice and Evie between 'em, clever girls, made me the cap to match.'

'Oh, Mary, mentioning John, I can still feel his presence today and it means so much to know he was pleased for me and Arthur. And that you came today – oh, my dear friend, it means so very much to me. It cannot be easy for you to look merry, certainly not feel that way – it is still too soon. Yet you are here. You and Evelyn and John Benjamin have been my dearest friends since that unhappy arrival day in Port Adelaide.'

'My dear girl, perhaps I should confess. As you know, I am something of a stickler for being correct – my dear father's influence, I feel. I spoke to dear Mrs Colton and asked her advice about coming to your wedding. Some Adelaide folk are rather dyed in the wool about traditions, you know. However, she assured me that for me to come to your nuptials, even though some might tut-tut as it is so close to dear John Benjamin's dying, would be, taking all the friendships into account, quite appropriate. I know she will let it be known that she approves too, so I am, my dear friend, even more delighted to be here.'

'Dear Mary, Mrs Colton sounds such a good friend to you and a sound advocate for your good works. But you know, when Arthur and I go to the river lands, I do hope you will visit. Certainly, if you work as hard as Evelyn says you want to keep on doing, you'll need a break now and then. Do take care of yourself, dear friend. I know already you are involved, and plan to do more, and you a recent arrival here. Yes, so am I, but you have already done so much trying to help young women and girls arriving in the colony. You are indefatigable, Mary. Evie gave me a list – a long list – of some committees whose works interest you, and you are planning to give your time to them, and I know how you are helping Alice, and I think that absolutely wonderful.'

She brought up an adjacent chair and sat facing her dear Mrs Lee. 'It has been a very strange 1880 to this point, Mary. My own experiences here have taught me how fortunate I have been. For you and others to secure places where young women, newly arrived from the northern hemisphere, can seek refuge until a genuine position comes along – Mary, that is wonderful work. I know how I felt lost, quite unsure of myself, masking my fears as I marked the changes in my life. I had no one of family to help me. Then the Lees stepped in. Had you not, well, it does not bear thinking about. Then I met these dear Bridgewater folk, and I will always be so very grateful.'

'Shush, Beatrice, my dear. I am but an ordinary woman with some experience of life I can put to use. And what you have just described – well, that was very nearly a year ago. Fancy that! And what an eventful year for us all it has been. My dear John Benjamin, yes, but he would be so happy if he's looking down on us today because he was so happy to know of you and Arthur… Oh dear.' She wiped a tear from under her eye with her lacy kerchief. 'But happier days are now with us and today especially, you, dear girl. I would ask perhaps, when you are established in your new place, that you will let Evie or me know how to contact you. You say for me to come and stay and I will but also, you never know, perhaps you may in the future be able to find positions for some of the young women I'm learnin' about. A healthy, country life away from the temptations of the city would, it seems to me, be a blessing for them. We'll talk again, my dear, if not tomorrow, as Evelyn and I will be leaving in the morning, then as soon as we can. But now, I do believe your new husband is looking for you, maybe for another dance before he whisks you off upstairs.' She actually gave a chuckle, then sniffed above a wide smile and took Beatrice's hand and squeezed it, still chuckling.

Beatrice bit her lip in emotion. 'Oh, Mary, dear Mary Lee, you are such a dear friend and you are so strong… But bless you, I will write, I promise.'

She looked over at the piano. Lucy was playing a selection of music after the eldest Rogers girl, Paula, had taken turns playing a phrase or two. The music had surpassed all Beatrice's expectations – these girls would carve satisfying niches in their chosen lifestyles, that much was certain. Really, perhaps, she had helped this to happen. Not on Mary's scale perhaps: a modest achievement, but nevertheless she had been truly fortunate.

Beatrice spotted Anderson whispering to Lucy and Paula Rogers. Anderson noticed her watching and nodded, by which Beatrice understood this was to be the last waltz. And those young girls deserved a break. It had been a long and busy afternoon and now, though not dark, dusk was happening. Perhaps they should wind up, as no one could leave until after the bridal pair, so had decreed Anderson.

She moved over to touch Arthur's arm. He smiled and nodded and they moved into a last dance. Not a waltz, it was a Prelude – she couldn't think which but thought it sounded like the 'Raindrop' – Chopin again.

She whispered to Arthur. 'Goodness, how ambitious of Lucy.' *And just when has she been able to practise? An odd choice perhaps, choosing a prelude to end the day. Or intended as a prelude to their marriage, happiness, perhaps?*

She almost lost her step.

Arthur gave her a slow wink. 'It's pretty, my love, light-hearted. As for me, I like the idea it's the prelude to our first night together… Let us now stop and signal our goodbyes then they can all close their day and we – well, I – can get you alone, Mrs Symonds. Grrrrrrr…'

He laughed and they clung together in a long kiss. A slow clapping began from the watchers.

Arthur whispered against her lips and relinquished his clasp, then grasped her hand. 'It's our signal, Beatrice. Let's smile, wave and…and flee!'

As the newly marrieds disappeared upstairs, Anderson grinned at Lucy, who rippled a few final keys. She was looking over at Rauf, who was gazing at her with – was that love? Well, admiration anyway – in his eyes.

Anderson tucked his thumbs into his braces and smirked in satisfaction as he watched the newly weds disappear from the top of the stairwell. *Yerse, yerse indeed. It's been a grand, a wonderful, happy wedding day.*

# 1882–1886

## 58

Mrs Lee fastened up her boots with the hook, and a measure of difficulty. She hated the idea of growing stout and, to be honest, there were times when the stays seemed to bring on a feeling of congestion. Since Christmas she'd had the thought off and on to eat less from her plate – well, not put it there in the first place – but she kept forgetting to tell Alice. Now she was regretting that piece of cheese at lunchtime; and the piece of bread; and the apple. She wished she was arriving home instead of going out to the meeting. Anyway, meetings should be in mornings not afternoons. Folk need a snooze in the afternoons this weather! And now she was almost sixty-one years old – surely she could sometimes wish…?

More and more, she welcomed climbing into bed at night in her nightgown and free of such contraptions as bits of whalebone. She could not afford to follow fashion, nor was she particularly interested but, thanks to Evelyn's persuasion, some of her dresses now had buttons in the newer style, instead of laces. Buttons were a problem because they would not always stay in line when fastened – well, when they were under stress; gaps were unsightly when one's shift could be seen beneath.

She remonstrated with her reflection in the looking glass. 'Come on, Mrs Mary Lee, you have things to do today! It could be an interesting one.'

She and her dear friend Mrs Colton were to visit the House of Mercy in Stephens Terrace, Walkerville – not far away, but they would be going in Mrs Colton's trap, the sun being at its zenith at the appointed time, and on an already hot day. *Oh dear, this heat and I do not agree!*

Mrs Lee, as a member of the ladies' committee of the female refuge, had been invited to accompany Mrs Colton, who had stated it was an exploratory mission on behalf of the Social Purity Society and at the request of the Reverend Kirby. The House of Mercy, also known as the Adelaide Retreat for Women, had only recently been instituted. It was intriguing for Mary Lee, who had already visited and helped organise aspects of the accommodation administration for young Jewish and Catholic girls, to visit an institution described as 'thoroughly unsectarian in character; opening its arms to those in need of help of all religions'. Mary liked the idea that the young women could stay with their babies for the first year of the baby's life and then choose to keep the baby, or place it in the babies' home ready for adoption. *Very Christian attitude, indeed. I like it, so I do. Makes me think of Beatrice. Wonder how her little girl is doing? She'll be three months old now…*

There were only six young women in residence on that day and according to the matron six was all they could accommodate at any one time. Recently, one girl had married the father of her child, some had gone home to their relatives and two had obtained positions as servants in good houses. Mrs Lee and Mrs Colton were of one mind as they drove home: to recommend the establishment as worthy of any help that might be forthcoming from the Social Purity Society…

Mary Lee arrived home to find a letter waiting from her friend Beatrice. 'Oh, this is lovely. Just when I was thinking of her.'

Alice placed a pot of tea on the table. She knew the handwriting and was curious. 'Do tell me, Mrs Lee, please, how is that baby of hers?'

Mary stopped reading. 'I've seen some lovely babies this very afternoon Alice, ones with no homes, or doubtful ones for some, at best. As for little Esther Symonds… just wait a minute or two and I may even let you read it for yourself… Oh, they have moved – this is from the town of Morgan. The train goes to Morgan, Alice, I know that. She says that Mr Symonds has renewed contacts with the paddle boats and steam engines and pumping water again. So she says, Alice. Also, Mr Symonds has gained a reputation with steam irrigators. Goodness me, I wonder what exactly all that means? She says they are living in a small lodging house and she is finding it hard not having a place of their own with the baby an' all. Also, it is using up some of their savings. It seems Mr Symonds has explored the idea of them all living on a peebee – what? Oh, I see, a paddle boat – but there is some prejudice against women on boats and it's only accepted if they own the vessel. Arthur – that is Mr Symonds of course – is looking for a property somewhere nearer to where the irrigation settlement will grow. And it seems some wealthy pastoralist has donated – donated? My goodness me! – about twenty thousand acres to the government, who are negotiating with some irrigation specialists czlled Chaffey to build an irrigation colony based on the area. It'll be called the Renmark Irrigation Trust. But it will take another two or three years she thinks and she wants her own home before then. Mr Symonds wants to be involved in all that and he plans to look for a house – and there are some but not many properties already settled there – so Beatrice can make a permanent home and he will work on the property and also use his skills as an engineer. Well, well, well, Alice. It seems everything is positive with them. She promises to write when all that happens. Now, do pour me that cup of tea even as you listen, please! That reminds me, Alice: there have been a few deaths in the hospital from typhoid.'

'Typhoid fever, ma'am? Isn't that from dirty water and... and...'

'Sewage? Yes, Alice. But Mrs Colton was saying her husband had been given a report in the House that it can be caused by a bacterium found in eggs. We must wash all the eggs we buy, Alice, before we break into them.'

1882 was a year when over a hundred and forty cases of typhoid were noted in Adelaide and there was an outcry from people believing the fault to lie with the operation of the new sewerage system set up in Islington. Ample washing and water supplies to flush the sewerage system properly were badly affected by the drought later that year, which carried on well into the next year.

*

Beatrice wrote fairly often, causing Mary to feel rather guilty that she did not write back as promptly as she should. Following the Easter holiday of the next year, Beatrice wrote to say they had moved nearer to what was planned to be the town of Renmark.

'Evelyn, listen to this! She calls her house Cumquats. What on earth is a cumquat? A tree? It seems yes, yes, yes. It is more like a farm and has vines and land and is by the river but there are no other houses for miles. Oh, goodness, it seems Beatrice will be looking after the vines and the vegetables and Arthur will be looking into irrigation for the crops. She says they have some land that straddles the border. Goodness me! How can that be? I didn't know they were near the border but it must be so because she says the Customs House is less than ten miles from where they are. I really should reply. Do remind me, Alice. She seems contented now, but oh my goodness! I don't see Beatrice as a farmer, I must admit. She writes they have help, though, a man and wife who lived there before. Sam and Nancy, she calls them. Oh, and although production on the new vines and the vegetable plot had been severely affected by the drought – the Murray river levels have been critical – the production of future Symondses is progressing healthily. She is expecting another baby!'

Evelyn was too busy in the administration of the Telegraph Department's involvement with the correct functioning of the Adelaide Telephone Exchange to comment other than to ask her mother to wish Beatrice well.

January 1884 brought a long letter from Beatrice, apologising for not writing since weeks before Christmas and the reason – or reasons – were her twin boys William and George! Mary and Evelyn were delighted and Evelyn spoke of going to visit.

But the next two years were busy ones for Mary Lee. She didn't manage to take time off to go to Cumquats. *Beattie will understand. She knows what I'm like…*

Mary was increasingly interested in the proceedings of the new Trades and Labour Council and, later, the State Children's Council. She wanted to understand how the one could help the working women discussed at times on one of her committees, and the other council, if they would change the age of consent. However, John Colton was also keen for that to happen and according to dear Mrs Colton it would be brought to pass in 1885.

Much to do…

# 1887

## 59

Mary Lee was once more contemplating her dress in front of the long cheval glass. 'I know Evelyn believes the easier, looser styles are more becoming but on an older woman like myself they are not so flattering. What are we now – 1887 – and another hot summer's day. Near the end o' January already. My goodness, how time flies, an' soon I've another birthday comin' up – I'll be sixty-six. Oh, my deed an' goodness. Well, since I came here, my waist has grown a little bigger, no denying, but one's figure loses its elasticity as one grows older, sure it does, and needs more support – so I tell Evie. Only yesterday morning when I went to pin on my cap, the seam of my dress gave way under the arm. I've had this navy blue one a while and the fabric's getting' thinner but I do think it's due more to the hot weather, so energetic is that sun at times. Oh, Mary Walsh Lee, it's a bad way you're in when you're talking to yourself. Aye, so I am, an' no wonder. An' no Evie to comment at my 'oi' sounds, impertinent so she is. I only ever put them on for fun, but she is so serious about her position, that girl… And who else is here to listen? So I'll save my voice and think instead!'

*Alice is out at her friend's and Evelyn's on her way to that Bridgewater place to be a godmother, Lord be praised! Then it's that Lucille's wedding. Well, she's a nice young lass, too. Evie says when Lucille comes to live in the city with her new husband – he's a German an' I met him at Beattie's wedding all those years ago – she plans to visit. And I thought they would have married much before now – Lucille must be twenty-three or -four – but Evie says her fiancé wanted to be established first. Well, that's commendable, I suppose…*

'Oh, this blessed new button! It's stuck an' Mrs Colton's trap will be here to collect me in a few minutes. Stuck or not, I'd better get me to the gate or the trap will be in the way o' the other traffic an' that gets noisy with the drivers arguing, so it does.'

She breathed in, pulled down her bodice to snare the button, and collected her quilted document satchel, stitched by Evelyn, from the table. *Evelyn's quite the favourite among some ladies of acquaintance for designing and stitching these bags; they're keeping her busy. She's made one for Beatrice, I know, as a present... Useful for my letters and papers, though.*

Mary sighed. She seemed to acquire more and more written notes to carry round for reference as 'Hon. Sec.', so she called herself. Unfortunately, the 'honorary' bit meant she wasn't paid for her work. Today's business was with the ladies' committee of the Social Purity Society, of which Mrs Colton was now ladies' president, with Mrs Lee as the ladies' secretary and Rosetta – properly entitled Mrs Charles Birks in public company – being the treasurer. The society had campaigned energetically in the last two years for reforms to stop the exploitation of young girls, a campaign facilitated in some degree by the raising of the age of consent – something Mary had hoped for and now enabled by the Honourable John Colton. In his capacity as premier and during his last year in office, 1885, he enabled the passing of relevant legislation, the Criminal Law Consolidation Amendment Act, which raised the legal age of consent in South Australia to sixteen. The Act effectively gave young girls in the colony a measure of protection from many kinds of exploitation. And it was now fact.

*Good man, that one. We've been worrying about that for a couple of years, even though dear Mrs Colton gave me the whisper a while back...Wonder if the rumours of his being knighted become fact also.*

Mary Lee and her contemporaries felt keenly for the plight of these children, some as young as only ten, who were often sent out to work at anything to bring in the pennies; unfortunately, that ominous 'anything' seemed more and more to involve unsavoury practices. Those girls who gained places as servants in households were the lucky ones, as they were usually cared for by their employers. Sometimes boys were taken on as yard boys or for other odd jobs and it meant good savings when they too were fed an' watered by their employers, so Mary felt, but girls were the bigger worry. And even now, despite the legislation, young girls were still being abused, sometimes in their over-crowded homes. Too many young girls in Adelaide had opted for a life of prostitution, selling themselves on the streets or in brothels.

Mary Colton was hoping to initiate a discussion at this afternoon's meeting about the issue of exploitation. Coincidentally, that same year the news had reached Adelaide about Eliza Armstrong, the thirteen-year-old daughter of a London chimney sweep. When she told Evelyn the story, Evie had actually suggested it was straight out of Charles Dickens. Mary was not a little shocked that her daughter could not believe that such unpleasantness existed, yet had to admit the tale did read like something Dickens would have scripted.

This Eliza was the innocent protagonist in a scheme whereby the editor of the *Pall Mall Gazette*, William Stead, of an investigative turn of mind, hoped to demonstrate the despicable ease with which young girls could be enticed, indeed sold, into prostitution. Stead elicited the aid of a prominent feminist, Josephine Butler, and Bramwell Booth of the Salvation Army in his plan, hoping to highlight the levels of depredation to which poverty-stricken young girls were subjected. They 'bought' young Eliza Armstrong from her mother to show how young girls under the age of consent were being lured – or abducted – to brothels on the European continent.

It was a reprehensible practice all round, Mary thought, and feelings were mixed over there about William Stead being sent to prison for a few months and young Eliza being returned to her parents by the Salvation Army. He meant well, so he did.

What intrigued Mary was the question whether it was a consequence of that case or purely coincidence that the social purity movement in Britain had sought to raise the age of consent to sixteen? There was a Bill pending here, too. Not before time, in Mary's opinion. This young colony of South Australia was ahead of the Mother Country in matters of sensibility and common sense, or so she was pleased to consider. Her complaint was that a lot of preparation went into planning good legislation yet it seemed to drag its heels into actuality. *I have only been here seven years and a bit and they have been busy ones, so that's how things get done. And there's always lots more to do.*

As she rushed down the path, her waist button popped open again. 'Well, no time to fix you now. I'll just carry my bag and then keep my glove in front…' *I'm sure Evelyn will mend it for me. Perhaps let out the bodice? Oh, I do not like that idea at all! Besides which, the seams will show…*

She wasn't the only one careful of expenses, however. She knew she was managing, especially with Evelyn getting paid, and the boarders paying their lodging fees. However, the state was in what was euphemistically called 'an economic downturn'; family breadwinners were losing their jobs and incidences of abuse and unsavoury job requirements of youngsters were reaching the papers. Just too many of them to help...

As the population of the colony increased, as many more women, daughters, sisters, single adults and wives arrived, giving weight to their arguments for fairness and equality, it became apparent to Mary Lee – and equally so to her colleagues– that many changes were needed in the law to raise women's legal status. It had been a small – but significant – move in 1883 when they passed the Married Women's Property Act.

Mary tried hard to enthuse Evelyn with the progress of the suffrage debate but Evelyn considered the matter was being pursued quite adequately by her mother and her friends! Under the Honourable John Colton's guidance, also in 1885, a motion had been passed in the South Australian parliament for the enfranchisement of women. This motion put the whole question of a woman's right to vote on the political agenda and was followed up the next year on the thirteenth of October by Dr Edward Stirling in the House of Assembly. He had daughters – in Mary's mind a decided advantage for understanding a woman's capabilities. She did wonder if his daughters were earnest followers of the cause. The Bill was passed on a second reading but with no absolute majority, and was therefore not being proceeded with – currently. Mary was becoming quite impatient!

# 60

All this was on her mind as she waited at her garden gate for Mrs John Colton. The trap arrived and, with it, an apology delivered by the driver. Mary sighed as she took it from him. Mrs Colton would not be attending the meeting as she had succumbed to a migraine but she knew 'that Mrs Lee was cognisant of her opinions and feelings in the matters for discussion and would have able assistance in the person of Mrs Charles Birks'.

Mary mused further on the local issues as the trap made its way to the community hall. She knew that the Honourable John Colton was to tender his resignation from the Assembly, imminently, as dear Mrs Colton had confided to her, because of – as she explained – 'a tiredness of all the procedural headaches'. Mrs Charles Birks – Rosetta – was quite recently returned from England and had already become a dear friend despite her many social obligations. Her husband had some years ago run a shop in Hindley Street with David Robin and then when that partnership was dissolved had established a larger store in Rundle Street. Charles and Rosetta ('please call me Rose') had married in 1879 but had lived in England a number of years and Rose had become a full-time stepmother to Charles's six children. Returning to Adelaide as they did in the jubilee year, when South Australia celebrated the colony's fiftieth birthday, and then of course being guests at the various Commemoration Day festivities just before New Year, dear Mrs Birks had found her social duties rather onerous.

'I love him dearly and his children are such darlings, dear Mrs Lee, but being the partner of someone re-establishing himself in the city carries quite a weight of duties, I feel, to the exclusion of my own personal interests.'

Mr Charles Birks had been called back to Adelaide to resume his management duties of the store that had become one of Adelaide's most popular and profitable department stores, no doubt thanks to that 're-establishing' Rose had mentioned. He was supportive of his wife's concerns and welcomed female employees in his store, recognising that, in some departments particularly, they were a decided asset. It was one of Evelyn's favourite haunts, that's for sure.

Reverend Kirby was at the meeting. He was newly made up as chairman of the Congregational Union in South Australia and a powerful voice in social reform, his views fitting neatly with those of the society. Unfortunately for the planned introductions on the agenda this day, Reverend Kirby's main concern was related to the youth – male youth – around the Port Adelaide area; his ideas and plans had today dominated the planned agendum. Little was therefore discussed about the matters of exploitation and training for young women migrants as mooted by Mrs Colton.

Mary Lee had also mooted a committee discussion about the failure of the last Suffrage Bill that Dr Stirling reintroduced into parliament the previous October. It failed to gain the required majority and now Mary was eager to gain some indication of a next move – unfortunately, only men could move such things in parliament!

But little was gained that day, and she was pleased to return home and loosen her stays. Even better, Alice greeted her with a welcome pot of tea on the table.

'No biscuits, thank you, Alice.'

'Saw you climb down from that trap, Mrs Mary. How was the meeting?'

Mary allowed that form of address from her trusted Alice when they were together and she outlined her disappointment with Reverend Kirby's domination of the meeting. One counterpoint to the ability of a widow to please herself in her opinions and activities was, she had discovered, a readiness on the part of worthy causes not to give her the recognition married women with 'important' husbands seemed to command, whether they deserved it or not.

Evelyn told her once, when she and her mother were arguing about Mary's frequent letters to the newspapers on matters topical, that she'd heard her mother referred to as a 'fierce Irish woman'. She would not reveal the source. Mary digested the remark and concluded that if not a compliment, it was a mixed blessing, as it was at least recognition of sorts.

Alice took away the biscuits. 'Never mind, ma'am. As you say to me, there are many more ways of killing a cat!'

Alice was now a proficient young housekeeper and, contrary to her earlier intentions of always being an independent single woman with a career, was 'walking out'. Freddy was a wharfsman from the Port and locally born with parents living in Hindmarsh. Mary had met the whole family and, as long as he did the right thing by her young charge, he was welcome in Barnard Street. Not that Mary wanted to lose Alice to him. If the relationship became more permanent, she planned to talk over with Evelyn the feasibility of the young marrieds becoming boarders, even at a reduced rate. There was a little room attached to the outside laundry which they could make into a respectable bedroom with a couple of chairs and a small table…

Mary already had two lady boarders who shared one of the larger rooms. At Mrs Colton's suggestion – she was a board member of the Nursing Sister's Association, which cared for needy mothers after childbirth, and before as necessary – Mary had applied and obtained a permit to take boarders, particularly ladies from country families wishing to attend city doctors. After the babes were born, the new mothers would return to Barnard Street for their lying-in or until they felt capable of taking the babies back to their remote country homes. With one in particular, Mrs Dawes, Mary and Evelyn became quite friendly and she came to stay for two of her babies. More to the point, though, in addition to their pleasant company of an evening, the boarders' regular payments helped Mary get by. As Mary would say to Evelyn and Alice – and anyone else close to her – 'Every little helps!'

Alice announced she'd serve her and Mary's dinner shortly in the small dining room but she'd take the boarders' meals into their room as they had asked that afternoon.

'Can you bring my writing things in shortly, please, Alice?'

Alice looked a little perturbed. Miss Evelyn had recently confided in her that her mother's letters to the editor tended to be imprudent when she was worked up about an issue. Evelyn worried that her mother would anger people she might later need on her side in an argument. Yet this very evening, Mary was planning another letter to the editor of the *Register* on the supply of proper training for young single women to enable them to profit honestly and properly by their industry.

'More than one way of killing a cat…' *Indeed, Alice! And as if you are not the very living example of what can be done, I don't know what is…*

# 61

In Bridgewater, on that same day, the atmosphere was one of enjoyment and reunion. Evelyn had visited the inn for a local ceremony during the state's jubilee year, and had consequently promised to visit again. Only a few months later and she was back in the little town to stay and as godmother to a little baby girl. And right now after an ecstatic welcome she was sitting in the baby girl's parents' house in the German village. Evie and Kate had been friendly since Kate's wedding but the Flachs had spent some years in the Barossa area and the women had only met up a couple of times since they returned to Hahndorf. Herbert learned coopering up there and Kate seemed to have babies regularly. It was so good to get together again! Kate's latest little girl had been born on Christmas after their return to Hahndorf and was named Evelyn Mary. Evelyn was thrilled at the choice and she was to stand as godmother the next Sunday.

She was staying at the inn, where all the news and talk was about Lucy's wedding to be held on the twelfth, the week after the christening. She was delighted to find that Anderson and Sissy were still mine hosts. Last year there had been rumours they might sell up when Lucy left, but apparently some new arrangement had been settled. Lucy – or Lucille, as she now preferred to be called – was equally delighted to see her and they had spent time that morning, she and Evelyn, discussing city fashions.

As a constant friend of 'dear Beattie', Evie was a welcome visitor and had persuaded Anderson to loan her the small trap for the afternoon. It wasn't far to the Flachs' place and she was a proficient driver, and so eager to catch up with Kate and meet her little god-daughter, that Anderson had been quite willing.

Over the years apart, Kate had written to both Evelyn and Beatrice – but not as often as she would have liked – and as soon as her children were settled around their tea table she and Evelyn enjoyed a most enjoyable chat, as Herbert called women's news-sharing.

Herbert wasn't present. He was now fully accomplished, with his own workshop and some apprentices taken from the Lutheran village; he consequently made a very comfortable living making and supplying beer and wine barrels. They were both looking forward to seeing Beatrice again and Herbert would have liked Arthur to come as well, but understood about him needing to stay for business reasons.

'That is my misfortune, *meine Liebe*. But you and Evelyn can find out all the news from her if I cannot see much of her myself, how his business is going, *ja*?'

Kate and Herbert had seen the Symondses some months previously on Cobdogla Station, a little settlement on the enormous property owned by the Chambers brothers. It had been a happy coincidence. She and Herbert were visiting there to look at some wood barrelling workshop equipment that was up for sale and they literally bumped into Arthur and Beatrice. Arthur, as usual, was sizing up the prospects of a huge pumping engine planned for that part of the river country and hoping that the manager, James Trussell, a keen irrigator, could answer some questions. Arthur was preparing a report for a British firm which had hired him to survey the area for them with a view to potential development. The men had gone off together and Kate and Beatrice had thoroughly enjoyed catching up on each other's news over a relaxed session in the extensive station kitchen with scones and tea. Now Beatrice was coming for the christening and the wedding, so they would be able to share some wonderful days.

It was not only Beatrice who lived far away; Kate's life in the Barossa had intervened too. Now, being the typical teacher, she stated the early days of February 1887 should be marked in history books for posterity – whenever Beatrice was able get there! It was all too long since the three young women had been together; their meeting here, where they had become close friends, was going to be just the happiest experience, declared Kate.

'So long ago! And soon Beattie will be here too. We can all three be together again but do tell me first, Evie, is your mother well? It's so long since I saw her but I do read about her in the newspaper. She cares so much about the young homeless girls and I empathise with some of that, even though I was one of the fortunate ones. Is she well? In herself, I mean. She must be well into her sixties now and yet still so busy…'

Evie said how her mother sent her blessings to the new little Evelyn and to Lucy for her wedding – she had met her at Beattie's wedding. Lucy was to be married on the twelfth of February, the Saturday after little Evelyn's christening. As Kate and Evie settled down to some lovely cheesy bites and a home-grown white wine, they speculated on how country life might have changed Beatrice's general outlook from the very upright person she had been on first arriving.

Evie recounted Beatrice's initial shock just after arrival in the colony when assured that wearing leggings under a hacking skirt was accepted, as was shedding a petticoat under her dress in the hot weather…

'But so commonsensical is she, she quickly realised the logic. Mam feels that in England she was brought up to be so correct by her mama that it would have been hard to accept some of Adelaide's ways.'

Evelyn thought for a while and sipped her wine. 'Nevertheless, I do find that in some ways the Adelaide society ladies are hidebound in inherited Britishness. My mother accepts it as part of her theory of it being a small world. I think I was helped to accept all the changes of our new city because I started work and met other people and learned from them, and my work kept me busy and I had money to spend on what fashions helped me to blend in. I do remember how Beattie agonised over how to demonstrate her mourning. Poor girl, she was even unsure whether she was mourning her mother more than James! I know Mrs Woof caught her covering all the mirrors one day and Beattie explained how it was a rigid custom in England. That was all Queen Victoria's doing, of course – she started doing that after Prince Albert died. Thankfully, my mam was always more relaxed about certain English customs. She is looking forward to seeing Beattie again as she goes back home through Adelaide. We all managed to adjust in our different ways, didn't we?'

'Well, I did grow up here, Evie, but you quickly adapted into the Aussie ways, didn't you? I had the feeling Beattie has too, now, after I met her and we talked in Cobdogla.'

'Where? Cob-dog–what?'

Kate grinned. 'It's a station. Breeds horses, I think. Massive place. I found Beattie looking quite at home in the river land surroundings but still the lovely warm and energetic woman we knew. She was so eager to have news of everyone. I hadn't written as often as I should perhaps but she had read in the newspapers of your mother's battles on behalf of working women.'

'She would have done. She wrote to me that she was remarkably certain Mam would win all her battles too. She follows all Mam's news from the papers – and her letters to the editor. Oh, I dislike some of those letters she writes, Kate, and dislike more some of the ones sent to her or back to the *Register*! She brushes off the criticism, but I feel it for her! Of course, like everyone else, she asks me constantly if I have found a special man – it is so expected and yet I do wish my friends would know I am happy as I am. I'm sure my mother thinks I must have a husband to be happy. I do have a very good friend, but we neither of us want to marry.' She bent as if to whisper. 'You'll think me strange perhaps but I really don't want children.'

'Goodness me, Evie, I didn't know but… '

Evie put out her hand and grasped her friend's. 'Kate, dearest Kate. I shall be the best, the very best godmother to your little Evie. I do like children, it's just that… Oh, I don't know. Maybe I am just selfish. I do know Mam would like grandchildren here to dandle on her knee, but I have not yet met any man who persuaded me and now I'm in my late twenties and too long in the tooth to change. I do love my work in the Telegraph Office, and I am paid well. At least I can help her in that way.

# 62

Kate was so happy to see Evie again – and to have the chance to sit and talk about things. *She may not like children but they certainly like her. Eloise has taken note of her hair, her dress and even cast an eye on her pretty suede boots, and she just a child! Bless her. Eloise was so good with the little ones and soon she would take them over to the watchful eye of Frau Wilhelm, her mutti's proxy mother, so they could play with some of the other little ones and her with seven-year-old Elsa. Baby would have to stay but she was so happy when awake and when asleep – well.*

Little Eloise was busy keeping the children under control at their table. Even Frank, her twin, bowed to her stately authority. At six years old, he recognised that in this house the women were the bosses. When he grumbled, his father explained that women ruled the home – inside the walls. But Eloise got his goat when she kept reminding him that she was born first anyway and it was her right to be Number One!

Kate was unaware of her children's rivalry; she tried hard not to show favouritism among them and, by and large, life went along smoothly and she was content. By and large, she had succeeded. Frank would be astonished to know his mother admitted to a favourite and that he was it! He certainly didn't want Joshua to join school yet, to begin growing up and trying to be boss, yet Mutti said Josh already knew his letters in English, and some in German. He could read in English and was mature enough for school. However, thankfully for Frank, Vati had decided Josh should wait till after Easter.

He thought that at least it was different outdoors when girls had to bow to the masculine will, but sometimes he was kept so busy with what his father called his manly chores he couldn't throw the weight of his authority around very much. And this next week he and Eloise were to start back at school. Frank was not too keen at having to learn to write and things like that. Writing and reading were girls' jobs, in his opinion! And maybe he could boss the little ones around outside but it was a nuisance having to watch them. Joshua was soon to be five and the only one not with a December birthday! Inga had been born in 1885 on the twins' birthday and this new baby had been born when Inga was only just one year old on Christmas Day and was soon to be christened. Miss Evelyn would be her godmother. The christening was to be held on Sunday in their Lutheran church. Even worse, thought Frank, only a week afterwards, Rauf was marrying that lady from the inn in Bridgewater there and he was expected – well, invited, his mother said – to be an attendant. He had to dress up two weekends and he hated stupid breeches! When he complained to his *großmutter* that dressing up wasn't manly stuff, she looked really angry and said any more complaints about manly duties and she would give the important wedding duty to Joshua. That baby!

Frau Wilhelm wasn't his real grandmother anyway but the pastor called her the Kommandant so she had to be obeyed, or so Vati ordered. And this man Rauf Schulze who was getting married, Frank didn't remember him, but he knew that like his Vati Herbert, he was really an orphan from an old country on the other side of the world. And that was why his own father and this other Rauf thought of the pastor as their real father. Vati's parents had died far away too, and so had Mutti's – but in different countries. It was all a bit confusing but Frank didn't care too much, because Vati and Mutti were happy and he loved them both, even when they told him what to do. Vati had explained how the Lutheran village had given Rauf a home too and he thought of it as his place and the church they had built themselves had played such a part in Rauf's life as well as Vati's… So that's why it was all to happen here.

Eloise took Josh and Inga by their hands to walk across the compound and Frank also scrambled over to the door.

'Children! Please say a polite goodbye to Miss Evelyn because she will be going before you come home. Frank, please carry Inga. Her little legs are still quite new to walking.'

The little ones held up their face for a kiss. Eloise planted a sloppy one firmly on Evelyn's cheek and Frank thrust out his hand to be shaken, copying his father.

Kate flopped back on her chair. 'Oh, lovely! Peace at last and even Baby's still sleeping. A wine, I think?'

'Oh, can you?' Evie wiggled her hand miming breast feeding, and Kate chuckled.

'She has not suffered yet. I am careful, of course, but she is so sturdy she is already eating groats, don't worry! Now tell me of the people at the inn. I haven't seen them for a couple of weeks. Is Lucy all excited about the wedding?'

They talked of Lucy and her Rauf and remembered how that affair had started at Kate and Herbert's wedding. The young Rauf Schulze was now practising some kind of law in the city and that was where he and Lucille Woof were to live after the wedding.

Kate confided that Lucy's mother had wanted her to marry in the little Bridgewater church but Lucy was quite happy to go along with Rauf. 'Sissy is taking on two new girls to learn the work in the inn. One is a Bridgewater lass, the other comes from this village. Beatrice will see some changes there, my word, she will. Lucy has already been passing onto the new girls all those nice little details Beattie taught her – serviettes and knives and fork and things like that.'

She leaned forward as if to whisper a secret. 'The inn has acquired an enviable reputation for its cooking and its musical events. Mr Anderson told the pastor that they are thinking of enlarging the hotel area so that people taking the train through from Adelaide can enjoy the events, stay overnight and then catch the train back to the city the next day.'

'Goodness! That *is* progress. I wonder if Beattie will bring her children with her? Esther is what – six? She's perhaps sensible enough to travel, but the little boys are only three, are they not? That would be a handful!'

William and George, Beatrice had written, were like chalk and cheese. Apparently each was fair-haired and grey-eyed like Arthur but whereas William seemed to develop a serious nature and later on was often trying to make things to please his father, George was always disappearing, chasing the chickens and being quite a handful. Esther and George argued incessantly, she complained, yet Arthur favoured George.

'They must be prospering up there, though, Evie. When Herbert and I met them in Cobdogla, Beattie said the children were left at home with…I can't remember her name, but she and her husband live on their land and he acts as manager for Arthur when he's away. I think this lady watches the children quite often. She has none of her own.'

'Beattie writes to Mam fairly often, Kate, which is nice. Mam told me she and Arthur are thinking of having a couple of girls to help in the house and asked Mam for advice. She will give them a safe home if they are up to scratch, said Mam. Apparently the manager's wife is lovely but she is older and has a hip problem and fears that she can't race after the little ones like she would like.'

Kate chuckled. 'That'd be right. Young boys can be the most trouble – they wander off on adventures… I suppose Beattie has to be outdoors quite a lot, too.'

'You are sooo right, Kate! Depending on the growth of the grapes apparently, Beattie has to spend most of her days in their vineyards. She trims the vines and works alongside Arthur in the fields – can you imagine? She is even learning how to add chemistry to the wines so that they keep well – or something. She could not do all that without help with the children, I'm sure.'

'Oh, it will be good to have her with us and she can tell us about her life. It really sounds so exciting and…well, different from what I would ever have thought Beatrice to adopt.'

Boing! Herbert's wall clock struck again and Evie literally shot from her chair.

'Oh, I promised Anderson I would return the trap before now! Please excuse me to Herbert, Kate. I'll see you again soon and hope I'll bring Beattie over with me – and certainly before Sunday!'

What a bustling around ensued! It woke the baby, who gave a hearty protest. Kate picked her up and walked her to the door just as Frau Wilhelm approached across the square with a toddler on each arm and a happy Eloise skipping and singing at her side. One of the village boys was readying the trap and its faithful old mare.

Evie clambered aboard, flicked the reins and clicked the horse on its way. Kate waved and took Baby indoors as Frau Wilhelm came into the house. Kate would be barraged with questions… Life was back to normal!

# 31 January 1887

## 63

The Symonds trap was a four-seater and Arthur strapped William securely on the cushions next to his own seat. It was Monday, the last day of January in 1887 – an auspicious year for those residents near the river because the long-discussed Renmark irrigation colony was to become fact.

'Now, stay strapped in, young fellow! If you fall from here, you could get a nasty head cut and I don't want to bring your mother back from her well-earned visiting. The paddle boat has only just taken off from Sheoak Landing and we've nearly ten miles to go home. Now, if you behave yourself, me and Nancy will be well pleased and she gave me a bag of bread and salty dripping to eat as we go along. Tell you what – you can look out for currawongs for me. Do you know what they look like? The big greyish-black one with a white bit on his tail?'

An energetic nodding caused the cushion around the little boy's ears to bob in unison.

'Right. Good man. Well, I need to think very carefully on some matters so I'd like you to count the birds you see until we get home. Quietly. See how quiet you can be. If you can do well, it's a chunk of taffy for you. I know Nancy was making some.'

A pair of wide-open grey eyes stared seriously at the father but no voice emanated from his wrappings. Bread and dripping was a favourite.

Arthur and Beatrice jointly owned a few acres southwards from what was soon to be recognised as the town of Renmark. After boarding in Blanchetown then renting in Morgan, they were eager to own a property of their own. When Cumquats came on the market, they looked it over, and that was that. It was actually a stone house, set low and with red stone quoins round the windows. Importantly, Beatrice loved it. The previous owner, Sam Bristol, was in his sixties and after years of building and developing the property in what had been even more of an isolated area, he was happy to hand over the reins, as he expressed it. He and his wife lived in a little cottage he'd built at the opposite end of the small home paddock from the main house. The Bristols had no children and accepted the Symondses' three children as their own. Sam had built the house and developed the property when they were the only settlers in the area and had been pleased to sell to the Symonds; even more so when Arthur asked him to stay on to act as manager and mentor. Sam had also invested in another land selection that straddled the border and had given the Symondses first option of purchase. Sam knew every inch of the acreage: which area flooded easily, which had the best soil, which dried out too quickly, and all the other thousand and one things Arthur wanted to learn.

Life on the land suited Arthur and Beatrice equally. Beatrice had the farming background and Arthur was learning to command the river and the irrigation needs of his land. The main problem at the moment, as Arthur saw it, was that the other selection not only abutted the Victorian border, but part of it deviated over into Victoria. This meant that the regulations of both colonies could affect his planning and there was the likelihood of future contention in water allocations. Not often, but occasionally, bureaucracies argued in Melbourne and Adelaide and Arthur felt he could be serving too many masters. The main problems concerning the river were the water allocations and use for irrigation.

He mused on the facts versus speculation on that homeward ride while little William looked for elusive currawongs. The more he and Beatrice learned of each other's capabilities, the more they felt they'd made a good decision in buying Cumquats. Beatrice was keen to develop the little vineyard and had already started to regenerate some old vines the Bristols had planted years ago. She had ordered books on the topic and was now looking into actually producing a wine. They'd sampled some this past year from the few bottles Sam had put down and it was highly drinkable. Her enthusiasms were spurred once again. She was now talking about markets. Not one for hastening slowly, was his Beatrice!

Arthur grinned as he wondered how she was liking the stately progress of the little paddle boat, called a peebee by the river folk, that was taking her downriver to Morgan. From there she'd go by train to Adelaide. The peebee was owned jointly by a husband and wife team and the wife lived on the boat also; this allowed Beatrice to travel too, for a short trip. There was a curious prejudice held by many river folk about women on any vessel. More to the point, she was one of Beatrice's ilk, so he thought, and they would get on well. He smiled to himself, thinking how Beatrice was not the most patient of women and its leisurely progress would try what patience she had, yet Neil promised they'd make the train in good time. He needed to, having taken on a train-despatch load at the Landing.

He grinned even more widely, looked down at his little boy she'd given him and impulsively gave his narrow shoulders an affectionate squeeze.

On a serious note, irrigation was essential, not only for her vines but also the oranges and other fruits already on the property under Sam's capable eye. Water flows needed steering where growers wanted them to go, and pumps properly fitted were the answer. Water supply could not be assumed, taken for granted. No one knew that more than a man with a background in pumping mechanisms!

And today was an auspicious day which could ease restrictions or reinforce them. This very day, later on, a meeting was planned in the local hall and would be sure to stir up some energetic discussion. Sam was to be there for Cumquats. On the fourteenth of February, the irrigation colony at Renmark was to be signed into fact as orchestrated by the Chaffey brothers under the auspices of the South Australian government. Renmark was not yet gazetted as a town, so it would have to be Adelaide. Sam would have the tale, but even so, Arthur intended to drive into the township as soon as possible and catch up with some knowledgeable friends. *Hmm, Beatrice won't be home by then. That's two days after the wedding and also Mrs Lee's birthday and I think she's going back with Evelyn, who wants to be with her mother on that day. Fine by me, but…*

'You're a good lad, young Will. Here's the sandwiches, and there's a jar of water to wash them down with. You can eat them all. I'm not hungry.'

'Can I still have some taffy, Pa?'

He laughed. 'You sure can, when we get home. That's if you stay awake!'

He slapped the reins, thinking hard. Originally, Alfred Deakin the prime minister had invited the Chaffeys to establish an irrigation settlement in the Mallee. The Chaffeys already had their sights on the old Mildura Station just over the border, which George Chaffey believed was ideal for the development in Australia of an irrigated fruit colony, one of which he had already established in California. The two brothers sold up in the USA and were to sign an agreement with the South Australian government to set up a fruit colony based on Renmark. It would be the first irrigation fruit settlement in the whole country of Australia.

Arthur knew that rivalry between the colonies was well entrenched. He already knew of mutterings from that direction – that the Victorians would sign up now South Australia had made the move. The skipper of Beatrice's little peebee transport this morning, being a former colleague, had confided as much.

'Currawong, Papa!'

The cry broke into Arthur's musings but he couldn't be too annoyed.

'Now start counting, Will, and quietly, or you'll scare any others in the trees.'

Arthur's mind veered to the tales of the massive pumps already being ordered by the Chaffeys from England, to be installed near the old Mildura Station, already under renovation. Arthur was vitally interested in these pumps. He knew pumps! *I want to know where they will be put; whether any effective analysis of the proposed irrigation scheme is available for public consultation, discussion – anything! What's the mechanical power of these pumps and just where will they put them to advantage all the river land properties? I'm no ignoramus on the topic – I've ridden the paddle boats up and down much of this river, seen rivers overseas, and I know darn well this Murray isn't as fast flowing or its levels as reliable as many foreign ones. I can see all kinds of problems arising and not only with the flows. What about the wretched arguments over sovereignty of the colonies? What about those properties accused of straddling the border?*

Arthur feared that if the pumps were installed near to the Chaffeys' property, the old Mildura Station, the consequent diversion of waters would affect those living downstream, such as himself and Beatrice. From his time spent at Echuca and other upstream ports, he knew that to the colonies of Victoria and New South Wales, 'downstream' meant South Australia, a separate colony of no great concern to the current authorities in Victoria and New South Wales.

'Hrumph! Hrumph!'

'Papa, can I speak now you are speaking?"

'Of course, m'lad. We're nearly home anyway and you've been very good. I've done my thinking and, you know what, you've earned your chunk of taffy!' He clicked his teeth. 'C'mon, old fella! Move along now and we'll get you in your stable. Hey, Will! Shall we give Molly the mare some taffy too?'

Giggles came from among the cushions. 'She's not having my bit, Papa!'

Fowls were running around the yard getting away from the hooves and wheels. Nancy was there, a stout aproned figure holding a trug of fresh eggs.

The door opened and out ran George, envious of his brother but eager to score a point. 'I got taffy, two chunks, an' you missed out, Will!'

'I never! Papa says I can have some. So there!'

Sam came and took Molly's bridle. 'I'll see to her, Arthur. Your little girl's wanting to see you indoors. Beatrice get away all right? Levels are down still after the drought. Hope we get some rain soon – summer's going on a bit long for my liking.'

Arthur went indoors with his little boys, Nancy following after. Little Esther, actually the first of his brood, looked up from her drawing at the table and gave him the sweetest smile; his heart jumped with love for her.

'Hello, Papa. One day, can I come and see Bridgewater where you and Mama met and were married?'

'Course you can, my Esther. But I met Mama first on the *Orient*. The fastest steam ship of its time, it was then – well, on this route anyway. But right now, I think we'll get these two little boys to bed. Hey, then you can tell me what story you want me to read. Mama's safe away and travelling down river to Murray Bridge. We'll see her again in about three weeks. You'll have to be my helper till then.'

She adored her papa. ''Course I will, Papa. I know Mama will really love seeing her old friends again, and going to a wedding. And a christening if she gets there in time! Now, would you like a bowl of soup, you and Will? We have it ready, Nancy and me, don't we, Nancy?' She stood and came over to him, wrapped her arms round his middle. 'Don't you worry about things while Mama is away, Papa. Me and Nancy will keep things in order and as for Mama, she will have a lovely time talking with her friends.'

Her papa smiled and ruffled her hair. He had no doubt!

# 3 February 1887

## 64

It was Thursday evening and Beatrice dismounted from the train at Bridgewater, near the mill. The station had not been there when she was here last; this was progress! It was small, but smartly painted with little pots of flowers – petunias? – gaily blooming in welcome, though closing gently as the sun faded. She hadn't been able to give Sissy a definite time of arrival, had hoped for the morning, but at least today was the expected day. *It will be good to settle into one place for a few days and nights. It is so good to be back.*

She collected her bag from the luggage van, walked out to the bottom of the hill and over the bridge. Here she could watch the water run and tumble and oh, how sweet and familiar its sound! She looked over, and down below could see the tumbling pebbles. There certainly seemed enough speed there to turn the big wheel. On the mill's wall across the bridge, the huge wheel was turning steadily. Still grinding so late in the day?

At home, in Cumquats, they'd heard of droughts on the plains and even in the hills during the recent summers and had themselves been affected by drought and waning river levels. She was relieved to hear the healthy rushing, bubbling and swishing noises of this busy little creek. It had become such a favourite hideaway during her first year in the colony, staying at the inn, and while she was at sixes and sevens, as Mary liked to say.

And there it was, almost at the top of the rise. The inn. Beyond and above, the early moon had risen and was suspended against a weakening blue. Closer, she could hear the snorting of a horse from the yard, the loud yell of one of the ostlers. Jack?

She pushed open the small gate set into the big wooden one and gazed happily at the rich frontage of what had been her first real home in the colony. Suddenly a squeal rent the air from the balcony and a flash of colour caught her eye as a skirt swished into the doors beyond. She smiled. *That can only be Lucy!*

Beatrice made haste into the reception area and there was Lucy skipping down the stairs. She almost skidded into Beatrice, then, almost unbelievably, gave a polite little bob before grabbing her in a most energetic hug.

'Oh, it is so good to see you, Beattie – Beattie? – and you haven't changed at all. You aren't at all fat.'

Fat? There was no time to respond before Sissy came bustling in, more hugs, then Anderson followed, a much stouter Anderson in a bright yellow vest that preceded him by quite a pace. He held out his hands and took Beatrice's in a warm, calloused clasp and with a wide happy smile boomed his welcome. Sissy was wiping her eyes – tears?

Lucy took control. 'Beattie, do you mind sleeping in your old little room off the deck? We have so many people coming up over the next few days but I thought you might really like your old room. Just to remember... Sort of...'

They walked over the deck, Lucy carrying Beatrice's bag. She jiggled it. 'Beatrice, is this all your luggage? Er, what are you wearing for my wedding?'

'I rolled up most of the dresses and skirts, Lucy, knowing I could use a flat iron here. And I have a favourite in there. You will like it when it's all pressed and freshened.'

'Anything...different? Erm...new?'

'You dear goose, Lucy. Oh, I believe it's Lucille now you're to be a respectably married woman... Of course I have something special for the wedding. I stopped off at Charles Birks's this morning just to have a look and I found a lovely two-piece. It's a peplum jacket and an ankle-length skirt. They're sending it up to the inn next Tuesday because I needed it taken in a little at the waist, and I wanted the hem shorter in the new style. You'll like it, and with my suede overshoes – you know, I'm looking forward to wearing it! Oh, listen!'

Outside her door were two magpies. One was a young one, still a grey-back. He clung nervously to the rail as the young women emerged from the door. The old one, with a sharply white back but a grey, gnarled beak, stretched his neck and warbled.

'Oh, Lucy! He has a twisted claw – surely not the same one! My old friend? How long do they live? But his warble sounds like a welcome. Oh, how lovely! Now do tell, Lucy: has Evelyn made a booking? I'm not even sure about private telephone connections yet. In some ways, we in the country are really out of touch! However, I did read that trunk line calls can be made from Adelaide to Port Adelaide and I just wondered…with Evie being in the Telegraph Department and all that…

'Oh, Beatrice, you don't know? Evelyn is here already! She has Mam's old room here next to yours because Mam has renovated the box room upstairs for herself. She likes to open the windows off the veranda on hot nights. She's here for the christening as she's standing godmother for little Evelyn Mary on Sunday. Then she's staying on for my wedding but she might go home Tuesday till Thursday, I think she said.'

She went down the deck a little further and knocked on the door.

'Who is it?' came a sleepy response. Then, 'Oh, my goodness, Lucille, did I sleep through dinner?'

The door opened, Beatrice called around the corner and out ran Evie, clad only in her shift.

Lucy smiled at their excited greetings. 'I'll fix you both a meal. Come in when you're ready…'

Later, after they'd eaten, the three young women monopolised the piano which, to Beatrice's delight, was the old one from the school, though well waxed and gleaming.

Lucy explained. 'Mrs Bones arranged for us to have it when some new management, the government, I think, took over the school from the church. They provided a new piano. Mrs Bones isn't there any more. The Boneses live in Kensington Park now with another relative. Now, how about "Greensleeves"?'

After Lucy demonstrated her piano prowess, they enjoyed a real music hall sing-song and Sissy and Anderson came in with their glasses of port.

Beatrice wanted to know who Lucille's attendants were at the wedding and was delighted the two elder Rogers girls were to fill the role. 'I'm so pleased I'm going to be able to catch up with everyone. But first, tomorrow I really would like to go and visit Kate. And, Evie, will you come too? I think it's so lovely the little one is to be named after you.'

'Beattie, dear, I've already had a lovely visit but will come with you again…'

'Good. I really must see little Eloise and Francis. I've brought a little gift for each of them because – you may remember, although it seems so long ago now – Arthur and I delayed our trip to the river land after our wedding so we could stand godparents the following Sunday for Kate and Herbert. I haven't seen the children since then and I am so excited to see them growing…'

'Oh, that's lovely, Beattie. I remember now, and though you had to go to Adelaide to check on some stores or something you fixed those up then came back. Goodness, you'll be surprised at Kate's family now. They are absolutely gorgeous. I am going to be the most wonderful godmother to little Evie, too.'

Anderson stirred from his chair and yawned. 'Don't know about you ladies but I'm off to bed. I've told Zed in the yard to have the trap ready for you to go to see Mrs Flach tomorrow. Just let him know when you are nearly ready.' He yawned again and waggled his fingers in a good night salute.

Sissy stood up to collect the port glasses. 'Come on, Madame Lucille, let us leave these two good friends to their own company for a while and we'll catch up on our beauty sleep!'

# 65

That same evening at 152 Barnard Street, Mary was taking a moment in the garden. The heat of the day was greatly lessened; the only problem were the gnats, or mozkeetos, as John Benjamin had called them. They had a nasty little nip and she was forever scratching around her hands and wrists. However, it was pleasant outside under the tree and carriage noises down the street weren't too noisy after many people had gone back home after work.

It was work that was on her mind – other people's. So many women were tied to working at home because of the children. The pay rate was abysmal. For a meagre living, the women had to sew well into dark and start early in the morning. Not only was it exhausting, some complained that the candles they needed to see what they were doing cost nearly as much as they earned.

Mary's work on the ladies' committee of the Social Purity League alerted her to case after case of destitution, ill health, failing eyesight and also accidents caused to children who were left in the care of others perhaps too young to act responsibly. It was a fact that the clothing trades in Adelaide were becoming increasingly mechanised and women flocked to apply for sewing in such conditions, where, for instance, the light by which to stitch was paid for by the factory. However, the very mechanisation which not only advantaged the women but also increased the profit margins of the owners, was one of the reasons given by them for not allowing young children on the premises, even under a mother's watchful eye. Sick or healthy, they were forbidden.

The mothers' peace of mind was something Mary had long pondered and now, thanks to her friend Mary Colton, there seemed to be some resolution. Working with Mrs Colton on what had been the foundation ladies' advisory planning committee for what later became the Adelaide Children's Hospital was a Mrs Laura Corbin, Adelaide born and bred and loving her city. Mary Colton had introduced Mary to Laura, and Laura was planning to found the South Adelaide Day Nursery. It would be for the children of women with day time work. The opening was planned for some date in May. *Only a couple o' months away. Good move, this.*

Laura had informed Mary that the fees had been costed at a minimum of twopence a day, still not easy for working mothers but if they could work a full day without worry, Laura felt that the mothers and the children would benefit. It would be for babies and children under six years old, and for between the hours of seven a.m. and six p.m. The children would be fed, bathed and taught simple play things. Mary applauded the idea, approving of any initiative that allowed women to work for their families with easy minds. She had promised, as had Mary Colton, to canvass the initiative amongst their various missions and committees, hoping for patrons as well as clients.

*As wife of a medical practitioner, this Laura knows what she's seen in her husband's surgery. Nasty cases I've seen myself but she'll have seen a fair few. She said there was a day nursery or crèche near Victoria Square some years ago. It didn't take off and was now closed. Pity that. No money around then like now.*

Alice came out to the garden as Mary slapped yet another bug from the back of her hand.

'Come on indoors, Mrs Mary. Those things can make a nasty bite if you scratch it, I'm allus telling you!'

'Thank you, Alice. Lot to think about. You know, I really don't know what I'd do without you.' She stood and turned to the lass. 'You know, I am so very glad your Freddy has agreed you can make your home here now you're wed. Very glad indeed, so I am. So's Evelyn… Righty-ho Alice, I'm comin'…'

*

Back indoors and debating whether to indulge in a cup of tea or a cocoa, Mary Lee considered again the limited options available to working women with children. The prevailing conditions under which they laboured were her priority for improvement, but she knew many were limited in their hours due to their children's needs; this day nursery promised to be a godsend.

Brought to the Social Purity Society were frequent complaints about some employer or other, the conditions in the place of employment, the pathetically low wages. It was not unusual that a lad whose only job was turning a wheel or doing some equally repetitive chore, one that did not demand a high level of skill and intelligence or initiative, would be paid twice as much as women who were operating intricate machinery. Some factories had no toilet facilities, no windows to let in fresh air, and had the workers in cramped conditions.

It was essential that working conditions be improved and monitored. So who…and how and when? Would Augusta be interested? Augusta, properly and publicly known as Mrs Wilhelm Zadow, had joked about her and Mary getting on so well, with so many ideas the same and both speaking English with an accent. Augusta had been a tailoress in London and married a tailor, too.

She and Augusta had quite a talk one afternoon at the Social Purity Committee. Augusta was a woman of indomitable spirit yet quite a bit smaller in height even than Mary, tiny in fact, but had experience of conditions in London where she had helped oppressed female clothing workers. Since coming to Adelaide in 1877, only a couple of years before Mary, she had worked hard to improve the lot of the number of females working in the increasingly mechanised clothing trades, the industry being, naturally, close to her heart.

*Yes, me and Mary Colton, that Laura Corbin and Augusta, we should make a good team to aim to get a Working women's trade union off the ground. That's badly needed. We'll have a talk, I think, then perhaps we can start making a good case against the greedy employers. It'll take a while. First, there's talk of another Women's Suffrage Bill being presented, this time by Robert Caldwell. Let's work on suffrage, I think, and from that other things may follow. Also, I'd better see if I can find a couple of girls for Beatrice and Arthur up at that Cumquats place. First of the firsts, I think, is a nice supper, then bath and bed. Though talking of them, I wonder if Beatrice is up at Bridgewater yet? I do hope I can meet up with her before she goes home again. A christening and a wedding – things happen up there, that's for sure.*

Tea and biscuits forgotten, she called to Alice. 'Let us have a nice cup of hot cocoa, Alice. Then bed for me, I think.'

# 4 February 1887

## 66

Evelyn and Beatrice thoroughly enjoyed their Friday visit to the Lutheran village. Beatrice's early impression was that the children had grown – in number also! The church had a fresh coat of paint and a couple of stained windows she didn't remember from before, but Pastor Wilhelm and his lovely cheerful wife hadn't changed at all.

Kate was as happy a wife and mother as anyone could wish to be. Her children were healthy and so well behaved, yet so lively when told to go out and play. The little ones were carefully watched by the bigger ones; all the children of the village were one happy family caring for each other. Francis was known as Frank and determined to lead the field (as Arthur would say) and Eloise a lovable little fusspot mother-in-the-making. Little Evelyn was a bouncing, chuckling baby; they'd run through the ceremony format and Frau Wilhelm had shown them with pride the cotton and embroidered gown the baby would wear.

They enjoyed a cheerful lunch, sitting along a large wooden table under the tree. At the clang of a bell, the children ran back to their classrooms, whereupon a wine was dispensed to the adults. The young women managed to talk among themselves, as the others had tasks to fulfil – other than Kate, whose little ones had gone off with their beloved and loving Vati, who would escort them to play at the pastor's house.

To Beatrice, it seemed an idyllic existence and she commented as much to Evie on the drive home. They talked of the village and its people and Evelyn remarked on the health of the children.

'They are all rosy-cheeked and I heard none with a cough or looking in any way sick. So different from some city children, where we read recently, Mam and I, of so many deaths from diphtheria and even typhoid – still, despite the sewerage improvements. Is it the healthy country air, do you think?'

Beatrice had noticed them and remembered the wonderful gardens yielding so many vegetables and fruits, the home-cured meats, the cows so well cared for in fresh fields to give milk. She remarked on how wholesome it all seemed.

The township of Bridgewater was another such place. It had certainly extended in all directions, to Beatrice's eyes, and the friendliness and industriousness of the people in both places had impressed them both. That led them to talk of Anderson and Sissy. Apparently they were now staying on at the inn, as Kate confirmed the young lasses to help Sissy were to start the following week, according to the mother of the Lutheran village girl. It seemed to be a happy arrangement all round. Beatrice was pleased to hear of that.

Living in Cumquats, with her own children, Arthur, and Sam and Nancy, she felt she had been there forever, so rapidly and happily it had become home. Their earlier months living in boarding houses and being unable to unpack her precious belongings to have them around her, had long ago faded in her memory. Cumquats was her place, and in its surroundings and within its community she knew the wonder of belonging, being a part of it all. Building friendships, an extended community, clubs and society were all on the agenda. Her own horizons were broadened and she realised her place within them; they constituted no longer the anonymous 'elsewhere' long associated with a migrant's uncertainty and insecurity.

'You know, Evie, here in Bridgewater again after so long away, the years have rolled back and I feel almost as if I have just arrived in the colony. I am looking upon it all as a visitor would see it yet memories are jostling around in my brain. I sense that old strangeness and it is somewhat unsettling.'

'I know how you mean, Beattie. I feel that myself sometimes. I think it's because we left so much behind that in a new place we have worked so hard to recreate that feeling of home, of belonging, that we have succeeded – to a degree. Yet it's only a veneer, isn't it? When we revisit our beginnings, we remember the early doubts and fears – well, we don't only remember them, they jump up and hit us in the solar plexus! I have spoken of much the same to some of my work colleagues who are also migrants, and I think it is common to all of us. We look for a constant in our lives and, you know what? In a peculiar way, I feel this little town is it, for me. Certainly it is for you. Now that I have a little god-daughter here, I feel that I am part of this place. I also know – because I've thought a lot about it – that I think more like a South Australian now, and less like a Kilnockian.' She chuckled.

'Evie, I do know what you mean but one aspect of warm evenings here I do not enjoy is the mozkeeto! They are eating me. But you put it so well, how we always remember our beginnings here. Now let's hand this four-legged beast over to Zed and see if we are still in time for dinner. Lucy will want to know all about the christening robe – and the arrangements – I do not doubt.'

# 5 February 1887

## 67

The following day was Saturday and there was great excitement at the inn. The bar sounded quite boisterous for the time of day.

Anderson was pleased at the busyness of the place and came to the girls at breakfast to explain. 'There's big hoorah in the bar, ladies. Got some breakfasts going so Sissy asks if you could help yourselves to what you want. There's going to be a football game, just a knockabout they call it. It's between some lads from around here and a team from Hahndorf. The Hahndorf Football Club is gettin' itself registered, so the men are sayin'. Next month it'll be hunky-dory then they can set up matches regular like. Today it'll be down by the school on Adam's field. They've set up some markers, but when they get all organised, Hahndorf is making a real oval with goal posts an' the like. It's under Australian rules – looks more like the rugby my dad useter play when he was young and told me about it. Rough game but good for burnin' off excess zeal, he useter say. But to get a real club hereabouts – that'll be good for the young men, a change from work an' mebbes more business in our front bar. Best go back…' and he gave his characteristic finger-wiggle salute and returned to the fray.

Lucy was kept busy in the inn all morning showing young Miss Rogers how to set tables, and Sissy was barking orders in the kitchen so Beatrice led Evie out the back and announced a trek down to the creek.

'Let's escape, Evie, and it's busy tomorrow as well. We'll commune with Nature. Come on, down to what used to be my special place, Evie, quite a sneaky little hidey-hole. I spent some thinking time down there that first year. So mind the step off the deck!'

'Oh, I remember, Beattie! Didn't you bring me down here before and oh, look! That magpie with the funny foot is flying along with us – and the other one. I've heard tales – do they swoop?'

'I know we have them in the trees near us at Cumquats and some of those do when they are nesting. They're very territorial, so old Sam told me. But this one – and it must be the same one but quite old for a bird now – he used to get quite pally. He'd wait for bacon crumbs and other bits of leftovers and take them from my hand. Lucy used to try and get him to talk – she said she'd been told they mimicked. I never heard him, though.'

'What a lovely place this is, and I can hear the creek bubbling along. Oops – need to be careful down this bank, though. A little footbridge would be good. Ow! The grass is dewy and it's slippery – oweee! Oh, darn it!'

Evie had done a long skid on the wet grass and come to a full stop on her derrière, her skirt underneath almost to her shoulders, shins bare, her whole body shaking with laughter. Beatrice stepped over, more nimble footed, to grab her friend's hand, helping her to her feet.

Evie wriggled, convulsing with giggles. 'Now my drawers are wet from the grass!'

They stood, arms round one another, laughing fit to burst, as Sissy would say.

'One of those rare moments, good friends coming together – literally,' sang Evie in a falsetto voice.

They dissolved into more laughter and fumbled their way back up the grassy bank to the little track, then down to the thinking stone by the creek.

Beatrice looked up through the gums at the blue sky then down to the creek and beyond the green fields. 'I spent ages here just thinking – when I had time from my duties, of course. This is where I decided to marry Arthur. It's where he kissed me, properly, later. The feel of the warm rock under me brings back the memories.'

Evelyn smiled. 'I am just content to have good friends and not a close relationship, Beattie. Nor marriage – or so I feel. I know Mam would like some South Australian grandchildren, of course. Ever since we came here, she has thrown herself into her work for us women – and girls. But here, especially, she needs the goals and to attain them. It's all about being an immigrant, proving our worth, as we were discussing yesterday. Yet you and I can look forward to a future. Mam has really had most of hers already! I am proud of her, I really am, but if she had some grandchildren here in the colony, to fill her days, I wonder if she would relax more. You know, this week – yesterday, I think – she was getting together with Mrs Colton and some others again to draft a motion to put later to the Social Purity League in the hope of getting a Suffrage League off the ground to work towards the female vote. Mam has such energy in this regard. I'm proud of her, never doubt it, but she does attract criticism of her approaches to issues at times. Some of it hurts her, I know, but she stays determined.'

Beatrice took her friend's hand and together they sat on the warm stone, leaning back against the big rock, Evie happy with the warmth of the rock against her derrière, each content with the other's quiet company. Beattie wondered how Arthur and Nancy were coping with the children, if the boys were quarrelling, if little Esther was playing mother in her usual way, if there had been any developments on the irrigation allocation debates to harass Arthur. She missed them all and it was still more than a week until she could see them. But meeting everyone again, everyone from her earliest days in the colony, and being able to measure her own migrant beginnings against what she had here and now, was fulfilling in a way she could not have envisaged.

Evie stood. 'Come on, my friend. I'll fall asleep if I sit for longer. Let's gird our loins and brave the footballers' noise – that's if they haven't left to go to the match!'

# 6 February 1887

## 68

Sunday – Christening Day – and the family from the inn, with Evie and Beattie, drove over in the carriage to the Lutheran village.

An air of suppressed excitement was evident. All the children with hair slicked down and clean shirts gave rein to a noisy welcome until Frau Wilhelm came among them, prompting a respectful silence. She directed them into their places at the rear of the little church. Beattie sat with Sissy, Anderson and Lucy, and Evie was ushered to a place by Kate and Herbert. Little Evelyn Mary looked like a gorgeous doll in the beautiful gown and bonnet and chuckled and smiled all through the ceremony,- until just at the end. Lucy's Rauf was not there – he couldn't leave his office, despite it being the Sabbath, as he was involved in a court case the next day and he was assisting so had to prepare, despite his own wedding only a few days away.

Beatrice remembered how she and Arthur had stood at that carved sandstone font making promises for Francis and Eloise, both now sitting demurely with the parents. The form of service was the same today. Baby Evelyn Mary cried on cue and Evie looked terribly solemn as she made her promises.

Lunch in the hall afterwards was as sumptuous as anyone expected. As they broke the loaves of bread, Beattie remembered the first time she'd come here with Kate and they'd been given the big rye flour loaves to take home. *Yes, lots of memories, lots of good times, good friends…*

On the way home, Lucy dominated the conversation. 'For my wedding, I do think the flowers would look best under that pedestal by the second coloured window. I wish old Mrs Rogers was still alive to supply them for me. And I do hope the wedding menu afterwards won't have that thick bean soupy stuff. Roast meats are enough on their own…'

'Lucille! You will remember that you have chosen a man with a different background. Those things are his tradition, and nice ones too.

I suggest you bow to the village wishes on this day. Tut tut, young lady. When you and Rauf are settled in your city house, then, and only then, you can arrange menus as you wish. Goodness me, girl, you've had your choice of dress and everything else. And let's remember the occasion we have just attended.'

'Sorry, Mam, er Mama. Erm, Miss Evelyn, I do think the choice of names for the little baby, after you and your mama, is really lovely. I expect your mother is delighted to have a little baby named after her. It is such an honour. And well deserved, I know.'

*

Well deserved or not, on that day in Adelaide, Mary was not feeling very optimistic. There was so much to worry about. She and Mrs Colton had managed to draft a workable proposal on the Suffrage League to put to the Social Purity committee, and that did look optimistic. They now needed clients for the day nursery to allow this one to prosper and had agreed on some names to approach for support.

This new draft proposal she would suggest Mrs Colton put to the next Social Purity meeting before she left for overseas. She decided that she could herself start raising support amongst her colleagues in the various committees and boards. She felt there were many opinions favourable to her own ideals but also believed they should all speak with one voice. The Suffrage Society, or League, would be geared to the one objective, gaining women the vote, and ultimately giving them greater authority and certain rights.

*Yes, we'll call it the Women's Suffrage League – that's unequivocal. I know Mary Colton is of the same mind. Pity she's going abroad for a while, but her point of view is well known to the Social Purity Society. There's Rose Birks, she'll be involved, I know that. And Catherine Spence, well she doesn't care much for my approach, I know, but we believe, generally, in the same goals for women so… Oh, and Augusta – well, like me she wants to start a Working Women's Trade Union. Perhaps let's go for the suffrage first and maybe one will lead to the other – suffrage is for all women, we hope, not only the workers. Yes, we'll start dipping a toe in the waters, get prepared, then maybe in a month or two…*

Mary sat back. She was in her garden again, enjoying the birdsong.

The little blackbird seemed to have found his voice again after the hot summer. His warbling whistle, as she thought of it, reminded her of her home back in Kilnock – or there was that place in Armagh they'd once walked... Here, she loved to watch the Australian native birds, and her garden was home to a pair of little green parrots, tiny things that would sit and nod on the branches above her head, but they all tended to make caw-caw noises, or so she thought.

Evelyn'll be home on Tuesday, though I can't remember why, since she'll be heading back on Thursday to be at Lucille Woof's wedding. That's on the Saturday. It will be good to hear all about Beatrice and the others. Seemed a long time since that wedding...but I never thought Beatrice would make it in this colony. Little ninny-pinny I thought her. I was quite wrong...

Alice crept out, glad that Mrs Mary was resting. She had seemed a bit fractious lately. A half hour snoozing in the garden would be a good thing. *When she's awake, she's got everybody else on her mind. She needs to look after herself more than she does.*

# 12 February 1887

## 69

Lucy's wedding day! All was frantic bustle in the inn. Lucille was to have had a bouquet delivered and it hadn't arrived. Sissy's hair was still in rags as she reminded everyone it was still two and a half hours to the wedding. Beatrice was in Lucy's bedroom (she couldn't get used to the idea of calling her Lucille) asking how she wanted her hair. To her distress, Lucy was almost in tears.

'Lucy, do stop the histrionics, my dear. Or I'll believe you don't want to marry Rauf after all!'

'Beatrice, don't be so hard on me! It's a big day for me and I just want it all to be perfect.'

'It will be if the bride stops her caterwauling and lets me comb her hair!'

Anderson burst his best braces; Sissy was trying to fix them while he blustered. Thankfully, Jack came in and told Sissy to get herself prettied up, he'd see to the boss… Chaos reigned.

Then the bouquet arrived. Lucille's hair looked glorious, said Anderson. Sissy looked like a glamorous young'n again, said Anderson.

'An' you're a fine figure of a man, Anderson,' said Sissy.

The Rogers sisters, as the bride's attendants, arrived in their lavender silks, Evie's recalcitrant locks had sobered under a par-bonnet topknot and Beatrice's two-piece with the peplum toned in beautifully, thought Anderson.

The church was full to bustin', so whispered Sissy. This time, to Beatrice's delight, there was an organist who teased notes of such clarity she would not have thought possible from the small but beautifully carved organ. So they had gained an organ and a new piano for the church and school. Well done!

Up near the lectern stood the rigid figure of the groom with his two best friends, all clad in the new short black jackets.

Not a lederhosen in sight! *Now remember, Beatrice, didn't Kate tell you of a*

*group who came from another part of Germany, or Europe, packing up to settle in a
part of the Barossa with their own traditions?*

The organ had a deep loud tone and practised it to perfection as
Lucille made her entrance on Anderson's arm. He looked so proud. Her
dress was beautiful in an ivory silk with a lace overlay on the bodice. Her
veil was long and trailed behind on the floor.

'Pity about that,' Sissy whispered to Beatrice and Evie in the row
behind. 'Gets awful mucky.' Ever the practical Cecilia.

'Sissy, she looks exquisite! You can be so proud.'

The breakfast was in the Lutheran hall, as last time, thought Beatrice,
and was a jolly affair as soon as the speeches were over – and they were
brief. Rauf's was so tender and loving, it brought more tears to Sissy's eyes.
Lucy, Mrs Rauf Schulze, ate the traditional bean soup with aplomb and
afterwards danced as heartily as anyone else on the floor. Pastor Wilhelm,
with old-fashioned grace, came over to Beatrice and invited her to take to
the floor. He danced a waltz with such exquisite timing, so slowly, she felt
quite relaxed as it ended. Then it was Kate's turn – with Herbert's smiling
permission – and then Sissy's! Kate whispered to Beatrice how she hoped
Sissy's sore feet – they had their own reputation – would stand up to the
strain! The two young mothers had to subdue a spontaneous giggle at the
shared thought, then caught Lucille looking at them, a twinkle in her eye.

'She knows exactly why we are laughing,' Kate almost hooted!

The bride and groom were to go by trap into Hahndorf proper to
a hotel there for a couple of days then back to the inn before leaving
for their new home in Adelaide. They disappeared for a short while to
reappear in their street clothes, to farewell their families and friends.
There was much shaking of hands.

'Quite the German custom,' whispered Kate. 'I'm used to it now and
prefer it to sloppy kisses.'

After they had gone, the Bridgewater crowd packed their traps and
carriages to make their way home before dark. Pastor Wilhelm shook
Anderson's hand and, with a click of his heels, squeezed Sissy's. Anderson
found their conveyance and announced there would be celebrations back
at the inn for whoever felt in the mood.

Much later, when sitting with her shoes kicked off and a glass of port
in her hand, Sissy started to cry.

She stood, and gave Beatrice a huge squeeze. 'It's all down to you, Beattie, that my Lucy has made a good match. That Rauf will be a rich lawyer one day and their children will move in the best of society. An' it's all down to you!'

'No, no, Sissy…'

But no platitudes would satisfy the proud mother. Beattie gave Sissy a kiss and a hug and, following Evie's example, went off to bed.

She lay there, reflecting on the day… No matter by whom or how, everything had seemed to work out well for Lucy and Rauf; their future looked bright. And also for those dear folk Sissy and Anderson. They gave her credit for doing so much and yet whatever she had done for Lucy, now and before, was not pure altruism. She herself had benefited from the distraction, and from the perceived successes.

It was a good feeling, though. Perhaps she, Beatrice, had made her mark here, after all. Tomorrow would be her last day with Sissy, Anderson and the others, but she would take some lovely, everlasting memories home with her. Who could say when next she could come this way?

# 14 February 1887

## 70

'I do hope my mother's at home, Beattie. There's a good chance – most of her meetings are in the afternoon and we're early enough. I let her think I'd be coming Tuesday, as last week. Want to give her a birthday surprise…

'Hello, Alice! Is Mam here? We took the train – would you believe its speed downhill?'

Beatrice chuckled. 'They have gears, you goose. All was under control. Hello, Alice.'

Alice was already leading the way down to the back parlour, where Mrs Lee was queening it (her own phrase) over a pot of tea.

She looked up in surprise, pleasure and delight moulding her mobile features.

'Oh, girls! How lovely! I thought tomorrow…'

'Mam, would I miss your birthday? Many happy returns, love. Today is your celebration. Tomorrow is when I start work – all the celebrations will be over and it'll be back to normal: oh, woe… But let's first share a pot of tea, and we can tell you all about the wedding. Young Lucille has done well for herself, Mam. He's a pleasant young fellow. And we brought you a lovely bunch of roses from Zed's garden behind the inn. He picked the best, called them late bloomers, but the climate's more forgiving in the hills. Just drink in the perfume of them, Mam.' She bent over and gave her mother a kiss on the cheek.

Beattie was carrying the big bunch of roses and tilted the soggy, newspaper-wrapped bundle of gorgeously brilliant, sweet-scented flowers towards Mary, who took them in both hands and then almost buried her face in them. Alice took them to the kitchen, also sniffing them appreciatively.

Beattie then moved towards the plump little figure sitting in her chair and took both her hands as she too kissed the wrinkled cheek. 'Happy, happy birthday, my friend, with many more happy returns.'

'Oh, Beatrice, it is so nice to see you again and you don't look any older! How is ex-Lieutenant Symonds – and the children?'

'I haven't heard Arthur called that in a long time! He is well, very busy puzzling about water pumps and irrigation rights, not so much with my vines and plants, so thank heavens for Sam and Nancy.'

They shed their bonnets and loosened their buttons to sit down. Alice came in with teacups and homemade biscuits and refreshed the pot. As she did so, Beatrice drew a special paper package from her quilted satchel – one of Evelyn's designs, Mary noted with approval.

'We had these taken not long before I left home. Went into Renmark'

'Photographs! Oh, lovely!' Mary cried in delight. 'Isn't it wonderful what can be done. Please…'

Beatrice spread them on the table. Evie sat back and enjoyed her tea – even the inn couldn't equal Alice's biscuits. She had seen the photographs already, of course – each time they'd been produced over the last week!

'Oh Beatrice! Look at Esther – she's so like her papa, isn't she? What colour is her hair? Is it fair? Yours is so dark.'

'She has a reddish tint to it in some lights. Apparently it happens often when one parent is blond – as they call it now – and the other dark-haired. But yes, her features are Arthur's but more delicate. Yet at times she reminds me of my mama. Esther's not delicate, though – quite a sturdy little lady and with strong opinions!'

Typical Mary, of course, had to ask, 'What are you plans for her, Beatrice? To marry well or have a career, as is becoming popular now. Would she like to teach, do you think? She has an intelligent, wide brow…'

They laughed. 'Oh, Mam, you are incorrigible! You'll have her in your Suffrage League, so you will, before she's in school!'

'Oh, what sturdy little lads, Beatrice. Both have the stamp of their papa too. William and George, isn't it? And they're three now, are they not? My word.' She placed the photographs carefully on the table. 'Who would have thought we could so easily and quickly take pictures like this? It is a beautiful thing to do…'

'Quickly's not the word, though, Mary,' laughed Beatrice. 'We had to pose seemingly for ages next to the table and perch on the chairs, and the photographer was behind the camera and it was on a tripod. He'd come up from Adelaide. He travels around the country for business wherever there are enough people and said he'd like to set up in Renmark if and when the population grows. Thankfully the children were intrigued, fascinated really, and did precisely what he asked. Well, other than George, who wanted to know what was what and all that. The photographer took quite a few and I thought if you would like to have these, I can leave them with you. You and Evie – and John Benjamin too, of course, God bless him – were so very good to me when I came here. All that business with James, the gambling, his death – God bless him too. You three were my rocks, the spur I needed to kick me along, to make decisions for myself.'

She sipped her tea. 'I'm so very fortunate, really I am. Arthur and I are happy and it seems things are just beginning for us in the country, with the plantings and everything.'

Mary wiped her eyes. 'Oh, I'm a big softy but I feared for you at times, Beatrice. You were so stricken at the start and I must admit I never thought you would be so capable, Beatrice, I really didn't… Oh, that sounds dreadful but… I think I spend too much time chasing echoes.'

Beatrice had to smile. 'I grew up rapidly and it was the Lees who gave me the much-needed nudge. But you, dear Mary, by echoes do you mean memories? Surely not failed ambitions?' She paused, steepled her fingers. 'You know, my dear friend, when I'm up there at Cumquats and I read about you in the papers, how you fight and work for so many good causes, I am so impressed and grateful for all our young women – like my daughter in days to come.'

Evie broke in. 'She does more for others than she does for herself and she makes some people like her less in spite of all her hard work because she achieves what they've been waffling around the edges of for years! If she has a fault it's that she's so plain spoken, calls a spade a spade – isn't that the phrase? Sorry, I get angry at times. But I can foresee Mam going down in the history books because of the gains she is making for girls, young and not so young; for women in their work and most of all, in petitioning for women to get the vote so we can all have a say in choosing the governments that rule. Yet there is resentment for that at times, for her successes. And you know what? No one pays her expenses – she's honorary this and honorary that. Unlike most of the others, she has no husband to support her, no private income. My mother knows and understands hardship from personal experience. So she gains some praise, every word well deserved, but words are cheap.'

'Evelyn! Please, dear, refrain from sounding cross on my birthday. Now you have come to see me, you and Beatrice, I am the happiest woman in Adelaide.'

'Oops! Sorry, Mam. On my soapbox again. None of the gloom today! Me and Beattie have arranged a special lunch for you, with Alice's help. We've brought cold goose, salad greens and even tomatoes from the inn gardens, with their blessings for you and birthday wishes. And we'll help prepare it and Alice will join us, won't you, Alice? Today is a very special day!'

# Early August 1888

## 71

Beatrice was enjoying an afternoon tea with others of the Ladies' Quilting Guild when Mrs Hall passed to her a recent copy of the SA *Register*, tapping a place on the page with a long bodkin.

'Isn't the Mary Lee they mention, her giving the speech, your friend? She's talking at a public meeting again. Goodness me, it's for women's voting again. They tried for that two or three years ago, didn't they, an' it didn't get passed. Men don't want it, that's why...'

Beatrice scanned the article. 'Why, this is all of two weeks old! She hasn't written to me about it but, on your other question, it was a man, a Dr Edward Stirling, who first moved a Bill in the parliament. It asked for women over the age of twenty-one, I think, with property, to be able to vote. It was strange to me that they had to be widows or spinsters and have property of their own. It was passed but didn't get the majority it needed. You know, Fiona, a lot of men are sympathetic to women's causes.'

'Huh – not for married women, I notice. We're excluded so our husbands can still benefit from their dowries. Or our earnings!' Leaving the paper with Beatrice, she sat down to resume her pattern, lips pursed, head shaking...

Beatrice read that it was at the inaugural public meeting of the Women's Suffrage League. 'Oh, that's all properly set up then! Wonderful! Now... erm...what is Mary saying... "Enfranchising assists women to redress the wrongs done to them – moral, social, industrial and educational." So they quote her and, yes, that sounds like Mary. Oh, it was Reverend Kirby who declared the Women's Suffrage League is now formed and...' Beatrice went on to read the article quietly to herself.

'Oh, here you are, Fiona! Mary's speech... It reads... erm... "Gentlemen of South Australia were heroes in the battle. Would they be the charioteers in the brave reform or would they wait to be ignominiously dragged in at the chariot wheels? [Laughter and cheers] She asked the men of the colony to support the franchise for women." Well, that does sound like Mary!'

Fiona gave her sewing partner a nudge. 'I know she's a friend of yours, Beatrice, but she does have an argumentative tone. I know some of my other friends at church think she lets women down by not being more… well, ladylike when putting her case. There are other ways and means…'

Beatrice smiled. 'I do know that there is not a more determined woman than Mary Lee when the rights of women and young girls are concerned. Specially in the city. She deplores the conditions under which many women have to work. She's told me of some and they are so foreign-sounding, extremely primitive and with no basic facilities. Many of these women are migrants. Some have suffered dreadfully yet are determined to lift themselves up and bring up their children in a clean and safe environment. Over the years, she and her friends – rather, I would call them co-conspirators –' she chuckled, 'have done excellent things organising places where children can be looked after and even learn basic reading and writing while the mother works. Mary's main interest is gaining advantages for working women. She wants women to have a say in their circumstances, their ways of working and ultimately a say in who they want to govern them. She believes most fiercely that working women should have a union or an association they can appeal to for any injustices. If you knew Mary, she would tell you of quite a few of those!

She gave a little shrug as she returned to her sewing. 'I can imagine now these first important steps have been taken, Mary will be well at the front of any campaign to ensure the eventual passing of the Bill. You know, I've been very fortunate in having Mary as a friend, and she still is. She is not one thing to some and another to others. She is straight and true with anyone she knows and a more decent, friendly and supportive friend would be hard to find. I know that if I needed her help, she'd be the first one I'd turn to. My present amicable company no exception!'

She smiled widely. 'Now, can anyone advise me on what best to give my Esther for her birthday? She will be seven in a few weeks, though quite mature for her age, and is pestering us for a trip to Adelaide. I'd like to take her to Bridgewater – it's a special place for Arthur and me…'

'Oh, Beatrice! I used to visit there. My aunt and her mother lived there for years. I thought Bridgewater one of the prettiest places to live and I made some friends there. Did you know the Boneses? Her old ma grew wonderful flowers and me and my brothers would help her by weeding and things she found hard to do...'

'Judith, what a coincidence! Mrs Bones – I never knew her Christian name – played the organ in the little church there, and she did so for our wedding. She let me borrow her Singer sewing machine to make some new dresses I needed badly. She also arranged for me to use the school piano there. She was so helpful and friendly, and that was when I was new to this country. I was so lucky in my friends in Bridgewater. I found out when I last visited that the Boneses'd moved to live in a city suburb, Kensington, I think, with some relatives. Goodness, it is a small world – as Mary Lee would say!'

Conversation centred safely and happily on various friendly townships in the state and soon the group was debating places for holidays and reasons why and reasons not, to spend time in the city. Beatrice stored her thoughts of Mary until she could talk them over with Arthur.

# 72

As far as Arthur was concerned, Mary Lee could do no wrong. He watched the newspapers for her political progress avidly. Arthur agreed that evening that Mary would, by now if the *Register*'s report was correct, be busy planning her campaign to ensure the vote, a view strengthened when he read out that it mentioned the second Bill for Women's Suffrage had been put to the House of Assembly by Robert Caldwell.

'Constitutional change is not at all straightforward, Beattie. Not sure how it'll work out but certainly this will need to be put to a wider vote, later. But it's all in the pipe line, my love. It's the middle of 1888 and things are happening – though no doubt they're too slow for Mary Lee, bless her. She and her cohort of ladies are going to have to work hard.'

They discussed going to Adelaide and agreed to make it a double figures birthday trip for Esther – that would be in 1891. By then, the boys would also be a little more sensible, or so they hoped.

'You know, Arthur, I can well imagine Mary will be – what's that funny saying of hers? 'Having ants in her pants.' She will be so energised. She once said she would tour the whole colony to get petitions. I can see it happening. I just wish she would write and talk to me about her plans. It's as if we are not supposed to be interested. She keeps it all to herself...'

# February 1889

## 73

They were correct. Mary Lee was energised. In February 1889, using her influence on the South Australian Wesleyan Conference, she persuaded them, as Secretary of the Woman's Suffrage League, 'to express a sympathy for duly qualified women to gain a vote in the election of members of Parliament'.

The Symondses also sensed her increasing influence – if not outright involvement – in many of the reports subsequently appearing in the newspapers which often described 'an impassioned speech'. The declaration for women's suffrage from the Women's Christian Temperance Union resulted in Mary Lee making yet another 'impassioned speech' in that September of 1889. A number of 'impassioned speeches' for suffrage were published in the *Register*, as were many letters on the cause from Mary and her powerful colleagues.

Beatrice rode into the township to the post office annex to obtain copies of all the relevant newspapers and she and Arthur avidly read each one, realising for themselves the complexity of Mary's campaigning. Beatrice caught young Esther avidly reading one of the reports in the newspaper and realised that young Esther was avidly following the constant campaign for, as she called it, parliament to stop women's suffering. Beatrice explained it all to her and what suffrage meant.

One evening after dinner, she overheard Arthur answering questions put to him by the little girl.

Arthur reported to her later. 'She grilled me, Beatrice! Asked me why women were not as important as men. Were William and George more important than her. You know my sympathies for the cause, but I got my tongue tied in knots! And she's only a child! Oh, my goodness, Beatrice, you'll have to put her straight on this business.'

Beatrice smiled. How could Esther not ask questions, child or not. And if Arthur were honest and outspoken, he would have to admit his favourite of the three children was Esther. *He actually hopes she'll be a doctor!* But the campaign for suffrage was being kept uppermost in the newspapers and in letters, whether for or against. It could not be avoided and she certainly would not forbid any of her inquisitive children the newspapers.

That night she wrote to Evelyn hoping for more detailed news of where and when Mary was, and within days Evelyn replied, though with little detail, that Mary had indeed done some travelling.

'I had wondered if Mary would be travelling anywhere near to us, Arthur. It would be lovely to have her here for a few days so she can see Cumquats and the children. Evie gives no suggestions. I do sense Evie gets a little upset at the publicity Mary gains, because not all of it is friendly. It seems Mary is all fired up and will take the criticism head on, but Evie feels embarrassed – to say the least. It has been so from the outset, I feel, though I could be wrong. I have to sympathise with Evie: she is trying to maintain a presence in her own position and it may well be aggravating to have a mother whose name is constantly on everyone's lips – lips not always curled in a smile.'

# November 1889

## 74

In the November of 1889, as Beatrice and Arthur were planning the next season's plantings and prunings schedule, they read of the second reading of the Women's Suffrage Bill being debated in the House of Assembly. The debate was adjourned and a motion that the Bill was to be read a second time failed in a majority so it could not be proceeded with.

'Oh, Arthur, Bills and Acts and second readings – I thought that was last year or sometime. I find it hard to understand the proceedings of parliament, I really do. And then…look at this: a statement that the following day a huge petition was presented in favour of suffrage. Petitions are coming in from all over the state, it says. Has Mary travelled to all those places, do you think, Arthur? Or have others taken on some of the travelling too? I do wonder. Most of her colleagues have husbands whose own public standing must be protected and households to care for, whereas Mary has spoken to me in the past of what she called her advantage: that she is free to live her life as she wants and not worry over a husband. Some numbers quoted here – numerous Port Adelaide women residents, and Gawler residents, women residents of Port Pirie and women residents in North Adelaide – all signing petitions in favour of women's suffrage. Oh my, oh my! These were presented to Legislative Council and were closely followed by two petitions – one with thirty-two signatures, and another with ninety-nine! All presented to the House of Assembly.'

Arthur declared, slapping one newspaper with gusto onto his knee, 'The flood gates are open! I have to admit, Beattie, your friend Mrs Mary Lee is a powerful woman for her age. My goodness, yes!'

Beatrice read out loud. '"On the fourth of December in the House of Assembly the Women's Suffrage Bill was presented and proceeded with. Debate was vigorous." Arthur, I'm really getting lost in all the technicalities – oh, my goodness, but it just seems to go on, and on, and on!'

# January 1890

## 75

As Beatrice knew, Mary had also been working hard to set up a women's trade union with her dear friend Augusta Zadow. Early in the following year it was hoped to become fact and indeed, as they later learned, in January 1890 it was signed, sealed and delivered, in Mary's language.

Later that year, the Working Women's Trades Union was founded, and Mary was to be the foundation secretary with Augusta as foundation treasurer. This was a positive move and Beatrice was so pleased for Mary she wrote her a long letter of congratulation.

'My dear Beatrice,' asked Arthur, 'do you really think you'll gain a reply to that epistle? It seems to me that all Mary's writing energies are exhausted by an endless onslaught via the *Register*, entitled "Letter to Women" – how many now?' He smiled but was content to leave all that business to Beatrice.

He was having problems himself. There were river issues threatening. He felt the local irrigation committee members were becoming too bureaucratic in their dealings with growers. He could not afford to lose any water allocation. It was becoming a real problem, yet the future of the river lands – maybe the economies of the state – depended upon making the best of what was becoming an increasingly rare resource – water. This summer had been an improvement on the last few but the extended drought of recent years had taken its toll. As for the well-being of the river Murray, that was a great concern.

# 76

Beatrice had problems of her own. Out in the vineyard one hot day early in 1890 – in fact, the day after they learned of Mary Lee's success with the union – Beatrice collapsed in pain. She had suspected she was pregnant. Thirty-four years old was a risky age, but there had been hours upon hours of manual labour in the vineyard and maybe she should have been more circumspect. Instead she had worked as hard as any of the labourers; she loved her vines! Fortunately, this day she had Esther helping her and she, being a very sensible young lass who apparently knew more about having babies than her mother knew she knew, realised the problem.

'Into the wheelbarrow, Mama. I'll help you... Can you lean against the slopey bit and just put your knees up... I'll help you in... Never mind your clippers – we'll get them later.'

'No, my sweet! I'll just rest a moment then you can help me walk back home.'

Her little daughter, demonstrating a strength her mother found incredible, gripped the handles and started to push.

'Mama, stop where you are, quite still. It's not far to the track and then you won't be bumping along the soils. Mama! Sit back, do!'

Beatrice knew what was happening; she was cramping up and leaning forward with her head banging on her knees and, to her great embarrassment, frustration and or sheer anger, knew she had to allow her daughter to help her – and she but a child!. She gripped her abdomen tightly and gazed at the determination and effort showing on young Esther's rosy face and puffed cheeks as she struggled to balance the wheel over a furrow or two.

'Darling girl, I'm so sorry and if I don't tell you often, just know I do love you.'

Unable to protest any more, she relaxed back in between spasms and gazed up into the trees as they were now along the track. Quite inopportunely a cluster of magpies, indulging in a territorial battle over some branches up above, halted their flapping wings, perched along a bough and started their glorious warble.

'Oh no! They're laughing at me! How could they?'

'Mama, hush! Don't be silly. They are only curious, you know that. I do believe they're yodelling in sympathy, Mama. They're the same mob that cluster in our yard and Nancy would tell you they know what's going on. It's sympathy, Mama, or empathy perhaps. Like me, I know what's going to happen, Mama, and that too, is only nature... Now we're here. Almost. Stay there, Mama. Don't move! Nancy! NANCY!'

It was her papa who came to the door. He realised the situation and broke into a run. 'My darling Beattie!'

Beatrice looked about to cry but made no comment. He called her Beattie! He never did that. She recognised he was too upset for her to make a protest or argue about his fussing, so she buried her face into his shoulder as he carried her into the house, calling for Nancy.

Nancy came running up the cellar steps, looking most harassed and with a chorus of 'Oh noes' the three of them went into the bedroom, closing the door behind them.

Esther sat down on the end of the barrow, tired arms dangling above the ground and turning her back on the blood-streaked barrow. She sat there for quite a few minutes – her brothers were not around and all other household action was with Mama. She could hear bustling from the front passageway of the house and Papa asking Nancy to bring hot water. Then it went quiet again. She knew, young as she was, there would not be another baby; well, not this time.

A loud and gruff 'Hoi!' echoed from the vegetable patch. It was Sam. 'I seen it all, m'dear. You are some wonderful young leddy, so you are. Come on, while they're busy, let's make you a cool drink... That's it. Got wobbly legs, have yer? Not surprisin'. Lean on me... That's it.'

Later, Papa came into the kitchen where his little daughter was almost asleep, head on hands over the big wooden table. He stroked her hair. 'You are a wonder, my Esther. Mama is resting now and I think you know what was wrong, don't you?'

She lifted a heavy head. 'Yes, Papa. No baby this time.'

He pulled her onto his knee. She rested her head on his waistcoat and didn't even mind the hard bump of his pipe in the breast pocket. *This is Papa.*

They sat together until Nancy reappeared with a pile of clothing for the wash.

Later, Arthur laid down the law. 'A week at least within these four walls, Beatrice. If not longer! Please, no physical labour at all.'

She complied. It was easier that way and anyway she could spend time reading everything that might appear in the newspapers about Mary Lee and her campaigning. Also, she spent time, more than had been her habit, talking to Esther. As she saw matters, her little daughter had been pulled from her innocence; she was growing up into womanhood and yet still a child – but demonstrating a wondrous common sense.

She wrote to her dear Mrs Lee, or plain Mary as their friendship allowed, but received no answer, not even from Evelyn. She was disappointed but, as Arthur suggested, she might after all be travelling around the country with Mary.

'She seems to have some flexibility in her position, Beatrice, and someone has to help Mrs Lee gather all those signatures – oh, yes, I know there are others!'

Beatrice conceded the point, was indulged and, after the prescribed extended rest, slowly resumed her activities, her respect for her little daughter immeasurably increased. Despite her lack of years, Esther was a mature young lady and deserved that promised trip to Adelaide.

However, they didn't go that year after all. Esther was working hard at all her lessons. Her school was extending to cater for older boys who passed certain exams and the community was pressing for girls to have an equal advantage. She was determined to be selected. Thirteen was the commonest leaving age among many families because it freed the children for working on the growing industries, and agriculture, of the area. There was a class for fifteen-year-olds who passed the exam – still too young to leave school in Beatrice' s opinion. University was Esther's goal, and teaching was her chosen career.

Beatrice just wished the boys were as studious. They were now six years old and attending the school, as it was permitted, in fact appreciated, in order to gain the numbers for government funding. The school had come about, as she understood, as a result of the Chaffey irrigation plans for the area. Beatrice and Arthur had taught their children at home until they could enter this school, and they were good at reading, writing and arithmetic – this latter thanks to their father. At school, William liked all the offered subjects, but George was more active in sports – he loved the new Australian football. Beatrice was content with that, thinking George needed to expend his energies somehow and football seemed to provide that outlet. Ultimately, he wanted to work on the farm, grow grapes and make a lot of money selling wine! William had talked to Arthur about being a lawyer and fighting for irrigation rights to the water in the river. Arthur was willing, although, according to his mother, it seemed an ambitious goal for such a little boy.

# May 1892

## 77

The months went by and the years turned. Surprisingly, in May of 1892 Mary actually wrote to Beatrice, apologising for not answering so many of her earlier letters.

Arthur brought the missive home from the post office. He chortled as he gave it to her. 'Things must be going slowly for her, maybe even at a halt altogether, that she has time to write to you, Beattie, love!'

'Mary is certainly not resting, Arthur! Goodness… You can read it after me.'

Mary wrote that her dear friend was now Lady Colton – her husband, now Sir John, having been knighted at the start of the year. Lady Colton was now to take on the presidency of the Women's Suffrage League, succeeding Sir Edward Stirling. Mrs Lee had been complimented for her industry and was now planning to travel to Broken Hill, where conditions were very bad for women; they had no rights when their men were laid off work and there was a history of strikes and a forecast of new ones. Her letter was full of plans. She was to go as a delegate from the Sick Poor Fund and the Working Women's Trade Union.

'Arthur, she is travelling up to Broken Hill by train! Imagine that, at her age. She is not a spring chicken any more. She writes…erm…she has a stop at Coxburn – I think that's what she calls it – then on to Broken Hill. And this in December! Oh, Arthur, it will be so hot… I wonder if Evie will go with her, if she can take time from her work?' Beatrice thought of Mary's upright nature and personal discipline. She would not shed a petticoat to be cooler, Beatrice knew that for a fact.

Later, Beatrice learned that Mrs Lee spoke to the populace at Broken Hill at their Theatre Royal but drew only a moderate attendance. Her main topic was women's suffrage, and men in Broken Hill were then apparently opposed – in the main! However, she did manage to get a number of signatures from women which were added to the petition for suffrage.

This monster petition was planned to be presented to parliament ahead of any third reading of the Suffrage Bill – whenever that might eventuate.

# November 1893

## 78

Beatrice and Arthur took the children to Adelaide in the November of 1893, before the twins' tenth birthdays, intending to be home again in Cumquats for Christmas. Mary was not at home because she and some others from the Woman's Christian Temperance Union were touring northern country areas; Mary was to speak in Quorn and Port Augusta, again encouraging support for women's suffrage and – according to Alice – Evelyn had travelled with her this time.

'Mrs Mary's well past seventy, Miss Beatrice. Miss Evelyn worries about her traipsing all over the country like this. Might not agree with her mam some of the time but she is very proud of her and a good daughter… I think it's nice for them to be together, like…'

Alice delighted in the boys, having one of her own, and Esther, now an assured twelve-year-old, enjoyed walking with her over the nearby parklands. They all stayed in the Barnard Street house for a few days. Beatrice remembered her other visits to that house. *Fond memories I have, indeed!*

Then to please Esther they travelled on the train up to Bridgewater and stayed at the inn. Anderson was still ruling his kingdom, although he presented as a much stouter Anderson now! Sissy was delighted to see the children, said she still suffered with her feet, and entertained them all hugely with stories of their mother's early days there. She was a grandmother three times over now, Lucille having a boy and two girls. Rauf was hoping the boy would take up the law, too.

'Goodness, Beattie, the little fella's still in skirts, so to speak, and already he's a lawyer in his father's eyes! Anderson an' me think it's this migration attitood you an' Mrs Flach useter talk about. Always wanting to work hard, aim for the top! An' his little girls, like peas in a pod they are, born so close, he never talks of them as much. Why is it that men must have sons? Mind, little Jeanie was born too small. She gets bad chests, something awful. Catches whatever's goin'. I worry about her I do with all this scarlatina thing spreadin' around some parts. The paper calls it the diftheria or something. Lots o' little ones get it and they got no chance. Doctors cost money an' some just don' 'ave the shillin's.' Sissy shook her head then bustled off, patting her aproned girth.

Esther was intrigued by the old square piano, seldom used now but placed in an empty room. The old school piano, well cared for, was the accepted musical instrument in the inn now.

They took the trap over to see Beatrice and Arthur's godchildren, Frank and Eloise – both now aged thirteen and the elder pair in a clan of younger children. Kate was delighted to see them. Herbert was away at his cooperage business, which was prospering, and Frank was to follow in his footsteps. He had no interest in further study and was eager to start an apprenticeship with his father. He did show an interest in Esther, prompting each of the mothers to raise their eyebrows. However, when Esther announced her intention of going to university, now girls could gain degrees at Adelaide university, he was less than impressed.

'Girls are homemakers, like my mutti – erm…mother.'

Hearing this, Kate reminded him she had been a teacher once.

'Only till you had me an' Lou, Mutti. Then you were boss in the house, Vati said so.'

Kate shrugged in apology to Esther but let him go. Esther thought him all right for a boy but one with very different ideas about the role of women. She was intrigued by his little carvings, though, usually of animals. He gave one to her later, said it was a keepsake. She was delighted. It was very clever and the detail realistic: a fox, slinking towards a prey. Kate raised her eyebrows at Beatrice – the symbolism striking them as rather obvious. Not least, their elder children were growing up!

Pastor Wilhelm and his family had moved to another parish in the Barossa Valley but the new pastor was a delightful young man. He took Arthur off to speak about raising water from the aquifer beneath the earth.

*Pumps again, no doubt. Arthur will be in seventh heaven!*

Beatrice thought Bridgewater was all so familiar and yet now so strange. It was no longer 'her' place – that was Cumquats with Arthur and the children and her community there. They no longer felt much like immigrants and, she felt sure, were not thought of in that way. Cumquats was a well-run, profitable property, they had worked hard and their labour had gained them quite a reputation. Next year, when her papa intended bringing his wife to visit, she knew he would be so pleased for her. *When Papa is here, Arthur wants to talk over the possibility of William having his farm as a home address so he can go to a feeder school for Oxford. I'm not too sure about how I feel about that. Plenty of time to think about it. We both know it's not what George would want, so...*

*She sighed. Esther wants to go to Adelaide University to be a teacher. Well, at least that's not too far away from home. Wonder if she could lodge with the Lees.*

## 79

Unknown to Alice, Mrs Mary Lee had spent some days that November resting in Crafers. Nor did Beatrice and her family, staying in nearby Bridgewater at that time, know of her nearness. At Evelyn's insistence, the Lees had spontaneously diverted their route at the end of the country trip. Mary was physically tired after her tour seeking support for women's suffrage and collecting country signatures – to add weight to the monstrous petition to be presented to the Legislative Council by the Kingston government.

Of course, critics of her efforts – and others'– on behalf of women's equality were vociferous on street corners and scathing in the newspapers, particularly so by certain writers to the editor in the newspapers. One letter in particular, published in the *Advertiser* of the twenty-seventh of November from someone calling himself Aristides seemed to have caught Mary at a vulnerable moment. While Mrs Lee and Evelyn were away in the country areas, a certain male reader had asked Mrs Mary Lee two questions she had not answered and this Aristides was – in Evelyn's words, 'beating the drum', asking for answers on behalf of the original questioner – or was it himself under a pseudonym? He asked, 'Who is Mrs Mary Lee and who is Mr Mary Lee?'

'Mam, do ignore it. You had not answered because you were up in the country campaigning. Just leave it, do…'

But Mary responded from Crafers, on the twenty-eighth November, writing to the *Advertiser*,

Mrs Mary Lee in reply to the Editor
I see no reason why Mr J.R. should not have an answer to his questions as far as I can answer him… I…shall have pleasure in giving him a full true and particular account of myself, birth, antecedents and family connections for many generations, providing of course that he can show some particular

claim to the information. As to his second question, I in common with many a lonesome mourner would be ah! too glad to solve that query both with regard to the one in question and three noble sons who have passed 'beyond the bar', one of whom has at least left some kindly memories behind him in Adelaide. As regards the public I have done what I could to serve them to the best of my knowledge and ability whenever and wherever I could, but having sought no service at their hands I cannot admit their right to question me. I am etc…MARY LEE

Crafers Hotel, Mt Lofty November 27, 1893*

# Christmas 1893

## 80

Evelyn then decided it was time to take her mother home to enjoy a peaceful Christmastide. At home they had invitations waiting from Sir John and Lady Mary Colton, which pleased Mary Lee and some from other worthies supporting the suffrage that Evelyn knew of from the newspapers. Also, friends not necessarily closely involved with the politics of the time, but true friends from church and other branches of their way of life, were eager to see them over the holiday.

These included a surprise visit from the Symondses, though only a short one before Christmas, Beatrice explained. She, Arthur and the children booked into an Adelaide hotel after leaving Bridgewater. Beatrice was hopeful that after their pleasant stay in Bridgewater, Mary and Evelyn might have returned. So it proved. With reminders from Arthur they really needed to leave Adelaide no later than three days hence, they walked out to Barnard Street. The boys were promised a ride on a tram later.

Mrs Lee answered the door, not Alice. Arthur had forgotten how tiny she really was! He held out his hand but she, Mary the so very correct, reached over for a hug. Beatrice thought she would never let her go when it was her turn!

Alice came running up the hall. 'Oh, how lovely seeing you again so soon! Boys, would you kindly round up the chickens for me, put them in the pen and see if there are some eggs? Just put them in the kitchen, please. I'll make a cup of tea for the grown-ups then I'll make you a glass of my lemonade…'

The boys ran off.

Esther stood by her mother and looked uncertain.

Mary put out her hand then took one of Esther's, encasing it with her two. 'You are Esther and I am so pleased to meet you. Come into the sitting room with us. I'm sure you like buttered teacakes. Our Alice makes the best ones in the world.'

It was a most pleasant couple of hours during which Esther, one of the new generation of women, met Mary Lee, whom she knew about and greatly admired. There was an instant rapport, and Mrs Lee invited Esther, should she wish, to board with them if she still wanted to go to Adelaide University after completing school. Esther was very happy to consider the plan. Rapport aside, she had followed and admired Mrs Lee's campaigning on behalf of women for quite some time now.

When they left, they all knew they were friends for, as William said, 'ever and ever and ever'.

# 1894

## 81

For Mary Lee and her colleagues, the New Year became tense with suspense and campaigning. They were spurred on by the successful passing of the Suffrage Bill in New Zealand.

In May of 1894, Mary Lee travelled once more to country centres within the state, speaking to huge crowds of people – men and women – whose interest had been reignited by the news of the passing of the New Zealand Bill. In July that year, Premier Kingston in South Australia brought before the Legislative Council a Bill for women's suffrage – unconditional, no strings attached. The Bill was passed by an absolute majority, to go through for a second reading.

Then in August, the Women's Suffrage League, aided by the Women's Christian Temperance Union, presented the long-planned monster petition to the House of Assembly. It bore 11,600 signatures gathered from around the colony. Mary Lee was certain such a gesture could not be ignored.

A third reading was scheduled for the seventeenth of December. Young Esther, infected by her respect and admiration of Mary Lee and the enthusiasm and admiration shown by her own mother, was riding her horse into the town as often as possible to check the newspaper. Then in the eighteenth December edition she read how every seat on the cushioned benches of the 'cushioned benches' was taken up by ladies! However, the third reading was to be adjourned until after midnight. Esther was determined to ride for the following day's paper. Their papers were a day behind. Surely by now... Oh, how frustrating having to wait!

Had she been at Barnard Street on the eighteenth, she would have witnessed Mrs Lee arriving home. The Bill had been passed at the start of that day's proceedings! According to the *Register* of the nineteenth of December there were three more votes than the required majority and 'the ayes were sonorous and cheery, the noes despondent like muffled bells'.

On that day, Mrs Lee had arrived home exhausted. It showed in her face as she flopped into her favourite chair.

Alice rushed to undo her boots. 'Mrs Mary! You've been sitting around that Parliament House days and hours on end lately. All that stress and tension! It's not doing you any good. Let's get your feet comfy… Now, shall I undo your laces or will you wait for Miss Evie…'

'Shush, Alice, do! Let me get a word in… It's happened, Alice, it's done! Early this morning an' the vote was three more than they needed! Alice, we've done it!'

Alice jumped to her feet. 'We have the vote, Mrs Mary? Like the men?'

Mary beamed and tears of happiness ran down her cheeks. She mopped them with a rather crushed red handkerchief. 'To my count, dear Alice, it's taken seven Bills, six that were all tied up and heavy with conditions and this one the premier – good man – guided through the stages to get accepted. We get the right to vote on equal terms with men, the right to send a vote in by post if we can't get to a place, and not only that: South Australian women will have the right to stand for parliament – to be a part of whatever government they vote in.'

Alice clapped her hands. 'Is it the Madeira, Mrs Mary?'

'It is, Alice, it is indeed. And one for you too. Now the next thing will be to encourage all women to enrol so they *can* make a mark when voting times come.'

'Not today. Mrs Mary, not today. Time now to relax until Miss Evelyn comes home. She will be so pleased…'

# 82

Beatrice met the coach in Renmark at the new Council Hall and, after excited hugs, helped her papa and his 'new' wife – *she has a friendly enough face but he's become so fat...* – into the hired brougham. Max the ostler did the driving so she could join in the excited chat all the way home.

The twins were waiting at the gate and Arthur with a rather hot and dusty Esther by the front door.

'Welcome to Cumquats, sir...'

Hands were shaken and clasped. Thirteen-year-old Esther, sweetly serious – though mysteriously, noted her observant mother, subduing a bubbling excitement, for she had only minutes earlier ridden home herself – nevertheless gave a polite bob in welcome.

From behind the brougham, Beatrice's papa surveyed his new family and was quite openly overcome with emotion, making quite a few 'hrrmph', noises so Arthur escorted him in, leaving Beatrice and her new mama to become better acquainted.

As soon as the second Mrs Fletcher was shown her room after electing to wash off the dust of the road, Esther whispered to her mother and thrust a copy of the *Register* up to her face.

'Mama, old Sam bought a paper and, you know what, it's dated the nineteent – that's quick! Mama! Mrs Lee has done it, Mama!'

Beatrice almost snatched the rolled-up paper from her daughter's grasp. 'The vote, Esther, the vote... Oh, yes!' And forgetting decorum she ran down to where her husband was preparing Papa a long cool drink. She waved the paper under his nose, and her papa jumped back in surprise.

She cried out, practically weeping in her excitement, 'Arthur, Mary's won us the suffrage!'

After that, there was great delight and more cool drinks. Mrs Fletcher came out of her room to hear and when told that South Australian women now had the vote was silent for a moment, shocked at the news. 'You have the vote? Women? Here in the colonies? Before we English do? Oh, my deary me…'

Beatrice and Arthur shared a grin.

Arthur raised his glass. 'A toast! To the indefatigable Mrs Mary Lee! Mary is determined in her goals and a good friend of all women of this state.'

For the benefit of the Fletchers, he explained their relationship with Mary, how good a friend she had been, as well as speaking of her achievements. 'I have not always agreed with her approach to her campaigning but certainly we are all the better for her generosity of spirit.'

*

A few days later, a long letter came from Mary to Beatrice. Its tone was nothing less than joyful; her words literally sang onto the page!

'Oh, Arthur, do listen. This is nothing less than joyful. Her words literally sing onto the page. She says, "We did it, Beatrice, we did it!" Arthur, she is so happy. She deserves to be, and so proud of her achievements. All women should thank her, profoundly. Esther, dear, you can be so proud that she is our friend.'

'Actually, Mum, she is a friend to all women in this state. I just hope that they all, everyone, come to recognise what she has gained for us. You know, some of my friends think it's all a fuss about nothing and women have enough to do without having to think who to vote for. Can you believe that! And Mum, Mama, she writes that some people thought she wasn't gracious in victory. Oh, for goodness' sake! There's no accounting for the intelligence of some!'

*

Beatrice was delighted for the Lees; of course for her dear friend Mary Lee, who worked so hard to gain the vote for women, but also for Evelyn, who worried about her mother so. Not only that, she was so very delighted about the news personally. She was equally so, to be able to tell the news to her new step-mama. As she wrote to Mary later, 'Step-Mama was quite miffed when she realised that women in this "remote little colony" – her words – had achieved what women in England look most unlikely to, for many years yet! Hurrah!'

Beatrice was becoming concerned for Esther too. She had only another year before she entered her school's final year and its age limit. She would receive a certificate evaluating her education level – the highest qualification her school issued – yet the girl would still be only fifteen. Esther did not want her education to finish. Nor was she yet of a standard to go to university. Arthur and Beatrice were concerned that she should have every chance to achieve her ambition, which was to teach – not as a governess but in a recognised scholastic and academic environment such as a 'proper' recognised school – her own description.

Beatrice did some searching and made enquiries and then Arthur was told of a girls' school in Adelaide that taught up to matriculation level so that she could be admitted to university. They already knew that Adelaide University had since 1880 allowed girls to undertake degrees.

When her step-mama heard this, she was shocked once more, for English universities, to her knowledge, did not allow females to gain a degree, unless for medicine, and then only perhaps at Oxford.

Esther suggested that perhaps dear Mrs Lee and Evelyn would allow her to stay with them if she went to that school. So Beatrice decided to write and ask, though she warned that perhaps Mrs Lee still had the new mothers lodging from the country areas. Beatrice's letter spoke at length of Arthur's successes with the irrigation pumps and, as usual, closed with urging her friend to take things easy.

Mary was delighted to receive the letter and thought she would speak with Evelyn about the girl boarding. They no longer had boarders; even her dear Mrs Dawes had returned to the country some time ago. And Esther did seem a lovely young lady…

However, Esther was able to attend a crammer set up in Renmark by a lady teacher formerly from Bendigo in Victoria. Very well qualified, this Mrs Faithfull had moved to the area to be near her own son and her grandchildren. She was recommended to Arthur by a fellow member of council and her school was to be for no more than four girls at any one time who were above the official school leaving age and wished to gain matriculation acceptable to Melbourne and Adelaide universities.

After some judicious investigation, it was arranged that Esther could stay Monday to Friday at her father's friend's home and ride home for weekends. Beatrice was happier that her daughter was nearer home for the time and the arrangement proved to be happily suited to everyone. Mary Lee was a little disappointed but was content that a young girl would gain her life's goal.

# 1896–1898

## 83

So the vote had been won and Evelyn had hoped her mother would settle down to a calmer routine.. However, in Mary's estimation there was still a lot to be done. She and Augusta Zadow had held a couple of informal meetings, sharing their concerns at the treatment of women workers in the 1894 Factories Act. It was written into law about the same time as the suffrage, which was of course Mrs Lee's main interest. Premier Charles Kingston appointed Augusta the Inspector of Factories in 1895. But dear Augusta had something wrong with her blood, so Mary heard, and she died of some complication after the influenza. Mary Lee felt incredibly sad that such a vibrant personality was lost to the welfare of struggling women. Premier Kingston attended her funeral; she was so valued.

He backed Mrs Lee's nomination to parliament but she couldn't stand for the United Labour Party and declined, preferring to 'work on the side of right, unfettered by pledge or obligation'. As her nomination was considered to succeed and she would receive a fee for her energies and enthusiasms, Evelyn asked her to reconsider.

That same month, a public donations fund was established for Mary Lee in recognition of the work she had done during the women's suffrage campaign. The monies raised – fifty sovereigns – were presented by Premier Kingston at a testimonial ceremony on her seventy-fifth birthday in February 1896. Another minister said she deserved all the applause.

Evelyn brought Alice to the ceremony and Mrs Lee made a speech in thanks and mentioned it was the proudest birthday of her life; that its memories would be among her proudest possessions.

'You know,' she would say later, 'for all those years I didn't get paid at all. Then Premier Kingston appointed me the female official visitor to the lunatic asylums. Catherine Helen Spence got the schools. He must've thought I was ready to enter one of those places, no? Just a joke! Turned out it was honorary – again. But I spotted quite a few deficiencies in that place so it's good to know I had some results. Perhaps I should have asked for recompense for expenses but I just never thought…'

Then in 1898 there was a national referendum on federation.

Esther was cross because she was not yet twenty-one – the age of adulthood and eligibility to vote. However she was intrigued by, and in favour of, the concept of federation. 'Mama, we are all one country, after all. What if I go to Melbourne University instead, which is a thought. If we are not one federation, would that be allowed? Or would I need a document of identity to say I was South Australian?'

It was reported that seventy per cent of South Australians voted Yes; NSW, Victoria and Tasmania all voted for federation also. Then in 1899 Queensland voted to be included.

Mary was critical of Western Australia, where the goldfields region asked to be a separate state within the Commonwealth. She complained to Evelyn over dinner. 'Their premier, Sir John Forrest, insists on five years' fiscal freedom – that's what he calls it – if they join the federation. However, apparently the West will be included in a delegation that will go to London soon for the submission to the Imperial Parliament of the Commonwealth Bill. Wonder when it'll all happen? The paper says the delegation will meet with the Queen at Windsor Castle. In March. Seems she is emerging from that long mourning of hers for Albert. She's been grieving for a long enough time, it says here, and, as head of the church and state, her country needs her.'

It was Esther who reported from an early reading of her newspaper that Queen Victoria gave her assent to an Act on the ninth of July 1900 creating the Federal Commonwealth of Australia. On the thirty-first of December, Mr Edmund Barton was sworn in as prime minister and the cabinet was also sworn.

Beatrice was more concerned about how William would be feeling, as he was still over in England and hoping to go up at Oxford. 'Will the public over there think of him as a colonial now? He's lived with Papa for long enough, according to Step-Mama, that he's speaking like an Englishman. With you and me as parents, Arthur, did he ever speak otherwise? However, it means at least that he won't suffer that "migrant colonial" label we read about. What do you think, Arthur?'

'Hrrmmph – just reading about the colony of Victoria offering to send two hundred men for service against the Boxers and there's no sign of those Boxers giving in as yet. Hrrmmph.'

# September 1909

## 84

A pleasant early spring day, enough sunshine to warm the air and enough cool breeze to stir it gently. Mary Lee had been reading her newspaper. An article caught her eye and sparked her memory. They were commenting on the anniversary of the death of former Premier Charles Cameron Kingston. *Another good man. Died only a year ago but he saw us become a federation and he was in Barton's first cabinet. His father came from my part of the old country.*

Mary lay back in her basket-weave chair listening to a blackbird somewhere in the high hedge blocking their small garden from the roadway. Wistfully, she recalled their Barnard Street garden, years ago now, and the tree in the middle for shade. Evelyn had liked Molesworth Street, but agreed Gover Street was now more central for shopping and moving around. Also, the rent was less, thankfully.

From indoors came the sounds of Alice boiling some laundry and directing her son Robert in turning the heavy mangle.

*I'm going backwards. I've been in the colony for almost thirty years and today I feel like one of those babies put out in the perambulators to benefit from the sun. What's the phrase – a second childhood?*

Alice was still part of the family, had been for thirty plus years. She had just turned forty-five, or so she thought, not ever having known her actual birthday. She was devoted to Mary, who was now in her eighty-ninth year. Alice didn't live in any more – she had her own home to run and a family to fill the rooms, but it was only a couple of streets away on the other side of Wellington Square. Mary simply didn't have the money to pay her for her work but Alice shared in the meals she cooked for them each dinner time and, to Mary's direction, did the shopping in the market, always working out the best deals. Sometimes it was just the two of them, sometimes they were three.

*Funny weather this. Head's hot, feet are frozen. Where's my wee bell?*

Even at the thought, Alice came into the garden with a letter and a glass of homemade lemonade. 'Nice one for you from Mrs Beatrice, just came to the door. She's only been gone from here a fortnight! This time she must've got round to writing soon as she got home. I opened it for yer. Hope it's happy news. An' the young postman, cheerful feller, he is...'

She sat down on the stool. 'Mrs Mary, you look a bit heavy-eyed an' I heard you coughing. I hope you haven't picked up that influenza that's goin' round.'

'No, no, Alice. And this lemonade slips down nicely. We had the influenza before, remember? You an' I caught it last time when it was going round and we recovered. They say you don't get it twice. This is just a between-season sniffles. Lovely to have a letter and I'm just in the mood for a chat. Alice, please ask Rob to bring you a drink and me another one and then stay with me a while? You're not too busy?'

Alice shot over to the doorway and called out to Rob then resumed her seat.

'Let's read what Beattie has to say – together. Aha, it's good news. She wants to visit again – well, so does Arthur, and the boys and Esther! Oh, that is lovely. So soon. She asks if I can book them in at the hotel. What dates...aha, from the twelfth of October. Good time to leave the property, she says. Seeing Esther in Melbourne first then coming to Adelaide to meet young William off the boat. He's finished with Oxford and been inventing machines or something – like Arthur, says Beattie. Oh, it will be so good to see those young men grown up. And Esther of course, lovely young lass. Oh, I shall look forward to seeing them again. I'm feeling really lazy today Alice. It's this balmy weather. I've had memories rolling round in my head, and thinking of the friends I've made and lost and what I've done with my life. We were a mixed bag, were we not? Most of us were immigrants, most of us were married. What would this country do without us migrants, Alice? Catherine Helen and me were the single ones, no husbands to worry about. Oh – water – thank you, young Rob. I miss the other Mary most. Lady Mary Colton as she was later – when was it? 1891, when her husband was knighted. Another good man. Her illness was a bit of a mystery to me. It was when I was still in Barnard Street. I remember I introduced her to Lady Windeyer of Sydney after Lady Windeyer resigned from the Suffrage League there. It was some conflict over policy and I was the one who'd suggested the policy to Lady Windeyer. I was upset about all that and couldn't bring myself to write to Rose Scott again. Good, though, that I could introduce the two Lady Marys to each other. That's enough of that, now. It's all well past.'

'Oh, yes, Mrs Mary, it was 'cause of Lady Colton I met Mr Hartley an' he taught me mathematics. Lovely lady, she was. Remember that little trap she was driven round in? High up to climb into. I watched you from the window a few times, but you managed.'

'Oh, I well remember! It was she who introduced me to Catherine Helen Spence. Well, our paths had crossed – but only that – earlier. Catherine and me were never friends, Alice. She was a writer, a journalist, and she wrote about everything she did, so everyone knew her name. Oh, don't mistake me. Catherine is a good woman, she's done women proud. It's just that she and I are chalk an' cheese. She was all for proportional voting an' I must admit I was concerned less with the way of it than the truth of it. And she fought for the children while I was all for the women's rights. Credit where it's due, Alice, she's a good woman. In those early years, the trouble young girls on their own had to face when getting off the ships! It doesn't bear thinking of, Alice. I think I did help, though, me and some of the others in the early days – and the Rabbi Boas of course. I beg your pardon…got to cough. Urgh, urgh huhhooo.'

'Oh, that cough's getting worse, Mrs Mary. Don't like the sound of it. Shall I mix up a honey and lemon tisane?'

'No, no, dear girl. I'm fine. Come back and sit, put your feet up for a while. It's the sunshine, bit bright but warm on your shoulders. That cough's given me a bit of a headache… Have we a Steedman's powder, perhaps? Yes, perhaps Robert could fetch one for me? You know, Catherine is still writing for the papers. Not just letters like me but she writes articles, everyone knows her and she gets thanks for what she's done… She's about five years younger than me. It did rankle a bit when some said she set a perfect womanly example in her labours, an' me they called outspoken. Patience was never a strong point of mine but getting things done is still what matters most. Oh, yes, that is for sure. I always said that my aim was to leave the world a better place for women than I found it.'

'Thanks, Rob. Here we are, Mrs Mary. Now, some water for both of us an' a Steedmans for you. Give your throat a rest, dear lady. You're sounding hoarse.'

'Alice, desist, do! It's good to have time to remember an' me an' you. We don't get much chance to talk nowadays, do we?'

'You'll never be forgot, Mrs Mary. Like Miss Evelyn says, you'll go into history books for what you've done for women.'

Mary squeezed Alice's cool and calloused hand. 'If I do, Alice, I wonder what they'll say of me. Another drink would go down well. Just water please. That's good. I seem to have quite a thirst. Hmm... Laura was the last of my good friends to go, only a couple o' years ago, it was. Do you remember Laura Corbin? She started the day nurseries for working women's children and then in the depression, that was 1893 or '94, can't remember exactly, she founded a relief fund for women. Augusta and I helped with taking food and other things to the really poor families. And *you*! Remember, my young friend, you helped too – you pushed the box cart.'

'I remember, Mrs Mary. I specially remember Mrs Beatrice wrote to you 'cause she saw the write-up in the *Register* of the fifteenth of February, the day after your birthday, when Mr Kingston gave you that parchment, the one hanging in the hall. You was seventy-five then. And all those guineas. She is so proud of you. An', Mrs Mary, so am I. It is good to take all these memories out an' give 'em an airing, just like what we are doin' now. But that cough worries me. Let me get you a spoon of Bonnington's Irish Moss. I bought a bottle this morning for my Sarah. It's one and sixpence so it must be good an' you can take it in warm water. Soothes the throat.'

'No, Alice. Please sit with me. It's just the warmth of the sun – an' me and you having a chance to talk for once. Listen to that blackbird: he's enjoying our company! Evie's favourite bird call, that is. I felt I was doing good. I know Evelyn laughs when I say there's no such word as can't. But I did consider saying it, once or twice. Wasn't much money to spare here on the home front, was there? Without Evelyn's support I could not have afforded to keep on, that's a fact. She is a good woman, that, and a dutiful daughter as good as any mother could want. And you, my dear girl, worth all the gold in China you are to me. Oh, Alice, come on... Dear girl, why the tears? I'm remembering things and on top of it all is how you have helped me, always. I don't tell you enough just what you mean to me. Oh, you want to go indoors? Get on with something? No? Well, that's good, because it is so enjoyable having the chance to chat like this with you. Nice to remember, so it is. Tush-tush, girl, I'm all right, stop the tears, do. What's got into you?'

'Mrs Mary, it just gives me a funny feeling, you talking like this. An' yer memories are jumpin' round all over the place... I know all you do and so do all your friends, but you don' often talk to me, or boast about it...'

'I'm just in the mood, Alice, and I do miss those who can't – oh, did I tell you? Rose is coming for tea. Sent me a note – Tuesday, I think. It'll be so good to see her. Soon she's off again, this time to Germany – Berlin, I think – for her Young Women's Christian Association. Folk call it the YWCA. Alice my dear, my face is a bit hot. Can I bother you for a feel of that wet flannel? Aah, thank you. Evelyn used to get annoyed with me and said I invited the criticism. The newspapers have quite a few of my writings, so they have, if they keep any of them. "Bad penny" someone called me, I believe. I embarrassed Evie, caused talk among her colleagues at work. Even the Reverend Kirby told me once on the quiet that strong opinions needed special phrasing when written.'

She placed the wet flannel across her brow. Then with her hands in a steeple movement in front of her nose, fingertips supporting the flannel, she chuckled. It developed into a throaty laugh and Alice handed her more water.

'Here, Mrs Mary, drink this fresh water. You need switching off for a few minutes. Now, how many times have I heard you say that about folk?'

Mary laughed again then broke into a fit of coughing. She dabbed her face with the wet cloth and wiped droplets off her chin. 'Just thinking, Alice. Just remembered that phrase...the time I wrote to the *Register* when I told the readers that if I died before the right to vote was won, the words "women's enfranchisement" shall be found engraved upon my heart. Sounds a bit pompous but I believed it then and I still do. I am as strong in my feelings now. However, we won the fight. That is such a very good feeling, my dear young friend. When I do have to leave this place, I shall go peacefully. I think I've played my part, Alice.'

'Please, Mrs Mary, don't talk like that. I'm feeling a bit funny, just hearing you...'

'Dear Alice, have a think on this, that most of the women I've known, and still know, put expectations on themselves and tried their hardest to live up to them. They do an' they did, whenever... And many – if not most – were guided here as immigrants, including me and Evelyn, and you and Fred with your Robert who's ambitious enough to want to have his own laundry business. And your little Sarah wants to be a teacher and write books. An' what about Beatrice and Arthur and their new agriculture projects? She always tells me I was her greatest support since her ma died. Took a while for her to realise she was made of the right stuff all along. Now look at her, with her teaching and lawyering offspring – she did well. We've all of us made our mark in this colony, Alice. You too. We leave it a better place for women than it was when we arrived. Now that does make me content. Yes, have to say, I'm pleased enough. So what's with all this sniffing, Alice? You know, it's been so good to reminisce like this with you – to add it all up, what we did with our years here, together. And I can talk to you freely about all of them, because you know them all too. And all those friends we've been talking about, they know that too, wherever they now are. I believe I can hear them chuckling with me. Not at me, Alice, with me. Listen, Alice, listen – indulge me, dear friend – cup your hand on your ear instead of rubbing your eyes. You know, Alice, I really can hear them. Yes I can...'

*

Some days later, in Renmark, Beatrice Symonds bought a copy of the *Observer* newspaper, albeit two days old. While waiting for Arthur to complete his business, she guided the trap to the shade of one of the pepper trees and settled to read. When she turned to page 38, she caught her breath and realised why dear Mary Lee had not responded to her latest letter. She quietly and unobtrusively shed copious tears for a very special life that had passed.

Mrs Mary Lee neé Walsh died on Saturday 18th September 1909 from pleurisy following influenza. She was 88. She had been 58 when she arrived in South Australia in December 1879, almost exactly 30 years earlier. She is buried in the same grave as her son John Benjamin, known as Ben, in the Smith Street Cemetery, Walkerville, South Australia.

# Epilogue

'In all the papers of the day there were obituary notices…and each gave details of Mary Lee's amazing life in the thirty years since her arrival in South Australia. Her remarkable public life during the years of the battle for Women's Suffrage was recalled and many tributes paid to her memory.'

Elizabeth Mansutti,
*Mary Lee, 1821–1909: Let her name be honoured*

# Bibliography & Further Reading

## Books

Australian Army, 1977, *Historical Record of the 27th Battalion 1877–1977*

Cartwright, Colin, 2013, *Burning To Get the Vote*, University of Buckingham Press

Christopher, Peter, 2006, *Australian Riverboats – A Pictorial History*, Axiom Publishing

Cuffley, Peter, *Chandeliers and Billy Tea – A Catalogue of Australian Life 1880–1940*

Flower, Cedric, *Duck and Cabbage Tree: Australian Dressing/Fashion 1788–1914*

Magarey, Susan, 'Sex & Citizenship: From Ballot Boxes To Bedrooms', in Robert Foster & Paul Sendziuk (eds), *Turning Points In South Australian History*

Gibbs, R.M., 1992, *A History of South Australia From Colonial Days To the Present*

Goldsworthy, Kerryn, 2011, *Adelaide*, New South Publishing, University of NSW

Isaacs, Jennifer, 1990, *Pioneer Women of the Bush and Outback*, Lansdowne Press

Jones, Helen, 1986, *In Her Own Name: Women In South Australian History*, Wakefield Press

Kearney, Robert, 2005, *Silent Voices: Story of the 10th Battalion AIF*

Magarey, Susan (ed.), 2005, *Ever Yours, C.H. Spence. Autobiography, Diaries & Some Correspondence*, Wakefield Press

Manning, Geoffrey H., *A Colonial Experience*, Register, 14 July 1885

Mansutti, Elizabeth, 1994, *Mary Lee, 1821–1909: Let Her Name Be Honoured*, Elizabeth Ho in association with the Women's Suffrage Centenary History Subcommittee

Monteath, Peter (ed.), *Germans: Travellers, Settlers and Their Descendants In South Australia*, Wakefield Press

Spence, Catherine Helen, 2005, *Ever Yours – An Autobiography*, Wakefield Press

## Informative extracts about some of the actual settlers mentioned in the story

Australian Dictionary of Biography: Online Editions, MUP

> Mary Lee (1821–1909), Vol. 10, 1986
>
> Rosetta Jane Birks (1856–1911), 2005
>
> Mary Colton (1822–1898), 2005
>
> Laura Mary Louisa Corbin (1841–1906), 2005
>
> John Anderson Hartley (1844–1896), Vol. 4, 1972
>
> Christiane Susanne Augusta Zadow (1846–1896), Vol. 12

Information about other persons mentioned may be found in State Library newspaper collections or online.